St. Urbain's Horseman

In 1967, whilst four hundred and fifty million people were starving and, in England, at least eighteen per cent of this happy breed lived below subsistence level, and society's golden rule was alcoholism, drug addiction and inchoate brutality, Jacob Hersh, descendant of the House of David, was paid £15,000 *NOT* to direct a fun film, made love to his wife on crisp clean sheets, sent his progeny to private schools and worried about corpulence gained through over-indulgence. He complained about his maid's indolence. He lamented the falling off in the British craftsman's traditional pride and a rise in the price of claret. While the rich got richer and the poor poorer, Jacob Hersh survived very nicely. As his best friend put it so pithily, if we're all on the Titanic, at least we're going down first-class.

One day, to his astonishment, Jacob Hersh finds himself in the dock at the Old Bailey, accused of rape (and worse) by a young German au pair girl.

Yet, the thirty-seven years of Jake's life had so far run in an unbroken line upwards from teeming St. Urbain Street in the Montreal ghetto to his present highly enviable position in London.

The issues are joined as Jacob Hersh, that man of our time, stands trial—perhaps, too, for his way of life, incomparably blessed in contrast to cousin Joey, St. Urbain's Horseman, who stalks enigmatically through Jacob Hersh's dreams, here as an avenger in Paraguay, seeking out the notorious Dr. Mengele of Auschwitz, there with the International Brigade on the banks of the Ebro, or in the battle for Jerusalem in 1948.

This deeply serious novel has an abundance of comic scenes and wonderful characterisations. Among them Harry Stein, the vindictive little book-keeper with rancorous eyes—the sort of man who makes obscene phone calls; Hannah, hawking newspapers and buttonholing startled strangers in her ceaseless search for her son; cousin Joey, who casually left home at eighteen; Herky, the toilet accessories manufacturer, who as a tourist was apprehended in Harrods, ecstatically photographing their 'Gents'; ebullient Duddy Kravitz on the high-road to his first million with *Dr. McCoy's Real Wate-Loss*; and bowler-hatted, stiff-collared, cherub-mouthed Ormsby-Fletcher, Jacob Hersh's solicitor.

Also by Mordecai Richler

THE ACROBATS
SON OF A SMALLER HERO
A CHOICE OF ENEMIES
THE APPRENTICESHIP OF DUDDY KRAVITZ
THE INCOMPARABLE ATUK
COCKSURE
HUNTING TIGERS UNDER GLASS (essays)

St. Urbain's Horseman

A NOVEL

Mordecai Richler

WEIDENFELD AND NICOLSON
5 Winsley Street London W1

Portions of 'September 1, 1939' and 'In Memory of W. B. Yeats' by
W. H. Auden are reprinted by permission of Faber & Faber Ltd.
Copyright 1940, renewed 1968 by W. H. Auden.

Portions of 'The Girl That I Marry' by Irving Berlin are reprinted
by permission of Irving Berlin Ltd. Copyright 1946 by Irving Berlin.

The puzzles for the intelligence test on pp. 346–49 are from *Know
Your Own I.Q.*, by H. J. Eysenck, Penguin Books Ltd., and *The
Mensa Puzzle Book*, by Nicholas Scripture, New English Library.

ISBN 0 297 00363 1

Reproduced and Printed in Great Britain by
Redwood Press Limited, Trowbridge & London

For Florence,
and my other editors,
Bob Gottlieb and Tony Godwin

Defenceless under the night
Our world in a stupor lies;
Yet, dotted everywhere,
Ironic points of light
Flash out wherever the Just
Exchange their messages:
May I, composed like them
Of Eros and of dust,
Beleaguered by the same
Negation and despair,
Show an affirming flame.

W. H. AUDEN

One

1

Sometimes Jake wondered if the *Doktor*, given his declining years, slept with his mouth open, slack, or was it (more characteristically, perhaps) always clamped shut? Doesn't matter. In any event, the Horseman would extract the gold fillings from the triangular cleft between his upper front teeth with pliers. Slowly, Jake thought, coming abruptly awake in a sweat. "He's come," Jake proclaimed aloud.

Beside him, Nancy stirred.

"It's nothing," Jake said softly. "Just the dream again. Go back to sleep."

The *Doktor* was reputed to keep armed bodyguards, maybe four of them. Certainly he kept a weapon handy himself. Say a service revolver tucked under his pillow or an automatic rifle leaning against the wall in his villa with the barred windows off an unmarked road in the jungle, between Puerto San Vincente and the border fortress of Carlos Antonio López, on the Paraná River. Even that doesn't matter, Jake thought. St. Urbain's Horseman will take him by surprise, gaining the advantage.

Jake couldn't get back to sleep. So, careful not to disturb Nancy, he slid out of bed and into his dressing gown, sucking in his stomach to squeeze between the bed and the baby in the bassinet.

Once in his attic aerie, Jake glanced automatically at the wall clock that had been adjusted to show the time in Paraguay—the *Doktor's* time. It was 10:45 p.m. in Asunción.

Still yesterday.

Jake stood back and studied his desk, ostensibly such a mess, but to his initiated eye an ingeniously conceived system of booby traps. The second right-hand drawer, for instance, which seemed carelessly left open, was in fact precisely one and three quarter inches open. The airmail envelope, which appeared to be haphazardly thrown over his diary, had actually been laid there at an exact thirty-degree angle to his desk lamp. Or was it sixty degrees? Goddammit. The trouble with Jake's snares, so cunningly set for his mother the night before, was that the morning after he could never recall the crucial measurements and angles, and he was too indolent to keep a written record. Scrutinizing the second right-hand drawer again, it occurred to Jake that maybe last night he had set it at two and three quarter inches. Or was that the night before?

Four a.m. Jake drifted downstairs to the kitchen, where he fixed himself a gin and tonic and lit a Romeo y Julieta. The hall mirror caught him . . . Jake tugged at his cap. He shook his head, rejecting the catcher's signal, reared back on his left leg, kicked, and threw. No-Hit Hersh's garbage ball. Inimitable, unhitable. Wondrous Willie Mays swung and missed and the umpire hollered "Strike three." *Gut gezukt*, Jake thought. And so much for Red Smith, who had put him down for trade bait.

There would be a three-hour wait at least for the morning papers, unless, Jake thought, I drive down to Fleet Street. Hell, no. Jake retired to the oak-paneled sitting room with yesterday's *Evening Standard*, pretending he had no idea what was on the back page, trying to sneak up on it by way of Londoner's Diary and "the page with the human touch."

CHIN UP! THE POLIO GIRL CAN COOK
For 15 years Betty Ward has wanted to cook her own

meals. And in her iron lung she has read cookery books
in the hope that one day her dream would come true.

Now with the aid of one of the latest pieces of appara-
tus for polio victims she can cook at her home in Esher,
Surrey. A remote control unit has been fitted in her iron
lung and it controls a hot plate and a frying pan. She
gives instructions to her mother about mixing the ingre-
dients and then controls the cooking by moving a switch
in different positions with her chin.

"My most successful dishes," said Betty, "are pancakes
and braised chops."

Nancy had ripped out the story with his photograph on the
back page. For the children's sake. Capital Units, Jake read, was
down another penny. So was M.&G. Modesty Blaise was in
trouble again, but there were no tit pictures. India ink nipples.
And in spite of himself, Jake began to feel horny. Should he
wake Nancy? No; the baby robbed her of enough sleep. He
began to scan the bookshelves, looking for something with an
erotic passage, one of his Traveler's Companion Books maybe,
before he remembered that whatever Harry hadn't stolen was
now an exhibit in Courtroom Number One. Like his Y-front
underwear.

Jake found a coin in his dressing gown pocket and tossed it, but
it landed heads. Two out of three. Three out of five, then. He
went into the kitchen and poured himself another drink. 4:15; a
quarter past eleven in Toronto. If he were there now he would
be shooting pool with cherished friends at Julie's, or be drinking
in the Park Plaza Roof Bar, enjoying being at home. At ease in
Canada. The homeland he had shed with such soaring enthusiasm
twelve years earlier. Thousands of miles of wheat, indifference,
and self-apology, it had seemed. And no more.

Jake recalled standing with Luke at the ship's rail, afloat on
champagne, euphoric, as Quebec City receded and they headed
into the St. Lawrence and the sea.

"I say! I say! I say!" Jake had demanded, "what's beginning to
happen in Toronto?"

"Exciting things."

. "And Montreal?"

"It's changing."

Tomorrow country then, tomorrow country now. And yet—and yet—he felt increasingly claimed by it, especially in the autumn, the Laurentian season, and the last time he had sailed the tranquil St. Lawrence into swells and the sea, it was with a sense of loss, even deprivation, and melancholy, that he had watched the clifftop towns drift past. Each one unknown to him.

Circles completed, he thought.

As a St. Urbain Street boy he had, God forgive him, been ashamed of his parents' Yiddish accent. Now that he lived in Hampstead, Sammy (and soon Molly and Ben too, he supposed) mocked his immigrant's twang. Such, such are the trendy's dues, Jake thought, as he added a couple of pieces to Sammy's unfinished Popeye jigsaw puzzle on the table, found the cards, and sat down to play solitaire. If I win, he thought, I'll be acquitted. If I lose, it's the nick for me.

With a shiver of fear, his hands trembling, actually trembling in BCU (like a lesser director's overstatement, he thought, something he would never countenance in a shooting script), Jake recalled how the portly, avuncular Mr. Pound had opened for the prosecution yesterday in Number One Court at the Old Bailey.

ZOOM in on Number One Court for MCU MR. POUND.

"My Lord, there is a letter and some pages of film script which I think I shall have to refer to in my opening address. Would it be convenient if they were handed up now and for them to be proven at the proper time?"

"Yes, Mr. Pound."

"May it please your lordship, members of the jury," he began, peering over his bifocals as he calmly outlined the case for the Crown, going on to explain that Hersh, "as you will hear, is affluent by any standards, sophisticated, rather a 'swinger' in current parlance, with a library that runs to the Marquis de Sade and a taste that includes gunmanship. A successful film director, he moves freely in the glamorous world of glittering first nights, opulent restaurants, and gaming tables. His attic-study walls are plastered with photographs of wartime Nazi leaders and their survivors. There is also a portrait, intentionally garish, of Field Marshal Montgomery. No equestrian himself, he keeps a saddle and a riding crop in a cupboard. But now I'm anticipating. We shall hear much about these artifacts later. For the moment, I would ask you to consider the letter and pages of script the clerk of the court has distributed among you. The letter reads as follows:

My dear Sturmbannführer,

I do appreciate, as does Dr. Goebbels, that you are a writer of integrity and do not wish to see the glorious past distorted. Though the victors must be generous, all of us at the ministry agree that we must not do too much to whitewash perfidious Albion. On the other hand, you know our quarrel was never with the British people, but with their criminal government. It is most unfair of you to suggest that we wish to soften the past, because we are concerned about box office potential in the liberated territories. Therefore, I beg you to reconsider, and to add the following sequence to your scenario in progress.

Heil Hitler!

JACOB VON HERSH

"The scenes I shall now read you presuppose, as I understand it, that these islands, which welcomed Hersh to their shores, were defeated in World War II; and that the Nazis were indeed victorious. The scenes are from a projected film called *The Good Britons*. They read as follows:

CU GENERAL ROMMEL

As he raises his field glasses to his eyes.

POV ROMMEL (THROUGH FIELD GLASSES)

The 8th Army retreating in disarray across the dunes.

ROMMEL OS

Poor bastards. They fight like lions, but they are led by donkeys.

• • •

EXT. DAY. LONG OVERHEAD SHOT. THE DESERT

A file of Good Britons in retreat as far as the eye can see.

EXT. DAY. DESERT. BRITISH COMMAND CAMP WELL BEHIND THE ENEMY LINES

A thrusting crowd of British and American photographers snapping shots of GENERAL MONTGOMERY, makeup men dabbing his cheeks with grit while others, behind, kick up desert dust to simulate explosions.

REVERSE ANGLE

Cynically, the battle-weary Good Britons smile.

INT. DAY. MONTY'S HQ

favoring stunningly beautiful, but obviously sadistic, MAJOR MARY POPPINS, ostensibly a WREN

POV MAJOR POPPINS

. . . MONTY, clutching his TEDDY BEAR, rocks in his chair, thumb in mouth.

> MAJOR POPPINS
> You must stop them here, Monty. They are to come no farther.

As MONTY, a shell of a man, shrugs . . .

TRACK BACK to reveal two MI5 THUGS, as they spring to attention. They are bearded and wear skullcaps.

> MAJOR POPPINS
> I will expect him in "the nursery" at 1400 hours.

> DISSOLVE TO:

INT. DAY. A DUNGEON

reconstructed to resemble a child's nursery. MONTY, on his knees, stripped to the waist. Terrified yet enthralled as MAJOR POPPINS enters, wearing only a nurse's cap, bra and corset, and high-button shoes.

> MONTY
> (slavering)
> Bernie's been a naughty-poo.

At once, MAJOR POPPINS begins to flog him. Thwack

> MONTY
> Yes! I deserve it, Nanny . . . Arggh! . . . Stop!
> Please, Nanny . . . Argggh! . . . I'll be good . . .
> I'll command the troops to dig in. Please, Nanny.

But she is too sexually aroused to stop now.

INT. DAY. A BEDROOM

MAJOR POPPINS, still in her Discipline Fatigues, picks up the telephone.

> MAJOR POPPINS
> (into phone)
> Get me Moscow. KGB HQ. Comrade Beria, please.
> (a pause)
> Shalom, Labish. It's Malka here. Tell Zhukie to
> stop quaking in his boots. They will keep Rom-
> mel occupied here for a while longer.

As she hangs up, her Jewess lips moist with sexual appetite, TRACK BACK to reveal . . .

. . . a row of battle-weary, glowering young SUBAL-TERNS, Cambridge Blues, lined up against the wall, bare-chested, and guarded by two MI5 THUGS.

> MAJOR POPPINS
> (bosom heaving)
> Mmmmn . . .

PANNING over the blond young SUBALTERNS, stopping at the most Aryan one.

MAJOR POPPINS
. . . you can wash that one for me, and rub him
down with chicken fat . . .

As the SUBALTERN, filled with disgust, is about to protest, one of the M I 5 THUGS steps up to him.

M I 5 THUG
So, am I right, Lord Tottenham, in believing
you've got a vife and child livink in Belgravia
yet?

CU LORD TOTTENHAM

Trapped.

2

Sammy's schoolbag trailed from the kitchen doorknob. Inside Jake found his homework book, a wizened apple, two pennies, a Puffin Book Club badge, and a *Man from U.N.C.L.E.* cameragun. Comes his bar mitzvah, he thought, no fountain pens. Instead his first nickel bag. "Today you are a man, *bubele*. Turn on." Or a syringe maybe. Jake got a fresh sheet of paper and wrote,

> AGENT S FOR SAMMY
>> MOST IMMEDIATE. IGNORE PREVIOUS MESSAGE. PUT PLAN XH5 INTO OPERATION IMMEDIATELY.
>>> THE COMMANDER
> PS THE COMMANDER'S AGENTS LOVE THEIR FATHERS

He inserted the sheet in Sammy's notebook and then, enraged with himself, he suddenly, savagely, retrieved it. Leave the kid alone, don't bug him. Jake crushed the sheet into a ball, swerved to avoid the onrushing Wilt Chamberlain, and backhanded it into the dustbin.

Another basket.

In the sitting room again, the bookshelves filled him with weariness. Books bought in Montreal. Books bought in Toronto. Books bought in London. Hideously expensive art books bought for

Nancy while he was pursuing her and never opened since.

"Marriage is a rotten bourgeois institution. It stinks. I keep up with the times, you know. But, Nancy, ours would be something special. A rock."

Books lugged from country to country, flat to flat, across the ocean, crated and uncrated, and still largely unread. There was a letter on Nancy's desk, from Mill Hill, Sammy's school. Next term he would require a cricket outfit. In three generations, from foxy Jews to fox-hunting ones. What next? Lord Hersh of St. Urbain?

Turning to the bookshelves again, Jake reached for Hugo's *Spanish Self-Taught,* an egg-soiled copy, and then with an ache he remembered his villa on Ibiza. That would be all of ten years ago, he realized, alarmed. Ten years ago, when time had not yet begun to count, all ambitions were to be realized, and somewhere past midnight Guillermo retrieved him from the bar at the Bristol Hotel. "*Vamonos,*" he said.

They fetched the girls from Rosita's brothel, rounded up some of the fishermen, and continued to Guillermo's apartment, which was on the top floor of the tallest building on the waterfront. While the others waited there, Guillermo drove Jake to his clinic, they tiptoed past sleeping patients, pried open a case of champagne, and returned to the apartment, laden with bottles. Most of the others had already shed their clothes. A nude guitarist with a dampsoiled pink brassiere tied to his head like a bonnet danced on the table. A couple was screwing on the floor. Jake turned apprehensively to Guillermo, but he wasn't at all disconcerted. He began to rip off his shirt, buttons flying.

Next thing Jake knew everybody was on the floor. Rolling, heaving. A wriggling smelly creaming tangle of legs, arms, breasts, and tongues. Girls moaned, they shrieked ai-aii-aii and called for their mothers; the men laughed and pounded buttocks openhanded and shouted imprecations. Jake was dizzy from drink. Flushed and embarrassed. Then it struck him that this is what they called an orgy, he was taking part, and his spirits soared. This is living, Yankel. Liberated rebel-without-a-cause living. He undressed and made a sporting half-hearted

grab for the body next to him when a moist stinky leg hit him
on the cheek. One leg, then another, locking his neck. Arms
driving his head toward a churning vagina, mossy and glistening. Suppressing nausea, Jake broke free, slid into his trousers,
and sat down on a stool by the bar. He drank slowly, his head
throbbing, as on the floor below they continued to thrash,
roll, and writhe. Kiss, suck, gobble, penetrate. What is it with
me? Jake thought. What ails me? If I saw this in an how-empty-
is-the-life-of-the-rich movie or read it in a lowdown-on-subur-
bia novel, I'd burn with envy, but now that it's happening to
me—Jake scooped up a bottle of champagne and stepped on
the terrace to watch the sun come up. The Mediterranean
sun. Spain. Grubby fishing boats were beginning to chug into
the harbor. Gulls swooped hungrily overhead or bobbed on
the shimmering green water alongside. Remember this, Jake
thought, cherish it, and he felt very ghetto-liberated, very Hemingway, as he raised a bottle to his lips, drained it, and flung it
into the sea. A moment later he was sick to his stomach.

*Listen, your lordship. They're twisting everything in this
courtroom. Jacob Hersh is no sex nut. I'm a respecter of institutions. An all-around good chap. A big talker, but a chicken.
Even in Paris, I remained a Canadian. I puffed hashish, but I
didn't inhale.*

Mr. Justice Beal is a fart. He would say, quite, Mr. Hersh.
Quite.

5:30. Jake slumped in his chair and dipped into a stack of
magazines, coming up with an old copy of *Time*.

SURGERY
How Not To Die Of Cancer

A whole generation has grown up since William Powell
was a matinee idol noted for his sophisticated suavity in
The Thin Man, The Great Ziegfeld, and *My Man Godfrey*. Many of today's moviegoers scarcely know him.
But less surprising than his fading reputation is the actor's
actual survival. Last week in Palm Springs, Calif., Powell
observed the 25th anniversary of his operation for cancer
of the rectum. And with the same smooth ease that made

him a hit on the screen, Powell spoke frankly of his illness and a treatment that most patients and their relatives find embarrassing to discuss.

"I began bleeding from the rectum in March 1938," he said. "The doctor found a cancer, smaller than the nail of your little finger, between three and four inches up my rectum. They recommended removal of the rectum. Then I'd have to have a colostomy and evacuate into a pouch through an artificial opening for the rest of my life. I didn't feel I could go for this. But the doctor said that for my particular case they could offer an alternative —a temporary colostomy and radiation treatment. I took it."

Surgeons made an incision in Powell's abdomen, brought out part of the colon, and cut it half through. "From then on," said Powell, "fecal matter emptied into a pouch round my middle."

Jake skipped breathlessly to the bottom of the page.

Few cases of rectal cancer are detected early enough to be treated as Powell's case was. Says Powell simply: "I was one of the lucky ones."

Son-of-a-bitch. When Jake had been to Dr. O'Brien about his own rectal bleeding he had been told not to worry, old boy, it was hemorrhoids. Sure, old boy, only probably while Jake was hoisting his trousers up again inside that freezer of a surgery, O'Brien was saying to his nurse, "You know that nice Mr. Hersh?"

"You mean the chap with the undescended testicle?"

"Exactly. Well, I jolly well hope he's carrying lots of insurance. No sense opening him up. He's swimming in it."

Now Jake stood nude, legs spread wide apart and back to the hall mirror, bent over with his head bobbing between his knees, probing his ass hole for cancer nails. Nothing, no early-warning sprouts yet, as far as he could see. Then Jake remembered how Gas Berger of blessed memory had raised his arm to shave one morning and there was this unnecessary little lump above the elbow. Goodbye Gas. Jake searched all his body's hiding places, rubbing, pinching, squeezing, and slapping, testing for tell-tale lumps and bumps, but he could find nothing anywhere. Nothing visible anywhere. More suspicious than relieved he went into the kitchen for another drink, decided against it, squeezed himself an orange juice, and jogged around the table three times.

Once more the hall mirror trapped Jake, and this time he stickhandled into the sitting room, feinting Johnny Bower out of position by winding up for a slapshot, dekeing him, and then gently shifting the puck back in front of the net for the kid to pick up. Naturally the kid missed and Jake had to cut around the net and flip in the rebound. He knew without looking over at the bench that Toe would be smiling, smiling inwardly, as he said to the others, "The old son-of-a-b—— can still make the big move."

If it isn't lung cancer it will be an airplane crash.

DISSOLVE TO:

CLOSE ON: DOLL'S SEVERED HEAD LYING AMIDST TWISTED METAL AND STILL STEAMING RUBBLE

TRACK BACK

EXT. DAY. A MOUNTAIN. LABRADOR

Sun, sky, clouds. Peaks . . . A HUMMING BIRD . . . PAN-NING TO . . . twisted wings. Torn engine and tail work. Bodies under blankets. Small fires being hosed down here and there. POLICE wandering in the wreckage.

CLOSE ON: JAKE'S EYES

TRACKING IN

They have seen and known so much. Now they are dead, unseeing.

HOLD ONE EYE

MUSIC: Orgiastic.

CLOSE ON: NANCY wiggling out of a half slip with an air of moist expectancy.

TRACK BACK

INT. DAY HERSH BEDROOM

NANCY cavorting in bed with JAKE'S BEST FRIEND. Both nude.

> JAKE'S BEST FRIEND (LUKE)
>
> (raising his champagne glass)
>
> Well, here's to him. Hope the shmock is having a good time in Canada.

CU PHONE

Ringing ominously.

MUSIC: JAKE theme. Very pure, lofty.

NANCY frees her breasts from JAKE'S BEST FRIEND'S hands.

CLOSE ON: Greedy clutching fingers. *Dirty anti-Semitic fingernails.*

CLOSE ON: NANCY

Answering phone.

Grief. Dumb agony. As she realizes, *too late,* she will never look on his (JAKE'S) like again.

Or my shriveling liver giving out. Or robbery with violence. Or DDT poisoning, already begun. Or my back, Jake thought, because his disc felt tender again. Or my heart. Groping for his pulse, he discovered that it was fast, hammering again, indicating acute tachycardia or, God help him, SOLDIER'S HEART (or Disordered Action of the Heart or Effort Syndrome), a set of symptoms arising under conditions of great stress, and consisting of palpitation, shortness of breath, speedy exhaustion, depression, and irritability. Damn. It seemed reasonable to Jake, that is to say, he was reconciled to the deaths (sad, inevitable) of others, but he couldn't understand why they wanted him.

6:10. Jake went into the living room, opened the French doors, and stepped onto the terrace and into the garden. Through the wire fence that ran along the southern border of his garden he could see Old Lady Dry Cunt's newly planted rhododendron bed. Old Lady Dry Cunt's bedroom curtains were drawn. Good, good. Jake filled a bucket with water, took it to the greenhouse, poured lime into the water, stirred, and emptied the solution into the tank attached to his spray gun. Then, pretending to water the dahlia bed on his side of the fence, he directed a spray of murdering lime solution through the fence at Old Lady Dry Cunt's rhododendrons. Even if she was watching from behind the bedroom curtains it would appear—he hoped—that he was treating his own bed with liquid fertilizer. British bitch. He'd teach her to write snotty notes about the noise his brash American children make in the garden.

Inside again, Jake made himself a cup of instant coffee. 6:30. Stock-taking time.

It began well, ritualistically well. You have a gorgeous wife. Three kids. You're loved. All the same you've managed to remain an alienated Jew. Modishly ugly. But at thirty-seven you are a disappointment to yourself, a wash-out, and—and—and—he tried desperately to control the wheel, sensing a catastrophic turn, but he was too late. And he had to admit, looking at things objectively, there were other men in the world who were more talented—no, no, who were *rumored* to be more talented or taller or richer or better in bed than he was, not that he would be so doltish as to let one of them into the house. Still, you couldn't blinker your wife, completely. There were always those adoring profiles of the latest golden boy that she could read in the *Observer*, her legs crossed, the skirt riding above the knees. Or the winners who prevailed like Luke at parties they went to. She sitting glowingly still and scented in one of those breast-popping Mary Quant creations and Big Eyes looming over her, Jake hissing, "He's queer. I can tell." Or this season's Mr. Thingee being cooed over on the telly. How he abominated them, the scintillating people who blazed with confidence on TV panels. Or who could churn out a funny column once a week. Or who had articulate, controversial opinions about everything. She, watching in her kaftan, refulgent Mr. Thingee making eyes at the world and his wife, Jake jumping up and down in front of the telly. "He's talking crap."

Worse (but inevitable) news. Luke luxuriating on the Frost show. Mr. Fat Cat meets Bugs Bunny.

"Is Canada boring? Well, let me put it to you this way, David. Other people find it boring. My friend Jacob Hersh . . . you know," he offered in parenthesis, "the television and film director . . ."

Frost, who obviously didn't know, nodded, anticipating.

". . . likes to tell the story of the New York publisher who amused himself by drawing up a list of ten books for a new firm that was bound to fail. Leading the list of unreadables was a book titled *Canada, Our Good Neighbor to the North*."

Then Luke convulsed the studio audience by reading them a scene from *The Good Britons*.

Fuck you, old pal. Remembering, Jake poured himself a drink. It's too complicated, life's too spiky for me, he thought. There have been too many betrayals. In the study again, disc aching, Jake lowered himself gently to the floor. *Your lordship, listen to me. Let's clear this courtroom of these expensive lawyers, Regina's and mine. Tell the jury to go home. We'll talk this over, man to man.*

Quite, Mr. Hersh. Quite.

The judge didn't understand. Nobody did. Even Nancy. Of course Jake suffered his agonies, his guilt, his attacks of fear, but there were also times when it was getting off that alarmed him more than going to prison for two years—say one. In Jake's absence his friends would support his family and feel all the better for it. Slowly, shiftily, his unit trusts would accumulate capital growth and income, just like those tantalizing sales promotion charts had promised. When he finally got out, decent people would feel touched by him (slender again, his temples flecked with gray) because he had suffered an injustice. The Sacco of the sexual revolution. Juicy girls would cream for him at parties. To no avail.

"No, dear. It's not that. You *are* beautiful. Young. Firm. A *mechaieh*, I daresay. But I'm not the sort to risk my hard-won happiness, my wife, my children, my home, for an afternoon's abandon. I'll just stand here and drip."

He could count on being asked to direct a documentary on prison life. Hand-held cameras, jump cutting. Old lags, their heads held discreetly in the shadows, calling a spade a spade. "What's obscene? You can collect stamps with impunity. With me, it's jock straps. I'm a pouch-taster. It happens to be my kind of loving and as a result I've been rotting in this cell for twenty years. You know what's obscene? General Westmoreland. The CIA. Factory farming." Probing, thought-provoking stuff it would be. *Très* ballsy, very *cinéma vérité*.

DISSOLVE TO:

END TITLE, "INSIDE," SUPERIMPOSED OVER WASTE WATER RUNNING INTO A PRISON SEWER.

TRACK IN ON SOCIALLY SYMBOLIC SEWER GRATING

HERSH (Voice over)

I wrote, produced, directed, edited and cut this film. I also composed and played the pro-test ballads and did the narration. My name is . . .

(a pause; then, self-effacingly)

. . . Jacob Hersh.

People who had dropped him would possibly start inviting him around again. "You should have known Hersh in the old days. He used to be so talkative, such a bouncy guy, but now

. . . he opens his mouth and out comes an aphorism." But if he was found not guilty they'd say, "Wouldn't you know he'd get off, the prick? They made Harry Stein the fall guy."

No.

3

With his bleeding colonial heart, charged as he was with war guilt, Jake, when he had first come to London twelve years ago, had asked everywhere about the blitz. "How you must have suffered . . ." But everyone spoke longingly about the blitz. "People were so friendly then."

Only Harry, his co-defendant, spoke with rancor about the blitz.

Say "evacuee" and Jake, in his Canadian mind's eye, instantly conjured up an image of huggable Margaret O'Brien, shrinking in the corner of a foreign station platform that was forever England, a tattered golliwog in her hand, only to be redeemed by Robert Young and Dorothy McGuire, parents enviable because, unlike Jake's, one didn't belch at the table and the other didn't nag.

Oh to be blitzed, Jake used to dream, orphaned and adopted by M-G-M; but it was something else for prickly Harry Stein. Even before the *Luftwaffe* struck, ten-year-old Harry, scruffy and sty-ridden, was uprooted from his Stepney council school, tagged, issued a gas mask, and shoveled into a train crammed with squealing mums and babes, other slum kids (some covered with septic sores, still more lice-infested), and frantic teachers;

a train without food and insufficient toilets, each one at flood-tide, the floor slithery; to be finally disgorged on a station plat-form in the outer wilds of Buckinghamshire, where the ill-tem-pered gentry, aghast to discover such urban pestilence in their midst, had nevertheless foregathered to take their pick.

"It was a bloody selection ramp," Harry was fond of saying, "but, in lieu of old Eichmann, there were market farmers and shopkeepers to poke and prod us, choosing the healthiest lads, the most promising-looking workhands. And unspeakable old biddies to snatch the girls who would make the best unpaid maids."

Insolent and disheveled Harry, naturally, was among those urchins rejected, still left shivering in the cold after the second pick, ultimately forced on a late-to-arrive family by an irate billeting officer.

"The way they looked at me, you'd think I was going to steal their silver or shit on their carpets."

Harry was immediately lowered into a bath and then de-posited in an unheated attic room, though decidedly more agree-able quarters lay empty. But he exacted retribution by slipping into the library and tearing pages out of the reactionary old bastard's collection of first editions. And wetting his bed tri-umphantly.

"You think the war was all fun and games, don't you? After the raid, cockneys crawling out of the rubble with a wisecrack. Churchill traipsing through the bomb damage and asking, 'Are we downcast?' the forelock-touching workers shouting back, 'No!'"

Unwisely, Jake once tried to tease Harry out of his denigrat-ing mood.

"Why, Hershel," he said, calling him by his Yiddish name. "Bai Jove, Hershel, how you disillusion me. I cherish the notion of you surviving the war at Greyfriars, admittedly not so much a swell as the Bolshy of the Remove. Thick with Harry Whar-ton and Billy Bunter, but standing up for the proles and nignogs all the same. Out there on the pitch, Hershel, proving your mettle to Fisher T. Fish and other cads, secretly proud of the old gray stones . . ."

His sojourn in Buckinghamshire cut short, Harry, like so many other East End kids, was returned to Stepney in time for the blitz, where his father, no Churchill-idolator but an avid Left Book Club subscriber, dragged him out to absorb all the anti-Semitic sights, from the walls scrawled with "It's a Jewish War" to the poster that read

> YOUR COURAGE
> YOUR CHEERFULNESS
> YOUR RESOLUTION
> WILL BRING
> US VICTORY

altered by the Mosleyites to read JEW VICTORY.

While Jake, in Montreal, learned Stuka recognition from chewing gum cards and thrilled to hear, on *Carry On, Canada,* that when Churchill returned to his post as First Lord of the Admiralty, out to the Fleet went the signal, "Winston is back," Harry, in Stepney, looked up to see the sky aflame and plunged into the throng rattling the gates to Liverpool Street tube station, where he was to bunk down almost every night of the blitz.

As Jake joined his father and mother, his aunts, his uncles, to huddle around the radio and hear the great man say, "Let us therefore brace ourselves to our duties, and so bear ourselves that, if the British Empire and its Commonwealth last for a thousand years, men will still say, 'This was our finest hour,'" Harry, a ferret in search of novelty, ventured from 'Mickey's Shelter' to fetid Tilbury, where around the darkening bend in the tunnel you either unzipped for a tart against the wall or squatted to defecate. Given unfavorable winds, the stench of urine and excrement was overpowering. Mosquitoes abounded, lice proliferated. But meanwhile—as Harry's father explained to him—meanwhile, in the bacchanalian cellars of the Savoy and the Dorchester, the rich stuffed themselves with smoked salmon and vintage wines, they danced, and consumed debs in comfort.

"Never in the field of human conflict," Jake was stirred to hear the great man crackle over the BBC, "was so much owed by so many to so few," but Harry had other tales to tell. "Did you know that among the Brylcream Boys, the so-called few, class distinctions more than survived?"

"No, Hershel, I didn't know. I count on you for enlightenment."

"If a pilot officer and a pilot sergeant, both flying Spitfires, shone in combat, the former got the Flying Cross, but the latter only a Flying Medal."

"Yes, yes. It's the rich what takes the plunder, 'arry, and the poor that gets the blame."

"A commissioned R.A.F. officer could travel free and first class, naturally, on the railroads, but a pilot sergeant had to go third class."

If, before rationing, the rich only ventured into Stepney to load their Bentleys down with sugar, now they streamed into the East End to see the blitz sights, especially the Tilbury Arches. Jake, in Montreal, laughed at the Happy Gang, and in London Harry became an ITMA addict, but the one real giggle of the war, Harry said, was Red Army Day, the Lord Mayor praising Stalin in the Royal Albert Hall and Harry Pollitt enthusing over Churchill, the Sword of Stalingrad being on exhibit in Westminster Abbey.

"This island race, this happy breed, did not stand alone in 1940, or ever," Harry liked to say. "We stood niggyback on the Empire, if you get my meaning?"

"Yes, Harry. I do."

"Did you know that in 1939 a penny an hour was a normal industrial wage in India and that their per capita income was something like seven quid a year?"

"I never question your figures, Hershel."

4

The baby's piercing hungry howl jolted Nancy awake, savagely, out of a sleep fathoms deep, her dream cut short.

"Jake, could you please rock the baby until I pee and—"

Not there. Nancy wavered only briefly, between bassinet and toilet—the baby's needs, hers—before she scooped him to her aching swollen bosom lest his screaming wake Sammy.

And Molly.

And Mrs. Hersh.

The very morning of his mother's arrival, Jake, his manner fiendishly sweet, had said, "I suppose we must reconcile ourselves to the fact that you're on one of those twenty-one day return flights?"

"I'm going to stay here for just as long as I'm needed, *ketzelle*."

Mrs. Hersh had flown over a week before the trial to be with them during, as she put it, "Jake's ordeal," and it fell to Nancy, as if she didn't have sufficient troubles, to obviate an ugly collision between them by filling tense silences with prattle about the children and tedious comparisons between British and Canadian life, the sort of small talk which propelled Jake, liberated but unappreciative, out of the room. Jake's behavior was atrocious, devious as well. He ricocheted between icy cruelty to his mother and what she, understandably, came to cherish as acts of filial kindness.

Nancy got used to him coming abruptly awake at three a.m.

"Didn't my mother say," he would ask, "that she was going shopping in the West End first thing in the morning?"

"Yes."

Then he would scramble into his dressing gown and shoot outside to make sure that there were no bicycles, scooters, or other potentially treacherous obstacles in her path.

"Imagine," Mrs. Hersh would say to Nancy, "this morning he insisted on helping me across the street to the bus stop. That's some son I've got there."

"He's one in a million, Mrs. Hersh."

And at night in bed, Jake, lighting one cigarillo off another, pouring himself yet another cognac, would say, "You let her go to bed without reminding her to take her medicine. Great, fine. That's a big help. Women her age get strokes just like that. Boom. Heart trouble runs in the family too."

"But she's your mother. In spite of everything she's—"

"You've got to watch her like a hawk. Like a hawk, you hear? All I need is for her to be with us for years . . ." Bedridden.

Then, only last night, his first question on coming home from the Old Bailey was, "How's my mother?" But once her continued good health was established, he devoted the rest of the evening to tormenting her with Old Bailey lore.

"Things have improved, Maw. I mean these days you can actually plead not guilty." And he regaled her, savoring each *oy*, rising gleefully to her heaviest sighs, about the Press Room that had once been set up beneath the Old Bailey for administering *Peine Forte et Dure;* and how prisoners had been spread-eagled upon the stone-flagged floor, their arms secured, and heavy weights laid upon their bodies until their ribs cracked or they pleaded to the charge on which they were being held. "Mind you," he added, closing in, "even this was tempered with mercy. Prisoners were allowed a wooden spike under their backs to hasten penetration. With the conspicuous exception of one Major Strangeways who, in 1658, refused to admit to the murder of his brother-in-law and was so strong as to withstand the iron and stones that were piled on his chest. Fortunately, Strangeways was blessed with good companions, and a soft-hearted warder gave them permission to stand on him, hastening death. And there, Maw, you have the origin of the expression a friend in need. Like my pal Luke. Isn't that right, Nancy?"

Mrs. Hersh, an early riser, usually lay in wait in her bedroom until she heard the children in the hall, a grizzly old hen perched on the edge of her bed, her flat brown eyes melancholy. So this morning, typically, when Nancy started downstairs with the baby in her arms at seven thirty, followed by Molly, followed by Sammy, Mrs. Hersh opened her door to join them. Mrs. Hersh was wearing pink flowery pajamas and slippers with baby-blue pompoms. The winged tips of her glasses were silver-speckled. "Good morning, my precious ones," she said.

"Got a present for me?" Sammy asked.

"Devil! Such a devil!"

"Me too, it's not fair," Molly said.

"You hear, it's not fair. Do you hear how I'm being threatened? Do you hear? Already yet. I could eat you. Both of you!"

Nancy discovered Jake asleep on the sitting room floor, moaning.

"Oh." Mrs. Hersh's big stricken brown eyes went from her son to the empty glass beside him on the floor. She brought a hand to her mouth, appalled. "Oh, my. I'll get the C-H-I-L-D-R-E-N out of the way immediately."

"He's asleep," Nancy said evenly. "He's asleep, that's all," and she shut the sitting room door softly behind her.

Jake surfaced to have his mother's voice come clawing at him out of the kitchen. She must have Molly on her lap again, he thought.

"Sweetie-pie! My precious one! Beauty! Such a face. Have

you ever seen such a face? Well, do you love your granny? Tell me."

No answer.

"Say I love you. I-LOVE-YOU."

"Ilubyou."

"*You hear?* She loves me! She loves me, the beauty."

"Would you care for some coffee, Mrs. Hersh?"

"Only if you're making."

"But I make coffee every morning, Mrs. Hersh."

"And who said no?"

Molly began to whine.

"I suppose it's uncomfortable for her, the dirty diaper. Maybe I should wake Jake."

"Jake has never changed a nappy in his life. Let's not wake him yet. And please, Mrs. Hersh, I'm not criticizing but—"

"Of course not, doll. Why should you?"

"—but when Jake comes in please don't give him the long sad look. As if this was his last day on earth. Ignore him. Let him read his newspapers."

"Certainly, doll," Mrs. Hersh said, sighing.

Seated with them at the kitchen table, Jake read,

THE CRIPPLED BOY WHO
WANTS TO
BACK BRITAIN

A 19-year-old cripple wants to back Britain but, in spite of the fact that every Thursday he goes to the local labor exchange and asks for a job, they cannot find him one.

But for George the half-mile journey from his home in Eden Street, Kingston, Surrey, is a supreme effort, for he has a disease which makes every step difficult.

Apart from his physical handicap he is registered as a blind person. Recently he—

The doorbell rang.

"Jake!"

Does she have to disturb him? It's such a pleasure to see him laugh.

Resentfully, Jake lowered his newspaper.

"I'll get it," Mrs. Hersh said, leaping up. "Let him read."

"*He'll get it.*"

Usually, Pilar would have answered the door. But she had picked this, of all times, to visit her family near Malaga, and so they would be without a housekeeper for another week.

It was the postman.

"Gorgeous day, isn't it?"

"Yes."

"I suppose you're grateful for this sort of weather?"

This was the flip side of a record they sometimes played. Then Jake was supposed to say, At home, I've seen blizzards in September, and the postman would shake his fat foolish head, astonished but grateful to have been born in such a temperate and civilized climate.

Screw him. This morning Jake would say nothing. But the postman didn't budge or hand over his mail.

"O.K., so you've seen the newspapers," Jake said.

"No."

"I don't see how you could have missed it."

There was, among other things, a familiar, yet all the same ominous-looking, brown envelope that had come OHMS. The tax inspector again.

"I'm sure the girl's lying," the postman said vehemently. Then he spoiled it by adding, "You're just not the type," but hopefully, quizzically.

"Neither was Christie," Jake said, shutting the door.

Molly said, "I ate my lunch."

"You mean breakfast, you nit," Jake said, yanking her curly blond hair.

Molly was only four, but Sammy was seven, so it was necessary to conceal the newspapers from him. Jake retreated into the sitting room and had already begun to rip open the long brown envelope when the door began to inch open tentatively.

"Is it bad news?"

"I haven't opened it yet, Maw."

"You're pleased I've come to stay with you. It's a help, isn't it?"

"Yes, Maw."

"I'm glad. The children love me, they're adorable."

Jake squashed the unopened letter into his dressing gown pocket.

"I've been here a week and you haven't once said how I look to you. Wouldn't you say I carry my years well? Don't you think I look young for my age?"

"Yes."

"Everybody says so. Dr. Bercovitch, he adores me, when I went to see him about the lump on my breast, this one, he was amazed. Simply amazed. *You're* sixty-two, he said. I don't believe it. With such breasts. And he's a doctor, you know. I get hot flushes, that's all. Nature is full of amazing beauty, but it can be cruel too. Well, the lawyers will cost you plenty?"

Nancy called from the kitchen. "Darling, would you like some coffee?"

"Coming."

Sipping coffee, pretending to be engrossed in the *Guardian*, Jake slid his foot along under the table until he touched Nancy. How he wished she would not nurse the baby at the kitchen table while his mother was there. Mrs. Hersh's hot appraising eye on Nancy's bosom enraged Jake. Suddenly Nancy let out a cry.

"Jake was a biter too, such a biter. I had tooth marks all around the nipples. He wouldn't remember, would you, *ketzelle?*"

"Do you mind," Jake asked, "if I take my coffee into the sitting room?"

But he could still hear her from there.

"Jake says I carry my years very well. He thinks I look young for my age. Of course," Mrs. Hersh added, probing, "maybe he was just flattering?"

This once, Nancy failed to deliver reassurances.

"My jaw's caved in a little, but listen, you can't tell with me, my teeth they're artificial. With others, they have them done up so white it's pathetic. With me it isn't vanity. Listen, I'm no fool. I don't kid myself or go in for blue rinses. To grow old isn't a pleasure."

"But one must retain a certain dignity," Nancy said in spite of herself.

"Yes, that's the truth. But it isn't like I was ever a raving beauty." Shooting Nancy a hot bright look, she added, "For a beautiful woman, it's worse, it must be utter hell to grow old."

The baby howled briefly as Nancy moved him to another breast.

"You must take care, doll. The milk can stretch the skin something awful. You want to take care of yourself."

Oh Nancy, Jake thought, Nancy my darling, and he began to sob. Without control. Without dignity. But with sufficient presence of mind to slip out of the sitting room and into the toilet. A torn section of the Saturday edition of the Montreal *Star* was folded over the radiator, opened at a full page Eaton's ad. Sports equipment and clothes.

Eaton's, Jake remembered, on a Saturday morning. It was Duddy, Duddy Kravitz, who took him there, only this time instead of trying to lift stuff in the toy department, they went directly to lingerie and when nobody was looking darted into the hall with changing rooms. Duddy pushed open the door just in time to gawk at a gorgeous girl stooping to snuggle into a black lace brassiere. A fat saleslady let out a shriek.

"I was only looking for my Aunt Ettie," Duddy whined, retreating.

The saleslady snatched Duddy by the arm. "I'm going to get the manager and have you sent to reform school for life. Filthy things."

"Aunt Ettie," Duddy hollered.

"Oh, let him go," the girl said.

Duddy stepped on the saleslady's foot and they were off, scooting between shoppers, and flying down the escalator. Outside, Duddy said, "Did you see her bazooms, butt? What a handful!"

"A lot of good it did you."

"*Shmeck!* Let him go, that's what she *said*, but did you see where she was *looking?* Right at my bone. One more minute and I would have had her up against the wall."

They found some butts, lit up, and climbed Mount Royal in search of couples in the bushes. "Everybody's doin' it, doin' it," Duddy sang, "pickin' their nose and chewin' it, chewin' it." He told Jake that once he discovered a couple stuck together, just like dogs, and had to summon the St. John's Ambulance man to get a kettle of boiling water to break them apart. Jake didn't believe him. *But there, your lordship, you have a scene from my early sex life.* How Hersh was first led astray, he thought, feeling better, much better.

Jake reached into his dressing gown pocket for a cigarillo, but came up with the most urgent of the morning mail instead. The letter from the tax inspector. The Grand Inquisitor, bless him, was keen to meet with Jake and his accountant for further epiphanies.

If only he had listened to Luke.

"I happen to know of at least three of Hoffman's clients who are being reassessed. If I were you, Jake, I'd move elsewhere."

"I'm scared to. He knows too much about me."

It was the sapient Oscar Hoffman who had first incorporated him, with a capital of one hundred pounds and three directors. Jake had come to him with a tangled and confused carton of accounts, receipts, and statements from his agent, which a bony little man, a bantam with steel-rimmed glasses, had gathered together, his smile servile, retreating from Hoffman's office as unobtrusively as he had entered. Then Hoffman had told Jake that from this day forward he would draw a salary of five thousand pounds from his company, PAYE being deducted at source. A further ten thousand pounds could be left in company accounts, for outgoings, as it were, and there would be no need for more inventive measures to be taken until such time as Jake's earnings burgeoned, as they certainly would, Hoffman assured him, beaming.

But at the end of the first year in the troubled life of Jacob Hersh Productions, Hoffman pondered the balance sheets and was displeased. "My goodness! Five thousand pounds in withdrawals!"

"Yes. I'm afraid so."

"Surely, you invested some of this in screen properties." Here he paused to peer at Jake. "Paying cash, you understand."

"Yes. Sure I did."

Which earned him a benevolent smile.

"And on your trip to Canada in February you hired a writer, I suppose. Took options on this and that. Kept a secretary, paying her in cash."

"Damn right I did."

"And here I see you were in Paris . . . 1959 . . . The George V, from the twelfth of April to the fifteenth . . ."

Nancy in a light blue Givenchy negligée with white lace cuffs and a high collar, tied in a bow around her neck, seated by the dressing table, head inclined, combing out her long black hair.

". . . was that not to meet with a producer, which would have made the trip deductible?"

Producer of my first-born son.

"Yes."

"Good. Very good, Mr. Hersh. Now you take these accounts home again and try to recall any other business trips, properties and options paid for in cash, and so forth and so on."

In his attic aerie, Jake opened the Horseman's cupboard and removed the journal. The entry on the first page read, "The Horseman: Born Joseph Hersh in a miner's shanty in Yellowknife, Yukon Territories. Winter. Exact date unknown." Following, there was a list of Joey's aliases. Jake flipped to another section, still sadly incomplete.

JEWS AND HORSES:

Babel, Isaac. *Sunset.*

LEVKA: You're an idiot, Arye-Leib. Another week, he says. Do you think I'm in the infantry? I'm in the cavalry, Arye-Leib, the cavalry . . . Why, if I'm even an hour late the sergeant will cut me up for breakfast. He'll squeeze the juice out of my heart and put me up for court-martial. They get three generals to try one cavalry man; three generals with medals from the Turkish campaign.

ARYE-LEIB: Do they do this to everyone or only the Jews?

LEVKA: When a Jew gets on a horse he stops being a Jew . . .

There was a cross-reference to Fitzgerald, F. Scott, *The Last Tycoon*. Monroe Stahr "guessed that the Jews had taken over the worship of horses as a symbol—for years it had been the Cossacks mounted and the Jews afoot. Now the Jews had the horses . . ."

Another entry, this one penciled in, read:

See Alberto Gerchunoff: *The Jewish Gauchos of the Pampas.* Also Rothschild's horsemen. The web of messengers.

The Horseman. Right now, Jake thought, maybe this very minute, he is out riding somewhere. Over the olive-green hills of the Upper Galilee or maybe in Mexico again. Or Catalonia. But, most likely, Paraguay.

"All right, then," Uncle Abe had said, seething. "Chew on this, Jake. From what I know of your cousin, if he is actually searching for Mengele, which I don't believe for a minute, if he is hunting this Nazi down and finds him," Uncle Abe had shouted, pounding the table, "he won't kill him, he'll blackmail him."

No, Jake thought, shutting out the obtruding voice, Uncle Abe was only trying to justify his own chicanery, *no, no,* and Jake imagined the avenging Horseman seeking out the villa with the barred windows off an unmarked road in the jungle, between Puerto San Vincente and the border fortress of Carlos Antonio López, on the Paraná River.

Joey, Joey.

In his mind's eye, Jake saw him cantering on a magnificent Pleven stallion. Galloping, thundering. Planning fresh campaigns, more daring maneuvers.

5

She continued:

"So I says to the fella, what do you think, I've never flown before, I don't know how *other* airlines do things? You're talking to a world traveler, a jet-setter yet. He doesn't even crack a smile, I tell you it takes all kinds. With Air Canada I says if you had to wait two hours for the take-off there would be sandwiches, *individually wrapped.* (We have this Saran Wrap now, I don't know if you get it here, I'll send you some, you can't do without it. Honestly, doll, what they can do nowadays, it's remarkable, who has to slave over a hot stove any more like I did?) With Air Canada I says to him, we wouldn't be treated like cattle, we would be served tea. Well, you should have seen him jump. *Yes, madame. Certainly, madame.* Good for you, the Indian lady says when I sit down again. Who even knew she could speak English, we'd been sitting side by side for an hour maybe? So I says I hope you don't mind me asking, but why is it you people paints dots on your forehead? Forgive me, I'm not the nosy type, but if you don't ask you never find out, isn't that so? Is it a Christian symbol, I says? No, she says, in India they're Hindu. You know, like the Beatles. And the dot means she's married. Oh, isn't that fascinating, I says. Now I've learned something. So we get to talking and she tells me that in India, you know, there is respect for the mother. Such respect. Her mother is a widow, she says, and they all live in one house, her family, her brother's family, her younger sister's family, all in one house, and the mother, well, the mother is the head of the family and everybody respects her, it's a time-honored Indian custom. Now isn't that interesting?"

As Mrs. Hersh and Nancy reached the top of the stairs, Jake flitted into the bedroom, unseen he hoped.

Heh-heh-heh.

The bedroom door opened. Oh God, no, Jake thought. But it was Nancy. "*Ketzelle*," she squealed, "nipple-biter, so there you are!"

Jake giggled.

"Let me come to court today."

"Absolutely no."

"Jake," she began tentatively, "there's something I've been meaning to ask you . . . ?"

"Harrod's?" he countered, grinning.

"Yes."

The handsomely appointed oak and marble toilets adjoining the men's hairdressing salon.

"They can't bring it up. It never made the charge sheet, duckie."

"And what about your friend Sergeant Hoare?"

"I no longer think it's bad luck that Hoare's involved. He's a surprisingly sympathetic type, really, and he's not holding a grudge."

"How can you tell?"

"Because we joked about it."

"Oh, you are such an innocent, Jake!"

Then, just as he was about to embrace her, Mrs. Hersh was with them. Immediately Jake stiffened.

"Good luck in court today."

"It's Harry who's going to need the luck today."

"May he rot in hell."

"He's my friend, Maw. We are in this together. Comrades.

Look at it this way, me and Harry, we're saints in the new order of things. *Lamed vovs.* Like Jean Genet. You explain that to her, Nancy." And slamming the door, he was gone.

Mrs. Hersh sunk to the bed. "You don't know what it is to be a mother. What an agony . . ."

"I have children too, Mrs. Hersh. And if he goes to prison—"

"You mustn't even think that."

"But I have to think that."

"I wouldn't go home, you know. I'd stay right here and stick by you for as long as I was needed. I'd stay, you can count on it. You married into a Jewish family, doll, and we stick together, you know. In a crisis we always stick together." Mrs. Hersh lowered her eyes and smoothed out her pajamas. "Many outstanding sociologists have observed that."

Nancy retrieved Jake's brown cashmere jacket from the floor and slid open the door to his built-in cupboard. Too late, she realized that Mrs. Hersh had come up softly behind her to peer inside.

"What is *that?*" Mrs. Hersh asked.

"Nothing," Nancy said, flushing.

"Nothing. *Some* nothing."

The military kit, including a rifle with a long-range sight, was stacked in a corner. With the body-building equipment.

"Oh, that," Nancy said, simulating laughter, "that's not Jake's. It's a friend's—yes, an actor's—he left it here."

"But the lying little bitch, I know she's a whore, yesterday in court didn't her lawyer say—"

"It's an actor's."

"Oh, an actor's. You mean it's for a play?"

"Yes," Nancy said. Emphatically yes. And glancing out of the window she caught Jake edging cautiously toward the terrace, where the baby, unsuspecting, was playing in his pram.

Smiling down at his five-month-old son, Jake extended his right arm surreptitiously and then flicked his fingers. No reaction. Shit, he thought, a clear case of LOCOMOTOR ATAXIA (also called Tabes Dorsalis or Posterior Spinal Sclerosis), a disease of the nervous system, manifested principally by disordered movements of the limbs in walking. Among the earlier symptoms are disorders of vision.

Perplexed, Jake brought his hand in closer, flicking his fingers again. Fiercely. The baby, who had been gurgling happily, frowned. His frown, Nancy witnessed from the window above, was just as severe as Jake's, and, unaccountably, her eyes filled with tears.

"Will you please stop tormenting the baby," Nancy called out.

"I'm playing with my son."

"I saw you. Now lay off, Jake."

Banging the window shut Nancy all but collided with Mrs. Hersh behind her. A hand held to her cheek, her eyes stricken, Mrs. Hersh asked, "Is he cruel to the baby?"

"Oh, it's nothing, Mrs. Hersh."

Sammy, still in his pajamas, slid into the bedroom—braking—*Topper* comics clutched in one hand. "What begins with an 'E' and has only one letter in it?" he asked.

"You hear," Mrs. Hersh said, her eyes filled with reverence, "at his age."

"Oh, Sammy, please. You must get dressed. You'll be late for school."

"There's a trick in it," Sammy said.

"A trick in it, you hear?"

"What begins with an 'E' and has—"

"I don't know."

"She doesn't know. Me too."

"Give up?"

"Yes, doll."

"An envelope."

"An envelope!" Mrs. Hersh clapped her hands, she hugged Sammy. "Delicious one," she said.

Nancy retreated around the other side of the bed to her bathroom but Mrs. Hersh followed her, scanning the glass shelves, sucking in every detail avidly, finally lifting a bottle of Arpège. "Such a big bottle of perfume."

"It's cologne."

Mrs. Hersh shrugged, lowering her eyes. Everything I do is wrong. Her gaze fell on the bidet; quickly, she averted her eyes.

To her way of looking, Nancy knew, the bidet was some sort of sinister gentile contrivance. For the orgies. "I'm going to wash now," Nancy said evenly. "Would you excuse me?"

"I'll get Sammy ready for school. It's my pleasure."

While he was waiting in the study for the black Humber with his solicitor Ormsby-Fletcher to come and pick him up, Jake flicked open the rest of the morning mail, hoping for a token of concern from Luke. Nothing. The first letter he opened was written on a round piece of stationery.

> Sept 21, 1967
>
> Dear Mr Hersh,
> I trust you will gather from this circular letter that I am no square, though all I ask is a square deal, not necessarily a great deal.

Jake began to skip.

> Despite the serious state of the Theatre today, I still have to live by my one and only talent, hence I throw myself at your mercy and beg you not to condemn me to a professional death.
> TV or not TV—that is for you to answer.
>
> Yours swingingly,
> JUDD WARD

Next came some overdue bills. Rose catalogues from the nursery in Sunningdale. Barclay's Bank reminder about his overdraft. Quarterly report from Investor's Growth Fund. Request for money from Anti-Apartheid Movement. *Saturday Night* magazine. DEBATE: OUR MONEY . . . or UNCLE SAM'S? ALSO FRENCH CANADIAN ATTITUDES TO SEX. There was a letter from the secretary of a recently formed minorities' society who wrote to say he

had been following Jake's case with keen interest and wished
him the best of British luck. He also asked Jake to lend his name
to a Sexual Bill of Rights that would be just the job for those
who require visual stimulation or who must inflict or receive
pain; for necrophiles and for those who enjoy troilism or trans-
vestism. The society's program called for the establishment of
clubs which would arrange meetings between so-called deviants
with complementary sex needs. Exhibitionists, for instance, would
be encouraged to expose themselves before a select audience of
voyeurs. The society also intended to petition M.P.'s, especially
the known deviants among them, for a start on the pornographic
social services. Taking the long view, it was hoped to establish
mobile brothels to provide for hospitals, institutions, the paralyzed, the crippled, the aged and the inhibited.

There was also the usual quota of obscene letters from
strangers who had been following the case in the newspapers,
but this morning only one correspondent had enclosed a photograph. It showed a lumpy nude lady, probably in her thirties,
kneeling on a mussed-up bed. She smiled grossly at the unseen
photographer, her hands cupping her enormous globular breasts,
squeezing the nipples. HOW WOULD YOU LIKE TO FUCK ME, PER-
VERT? was scrawled over the photograph with lipstick.

Sammy skittered into the room, demanding, "Why aren't you
taking me to school this morning?"

"I can't. I've got to be in the West End early again. Granny
will take you."

"Have you got a hangover?"

"Yes." Jake motioned him closer. Lowering his voice, he asked,
"Anything new on Tibbett?"

Tibbett, a schoolmate, was splendid at football.

"You won't tell Molly?"

Jake promised.

"He's being transferred to Leeds. They got twenty-one pounds
for him."

"But he must be worth more than that."

Mrs. Hersh was calling.

"Will you take me to school tomorrow, then?"

"Tomorrow's Saturday . . . Oh, Sammy!"

"Yes."

What do you say to him? I never got to know my father and now it's too late. Or, look here, starting next week I may be a boarder at Dartmoor for a while. Until I get home, walk tall.

"I enjoy you. I like taking you places with me. You've got style. Now hurry or you'll be late."

Five minutes later the doorbell rang and Jake opened his window and shouted down to Ormsby-Fletcher, "Coming."

Your lordship, look at it this way. There's a sexual revolution going on outside. All this switched-on lean hungry alienated white Negro cat wanted—

Quite, Mr. Hersh.

Ormsby-Fletcher, disconcertingly cheerful this (and every) morning, continued to chirp, making reassuring noises, as Jake alighted from the black Humber before the Old Bailey.

Cut into stone over the main entrance was the inscription:

Defend the children of the Poor;
Punish the Wrong-doer.

And if the Wrong-doer, like Harry, is a child of the Poor? Ormsby-Fletcher gave Jake the thumbs-up sign and Jake responded with a wink. His most ebullient wink.

Jew boys and WASP Canadians, Jake knew, had a long and dishonorable association with the Number One Court of the London Assizes. He wasn't the first.

In 1710, when Jonathan Wild, the Prince of Robbers, was the unquestioned *numero uno* of the London underworld, his indispensable aide was a *macher* named Abraham. "This Israelite," according to the Newgate Calendar, "proved a remarkable, industrious and faithful servant to Jonathan, who entrusted him with matters of the greatest importance." Traditionally, coiners and highwaymen, footpads, sharpers, and rogues of every description, pleaded—once apprehended—that they had flogged their ill-gotten gains to a Jew boy in Whitechapel. And, speaking of Jews, latter-day Jews, there was also Lord George Gordon, instigator of the riots of June 2, 1780. Lord Gordon's followers set fire to Newgate, laying it in ruins, and plundered the Sessions-house at the Old Bailey. Lord Gordon himself went on to libel Marie-Antoinette and Count d'Amédar, but did not reveal himself as certainly deranged until he ". . . was discovered, in the habit of a Jew, at Birmingham, with a long beard; and having undergone circumcision . . . (having) firmly embraced the Jewish faith." Once Lord, now Reb, Gordon lingered on in Newgate for some years, praying daily, keeping a kosher cell, until he died of jail fever. Once the most popular idol of the mob, he perished, as the Newgate Calendar put it, in the company of the very refuse of society, ". . . negros, Jews, gypsies, and vagabonds of every description."

The social tone hadn't much improved by 1880, when the fastidious Montagu Williams, Q.C., complained in his memoirs of the "shabby Jews with anxious faces" who loitered outside the courthouse. Shabby Jews who had knit into defiant gangs, in 1903, and declared their intention to free the accused murderer Lipski, which obliged the warders of Newgate to carry guns for the first time in history on the Polish Jew's hanging day.

Among WASP Canadian precursors, Jake, of necessity, identified most closely with the cross-eyed sex nut, junkie, and McGill alumnus, Thomas Neill Cream, debauched habitué of the fleshpots of South Lambeth about which Hollingshead wrote in *Ragged London*: "The houses present every conceivable aspect of filth and wretchedness" and "the faces that peer out of the narrow windows are yellow and repulsive: some are the faces of Jews, some of Irishwomen . . ."

Thomas Neill Cream, begot in Glasgow, in 1850, came to Montreal as a child and, at the age of twenty-two, entered McGill, emerging four years later, another immigrant fulfilled, with his M.D. degree. "An excellent worker, a brilliant boy," his professor wrote, "but he has some queer ideas: monstrously queer ideas, and I don't know which way they may lead him."

They led Tommy, for openers, to murder with morphine the Toronto girl an irate father forced him to marry at pistol point. As the girl lay dying in Cream's arms, he sobbed in apparent grief, and then lit out for Illinois, where he did in an elderly rancher with strychnine, the better to savor his rambunctious wife, for which indulgence he endured ten years in the pen, after which he sailed for London. Swinging London (Eng.), where the cross-eyed doctor poisoned at least six *filles de joie* within a year, four of whom died in agony, before he was apprehended and hanged in 1892, falsely claiming on the gallows to be Jack the Ripper.

Yet another Canadian bigmouth trying to make his mark in London.

Possibly, Jake reflected, sitting in the dock, lowering his eyes demurely whenever a juror glanced at him, possibly colonials coming to London have always had a taste for nymphs of the pavements, and he sang to himself,

> "I'm not a butcher, I'm not a Yid,
>   Nor yet a foreign skipper,
> But I'm your own light-hearted friend,
>   Yours truly, Jake the Ripper."

6

Jake had only been gone an hour when the phone rang. "Yes," Mrs. Hersh said, "she's here. Who shall I say is calling, please?" But before the man on the other end of the line could identify himself—

"Is it for me?"

"Yes," Mrs. Hersh agreed, proffering the phone.

Nancy took it, yielding the baby to her mother-in-law. "Could you take him into the kitchen, please? You can give him some mashed banana, if you like."

Suddenly, without a struggle, Fort Knox surrenders its gold. Suddenly I'm not too unhygienic to feed my own grandson.

"Yes, certainly," she heard Nancy say, "as long as I'm back by five. He phones as soon as court adjourns . . ."

"You're going out?" Mrs. Hersh demanded, appalled.

"So it seems," Nancy agreed icily.

"What shall I say if the lawyer phones at noon?"

Say I've gone to Forest Mere Hydro for a colonic irrigation. "I must get a breath of air, Mrs. Hersh. I need it."

Nancy retrieved the baby, nursed him, and sang him to sleep. Mrs. Hersh kept Molly occupied in the kitchen, helping her to make a Lego building, until Nancy reappeared, no longer in slacks, but dressed to kill, wearing her Schmucci-Pucci, if you don't mind, and smelling like a perfumery. Yankel's Princess. She bestowed a smile on Mrs. Hersh. A small smile. "Now please don't worry about a thing. Molly will play in the garden, like a good girl. Ben's next feeding is at four. I'll be back long before and he should sleep through anyway."

Alone in the house, Mrs. Hersh did not sift through Nancy's wall-to-wall, cedar-lined cupboard this time, for its extravagant contents, out of Dior and Simonetta, Saint Laurent and Lanvin, had already been revealed to her. Neither did she bother with the umpteen drawers of lingerie, which were no longer a mystery to her either. For Yankel's Princess, silk panties yet. If she ever got a splinter in her ass, that one, only rosewood would do.

Mrs. Hersh hugged Molly, sent her out into the garden with the promise of a present after lunch, and climbed into Jake's attic aerie, where he did not keep a photograph of his mother. His father, the prize idiot, yes. Nancy, naturally. Why, there was even sufficient room on the walls for photographs, plucked from German magazines, of the Von Papen family, Mrs. Goering out shopping, and an S.S. general, as well as an absurd painting of Field Marshal Montgomery. But little me? No.

One cupboard was almost bare. For the riding habit and saddle he usually kept there were both being held at the Old Bailey. Exhibits for the prosecution. But in the other cupboard she was astonished to discover stacks and stacks of tinned food. Shelf upon shelf of cans. A regular supermarket. Soup-size tins, pilchard-type cans, sardine tins. What was so baffling was there was not one tin with a label on it. The labels had been peeled from every single tin. Mrs. Hersh took a can that seemed to be salmon or tuna, either would do, and descended to the kitchen, which she knew from sour experience would be stuffed with *dreck*. In the fridge, bacon and sausages from Harrod's, some smoked eel maybe, and a larder crammed with tins of crab and lobster, mussels, snail shells, pork beans and other *traifes*, but no gefilte fish or kosher salami. Her Highness had forgotten to phone Selfridge's, dialing with a pencil, heaven forbid she should break a nail, they're a foot long. Anyhow there was bound to be tomato and lettuce, and salmon would be nice. But when Mrs. Hersh opened the unlabeled tin she was amazed to come upon a gooey, stewlike substance with a decidedly nasty smell.

It must be pork, she thought, shoving it aside hastily.

7

When Nancy had first met Jake, at one of Luke's parties, she had asked him, "Are you a writer?" swallowing the too.

"No," he had replied, affronted, "I'm the director."

Which was awfully conceited, yes, but preferable to how he had recently come to identify himself.

"I'm a director. Not the kind you send for—the type you use if he's in town."

1959 it was, following Luke's Royal Court triumph and while Jake was teetering in limbo, drinking prodigiously as he awaited the opportunity to direct his first film.

On arrival at Luke's party, only a day after she had flown into London, Nancy, thrust into a roomful of jabbering strangers, was instantly aware of a dark, slouching, curly-haired man watching her. Unevenly shaven, his tie loosened, his shirt riding out of his baggy trousers, Jacob Hersh hovered on the edge of whatever group she joined. Scrutinizing the tilt and fullness of her breasts, appraising the curve of her bottom, and searching for a flaw in the turn of her ankle. When she sat on the sofa, crossing her long legs, in animated conversation with an actor, she was not altogether surprised to catch him sinking to the floor opposite, drink in hand, edging lower and lower. Shamelessly seeking

out her stocking tops. Infuriated, flushing, Nancy briefly considered hiking her dress, shedding her panties, and flinging them
in his mournful face. Instead she drew her legs closer to her, tug-
ging at her dress. It wasn't, she grasped, so much that he was a
dirty little man as that he probably felt she was inaccessible to
him and was therefore determined to find fault with her. Being
a singularly lovely girl, she was in fact used to the type, having
suffered considerably at their hands at university. And Jake, more
than anything, reminded her of those insufferably bright boys on
campus, self-declared intellectuals, usually Jewish, charged with
bombast and abominable poetry in lower-case letters, who were
aroused by her presence, and yet were too gauche (and terrified) to speak out and actually ask for a date. Instead they sat
at the table next to her in the student union, aggressively calling
attention to themselves. Speculating loudly on what they took to
be her icy manner. Or they slid belligerently into the seat next to
her at lectures, trying to bedazzle with their questions. They
also ridiculed her to girls less happily endowed, wreaking vengeance for a rejection they anticipated, but were too cowardly to
risk, and bandied suggestions about her secret sexual life sufficiently coarse to make her cry. No matter that she took immense pains not to be provocative, swimming in sloppy joe
sweaters, sensible skirts, and flat shoes. Going out of her way to
discourage boys the other girls coveted. For this only proved
that Nancy Croft was remote; splendidly made, yes, but glacier-
like.

Drink in hand, Jake trailed after her everywhere, always on
the rim of her group. If she so much as ventured an observation
on London, or remarked on a play she had seen, he didn't comment, but smirked condescendingly, as if to say, idiot. If she
was trapped into conversation with a bore, he condemned her
with his eyes for tolerating him, raising his eyebrows, as if to
say, only a dolt would have time for him. Loping after her
from room to room, he twice made forays into her group. On
the first occasion, as a man, whispering in her ear, made her
laugh, he barged in, gratuitously rude, and when that failed to
demolish him, inquired pointedly after the man's wife and chil-

dren. On the other occasion, adjudging her too responsive to the flirtations of a man more handsome, taller, he actually plucked him by the sleeve and called him aside on one pretext or another. Jacob Hersh would not let her out of sight, even to refill his glass, until she was safely in conversation with a homosexual, when he would lurch off grinning widely.

Finally, Nancy thrust her empty glass at him. "Would you mind getting me a drink?"

"Who? Me?"

"Yes. You."

"WehaventmetmynamesJacobHersh."

It was then she asked him, Are you a writer, swallowing the too, and he replied, no, I'm the director, which allowed her a chance to smile.

Vengefully, he countered, "Don't tell me you're an actress?"

"No."

Redeeming her glass, she turned her back on him to chat with somebody else, responding with exaggerated warmth. Then, as she could sense his eyes raking her back, lingering on her bottom, she resisted her first impulse, which was to wiggle it at him, and slid away, her back against the wall, a man between them, so that Jake could not see and judge any of her. And as the man proved a bore, yet another competitor among so many jousting egos, she excused herself abruptly and went to fetch her coat.

"Would you call me a taxi, please, Luke."

Fumbling hands helped her into her coat. "I've got a car," Jake insisted.

"I think I'll walk. I could do with some fresh air."

"Me too," Jake chipped in cheerily and, without waiting for an invitation, he followed after.

Not a word was said until they started down Haverstock Hill together, Nancy's black hair flowing, her pale oval face bemused.

"What a beautiful girl you are," Jake allowed angrily.

"Thank you."

"Well, it's not the first time you've heard it," he muttered, shrugging.

"No. It isn't."

"But it's the first time you heard it from me," he hollered, waving a finger in her face, "and I don't say it to everybody. Like Shapiro. That glib prick."

"Who's he?"

"The one who was licking the wax out of your ears."

"Oh, him," she exclaimed with simulated warmth.

"Are you living in London or just visiting?"

"It depends on whether or not I'll like it."

"You'll like it," he assured her.

"It's settled, then?"

"Are you being sarcastic now?"

"I'd have to find a job."

"Maybe I can help. What do you do?"

"Strip at parties."

"Seriously, what do you do?"

"What's the difference?"

"You're not, for Chrissake, a social worker?"

"Why are you looking for reasons to dismiss me?"

"Or, God help us, a child psychologist?"

"Guess again."

"You rich?"

"My father's a shoe salesman."

"Attention must be paid."

"Oh, but you are a funny fellow!"

Which brought them to the front door of her flat on Arkwright Road. As she drove the key into the door, he lingered.

"All right. You can come in for a nightcap," she said, "if you promise not to be awkward."

He nodded, acquiescing, but she didn't care for his smile.

"So long as it's crystal clear," she said, "that I'm not inviting you into my bed."

While she fetched the drinks, she could see him, through the kitchen hatch, lifting up magazines, like a judge sifting evidence. Two years detention for reading *Vogue*. Six months in solitary for *Elle. The Ladies' Home Journal*, off with her head. Next he stooped to scan the bookshelves, probing for bad or modish taste, and snickering with delight to find evidence of both. Enjoying herself, she did not protest that she had sublet the flat. Then Jake stumbled on *The Collected Stories* of Isaac Babel lying on the coffee table and seized it, taken aback. "Are you reading this?" he demanded accusingly.

"No. I hoped I'd be able to bring you back here and I left it out to impress you. Do you recommend it?"

Jake retreated, narrowing his eyes. His manner softened. "I'm sorry," he said.

"You've been judging me all night. What right have you?"

"None. Come to dinner with me tomorrow night."

But she already had tickets for *Hedda Gabler.*

"It's a terrible production," Jake exploded. "An abortion. That bastard couldn't direct traffic," and he carried on to denounce Binky Beaumont, The Royal Court Theatre, Donald Albery, J. Arthur Rank, Granada, and the BBC. Until finally, she said: "I'm very, very tired. I only arrived yesterday, you know."

Leaping up, Jake emptied his glass. "I didn't make a pass, because you said—Maybe I should try. Maybe you didn't really mean it."

"I meant it. Honestly."

But he attempted to kiss her anyway. She did not respond. "O.K., O.K., you meant it. Can I pick you up at the theater and take you to dinner after the play?"

"I'm going with someone."

"You are. Who?"

"Is it your affair?"

"You're not ashamed, are you?"

And so she told him who.

"Him. Oh my God," he exclaimed, clapping a hand to his forehead, "you poor child. He's a hopeless prick."

"Like Shapiro?"

"Worse. He's one of the biggest phonies in town. He'll call you darling and send back the wine and flatter the hell out of you. Why are you going out with him?"

"If you don't mind—"

"What about Thursday night?"

"Luke's taking me out."

Which seemed, quite abruptly, to crush him. He didn't protest. He wasn't rude. He turned to go.

"I'm free Friday night," she said.

"All right. Friday night."

But, on Thursday, only ten minutes before Luke was to arrive, Nancy's phone rang.

"I'm in my bedroom," Luke said, "and I've got to talk quickly. Jake Hersh is here. Remember him?"

"Yes, indeed."

"He came by to invite me to dinner. It's awkward. He's in a truculent mood. I told him I had a date, but he said we could both come. Would you mind, terribly?"

Within minutes, Jake sat beaming on her sofa. Luke, agitated, was flicking his thumbnail against his teeth. Nancy poured drinks.

"I'll get the ice," Jake said, jumping up. "Don't you bother, Nancy. I know where it is."

"I will get the ice," Nancy said evenly.

"My God, I hope I'm not intruding."

But, once at Chez Luba, it was Nancy who began to feel curiously redundant. As the two friends vied for her approval, flicking stories off each other like beach boys with towels, ostensibly in fun, but stinging each time, she was, at once, immensely entertained but hardly ever allowed to get a word in herself. Luke told amusing anecdotes about the actors in his play, evoking her laughter, Jake's bile.

"Tell her about the New York producer," Jake said, glaring over the rim of his wine glass. "You know, and the girl who was there especially for you to—"

"Jake never betrays a confidence," Luke interrupted.

Then Jake told her about the time he had directed a play, for Granada TV, and one of the leading actors had died of a heart attack during transmission, and how from there on in he had had to improvise with his cameras.

Luke invited her to spend an afternoon watching them shoot at Pinewood Studios and Jake asked her to see a television play from the control booth.

On and on they volleyed, slamming at each other, and Nancy,

exhausted, was grateful when it was finally time to go, Jake seizing the bill.

"We'll take a taxi," Luke said, taking Nancy's arm.

But Jake, betting on Luke's stinginess overriding all, said, "No, I'll drive you. It's on my way home."

Jake held the front door of his car open for Nancy, but she slid gracefully into the back seat, close to Luke. Bitch, whore. "Who shall I drop off first?" Jake sang out.

"We're going to Nancy's place."

She didn't invite Jake in for a nightcap when he braked hard outside her front door. "Shall I wait for you here?" he asked Luke.

"Good night," he said, whacking the door shut, "and thanks for dinner."

Ungrateful bastard. Second-rate talent. Jake swung around the block, waiting out a red light and obliged to make a short detour to avoid a one-way stream, before he pulled up on the other side of the road and doused his lights to wait. *Adonoi, Adonoi,* Jake prayed, let this be her time of month. Make her bleed. *Not that he'd mind, the filthy goy bastard.*

A half hour passed. The living room lights went off and the bedroom curtains were drawn.

—Oooo, she moans, oooo, your hands are driving me crazy. Please come inside me now.

Trembling with excitement, Jake lit one cigarette off another.

—But why are you still small?

Heh heh. Jake laughed out loud, slapping his knee. Second-rate talent, a miser, and can't get it up, either.

—Let me eat you, then.

Oh, no. Don't, Nancy. He's got trench mouth.

An hour. The bedroom lights out. Come to think of it, Jake decided, she's not that bright. Or beautiful. Her teeth are uneven.

Two hours. And Jake, loathing her, enraged with himself for sitting there in the dark like a moonstruck teenager, reflected, if I die before I wake, and the Lord my soul does take, I will be buried without ever having directed Olivier, had a black girl, seen Jerusalem, delivered my speech turning down the Academy

Award, tried heroin, fought for a cause, owned a cabin cruiser, had a son, been a prime minister, given up smoking, met Mao, had a homosexual experience, made a film of the Benye Krick stories, rejected a knighthood, had two ravishing girls in my bed at the same time, killed a Nazi, brought Hanna to London, sailed first class on the *Île de France*, cast Lauren Bacall in a thriller, met Evelyn Waugh, read Proust, come four times in a night (do they, really?) or had a season of my films presented at the National Film Theatre.

At your age, Orson Welles was famous. Dostoevski had written *Crime and Punishment*. Mozart had done his best work. Shelley, dead.

> It was never my wish
> To be Sir Bysshe

Ineffably depressed, Jake started the car and drove off. Swinging around a corner, past Luke's flat, glancing up at the windows automatically, his heart leaped with sudden joy to see the bedroom light on.

Luke came to the door in his dressing gown.

"What are you doing here?" Jake demanded.

"I live here."

It was four a.m.

"And what, if I may be so bold as to ask, are you doing here?"

"I couldn't sleep."

"Me neither. Would you care for a drink?"

They talked about Luke's play transferring, a script Jake was considering, Senator John Kennedy's chances, and whether, futile as it seemed, they should squat in Trafalgar Square with the others next time. They talked about everything but Nancy. Finally, Jake asked, "You didn't stay with her very long, did you?"

"Left almost immediately. She had a headache."

"Too bad."

"Yeah. What did you think of her?"

"Not much. You?"

Which, over the years, evolved into a private joke between the three of them. One of the moments that bound them together.

The next evening, Nancy remembered, Jake arrived early, early and contrite, expecting to find her in a temper.

They flew to Paris together in the morning and only there, as she lay in his arms, did Jake reveal that if she had reprimanded him for ruining her evening with Luke, or threatened to send him away, he had planned to pretend to slip his disc.

"Then I would have stayed a week—helpless in your bed— unable to resist your most perverse designs on my loins."

Remembering, Nancy smiled to herself in the taxi.

1959 it was.

Now there was Sammy. Molly. Ben. Eight years swallowed whole.

Oh, Jake, Jake, my darling, why did you have to go and make such a fool of yourself? And me.

As Luke swept into the Duke of Wellington, late and breathless, his head bobbing over the other drinkers, it was an instant before he espied Nancy, and in that instant she saw him through Jake's jaundiced eyes. Luke's once oblong head rounder and wrinkled, fleshy, thinning flaxen hair buttressed by sideboards and a Fu Manchu mustache. Luke wore a yellow turtleneck sweater, a brown suede jacket, and punishingly slender hipsters with patch pockets that could only have been tailored by Doug Hayward. Our friend, the Trendy, Jake would say.

Well, why not, Nancy objected, resisting Jake's opprobrium, resentful that after eight years his prejudices should impinge first of all, even in his absence. Luke, she argued with herself, was still a delight, he likes me and always remembers my name, unlike so many of the others. Besides, they're all fighting forty now.

Luke gathered Nancy to him. "How did it go yesterday?"

"Let's not talk about it yet. How was Canada? Were you lionized everywhere?"

No, not everywhere. But all their old friends in Toronto, he said, had wanted to know about Jake's trouble, oozing sympathy but hungering for dirt. "Now look," he added hastily, "there's something I want to make clear. I don't think for a minute Jake is going to be sentenced to anything more than an embarrassing reprimand, but you are not to worry about money. I can tide you over without even feeling it."

The understatement of the year. All the same, Nancy was touched. Tears welled in her eyes. "Yes, I'm sure you would."

"Are you being sarcastic?" he asked testily.

"No. Honestly. But I couldn't. Jake wouldn't like it."

Luke didn't insist. "It's crazy," he said, "the whole business. I don't believe a word of it. Do you?"

Nancy looked at him sharply. "I didn't think you'd be in need of reassurances."

"Hell, no, we shared a flat for three years, remember? I know there's nothing kinky about his sexual proclivities. If anything, he's a prude."

"Yes. But he's not in this mess alone."

Harry had been to prison twice already, once for blackmail, and she told him about it.

"And what does Jake say to that?"

"He thought Harry was bragging, and when he discovered it was true, he was impressed. It seemed so inventive and bitter," and saying as much, she had to laugh too. So did Luke. "Who would have thought Hershel had the nerve, Jake said." Harry, she added, had already approached *News of the World* to sell them the inside story after the trial.

"And what did Jake say to *that?*"

"He's endlessly amused by it. Harry fascinates him."

"He's crazy."

Nancy tightened.

"I'm joking. I mean it, well, affectionately. The whole damn thing is ridiculous. The lawyers will explain how he has always collected strays, that he was Harry's benefactor, and how he had just flown over from the funeral in a distressed state and you were in Cornwall with the kids and—"

"What if he wants to go to prison?"

"Oh, come off it, Nancy."

"But you hardly know him any more, Luke."

"He made it impossible. The jokes got more and more gritty. About my girls. My style of living. Everything. O.K., to put it coarsely, I've made it. But that doesn't necessarily mean I'm corrupt. To see him was to apologize for myself. Especially the so-called name dropping. Hell, I'm no name dropper. I just happen to see those people all the time."

"But he doesn't."

"We were like brothers once, you know. Shit. Would you care for another drink?"

"I mustn't."

"Try to think of it as funny."

"Ha ha."

"It isn't now. I know, I know. But once it's over—Oh, hell. We were young together," he thought aloud, "full of hope and promise."

"Not all the candidates pass."

Which is what Jake had said.

8

Mrs. Hersh rapped on the window, summoning Molly from the garden, and the two of them ate eggs and toast together, boiled not fried, because she knew better than to so much as touch the First Lady's omelette pan again, it was so oily you could skate in it, but to have once given it the scrubbing it needed with hot water and soap was a criminal offense in her books.

Then, once she had settled Molly into bed for her afternoon nap, Mrs. Hersh, still enduring hunger pangs, prepared herself a cup of instant coffee. She just happened to be standing by the living room window, she was not spying no matter what Nancy thought, when the car pulled up. A low-slung, very, very expensive type sports car. The man who slid out and walked around to open the door for Nancy (you bet she couldn't turn the handle herself, the little *tzaske*) was taller than Jake, a skinny one, a *loksh*, with straw-colored hair and glasses.

A *goy*.

He embraced Nancy, he stroked her long black hair.

"Everything's going to work out."

"I mustn't lose my milk."

Luke held her tight.

"If I lose my milk, I'll hate him."

"You won't," he said, rocking her. "You couldn't."

"I'll hate him no matter what, if I lose my milk."

Then, instinctively, Nancy looked up, saw her mother-in-law's ashen face peering out of the window, and froze.

"Fuck!"

Oy veh iz mir. Mrs. Hersh retreated to the kitchen and sank into a chair, overwhelmed by hot flushes, her heart pounding. She heard the front door open, Nancy slip out of her coat, taking ages to hang it up, and then drift into the living room. Now there was the clink of a bottle against the glass-topped Italian table with the gold-painted flowery base. A cigarette lighter flicked, failed. Flicked again. Finally, Yankel's Princess floated into the kitchen, delicately holding a glass in a hand with long silvery fingernails. Three children and still she managed the hairdresser once a week and witch's fingernails. Nancy reeked more of the hard stuff now than perfume. Her eyes were swollen.

"Were the children any trouble?"

"How could they be any trouble, they're my precious darlings. I live only for them."

"I love them too, Mrs. Hersh, but I certainly do not live only for them."

You. You whore. Mrs. Hersh shoved the open, smelly can at Nancy. "What's this?"

"Dog food."

"Yes, that's what I thought. I said to myself, it's dog food. But you haven't got a dog."

"No."

"You had one then?"

"Never," Nancy said, beginning to enjoy herself.

"I opened it by mistake. I wasn't wearing my glasses. I'm in such a state, just thinking of him in court right now. Naturally, if I'd read the label . . ."

"But there was no label. There's no label on any of the cans in his attic."

Tears filled Mrs. Hersh's eyes and, all at once, Nancy relented. Her tone softer now, conciliatory, she said, "Don't you know that everything in his office is kept in a special order. He can tell if anything has been touched."

"What's it for, my God, the dog food?"

"For Ruthy."

"Ruthy?"

"Mrs. Flam. Harry's betrothed, as it were. It's of no importance. But please don't go through his things, Mrs. Hersh. For your own sake, please don't."

"I wouldn't in a million years—" She rose, stumbling. "It's the flushes. I think I'll lie down."

"Let me help you," Nancy said, taking her arm.

9

Jake's past, which he had always taken to be characterized by self-indulgence, soaring ambition, and too large an appetite, could at last be seen by him to have assumed nifty contours. A meaningful symmetry. The Horseman, *Doktor* Mengele, Harry, Ingrid, all frog-marching him to where he was to stand so incongruously, stupefied and inadequate, on trial in Courtroom Number One at the Old Bailey.

Yesterday the case against him had looked shaky, very shaky, but today, Friday, Harry was to be summoned to the stand for the first time. Harry, the idiot. And Jake, fear enveloping him, recalled their first meeting or, rather, what he had ruinously taken to be their initial encounter, the aggrieved Harry correcting him before leaving the house.

"You don't remember having met me before, do you?"

"No. Sorry."

"Not to worry. Very few people notice me. I'm used to it, don't you know."

But even then he hesitated at the door.

"You say you haven't got the money, Mr. Hersh, and that even if you so desired you couldn't spare it. A pity, that. For is it not a fact that at the moment you are being paid more monthly not to work than I take home in a year?"

"Who told you that?"

"I put it to you that you have lied to me."

"Where have we met before, Harry?"

"I take it you are implying that we couldn't possibly move in the same circles."

"Inferring," Jake said, the nastiness rising in him.

Harry's cheeks bled red.

"Now tell me how come you know," Jake asked, "or think you know about my private affairs?"

"If you lied to me about that, I say you are also prevaricating about your cousin. You know the present abode of Joseph Hersh. Or de la Hirsch," he added snidely, "and you are protecting him."

Standing in the dock, Jake, in his mind's eye, conjured up Harry as he had struck him on his first visit to the house.

Sneering, ferret-like Hershel. A Londoner born, a Londoner bred. National Health had been enacted in time for the steel-rimmed glasses, but too late to mend the crooked tartar-encrusted teeth. Harry's brown hair was thin and dry, his skin splotchy and almost as gray as his mac, and there were little tufts of hair spurting out of his ears. From the dampness, probably, Jake had thought at the time, like the shoots that grow in potatoes if they are abandoned under the sink.

Bony little Harry, a veritable bantam, wore a pullover under his jacket and a CND badge on his lapel. The badge was redundant, for his manner bespoke sufficiently of inherited discontent exacerbated by experience. Black, wintry experience. Jake immediately recognized in him the deprived man seething at the end of the bus queue in the driving rain. As he hurtled past in a taxi. It was Harry who called on his way home for a gallon of Esso Pink and lit the Aladdin before setting out the Birdseye frozen potato chips and Walls sausages for his solitary supper. While Jake upbraided the butcher at Harrod's, demanding and getting a thicker, better-hung slice of Scotch rump. Harry who joined the Christmas club in July and endured tallymen and was not chagrined by the cutback in bank overdrafts. Or the waiting list for Jaguars. Or the ski conditions at Klosters. Or the punitive capital gains tax. Harry whom the world insulted. His gray eyes were perfervid and brimmed with rancor. When he settled into the new winged armchair from Heal's, Jake couldn't help noticing the shine on his trousers and the leather strips sewn into his cuffs.

"Nice. Very nice," Harry said, taking in everything in the living room. "Ruthy would fancy a place like this."

Ruthy who was still collecting points on the council waiting list.

"But she can't afford it. Between you Yanks and Rachmanism the rents have been forced up everywhere."

"I'm a Canadian."

The world seemed especially ordered to tantalize Harry, mock and inflame him. Wakening, the morning after his first visit to Jake's house, to light his smelly heater and wait for the kettle to whistle, he read on the front page of the *Express* of the latest goddess to descend on Heathrow, Gina Lollobrigida, snug in her coat of jaguar and silver fox. "In addition to the coat La Lollo the Magnificent wore on arrival, she brought another three—a tiger, a sable, and another jaguar. And security staff at the Savoy Hotel were guarding the star's suite last night." There was also a photograph of the latest in *Avenger* girls, stooping to reveal a deep enough cleavage to ram it into, given a chance. Then there was a picture of some Swedish bit, the wind billowing her mini high as her cunt. Oh, to stir it into a swamp, and plug it once and for all.

And Harry only had to flip the page, making a mental note to drop off his seed-stained sheets at the laundromat en route to the office, before other people's good times obtruded.

MY LIFE AND LOVES
By Air Canada Steward on Sex Charge

Air Steward Paul Crane of Kingston Hill, Surrey, accused of raping an air hostess, told yesterday of the women in his life.

He said he had his regular girlfriend at Surbiton and he would take out air stewardesses between flights.

There was his girlfriend at traffic control and he also took out one or two other stewardesses.

His counsel asked: "How many of them do you sleep with?"

Crane: "I sleep with nearly all of them."

Those stewardesses, Harry was well aware, were not picked for their language skills but were selected for tit size and enthusiasm for taking it from behind, driving it in themselves, impaled on the captain's lap at thirty thousand feet while the plane was on automatic pilot. Which you could tell just sniffing it on them as they hobbled out of the flight cabin to the loo for a rinse, and if you so much as asked them if there were any cartons of fags or flasks on sale, even if this was the yabbo's cheap midnight flight to Paris, they gave you the I-know-you're-dirt look and said, "I've only got two hands, haven't I?" And Harry knew what they'd just been at, tuppenny whore.

Harry, enjoined to begin his day with a pinta, end it with a Horlick's. Whom Guinness Was Good For. Backing Britain. Because Labor had Soul. Harry, urged to go to work on an egg.

Into the crammed underground, old bastards gargling their phlegm ("We're on our way, brothers!") and mustachioed girls depositing their gum everywhere (Gala Is A Girl Like You), he was assailed again by posters of bikinied girls, their legs widespread for entry, enticing him to the beaches of Malta or Majorca. Girls clutching a bottle of sherry to their bare breasts, fondling it, beseeching him to "Drink . . ." Girls with the longest legs imaginable, lubricant girls, rolling nylons on like condoms. Girls snuggling into bras and rising from the bath, towel ready to drop, if only he'd hurry and join the queue outside the Old Compton or the new Windmill, unzipping and sliding his mac over his lap to whack off for the big scene.

Yes, yes indeed, everybody else, everywhere else, was getting his. Everybody with money that is.

Ascending at Oxford Street, squeezed into an escalator spilling over with tit and bum, with self-satisfied teenage girls in minis.

Sleepy-eyed and no wonder. Grudging insolent shorthand/typists or shop assistants by day they were, but pill-crazed groupies by night, plaster casters maybe, the window ledges of their bed-sitters choked with the imprints of lumpenproletariat cocks. But with no time for Harry, born too late. Who didn't strum the guitar badly or wear his hair down to his shoulders. Who just happened to prefer Beethoven to the Rolling Stones. Who had a social conscience.

Drawn to the newsstand, buffeted as he vacillated, Harry, un-able to pass it by as he had yesterday and the day before, not buying *Mayfair*, snatched it in a rage this morning, if only to see what lies they were purveying now. THE NUDEST NATHALIE DE-LON. SUSAN STRASBERG STRIPS. SCRUMPTIOUS SALLY'S ALLEY IS A SENSUAL PLACE TO BE. Stuffing the magazine into his briefcase, Harry turned into Soho Square, then the lift, off at the fifth floor and right to his cell, where basketsful of other people's prodigious expenses awaited his incomparable fiddling.

Come noon, Father Oscar Hoffman, A.F.A., A.A.I.A., breezed past, raining smiles like blessings, off to a two-hour business lunch at the White E.

—I'm told, Eisenthal says, his eyes watchful, that Triplex Tube is ripe for a takeover. What do you hear, Oscar?

—Bricks and mortar. Put it in bricks and mortar and you can't go wrong.

Harry, in a playful mood, invited the enormous Sister Pinsky to lunch, trying not to imagine how many pleats there were in her stomach and what agony it must be to support such pie-size breasts. "Come away with me, Sandra, we'll pool our vouchers and have us an orgy."

"Oh, you're a terror, Harry."

A ton of flesh quaking away.

"Would you drop your knickers to pose for a magazine, Sandra? Like Nathalie Delon?"

"For me," she replied, heaving, "it would have to be a double-page spread at least."

Sister Pinsky was reading a biography of King Farouk, of all people.

"For me," she said, "it symbolizes a classically misspent life."

Oh, Sandra, give me Farouk's life, and I shall take his squalid death. Allow me thirty-room hotel suites, belly dancers, and beauty queens. Make me squander my nights gambling a hundred thousand pounds away. Let me know every call girl in Rome by name and pubis and you know what, darling, you can have my office to call your own. Everything in my building society account. My insurance. My pension scheme. My cameras. My past, my present, my future.

Back to his cell and the never-ending other people's bills and ledgers and fiddling.

It was three thirty before a merry Father Hoffman sailed past, tacking to say hello.

"Do you know who was sitting at the next table?"

Harry attended with a smile.

"Warren Beatty with a real sex pot. He breaks off a piece of bread, chews it, and slides it into her mouth with his tongue. Right in the restaurant. Rye bread."

Finally Brother Bloom shuffled into Harry's cell with the revised accounts he had demanded. Harry flung them aside, saying, "We've got to get a computer in here one of these days, don't you think?"

"You're a born *momzer*," Bloom said, knowing how it grated on Harry to be spoken to in Yiddish. Claimed. Especially if Miss Bailey was within range.

And then it was time to go and Harry pondered alternatives. He could squeeze in a session at the Graphic Arts Society or take in the new flick at the Cameo-Poly. Or see Ruthy. He opted for his digs and the telly, remembering to pick up his laundry first, and settling into the *Evening Standard* with his fried eggs and beans. When David Bailey goes shopping, he read, if the bill comes to ninety-and-something pounds, he hastily buys more items before making out his check, because he doesn't know how to spell ninety. David Frost is giving another breakfast party for thirty at the Connaught. Everybody who counts is in a dither about what to wear at Lady Antonia Fraser's masked ball next Wednesday. Forty-year-old Bernie Cornfeld, head of I.O.S. with a personal fortune of more than a hundred million, is accompanied on all his travels by at least four mini-skirted lasses of *Playboy* pulchritude.

Harry dialed the Savoy. "May I speak with Miss Lollobrigida, please?"

"Miss Lollobrigida is not accepting any calls. Would you like to leave a message, please?"

"You better buzz her, baby, and see if she will accept a call from . . . John Huston."

"Yes, sir." A pause, then, "She is unavailable at the moment, Mr. Huston. Would you mind calling back in ten minutes?"

"Haven't you got phones by the bathtubs there yet?"

A giggle earned.

"Well now, lemme see. I'm just leaving here. Could you please ask Miss Lollobrigida to stay right where she is. I'll be along with a towel and my riding crop in ten minutes."

Sprawled on his bed, unzipped, Harry reached for *Mayfair*, "a wedding night tussle for Susan Strasberg and film husband Massimo Girotti." In the photograph she lies nude on the sheets, head arched back tensely, the hairy dago sucking her nipple. "Above right: see-through temptation fails to arouse her husband's ardor quite enough. Below: the result—the husband's cousin moves swiftly in." She is spread on a bench, nude except for leather knee boots, and the cousin's head is buried busily in her crotch. Lapping it up.

Harry turned to another page, "Quest," a survey on the sex life of single girls in London today.

> . . . I was sitting on the floor and he came over and kissed me and pulled me down on the floor with him. He pulled my dress off over my head and I suddenly realized I was blushing like mad, but he was ever so gentle. He put his arm under me and unclipped my bra and started to kiss my breasts and he rolled my nipples between his fingers to make them stand up. We were pushing our tongues into each other's mouths as far as we could and I could just feel the edge of his thumb and fingers on my panties. They were only a tichy pair of paper panties and he tore the

front of them open in a slit. His hands seemed to be everywhere, it drove me mad. I lifted my legs over his shoulders
and rubbed my calves against the side of his head and then
we made love—through my panties. We did it three times.

Afterwards, Harry dipped his fingers in his seed and smeared
Susan Strasberg's mouth and breasts with it, then he tore *Mayfair* to shreds, dressed hastily, and started up Haverstock Hill,
toward the pub.

Harry paused at the corner of England's Lane, looking for a
phone booth, his little book of ex-directory numbers in his breast
pocket, when he noticed a Silver Cloud Rolls Royce parked
down the street. There was no driver in attendance. Drifting
past, ostensibly without purpose, Harry opened the knife in his
mac pocket and ran it the length of the Rolls, walking on some
distance before wheeling around to slash the body paint on the
other side, continuing back to Haverstock Hill. When he
emerged from the pub and went to look for the Rolls, it was
gone.

10

Mr. Pound tried to skewer Jake on the stand.

"Would it be correct to say that you, personally, find Germans abhorrent?"

"But—but—Mozart was a German," Jake had ventured. "Beethoven. Why, even Karl M——I mean, Kant was a German."

"Even so, you abominate them. Is that right?"

"Why," Jake had replied, seemingly appalled, "that would make me a racist, sir."

Out there, he had thought, resuming his place in the dock. Out there, riding even now. St. Urbain's Horseman. Deprived of his Barnaby "International," without his bespoke riding habit from Jos. Monaghan Ltd. of St. Stephen's Green, Dublin. Galloping, thundering. Over the olive-green hills of the Upper Galilee. Or possibly already in Paraguay. Out on the steaming flood plains of the Paraná, neck-reining his magnificent Pleven stallion with his bridle hand as he reaches into his goatskin saddlebag for his field glasses, searching the savannas below for the unmarked track that winds into the jungle, between Puerto San Vincente and the border fortress of Carlos Antonio López, where the *Doktor* waits, unaware.

Beware Mengele, beware, for it is the Horseman who once

strode St. Urbain, bronzed as a lifeguard, trousers buckled tight against a flat stomach. Exhorting the men, mocking them, demanding vengeance.

How, Jake was asked again and again, as if it were perverse of him, could he still hate the Germans?

—Easily.

—Now look here, Nancy would reason sweetly, can you hate Günter Grass?

—Without any trouble whatsoever.

—Brecht?

—Unto the tenth generation.

Which Nancy, barely seven years old on V-E Day, could not comprehend.

And so how could he tell her, without seeming psychotic, about his Jewish nightmare, the terror that took him by surprise in his living room, striking only on those rare evenings when he brimmed over with well-being, a sense of everything having knit mysteriously together for once, his wife, the children they had made, so that he could even contemplate his shortcomings, his failures, his own rot and dying and, all things considered, it was tolerable.

If he attempted to explain it at all, he would have to begin with his living room and its commonplaces. Bourgeois commonplaces which, he had to allow, would have been anathema to him fifteen years ago.

It is a Friday night and although they didn't light candles or perform such ablutions that would enable them to welcome the sabbath like a bride, something remained, and on occasion it stirred within him. Most likely after a good dinner. Roast rib of beef and baked potatoes, salad, cheese and wine. He reclines on the sofa, freshly ground coffee set before him, brandy in a snifter; he is overcome with languor, but trying to grasp whatever script he is considering. Nancy's curled into an armchair, legs tucked under, listening to David Oistrakh play a Mozart concerto. Catching up on the Sunday newspapers at last, she tears out a recipe or an article on herbaceous borders made easy. Or she deliberates over the latest National Film Theatre program, knowing exactly what he wants to see. Curly-haired Sammy is lying on his stomach on the floor, fist jammed against his chin, blue eyes pensive, contemplating his jigsaw puzzle. Crayoning, Molly frowns. Only Ben isn't there. He's adrift in his bassinet, stoned on mother's milk. Once the children have been tucked in for the night and should his lethargy pass, he will rouse Nancy, caressing her, and they will climb to the bedroom to make love, pausing by the maid's door to say good night. She will flatter him in bed and he does not feel comparison-shopped. They come together. Afterwards, they plan holidays. Shall it be the Costa Brava this summer or the Loire Valley? Other, less fortunate, marriages will be a subject for self-satisfied speculation. Friends will be forgiven their inadequacies.

Or, possibly, Jake will succumb on the sofa, drifting into snores. Boorish, but at home. Meanwhile, if he wants a peach or an ashtray brought nearer, or cherries on a saucer maybe, Sammy will bring it. If he decides on a cigar, Molly will fetch it.

Somewhere else, there is war and rape. Famine. Rats gnawing at the toes of black babies. Outside, bestiality. Fire raisers. Enemies. This is the shelter he has provided for his family. They use it well and are at ease. The shattered greenhouse window was Sammy's doing, a badly-placed goal. Nancy tends to the rose beds and tomato plants. He weeds. The persistent whirring from the kitchen is the nocturnal Mr. Shapiro, Molly's hamster, racing nowhere on his wheel. Jake's responsible for the stained wallpaper in the dining room, a champagne bottle's eruption. The sideboard was Nancy's folly. Her first auction. There's food in the larder, wine in the pantry, money in the bank. His wife is the woman he wants. He enjoys the children.

—So, Yankel. How are you doing?

—I can't complain.

Then there obtrudes the familiar photograph of a bewildered little Jewish boy, wearing a cap, a torn pullover, and shorts, his eyes aching with fear as he raises his arms over his head. There are other Jews huddled together on this narrow street in Warsaw. Wearing caps, supporting bundles. All of them, with arms raised. Behind them, striking a pose for the unseen photographer,

are four German soldiers. One of them casually points his rifle
at the petrified little Jewish boy.

"*Children scratched their arms and with their own blood
would write on the barracks walls, as did my nephew, this child
here, who wrote: 'Andreas Rappaport—lived sixteen years.'*"

There is another photograph, this one of an astonishingly beautiful Jewess, squatting nude before a pit, the soldiers behind
smirking. She is staring right into the camera without anger or
reproach, but sorrowfully, attempting to conceal her pendulous
breasts with her hands. As if it mattered. As if she wouldn't be
dead within seconds.

"*How many do you estimate were murdered in Auschwitz?
You were in a position to know.*"

Boger: "*I believe that it was approximately the number given
by Höss.*"

"*That is, two and a half million people?*"

"*Two million or one million,*" Boger gestures. "*Who can tell
today?*"

Then, in Jake's Jewish nightmare, they come. Into his house.
The extermination officers seeking out the Jew vermin. Ben is
seized by the legs like a chicken and heaved out of the window,
his brains spilling to the terrace. Molly, whose experience has led
her to believe all adults gentle, is raised in the air not to be
tossed and tickled, but to be flung against the brick fireplace.
Sammy is dispatched with a pistol.

"*A terrible stench came out of the car, like the plague. These
prisoners were loaded onto the trucks directly and dumped into
the pits next to Crematory 11.*"

"*Were any of them still alive?*"

"*Yes.*"

"*Mengele cannot have been there all the time.*"

"*In my opinion, always. Night and day.*"

11

Friday.

After Thomas Neill Cream, following Lipski (the *Poilischer paskudnyak*), in the tradition of Dr. Crippen, the Seddons, Neville Heath, Christie and Stephen Ward . . . Jacob Hersh, former relief pitcher for Room 41, Fletcher's Field High (lifetime record, 2–7), stood in the dock of Number One Court, having been delivered thereto once again from the cells below to stand beside Harry, a taciturn prison officer posted on either side.

Number One Court was dominated by an enormous circular skylight. The walls were paneled in oak. The Sword of Justice which hung above the judge, a *very fayer and goodly sword well and workmanly wrought and gylded*, presented to the City by a cutler in 1563, was suspended hilt downwards. A fresh bouquet of posies and sweet herbs, the traditional antidote to gaol fever, the vicious stench that had once emanated from Newgate below, had been set before the plum-cheeked Queen's justice of Oyer and Terminer. The jury shifted from buttock to buttock on seats so obdurate as to surely make them surly, resentful, Jake feared.

Jake wore his cheapest, most conservative suit, something gray with hire purchase, shiny with virtue. His drip-dry shirt, especially chosen to ingratiate him with the jurors, was an Arrow. He had deliberated for more than an hour before settling on a tie, just the trick, from the sales rack at John Barnes.

Only yesterday the astute Mr. Pound had summoned Ingrid to the stand. Ingrid, appropriately pale yet fetching in a severe black suit, the hemline cut just a hint above the knee.

"What is your occupation, Miss Loebner?"

"I work as an *au pair* girl. I am a student."

In short order, the bewigged Queen's Counsel established that Ingrid was twenty years old, had been in the country for seven months, and came of impeccable family, her father being a dentist in Munich. On the night of June 12, she had been to see the film at the Swiss Cottage Odeon and had then stopped for a coffee at The Scene on Finchley Road. A stranger had approached her table.

"He purported to be Jacob Hersh and said that he was a film director."

"Yes, sir."

"Why did you believe him?"

"He showed me an identification card and a newspaper review of his last film."

"And then what happened?"

"He asked me if I was an actress."

"And what did you reply?"

"No. But he seemed excited. In a nice way, you understand. And he said I was just the girl he was looking for."

"And then what happened?"

"He asked me to come to his house, yeah, to read from a script. He wished to know if my English was good."

"You agreed?"

"There seemed no harm in it. He said Elke Sommer was also an *au pair* girl in Hampstead when she was discovered."

"Miss Sommer is a screen actress of German origin. Is that right?"

"Yes, sir."

"And are these the pages of script he asked you to read? Please examine them carefully before you answer."

"Yes, sir."

"The girl in the script is said to be attired, I quote, in only a nurse's cap, a bra, a corset, and high-button shoes. She wields a riding crop, unquote. Did you wear such a costume?"

"I read the lines for him many times first, yeah. He seemed very serious, sir."

"Then what happened?"

"He asked me to wear the costume as described in the script."

"And what did you do?"

"I did as he asked. I read the lines in my bra and panties. He had no nurse's cap, but there was a riding crop."

"I see. And who played the other part, as it were?"

"He was the General Montgomery."

"If it please your lordship, I will now hand up some further pages of script to be proven at the proper time . . ."

Jake stared at his shoes, squeezing his hands together. *Never apologize, never explain.*

The next witness was the long stooping cop with the correct face who had come to arrest Harry.

"And then," Sergeant Hoare said, "I asked him once more if his name was Harry Stein and he said this is not Germany and he would not tolerate Gestapo tactics."

"He refused to tell you his name?"

"He said he had chums in Fleet Street and he was familiar with police brutality. His exact words were, 'No Cossack is going to plant a bloody brick on me.'"

"I see. Go ahead, please."

"Then I asked him yet again if he was Harry Stein and if he knew a young lady called Ingrid and he replied this was still a free country in spite of Polaris and the American bases."

"*American bases?*"

"He was wearing a CND button on his lapel. He tried to shut the door in my face."

As the clerk brought Harry Stein the New Testament to swear on, the usher coughed and asked in a small, courteous voice, "Religion?"

Harry's silence was not merely hostile. It scorched.

"Are you, ah, Jewish?"

Before Jake's eyes the ruinously expensive legal advice, the cajoling, the rehearsals, the tranquillizers, all went up in smoke.

"For purposes of census, taxation, and pogroms," Harry proclaimed in a swelling voice, his St. Crispin's Day voice, to the somnolent court room, "I am a Jew."

It's the rope, Jake thought. *It's the rope for sure.*

The bewigged Mr. Pound fixed Harry with his most piercing look. "When you forced the girl upstairs into Hersh's bedroom," he asked, "was Hersh—"

"I didn't force her."

"When you *led* the girl upstairs, was Hersh already undressed?"

"I don't remember."

"You don't remember?"

"He had his underwear on."

"*Powder-blue* underwear?"

"I beg your pardon?"

"Powder-blue. The color."

"Yes."

Yes, yes. Sweat oozing from every pore, Jake forced himself to stop listening, already adjusting to prison life. He saw big goysy queens goosing him on the way to chow. Psychopaths calling him chicken because he wouldn't join in the escape plan, maybe murdering him because he was unlucky enough to overhear the plot. No sitting in a centrally heated toilet with the avant-*Guardian* after breakfast. Instead a bucket fermenting in the corner of the cell all day and he too sensitive but agonizingly constipated. "Go ahead, dearie. I won't look." Depraved warders jew-baiting him. "You want smoked salmon? Chivas Regal? Monte Cristos? Matzoh-ball soup? Sure, Yankel. Just write your missus to send us a check on the numbered Swiss account." And naturally he would fail to prove himself in the exercise yard. "There goes Hersh. Fainted at the carve-up. What a giggle."

12

Twisting dizzily on the bed, everything swaying, pounding, Mrs. Hersh prayed, offering five years of her life if only they wouldn't put him in prison, he got rid of her, the *choleria*, and returned to Montreal with the children, they were such a burden to her, to make a fresh beginning.

Then, just as she was drifting off to sleep, she was startled by a knock on the door. "Yes?"

"I'm sorry if I wakened you," Nancy began, determined to be gentle, "but—"

"Who can sleep?"

"—Jake just phoned to say he'll be late."

A hand held to her cheek, Mrs. Hersh asked, "Oh, my God, what's happened now?"

"Nothing," Nancy replied, mustering a reassuring smile. "He and Ormsby-Fletcher have a lot to talk about. They've gone to a pub. He could be very late, Mrs. Hersh. Here you are," she said, setting the tray before her. "I picked up some kosher salami and rye bread for you."

The salami sandwich was garnished with sliced sour pickle, radishes daintily cut, tomatoes and lettuce. There was also a pot of tea with lemon and a freshly cut rose standing in a tall wine

glass on the tray. Mrs. Hersh lifted the topmost slice of bread
off the sandwich, sighed reprovingly, replaced it and pushed the
tray aside. Impulsively, Nancy rammed the tray right back at
her. "Eat it," she demanded.

Mrs. Hersh stared, amazed. Pogrom, pogrom.

"I had to go to three shops before I could find kosher salami.
Now you eat it, Mrs. Hersh."

"I can't."

"I'm going to sit right here and you're going to eat the sandwich. Every—last—mouthful."

"I can't."

"*Eat it.*"

"But you buttered the bread."

"What?"

"It isn't kosher. I'm not allowed to eat butter with meat."

Shit. Shit, shit. "You are not to spy on me."

"I didn't see a thing. So help me God."

"You were watching by the window. Wide-eyed."

"Me, I committed a crime."

"You are not to say a word to Jake. Do you understand?"

"Oh, I understand. Don't you worry."

"No, you most emphatically do not understand. Not for a
moment. Do you actually think Luke is my lover?"

"Who said a word?"

"I have lots, you know. Troops. Between pregnancies. When
I'm not nursing babies or changing nappies. Whenever Jake's
out for lunch they arrive by the charabanc-load to fuck me
black and blue." Oh, no, Nancy thought. *Oh God, stop, what
are you saying?*

"That's a word from the gutter."

"If you can't eat butter on your salami sandwich," Nancy
charged, unable to contain her tears any more, "how come you
can have eggs with your hot dogs?"

"Eggs are *parve*," Mrs. Hersh returned haughtily.

"Oh! Oh! Oh!" Nancy stamped her foot. She stamped it
again. "Sometimes all your Jewish hocus-pocus—"

Six million isn't enough for them.

"I'm sorry."

"Don't be sorry. Open the sewer gates. Let's hear it all."

Which is when Molly catapulted into the room, flying into Mrs. Hersh's arms. "What's the matter?"

"Nothing, precious one."

Somehow, Nancy contrived to light a cigarette.

"And how did it go today?" Mrs. Hersh asked. "Did he say?"

"It couldn't have gone very well," Nancy said, "or he wouldn't be out getting drunk somewhere."

And she slipped out of the room, hurrying to Ben, who had begun to cry indignantly. Squashing out her cigarette, she scooped him up, digging her nose into his cheek and inhaling deeply, showering his bottom with little bites salty with tears. *I mustn't lose my milk. No matter what, I must not lose my milk.*

Slowly, methodically, Nancy emptied a pail of nappies into the Hoover, folded the dry set, and had only just escaped into the toilet when Molly began to pound on the door.

"Wanta come in."

"Go get your coat, dear. It's time for us to pick up Sam."

"Wanta come in, wanta come in."

So Nancy opened the door.

"Plop," Molly squealed, standing over her, giggling. "Plop-pety-plop."

13

"Mr. Hersh," the publican hollered, "telephone for Mr. Jacob Hersh."

But it wasn't Nancy.

"Is Harry with you?" Ruthy asked, her voice quivering.

"No."

"He was supposed to be here for dinner more than an hour ago. I don't know where he is."

"Calm down." If he's skipped bail, Jake thought, it will only cost me 2,500 pounds. Well, in for a penny, as Ruthy was so fond of saying, in for a pound. "I'm sure he'll turn up soon," he lied.

"What if he's done something to himself?"

Too much to hope for. "He's out walking somewhere, Ruthy. Or maybe he's fallen asleep."

"Don't you think I tried his flat?" she asked, breaking into sobs.

"Do you want me to come over?" he asked wearily.

"But if he found you here with me, he'd be furious."

"Yes, that's right. Take something, Ruthy." Cyanide. "He'll turn up eventually. Nothing's happened to him. If I know Harry he can hardly wait to sit in the stand again tomorrow."

"That's nasty."

"Yes, Ruthy. No, Ruthy. Good night."

But Ormsby-Fletcher, concerned, felt that Jake should not antagonize either of them, and he insisted that he look in on Ruthy. So they finished their drinks and walked to the car park behind the Old Bailey, assuring each other once more that it had been a most encouraging day in court. Ormsby-Fletcher dropped Jake off at Ruthy's place.

"Has he come yet?"

Ruthy shook her head, biting back the tears.

"Have you got anything to drink here?" Jake asked, sinking into the only chair that wasn't buried in clothes waiting to be ironed.

"There's some Shloer's. I've also got a bottle of Babycham."

If only, Jake thought, Remy Martin went in for contests, and, remembering, he dug into his jacket pocket. Hoping to mollify Ruthy, he made her a gift of a dozen Kit-i-Kats and six Knorr labels, withholding his five Beefeaters for the moment.

"Would it be too much trouble to make me a cup of coffee?"

The children were in bed, alas, and so, as she prepared the instant coffee, Ruthy was free to run through her dolorous litany of complaints again. Harry had wanted to mend his ways and settle down, he had given up that sort of girl, and the photography, until Jake had taken him to C. Bernard Farber's, *that* party, thrusting him into temptation.

Jake, playing his part, wearily pointed out that he was doing all he could for Harry. He sprang awake only when Ruthy tried a new twist.

"Harry brought the girl to the house for you. He didn't want her at all."

Suddenly, all the ugliness inherent in the trial, the coarseness, the necessary lies, crystallized for Jake in the buxom shape of flatulent Ruthy. "My dear Mrs. Flam," he said quietly, "listen to me. I've got a wife and three children. I'm risking more than I should for Harry's sake. All I want in return is the truth. No last minute tricks."

"You say one thing, he says another. How do I know what happened? I wasn't there."

"Even you can't be that stupid, Ruthy."

"Ta."

"Why would I have Harry bring a girl to my house for me?"

"You're a man, aren't you?"

"If I was going to have a girl while Nancy was away, I wouldn't have Harry there too."

"How would I know what sort of games you fancy?"

"Oh God," Jake said, rising, and he shoved the five Beefeater labels at her just as the doorbell rang.

"It's him! It's Harry!"

Harry stared at Jake, his eyes narrowed with suspicion.

"Well, hello. And where have you been? Out murdering somebody?"

He didn't answer.

"Or was it just a little rape round the corner that kept you?"

Pinched and pale, Harry said, "What are you doing here?"

"Ruthy was worried. I came to comfort her."

"To bribe her," Harry said, pouncing on the labels, "to turn her against me."

Don't antagonize them, Ormsby-Fletcher had said. Jake reached into his pocket and came up with a small bottle of pills. "You're not to take more than two, Harry."

Harry snickered.

"It went well today," Jake said. "I think we're going to be all right."

"You'll be acquitted on Monday, mate. Not to worry. It's me they want."

"Why is your barrister a Q.C.," Ruthy asked, "and Harry's isn't?"

"They work as a team," Jake said.

"You're fucking right they do. Against me."

"That's just not true, Harry."

"You're home free."

"He's got connections," Ruthy said.

"Right. And failing everything else, I'm sure to get a Queen's pardon. I spoke to Phil only yesterday. He promised. Good night. I'll phone in the morning, Harry."

"Don't worry. I'm not doing a bunk."

"I am not worried. I will phone to see how you are."

"He's ever so thoughtful," Ruthy said.

14

It was dark when Mrs. Hersh wakened to the sound of clinking glasses and their heightened voices.

"Jake, I never bug you about your drinking, but please don't pour yourself another one."

"In spite of everything I'm doing, Harry thinks he's being sold down the river. He thinks his lawyer is working for my interests. Christ Almighty, how could I ever get us into this mess?"

"Yes. Why did you do it, Jake?"

"Do what? What did I do? You think I laid into her with that riding crop?"

"No. Certainly not."

"Does it excite you? Should we try it?"

"Go to hell."

"I'm not being vicious. Honestly, when I listen to some of the testimony in court, I actually get a hard-on. I think, jeez, that sounds like it was fun. Wish I'd been there. But I was there and it was not like that at all."

"I believe you, Jake. For the umpteenth time, I believe you."

"Where's my ever-loving mum?" he demanded, his drink spilling over. "Why do you keep her from me?"

"I told you she's lying down."

"Harry will crack if they send him to prison again. He can't stand it. It would be the end of him."

"But you're looking forward to it. It would be an adventure."

"It doesn't matter. Who cares? You, me. It doesn't matter. You know what's important to me? Really, really important to me? Dr. Samuel Johnson. I keep wondering, if I had lived in his time, would he have liked me? Would Dr. Johnson have invited me to sit at his table? Luke's back, you know."

"Is he?"

"It's in the *Standard*. Not the court page, but Londoner's Diary. His arrivals and departures are news. He's a big talent, our Luke."

"Please don't drink any more."

"How are the kids?"

"They're all right. I'll make you an omelette."

"Nancy," he said, reaching out for her.

"Yes?"

But starting for the kitchen together, they ran into Mrs. Hersh.

"Hullo, Maw. *A guten shabus.* You know my mother used to light candles on Friday night? Every Friday night, when I was a kid, she lit the candles."

Mrs. Hersh glowed.

"Did you remember to take your pills today?"

"I was a good girl."

"Nancy's eyes are red. Your eyes are puffy. There's nothing to worry about, honestly. It's in the bag. Once this is over, I'll probably sue for false arrest."

"Your mother and I had words."

"It was nothing. A little misunderstanding. Let's not upset Jake."

"Why not upset Jake? I met Luke for drinks today. I broke down, he drove me home, and your mother saw him kiss me outside. She thinks we're having an affair and that's why I asked her not to tell you."

"I didn't say a word, so help me God."

"Would you please explain to her that you are jealous of

Luke not because of anything between us, but because he's so successful."

"Hey, hey. I'm not on trial here. I'm on trial there."

"Oh, why don't the two of you sit in the kitchen without me," Nancy cried, fleeing, "and eat something *parve* together?"

"What?" Jake called after her, baffled.

He found her lying on the bed, sobbing, and sat down beside her and stroked her hair. "Nelson Eddy's dead. It was in the *Herald-Trib* today."

Once her tears had abated, he held a glass of cool milk to her lips.

"I don't bully old ladies," she cried, beginning to heave again. "Or say—or say 'fuck' to them—or—it's not like me. I made such a—such a fool of myself today," and fitfully, between tearful outbursts, she told him what had happened.

Jake touched her cheek. "I was going through my desk yesterday," he said, "and I found a snapshot of you taken maybe ten years ago. You were twenty, I guess. Standing under an elm tree, wearing a summery dress and brushing your hair out of your eyes. You looked absolutely achingly beautiful and I hated you for it, because I didn't know what man you were smiling for, and what you had to look so pleased about before you met me. Now I know." He kissed her. "Please try to get some sleep, the baby's bound to have you up half the night."

Jake slipped past his mother's door, down the stairs, and into the living room, where he poured himself another brandy. Wrong place, wrong time. Young too late, old too soon was, as Jake had come to understand it, the plaintive story of his American generation. Conceived in the depression, but never to taste its bitterness firsthand, they had actually contrived to sail through the Spanish Civil War, World War II, the holocaust, Hiroshima, the Israeli War of Independence, McCarthyism, Korea, and, latterly, Vietnam and the drug culture, with impunity. Always the wrong age. Ever observers, never participants. The whirlwind elsewhere.

As Franco strutted into Madrid, a conqueror, Jake and his

friends sat on the St. Urbain Street stoop and mourned the benching of Lou Gehrig, their first hint of mortality. The invasion of Poland was photographs they pasted into the opening pages of World War II scrapbooks, coming in a season they cherished for *The Wizard of Oz*. Unlike their elder brothers, they could only conjecture about how they would have reacted in battle. They collected aluminum pots for Spitfires and waited impatiently for the war's end so that Billy Conn could get his second chance. The holocaust was when their parents prospered on the black market and they first learned the pleasures of masturbation. If, as secure and snotty ten-year-olds, they mocked those cousins and uncles who were too prudent to enlist, then it was an apprenticeship appropriate to encroaching middle age, when they were to exhort younger men to burn their draft cards. From pint-size needlers, callow fans in the wartime bleachers, they had matured to moral coaches, the instigators of petitions, without ever having been tried on the field themselves. The times had not used but compromised them. Too young to have marched into gunfire in Europe, they were also too old and embarrassed, too fat, to wear the flag as underwear.

"When they tote up our contribution," Luke once said, "all that can be claimed for us is that we took 'fuck' out of the oral tradition and wrote it plain." In lieu of *Iskra, Screw*. After Trotsky, Girodias-in-exile. "And sooner or later we will put it on stage, where you can win applause as well as pleasure from the act."

As it seemed to Jake that his generation was now being squeezed between two raging and carnivorous ones, the old and resentful have-everythings and the young know-nothings, the insurance brokers defending themselves against the fire-raisers, it followed inevitably that, once having stumbled, he would be judged by one when accused by the other. Ingrid would sing, Mr. Justice Beal would pronounce.

What he couldn't satisfactorily explain to Nancy was that he was more exhilarated than depressed by the trial because at last the issues had been joined. Joined, after a fashion. From the beginning, he had expected the outer, brutalized world to in-

trude on their little one, inflated with love but ultimately self-
serving and cocooned by money. The times were depraved.
Tenderness in one house, he had come to fear, was no more
possible, without corruption, than socialism in a single country.
And so, from the earliest, halcyon days with Nancy, he had
expected the coming of the vandals. Above all, the injustice-
collectors. The concentration camp survivors. The emaciated
millions of India. The starvelings of Africa.

> It took from the beginning of mankind until the year
> 1830 for the world's population to reach 1000 million.
> The next 1000 million came in only a hundred years.
> The third 1000 million took only 30 years. And by the
> end of this century there will be 6250 million people in
> the world, nearly twice as many as there are now. Al-
> ready half the world's people are undernourished and
> about 450 million exist at starvation level. What is going
> to happen in the next 35 years?

Well, I'll tell you, Jake thought, the demented Red Guards of
China are going to come, demanding theirs, followed by the
black fanatics, who live only for vengeance. The thalidomide
babies, the paraplegics. The insulted, the injured. Don't bother
barring the door, they'll spill in through the windows.

Jake was not surprised that out of his obsession with the
Horseman he had been delivered Ruthy.

Who had sent him Harry.

Who had served him Ingrid.

Elijah the Prophet had disappointed him, never coming to sip
from his silver wine cup at the Passover table. Not so the vandals.
After years of waiting somebody had at last come to ask him,
Jacob Hersh, husband, father, son, house owner, investor, sybarite, film fantasy-spinner, for an accounting.

"In 1967, while 450 million people were starving and, in England, at least 18 per cent of this happy breed lived below subsistence level, and society's golden rule was alcoholism, drug
addiction, and inchoate brutality, I, Jacob Hersh, descendant of
the House of David, paid £15,000 *not* to direct a fun film, made

love to my wife on crisp clean sheets, sent my progeny to private schools, worried about corpulence gained through overindulgence and play hours lost through overimbibing. Furthermore, I envied friends more successful and cursed those invited to more parties. I complained about our maid's indolence. I lamented the falling off in the British craftsman's traditional pride and a rise in the price of claret. While the rich got richer and the poor poorer, I survived very nicely. As Luke once put it so pithily, if we're all on the Titanic, at least I'm going down first class. Amen."

The slap of slippered feet wakened Jake. It was Mrs. Hersh.

"Does Nancy know you send money every month to a woman in Israel?"

"Maw, if I thought you were going through my mail, I'd hit the roof. I really would."

"The letter was lying on the floor. I picked it up. Is the child yours?"

"I already have a *kaddish*. Haven't you enough grandchildren?"

"That's no answer."

"All right then, no, it's not mine."

"So why does she send photographs?"

"Everybody wants to be cast in a Jacob Hersh production."

"The way people live today, I don't understand. I just don't understand."

"Once," Jake said, "my father talked to me about careers I might take up. He advised me not to become a doctor because I'd be at everybody's beck and call. Even in the middle of the night. Dentistry, he said, would involve me in expensive equipment. Become a rabbi, he said, and you don't need to make any capital outlay. All you need is what I already had, a big mouth. Do you think I would have made a good rabbi?"

"You could have been anything you set your mind to."

"With a house in the higher reaches of Outremont and a good Jewish girl for a wife."

"I've never said a word against Nancy."

"And it's best that you never do," he said, "because I love her. And so long as she loves me, I cannot be entirely bad."

Watching him stagger off to the glass-topped table, seeking his bottle, she thought, why, oh my God, why did he ever leave Montreal, the fool? In those years, after the war, who wouldn't have given his right arm for a Canadian passport? What Jew wasn't on his knees to be let into such a good country?

"Here it is," Jake said, rocking with the book in one hand and his glass in the other. He read aloud. " 'When I survey my past life, I discover nothing but a barren waste of time, with some disorders of the body and disturbances of the mind very near to madness, which I hope He that made me will suffer to extenuate many faults and exercise many deficiencies.' " Clapping the book shut, he announced, "From the diary of the late, great Reb Shmul Johnson. Easter Eve. 1777."

Two

1

How it maddened Jake when he remembered, standing in the dock at the Old Bailey, that his abortive trip to New York years ago, the true beginning, albeit inadvertent, of what was to become his ride to ruin with St. Urbain's Horseman, was, looked at baldly, no more than an immigration officer's clerical error.

1951 it was and Jake, who had been studying at McGill for three years, had decided not to register for the autumn term, beginning tomorrow. New York, New York, was his heart's desire. If only, he thought, lying on his bed, smoking, I can raise the fare. And money to keep me for a month.

His mother entered his room without knocking. "You should tell your father what you've decided to do. He's so bloated. I saw him on the street, he looks like a frog now. I wouldn't say a word against him, after all, he's your father, you hear? *Where are you going suddenly?*"

Compulsively, without design, he drifted all the way down to St. Urbain Street, entering Tansky's Cigar & Soda to phone his father, who had lived in a room nearby, ever since his parents had finally divorced four years earlier. Mr. Hersh came to fetch him in his battered Chevy, the back seat, as ever, buried in samples. Stationery supplies, ballpoint pens, calendars, blotters.

Another inclement Montreal winter had eaten into the body work since Jake had last seen him. The car was rusty and rotting. "How are you, Daddy?"

Issy Hersh looked at his son and groaned. "*Oy veh.*"

Jake wore a blue beret. He had grown a scraggly beard and favored an elongated ivory cigarette holder. He suggested they drive to a delicatessen on the Main, as in the old days.

"But nobody goes there any more. It's not the style."

Reluctantly, Issy Hersh drove Jake to Hy's Delicatessen on the Main. Smoked briskets were stacked like loaves in the window, red grizzly beef tongues heaped alongside. Salamis rocked on a line when Jake banged the door shut behind him. The aroma was even more maddeningly appetizing than he had remembered.

"It's very *simpático*, this," Jake said warmly.

"Come again."

"It's nice."

"It's a delicatessen. Big deal."

"No. I mean just the two of us, going out to eat again."

"I haven't got any money, if that's what you're after." Mr. Hersh ordered for both of them. Two lean on rye each, sour tomatoes, and knishes—if they were today's. "What sort of camel shit is that you're smoking?" he demanded, irritated.

"Gauloises."

"Feh."

"Do you still read *Northern Miner?*"

"Yes, I still read it. So?"

"What about your stocks, then?"

"What about my stocks? Right off the bat. What about my stocks? The stocks are not so hot. I don't understand it, I really don't. Your uncles have such luck on the market, but with me it never works. If people give me tips, it's out of spite. I've lost maybe eighteen hundred smackeroos, eighteen hundred, in the last year."

"That's terrible. I'm sorry."

"*C'est la guerre.*" Mr. Hersh motioned Jake closer. Narrowing his big frightened eyes, he searched out the farthest corners of the delicatessen for eavesdroppers. "I've got one stock"—his voice fell to an all but inaudible mumble—"Algonquin Mines—"

"Al-what mines?"

"Don't say it, big mouth."

"Say what? I didn't even hear you."

"You have to know the name of the mine? If you don't, your heart will stop ticking over?"

"No. Of course not."

"I've got an ock-stay—X-mines," he said, his voice gathering volume and booming like a bowling ball across the delicatessen, "it's just gone from a dollar nineteen to five ten . . . IN THE LAST WEEK . . ."

Immediately Hy switched off his automatic meat slicer. At the next table, an old man's spoon clattered in a bowl of kreplach soup.

"The trouble is," Mr. Hersh said, his voice shriveling again, "I bought it at eleven fifty-five."

As a boy, Jake remembered, he had used to lie in wait for his father with his grammar text, terrorizing him by demanding help with his homework. Each time his father flubbed a word, Mrs. Hersh laughed, her manner exultant. If not for Rifka and him, Jake realized, they could have been divorced years ago. Issy Hersh needn't have waited. Impulsively, Jake reached across the table to stroke his father's cheek.

Had anybody seen? Mr. Hersh, his eyes shooting in all directions, hastily knocked Jake's hand away. "What's that," he asked, "something you learned at McGill?"

Jake lit another Gauloise.

"Everything's on me," his father added hastily. "Today it's Daddy who pays."

"We should get together more often. I like you."

"I'm your father, for Chrissake. What should you—hate me?"

"When I was a kid, you had a gift for making me laugh. Once you made me lead soldiers on the kitchen stove. You bought the molds from a junk yard, remember?"

"Well, you're no longer a kid," Mr. Hersh said, bewildered, "and let's face it, it's turned out you're not such a fart smeller. Smart feller, I mean."

But he didn't earn a laugh, not even a smile.

"All right! That's just about enough out of you. Now what did you want to talk to me about? You haven't got the syph or anything like that?"

"No. You don't have to worry about fees any more. I've quit McGill. I'm not going back."

"Why?"

"It no longer suits my *Weltanschauung*."

Mr. Hersh slapped his cheek. He rocked his head. "Boy, did you ever turn out a *putz*. You're what-in-shtunk?"

"I'm bored," Jake said hotly. "I didn't like it there."

"What did you ever like? Everything you criticize."

"The movies."

"*What?*"

"I want to get into the movies."

Genuinely amused now, Issy Hersh shook with laughter. "Well, your ears are no bigger than Clark Gable's. That's a start, isn't it?"

Jake laughed too.

"Listen here," Mr. Hersh said, leaning closer, "you don't just decide I-want-to-be-in-the-movies. *You have to be discovered.*"

"I don't want to act. I want to direct."

"You think I like selling. I'd rather own the factory."

"I thought I'd go to New York for a start and look around. It's time I found out who I am."

"What do you mean, who you are? You're Yankel Hersh. You want to bet on it, I'll give you odds."

"The trouble is, I haven't even got the fare."

"I knew we'd get down to brass tacks sooner or later. The movies yet."

Mr. Hersh paid on the way out, scooping up a handful of change. Outside, he screwed up his eyes to glare at each coin before he dropped it into his pocket.

"Anything wrong?" Jake asked.

"Ssh. One minute."

A couple passed. Then a hawkish old lady hugging a parcel of fish, followed by some teenagers sporting shimmering A.Z.A. windbreakers. Finally, they were alone.

"You see this," Mr. Hersh said.

"Yes."

"It's an American nickel."

"So?"

"So? What were you, born stupid? If this nickel was not a Jefferson but a 1938 Buffalo, with a tiny S and a D . . . S for San Francisco, D for Denver . . . it would be worth plenty. Only last summer, Max Kravitz picks up a drunk in his taxi and he drives him to Aldo's. The fare is two ten. The *goy* hands Max a four-dollar bill. Yes, a four-dollar bill. A Bank of Upper Canada note, dated December 1, 1846. You know what that's worth?"

"Oh, Daddy, give up," Jake said fondly. "You're never going to be rich."

"In your books, that's everything, being rich. I'd be your pal then, wouldn't I? We could sit together in a swell restaurant, they have kosher Chinese food now in Snowdon, and you wouldn't be ashamed if your highbrow friends spotted us. Well let me tell you this much, not that you'll listen. What do I know, I'm just your father. Making money isn't everything. The president of the largest steel company in the world, Charles Schwab," he said, numbering him off on a finger, "died a bankrupt and lived on borrowed money for five years before his death. The man who in 1923 was president of the New York Stock Exchange, Richard Whitney, is still in Sing Sing. The greatest bear in Wall Street, Jesse Livemore, died a suicide. You know what you need? You need a job. Self-respect. Here," he hollered, ramming two ten-dollar bills into his chest, "you know what I am? Crazy."

"One day you'll be proud of me. I'm going to be a great film director."

"Don't shoot me the crap," he protested, appalled. "You want me to be proud? Earn a living. Stand on your own two feet."

• • •

Rather than drive back with his father, Jake wandered down St. Urbain again, as far as his old school.

Fletcher's Field High, wherefrom, three years after the war's end, he had graduated into McGill.

There's nothing, Jake's mother drilled into him, like a university education.

Yes.

It's not what you know, Jake's father corrected her, it's who you know.

Yes again.

Jake cultivated a *New Statesman* outlook, he wore a tweed jacket with leather armpatches, crammed his shelves with Penguins, and let his hair grow long. Whenever he could afford it, he ate at Italian restaurants. On each table there was an empty Chianti bottle plugged with a colored candlestick. Jake recommended Angelo's Trattoria to an old school friend, Duddy Kravitz. "They serve the most exciting scampi," he said.

Jake's older sister was embarrassed by him and his irreverent friends. Suspicious, hostile, Rifka began to ask what seemed like absurd questions.

"Do you drink sherry?"

"Well, sometimes. Tio Pepe."

He was, at the time, reading *The Quest for Corvo.*

"Ah ha. And what do you and your longhair friends do until four o'clock in the morning? Read poetry aloud to each other maybe?"

"Sometimes. Or we listen to records."

"*Classical?*"

"Well, yeah. So?"

"Tell me, are you scared of snakes?"

"*What?*"

Finally Jake discovered what was behind the inquiry. An issue of *Esquire* on his sister's dressing table with an article titled, "Is Your Kid Brother a Homosexual?" His future brother-in-law had given Rifka the magazine. Herky had already suggested that Jake do something about his blackheads. Before the wedding.

"It's going to be a formal affair, you know. And you're the best man."

"I won't pop any during the ceremony, O.K.?"

Jake took to walking about the house with his hands held in front of him, the wrists limp. At the supper table, he said to Herky, "Be a dear, will you, and pass me another knish. *Merci.*"

"Easy there," Herky said.

Money.

"It's for New York, Uncle Sam. Until I get settled there. I need two hundred and fifty dollars."

"Money. Ach, you've got your health, it's worth a million. I envy you to be your age."

"I could pay it back within a year."

"Look at us. You're an intelligent boy. We sit here . . . friends, family . . . You want another rye and ginger ale? Take. Who's counting? It's open house here. Isn't that so? Then I lend you money and you tell me I can have it back within a year. Right?"

"You've got my word."

"Then God forbid a year goes by and you haven't got the money. Then what happens? Tensions. Bad feeling. We no longer sit together, my rye and ginger ale between us—"

"But I promise, Uncle Sam—"

"You promise? Who comes to borrow money and says I won't pay you back? It's not my policy to lend. It only makes enemies. Specially family. You see my point of view?"

The sign behind the desk in Uncle Jack's office read:

ALI BABA WAS A FORTUNATE MAN, INDEED
—He Only Had 40 Thieves To Deal With

Uncle Jack said no, he couldn't lend money, not at the moment. So Jake tried Uncle Lou.

"I'll come right to the point. I need two hundred and fifty dollars."

"That's some stench of humor you've developed."

"This is serious, Uncle Lou. I've knocked up a *shiksa*."

"Oh my God, I could tell you were in trouble. Just looking at you I said to myself, the kid's in hot water, a tankful. I've always liked you."

"Either I raise the money for an abortion or I've got to marry her."

"Two hundred and fifty dollars?"

"That's the size of it."

"Don't brag."

"What?"

"A joke. I try to see the humorous side of everything. It's my philosophy."

"Oh, I see."

"Listen, my Ida's brother-in-law, the doctor in Hamilton, you remember him I'm sure. He'll do it for you, it will cost you only two hundred tops."

"I'd hate to have to bargain about a thing like this. It's not my nature, Uncle Lou."

"I understand. I'm the same. I'll phone him myself and settle it for you."

"Could you let me have the two hundred then?"

"There's no need. He's in to me for more than that. I'll wipe it off his account."

Only Uncle Abe was left, scornful Abe, the apogee of Hersh achievement; the guiding intelligence of Hersh, Seligman, Conway, Bouchard & Wiser, Advocates-*Avocats*. With offices in the Dominion Square Building and a stone mansion in Outremont. Not, Jake had to allow, utterly without conscience, for during the war he had championed the cause of the orthodox Jewish refugees, arguing for their legal rights, raising funds, finding them homes and jobs. But with a daughter Jake abhorred, the insufferable Doris, and a late-born son Uncle Abe devoured with love. Scornful Abe would bounce his six-year-old Irwin on his lap, and, inviting Jake to admire him, ask the boy to name Canada's nine provinces, drenching him in kisses once he had responded correctly. "This kid, I tell you, this is some kid." No, he had no intention of asking Abe for money.

Herky? Mn, maybe. Worth a try. Jake phoned him and asked if they could meet for a drink. Can do, Herky said, and he drove him to a roadhouse.

Jake and Herky did not go directly to their table. Hooking him under the arm, Herky said, "Got to check out the cans first. Come on."

Herky manufactured liquid soap and towel dispensers and deodorizing solutions for urinals. He never went to a restaurant or nightclub or a hotel without first inspecting the toilets and reporting back in full to the table. "It's from the Stone Ages here. You know what they've got in the urinals? Ice cubes." The roadhouse was not one of Herky's clients. "This isn't a toilet, it's a storage tank for last week's farts. Take a deep breath, kid."

"I believe you."

"It's a shame, a crying shame. You know why, but? In their books, the toilets are nonproductive units. They don't turn over a profit. But that's short-sighted as all hell, because if a guy comes in here to comb out his hair and gets a whiff of last week's crap, he doesn't complain about the toilet, that would be undignified, he tells everyone the steak isn't juicy. You read me?"

"Yeah, now let's go."

"O.K., O.K.," he said, leading Jake into the bar. "But facilities should be spotless. Above reproach. Like Napoleon's wife. It's the kind of investment that pays off."

"Goddammit, Herky, you don't have to sell me."

"We did a survey. The average guy, if he's in a restaurant or a nightclub and he has to crap, he skips the dessert and cancels the next round of drinks, so's he can let rip at home. Sorry, what are you drinking?"

"Scotch."

Herky ordered two Scotches. "Public toilets," he continued, "have a bad image. Now tell me a toilet's nonproductive. I mean when you add up a year's skipped desserts and drinks, well, what's the use of booking Lena Horne for a million dollars a week? We made the findings part of our sales kit."

"It's a strong argument. Are you rich, Herky?"

"It's all tied up." Herky put a hand on his heart. "I'd love to help out, kid, but—"

"I'm not asking for money."

"—you see, I shovel everything right back into the business. Rifka's very active, you know. Socializes like hell. She used to be in cancer, but she didn't care for the *kvetchy* president there. So now she's in heart ailments. In fact, as of last week she's running her own artery. They do a lot of good work, you know."

"I'm sure."

"Hey, tell you what. You want some stuff? That I can fix."

"Stuff?"

"It's free. Charna Rosen. You remember her. Well, now she puts out. She'd be glad to see you. *She reads Dylan Thomas.* Hand her some of the longhair stuff."

"Herky—"

"Aw, don't tell me. You're getting it regular. A college boy; an assimilationist. *Soixante-neuf.* Oh la la. Well you don't have to spit on us. Me and Rifka, we're the nonconformist type."

Jake fixed his brother-in-law with an earnest, melancholy stare. "Herky," he whispered, "I'm glad you said that."

"Oh, yeah," Herky said, full of anticipation.

"You see, I'm not interested in girls."

"*What?*"

"Remember you once put Rifka up to asking me funny questions. Like was I scared of snakes?"

"Let's get the hell out of here," Herky said, grabbing him.

They huddled together in Herky's Chrysler in the parking lot.

"You mean to sit there and tell me you're a *faigele?*"

Jake nodded.

"We've been to the YMHA pool together," Herky shouted, shaking a finger at him. "In the old days. Oh, you filthy bastard!" Herky bit his lip. "It would kill Rifka. Hell, if she found out . . ."

"It's no bowl of cherries for me either, you know."

"Yeah. Sure."

"Look at it this way, you go to a dance at the golf course and feel up Charna Rosen or somebody else's wife and the other guys just give you a big wink, but if I turned up and wanted to neck with one of the waiters or caddies—"

"Listen here, you little son-of-a-bitch—" Herky stopped short. He rolled down the window. "Couldn't you see a psychiatrist?"

Jake didn't answer immediately.

"Well?"

"Rifka says your new rabbi is brilliant. Very up-to-date. Maybe I should ask him, well, for guidance?"

"I wouldn't if I were you. He's not reform, you know."

"Herky, I think it would be best if I left town."

"Well," Herky said, starting up the car, "if that's how you feel . . ."

"I've been thinking of New York. The problem is I'm broke. I haven't got enough money for the fare."

"We all have our problems," he said frostily.

"Herky, you don't understand. My passions—"

"Shettup about it, will you! I'm driving."

"—get out of control. The cops are bound to pick me up one night. On the mountain . . . or in Outremont . . ."

"You want to borrow money from me, is that what you're getting at?"

"I'd pay you back. Honestly, darling."

"I should break your neck. I should pull you out of the car right here and cut it off for your own protection."

"Two hundred and fifty bucks would see me through nicely."

"I've always suspected you. You know that, don't you?"

"You're brainy, Herky. There's no denying it."

"Oh, you snake! Sewer! You really neck with other guys?"

Jake blew him a kiss.

"You take that back. You take that back, you filthy thing."

2

Every autumn, since childhood, he had watched the birds, the cunning birds, fly south, and this October, at last, Jake was following after. Across the border, to the sources of light. For his uncles, Miami, the Catskills; for his aunts, the wonder doctors of the Mayo Clinic. New York. It had always been their true capital. Ottawa? Quebec City? Those were bush league towns where you went to pay off a government *goy* for a contract or a building permit. They were the places the regulations came from, not life's joys. New York, New York. There wasn't a cigar store between Park Avenue and the Main that did not carry the obligatory New York dailies: the *News*, the *Mirror*, and the *Daily Racing Form*. Ed Sullivan, Bugs Bear, Dan Parker. *The Gumps* and *Smilin' Jack*. Dorothy Dix, Hedda Hopper. But, above all, Walter Winchell.

Jake had only been a boy during the war. He could remember signs in Tansky's Cigar & Soda that warned THE WALLS HAVE EARS and THE ENEMY IS EVERYWHERE. He could recall his father and mother, his uncles and aunts cracking peanuts on a Friday night and waiting for the United States, for those two un-equaled champions of their people, Roosevelt and Walter Winchell, to come off it and get into the war. They admired

the British, they were gutsy, but they had more confidence in
the U.S. Marines. They could see the likes of John Wayne,
Clark Gable, and Robert Taylor making mincemeat of the
Panzers, while Noel Coward, Laurence Olivier, and the others
seen in a spate of British war films had all looked too humanly
vulnerable. Like you, they could suffer heart failure, rectal
polyps, and disrespectful children. But Winchell, marvelous Walter, was proof against plain people's ailments. Out there in Manhattan, night after night, he was always ready to award orchids
for the best, regardless of race, color, or creed. Ever-watchful
under a broad-brimmed fedora, Walter Winchell cruised in a
radio police car, uncovering America-Firsters, giving FDR-bait-
ers what for, and smashing Hate-mongers in their lairs. Who was
there, if not WW, to tell Mr. & Mrs. America and all the ships at
sea about the Jewish war effort? About Barney Ross. About Irving Berlin and Eddie Cantor, giving so unselfishly of their time
and talent. Or that the bombardier in the first airplane to sink a
Nip ship was a Jewish boy, good enough to die for his country,
not good enough for some country clubs WW could name.

New York was quality, top quality. It sent Montreal Jenny
Goldstein and Aaron Lebedoff. When *Abie's Irish Rose* finally
reached His Majesty's Theater and uncles and aunts went not
once, but twice, the signs outside, a veritable guarantee, read
. . . DIRECT FROM NEW YORK. From blessed New York, where
Bernard Baruch sat on a park bench telling presidents and prime
ministers when to buy cheap, when to sell dear. Where Mayor
La Guardia could speak a Yiddish word. Where there were
second cousins on Delancey Street or in Brownsville. Where
the side-splitting Mickey Katz records were made. Where Pierre
van Paassen flew in from, exacting sobs, demanding donations, as
he told an SRO audience about the Hagana fighting off Rommel
in the desert, sometimes isolated for days and being driven to
drinking their own urine.

—Piss. Is that what he means to say?

—Sh.

—Imagine, Jake's mother said, imagine. What a piece of work
is man.

It was where Jake's father went for his best material. For only fifty cents a While-U-Wait newspaper headline that read RITA HAYWORTH LEAVES ALY KHAN FOR ISSY HERSH. It was where Jake's father bought his itching powder, metal ink spots, and the business cards which he handed out at Rifka's wedding.

KELLY'S TOOL WORKS
Does Yours?

America, the *real* America, was a chance for Jake to see the cream of the Montreal Royals (Duke Snider, Carl Furillo, Jackie Robinson, and Roy Campanella) at Ebbets Field. It was *Partisan Review, PM,* and the *New Republic.* It was the liberating knowledge which struck him one day at the university that he was not necessarily a freak. There were others, many more, who read and thought and felt as he did, and these others were mostly in New York. On the streets of Manhattan, where you could see them, real as relations, and maybe even get to touch some, talk to others.

As he packed his suitcases, and promised his mother, yes, to write once a week, as he assured his father that he really meant to find a job, he already saw himself chatting up a cashmere-sweater girl on Kafka in the bar at the Algonquin when the man with the gleaming bald head seated next to him said, "Couldn't help overhearing. Wow! Have you ever opened these tired old eyes! I wonder if you'd be willing to put that down on paper for us?"

"Us?" Jake says coldly.

"Oh. Sorry. My name's Ed. Ed Wilson." (Or would he say "Bunny"?) "I'd like you to say hello to Dorothy here . . . S. J., he's the one with the Groucho mustache . . . E. B. and Harold."

Or he's having a quick drink at Jack Dempsey's bar and a young Italianate man gives him a shove ("Move over, Hymie.") and Jake flattens him with a punch (the feared Hammer of Hersh, the very whisper of which is enough to turn champions to jelly), upsetting the Italian's middle-aged companion no end.

"Rocky, speak to me. My God, you've broken his jaw. He was going against Zale in the Garden tomorrow night. Now what am I going to do?"

Rising with the birds, the migrating birds, Jake caught the early morning train, thinking, I'm not going away, I'm heading for my spiritual home.

He's eating *latkas* or cheese cake or whatever it is Lindy's is famous for, reading that WW has wished him orchids again, Leonard Lyons ditto, when Lauren Bacall drifts over to his table, crossing her legs showily, trying to lure him to her hotel suite, anything to get Jacob Hersh to direct a film for her.

"Sorry," Jake says, "but I couldn't do it to Bogie."

Or even though he went twelve innings in the series opener the day before yesterday, allowing only two cheap hits, Leo looks at the loaded bases, Mantle coming up, their one-run lead, and he asks Jake to step in again.

Jake says, "On one condition only."

"Name it."

"You've got to tell Branch I want him to give the Negroes a chance in the big leagues."

At ten o'clock, as they were approaching the border, the latest Italian star, even sexier than Lollobrigida, began to shed her clothes in Jake's penthouse. *They've got to stop doing this*, he thought. Zip, zip. Then the fall of silk. No, a cascade. Ping goes the garter belt. Snap goes the bra clip . . . And Jake, looking down at the sudden upspringing of a pup tent between his legs, hastily covered his embarrassment with Norman Vincent Peale's column in *Look*, coughed, and lit a cigarette, as he was startled by a tapping on his shoulder.

"Yes?"

An American immigration officer with a sour purple-veined face, tufts of hair curling high on his cheeks, loomed over him. Sucking at a stubborn sliver of meat caught between his yellowing teeth, he asked to see his birth certificate. He looked at it, grunted, scribbled Jake's name down on a pad, and waddled away, rocking with the train. Fifteen minutes later, just as the

Italian star was pleading for help with a troublesome zipper, Jake was tapped on the shoulder yet again with a chewed-out pencil.

"You get off at the next stop, fella."

"*What?*"

"The desirability of your presence in the United States is suspect. The next stop will be St. Albans, Vermont. You get off there so that immigration officers can make a more thorough appraisal of your desirability," the officer said, waddling off again.

Jake sat for a minute, petrified, remembering that he had signed the Stockholm Peace Appeal and a petition asking for clemency for Julius and Ethel Rosenberg. Oh, you fool, you goddam fool, hadn't you ever heard of Senator McCarthy? Jake, having decided to go forward in search of more information, jumped up, *Look* spilling to the train floor, the tent between his legs remembered and prominent. Oh, my God! Mindful of the other passengers, Jake's hands went swiftly, instinctively, to cover his groin and just as swiftly retreated again, as he grasped that he was only drawing attention to his hard-on. Jake collapsed, cheeks burning red, into his seat.

Goddammit. Closing his eyes, concentrating, he lifted *Look* onto his lap again and willed the star back into his penthouse.

—Get your filthy hands off that zipper, she said.

—You've been leading me on. Why did you come here, then?

—I didn't realize you were so short and funny-faced—

(The throbbing abated.)

—so jewy—

(Good, good.)

—and besides I'm a lesbian—

(aaaaahhh)

Relieved, clearing his throat, and lighting up again, Jake went forward. He found the immigration officer sitting in an empty coach, working on his teeth with the edge of a bookmatch as he scanned a book full of names the size of a telephone directory.

"Why am I being taken off this train?"

"You will have to make a formal application for admission to the United States in St. Albans. If you pass the examination there, you will be allowed to go to New York tonight. If not, you will be sent back to Montreal."

"What's all this about?"

"We have reason to believe you might be an undesirable person."

"What reason?"

"I can't tell you."

"How long will the trial take?"

"It's not a trial."

"How long will *it* take?"

"As long as it does."

"The only reason why I ask, sir, is today is Friday. I'm, well, Jewish . . . Our sabbath begins at sundown and then it would be against the articles of my faith to travel."

The immigration officer peered at him with fresh and, Jake dared to hope, benevolent interest.

"If there's anything political in this, sir, I think it would be less than honest of me, if I didn't admit that at the university I was secretary of the Young Conservative Club."

"We arrive in St. Albans in ten minutes. I'll meet you at the exitway to your coach."

A dense downpour started just as the train was rounding into St. Albans. The immigration officer pointed at a three-story building at the crest of a hill and started to climb toward it. Jake followed behind, his two suitcases bouncing off each other and his legs. He finally made it to the stone building, panting and drenched. Over the main entrance he recognized the insignia of the U.S. Department of Justice, which he remembered from *T-Men* with Dennis O'Keefe. The immigration officer led Jake to the second-floor landing and left him there, dripping on the brown lino, while he conferred briefly with another man. Then they continued to the third floor, where all the corridors, as far as Jake could see, were choked with filing cabinets of the small-card variety. The officer asked Jake to step inside for a minute, politely holding the door open for him. It looked like a hospital ward. Three neatly made up double bunks and, off to the left, a bathroom. Suddenly Jake heard the clang of metal behind him and whirled around to discover he was imprisoned. The officer went away without a word.

Rain, rain, rain. A window, the bars greasy, looked out on a grubby inner courtyard. Jake lay down, deflated, on a lower bunk. "H.W. was here" and other initials had been cut into the brown metal bedpost, and on the underside of the upper bunk an earlier prisoner had scratched *"baise mon cul, oncle sam."* The radio transmitter in the room next to his crackled and squawked as the operator rasped out messages to border agents. "Watch out for Anafukobroplis, Anafuko—A as in Able, N as in —Yeah, he's a Greek. He's expected to try to enter from Montreal in a party of forty roller skaters."

Outside Jake's room, male and female clerks passed again and again, forever opening and kneeing shut metal files. Whirr, pause, clang. Whirr, pause, clang.

"Hear this," the radio operator said. "We expect those baby smugglers to make another crossing in two days. So this time let's get with it, eh, fellas?"

At noon the immigration officer returned, unlocked the door, and pointed his chewed-out pencil at Jake's head. "No *chapeau,*" he said.

"What?"

"I know about orthodox Jews. Read up on them in *Life* magazine once. No hat. So you'd travel after sundown too, wouldn't you, fella?"

"You're very observant. I'm sure one day Edgar Hoover will take notice."

The immigration officer led Jake out of the building and across town to a rambling, boxcar brown, clapboard unit that had been set up alongside the tracks. Jake followed the officer's shiny trouser seat up the wooden stairs to an office with four desks and a pot-bellied stove, where the interrogator sat. Hair parted straight down the middle, dead eyes, almost no lips, and a slightly soiled shirt collar curling at the edges. One heart-sinking glance and Jake knew he was done for.

Full name, the round-shouldered interrogator asked. Age?

"Twenty."

Father's full name? Place of birth? Religion?

"Jewish."

"Employer?"

"None."

"Uh-huh. Have you ever belonged to any of the following organizations? I'll read them over slowly. The Young Communist League?"

"I should say not."

Friends of the Spanish Civil War Refugees? The League of Canadian Consumers? Students For Peace?

"I'd like to make a statement."

The interrogator leaned back in his swivel chair and waited.

"One of my enemies at the university used to sign my name to left-wing petitions."

"What's his name?"

"It was a joke. He thought it was a funny thing to do."

"I see. The Progressive Book Club?"

"Um, one minute. Let me think . . . I'm not sure. The Progressive Book Club?"

"Yes or no?"

"Yes."

Next the interrogator read out a seemingly endless list of newspapers and magazines, and asked Jake if he had ever subscribed to any of them. All of Jake's replies were typed out in quintuplet and then he was asked to check his answers for inaccuracies and misspellings before he signed each copy.

"It says here . . . religion 'Hebrew.' I clearly remember saying 'Jewish.' "

"So what?"

"He's a fresh guy," the immigration officer said. "I warned you."

"I'm sure you wouldn't want me to sign a false statement."

"Christ Almighty, but you believe in making things tough for yourself; O.K., I'll write in Jewish over Hebrew. You initial each copy where I've done that."

"Roger," Jake said, winking.

"Now listen here, kid. You cut that out."

Jake signed the copies. Then he was fingerprinted and brought back to the office. "This hearing is now closed," the interrogator said, "because you are considered undesirable to the United States. Your application for admission has been refused and you are temporarily excluded under the provisions of Section 235 (c) of the Immigration and Nationality Act. You will be returned to Montreal this evening at 7:30."

"You still haven't given me a reason."

"We are not authorized to divulge information on which we pass exclusion."

Jake was driven back to his place of detention and found there was now a thin old man with a sunken pot belly perched on the edge of the upper bunk opposite him, spindly legs dangling in mid-air. The man was wearing a natty straw hat and a checked shirt at least two sizes too large for him and split running shoes. He had enormous pop eyes, opened, it seemed, in an attitude of perpetual amazement; and he held a walking stick over his head. "Don't move," he said, shaking his stick at Jake. "Not an inch closer."

"Jesus Christ. Who are you?"

"As if you didn't know."

Jake sat down tentatively.

"I knew they'd send somebody. Cockroach. Vermin. That's you."

"Would you mind telling me what this is all about?"

"Admit it. Feigelbaum's paying. Or is it Shapiro?"

"Nobody's paying. Nobody sent me here. I'm a prisoner. I'm being sent back to Montreal tonight."

"To keep tabs on me. Well, I'm on to you. Human trash. If you so much as reach into your pocket for a weapon, I'll scream for the guards."

"I'll stand up with my arms over my head and you search me."

"Oh, no you don't. No sirree. That's when I get the judo chop."

"Why would I want to kill you?"

"For the money. Five million."

Jake whistled.

"Didn't they tell you that much?"

"I'm not completely trusted."

"They'd stop at nothing to put me out of the way and you know it. My case is before the Supreme Court in Manhattan right now. Calendar number 33451/1953."

"I wish you luck."

"It's my father's money. It belongs to me. I know where Feigelbaum is and I've located Shapiro, but I still have to find Czucker and Leon Feigelbaum."

The man's eyes, to Jake's astonishment, appeared to open even wider. They might actually pop, he thought.

"I'm willing to share the money with anyone who helps me recover it and brings the criminals to justice."

"Cigarette?"

"Not one of yours, thank you. Are you crazy?"

"Surely you don't think my cigarettes are poisoned?"

"Last time Feigelbaum tried to murder me it was with supersonic rays. They paralyze and destroy the bodily organs. They're not trying to kill me themselves. No sirree. Instead they hire people to try for them. Human excrement, like you."

Suddenly a metal clipboard was banged against the door and a man peered in the barred window. "What did you say your mother's maiden name was?" he asked Jake.

"I already told you in quintuplet."

The old man leaped down from the bed and threw himself against the door. "You've got to get me out of here. I'm not like him."

"We want the name again."

"He was put in here to murder me. He's a hired killer."

"The name, please."

"It's on the form. You've got it right there."

"Spell it for me, will you?"

"Belloff. B-E-L-L. Off. Like in fuck off."

"You'd better watch it, buddy." But he opened the door for Jake all the same. "You can go now. Train time."

"Don't put me on the same train," the man whined, retreating.

"Don't worry, grandpa. Somebody's coming for you."

Somebody's coming. The man slid to the floor, holding his head in his hands, and began to sob.

"Can't you do anything for him?" Jake asked, exasperated.

"Got any ideas?"

The door shut behind Jake and he was led downstairs and put in the care of another officer, a young plainclothesman with a clean crisp feel about him and a most disarming smile. The young man immediately stooped to relieve Jake of one of his suitcases. It was a small gesture, done without fuss, but the kindness of it all touched Jake, and it occurred to him for the first time that he was sweaty and rumpled, and that in the eyes of this pleasant young man he must seem a small-time con artist or maybe even a nut, like the man Jake had left behind. After such a long day's squalor the young man came as a shock to Jake. He looked so wholesome, such a good credit risk. As Jake and the young man stepped outside together into the fresh air he dared to hope that passersby would take them for friends, not a prisoner and his guard, and he was filled with a need to dissociate himself from the day's seediness and make a good impression.

"Pardon my asking," the young man said, "but you're a political, aren't you?"

"Well, yes, I mean that's the charge."

"I don't mind the politicals. They're educated and are really, well, idealistic sort of. It's the junkies and faggots that I find so degrading. Or do you think of them as . . . sick?"

Jake shrugged.

"What were you going to do in New York?"

"Overthrow the government by force."

"That's rich. That's a good one."

"Me and my little supersonic ray gun."

"You were put in with him, then? Now isn't he something?"

"You with the F.B.I.?"

"Hell, no. Nothing like that. Say, I must tell you how much I admire things Canadian. In our house, we always listen to the CBC. It doesn't insult your intelligence, if you know what I mean? They allow for nonconformists. Like that, um, Professor McAllister who sometimes debates on foreign affairs."

McAllister lectured at McGill. A tiresome, literal socialist.

"Would you know McAllister personally? Coming from Montreal?"

"No. They said somebody was coming for the old man. Who?"

"Oh, him. Hell, we've had him three times already. His son, I suppose. He's a very distinguished dentist. Say, did the old boy show you the numbers on his arm?"

The numbers? "No," Jake said, nausea rising in him.

"The Dodgers are going with Erskine tomorrow. The ole perfesser's going to put in Whitey Ford."

"Mn."

"When the train pulls in you just get on ahead of me. No need to embarrass you, is there?"

"What numbers? What are you talking about, you goddam fool?"

"It was something they did to them during the war. In concentration camps. Didn't you know that?"

Jake suppressed an urge to hit him with his suitcase.

"The irony of it is that now some of those same Germans are back in office in Western Germany. Now what do you say to that?"

"Kiss my Royal Canadian ass."

"Be friendly. Come on. There's nothing personal in this." He offered Jake a cigarette. "Off the record, I'd even say there was something to it."

"To what? What are you talking about now? Concentration

camps? The World Series? Is everybody crazy in this country?"

The young man stopped, his pleasant face aching with high seriousness. "Would you say that?"

"That? This? What are you talking about?"

"Communism. The original idea. Brotherhood. Well, I buy it. But you can't make it work. It rubs against human nature."

Jake stared at the tracks, willing the train into the station.

"I suppose some of your buddies were going to meet you in New York."

"A parade was planned. A big demonstration."

"Can I phone anybody for you to explain why you didn't turn up?"

"I'm going to be sick. I've got to sit down."

Jake slumped against a pillar.

"Here comes the train. You just get on ahead of me. We don't need to sit together."

The young man settled in five seats behind Jake, and when they reached the border he got up and jumped off the train. Jake caught his eye as he stood on the platform, lighting up. The young man waved, his face broke into an infectious grin. Jake's heart thumped crazily, his head was pounding and, to his own amazement, he spit venomously on the window just as the train lurched backwards, vibrated, and jerked forward again. The young man looked after him, shaking his head, appalled. And Jake, consumed with shame, realized that he had done it again. Shown himself one of the oily ones, an off-white. He had done the wrong and childish thing, made a fool of himself, when hitherto all the right had been on his side. So that when he remembered this day and came to talk about it at dinner parties years later, he would recall with stinging shame his stupid spit on the window, but he would always leave that out of the story, except when he told it to Nancy.

Back in Montreal Jake made straight for the bar in Central Station, ordered a double whisky, and paid for it with American money.

"Montreal is the Paris of North America," the waiter said. "I trust you will enjoy your stay, sir."

Jake stared at his change. "What's this," he asked, "monopoly money?"

"It's Canadian."

Jake laughed, pleased.

"Canada's no joke. We're the world's leading producer of uranium. Walter Pidgeon was born in this country."

3

On his return to Montreal, Jake, trying to salvage at least a splinter of satisfaction out of the New York fiasco, assumed— gleefully assumed—that he would be the root of more Hersh border trouble. Gleefully, because it gratified him to think that his inchoate political past might deprive his uncles and aunts of Miami. Like him, this winter even the most affluent Hershes might have to suffer sub-zero Montreal. Sniffles, blizzards, frostbitten toes. Then, only a week after his return, Cousin Jerry was held at the border, questioned, and allowed to continue on to New York. It wasn't Jerry or Jake the immigration officers were worried about. It was another J. Hersh, Cousin Joey, and Jake's uncles had known this all along. Uncle Jack, the most unswervingly orthodox of the Hershes, a myopic furrier whose revolutionary activities had been confined to a failed uprising against the too permissive *apparat* of the Shaar Zion synagogue, told Jake how he too had once been stopped at the border and questioned for two hours before being cleared. "I'll bet," he said, "you got smart with them. You make more trouble for yourself than anybody can ever make for you."

"What have they got against Joey? A criminal charge?"

"He's a communist, a *roite*."

Jake, immersed in his own unpromising state, shrugged the idea off with a deprecating laugh. That Cousin Joey had been a gambler, an actor, probably a gangster, once, all this Jake could dimly recall, but a communist?

Nonsense.

1937, Jake recalled, was the first time he had ever encountered his cousin Joey.

Joey had been eighteen, Jake only seven years old.

Hanna had delivered her progeny, Joey, Jenny, and Arty, to Uncle Abe's cottage on the lake on a sweltering Sunday in summer that was, to begin with, a Sunday like any other. Jake and his cousins leaping shrieking off the raft, querulous aunts playing Mah Jong as they washed down liver knishes with Cokes, hefty uncles at the poker table under the shade of a maple tree, the women squealing, the men quaking with laughter, teenage cousins stomping to a boogie-woogie record, babies howling . . . when all at once there was an uncharacteristic stillness on the shore and Jake, curious, turned to look and saw Hanna and her three children. Hanna, compared to his aunts, appeared shockingly thin. A black winter twig. Her two youngest children, amazingly pale for June, wore ill-fitting dark city clothes, but not Joey, who was the eldest.

Cousin Joey, standing apart from them, smiled scornfully. His black hair had been ruthlessly brushcut and he wore a discolored blue work shirt and faded dungarees, the uniform of the Boys' Farm, the detention home for delinquents in Shawbridge. Jenny, her forehead encrusted with angry pimples, pointedly ignored the other teenagers. Arty, considerably younger, only three years older than Jake in fact, clung to Hanna, squinting against the sun. Uncle Abe led the sullen newcomers magnanimously from group to group and Jake noticed that his aunts and uncles recoiled stiffly, suspiciously, and took to whispering among themselves as soon as Abe had passed. Hanna and her brood did not eat lunch with the others; they were fed in the kitchen.

"Who are they?" Jake asked his father on the drive back to the city.

"Your second cousins. Baruch's bunch."

"And who's Baruch?"

Ignoring Jake's question, he turned to Mrs. Hersh and said, "Abe's Parker 51 is missing already. It's a crazy idea, a mistake."

But Jake's mother cut him off and the two began to quarrel heatedly in Yiddish.

"Why is the boy's head shaven?" Jake asked.

"You've heard of a de-icing? Well, he's just had a de-licing."

The new Hershes were shoveled into a cold-water flat on St. Urbain, one of Uncle Abe's properties on the same block as Jake's, and Cousin Joey, who was said to be sickly, did not go out to look for work. Instead he slept in late, obliged, as Dr. Katz put it, to stoke energy into the furnace of his body, enabling him to best resist the wintry blasts ahead. Joey usually slept in until noon and then he went out and no matter how late he ultimately came home, Hanna, it was reported, still waited at the kitchen table, her callused knobby feet soaking in a steaming basin, making a crochet tablecloth or knitting diamond socks for her most cherished radio comedian, ready to quiz Joey about aches and pains, the time and texture of his last bowel movement.

Four months after they had settled on St. Urbain, the snows came, the earth froze, bedsheets hung stiff as glass on the backyard clothesline, and Joey left home. He said to Hanna, "Going to Tansky's for a Coke. Back for supper," and he was gone.

Max Kravitz saw Joey at Tansky's. "He tried to borrow a sawski from me and I said no." Saying no to Joey was St. Urbain Street policy since Uncle Abe had ordained that he was no better, potentially worse, than Baruch, Joey's father. So it was no when Joey wanted to buy a guitar and no again when Hanna sought money so that Joey could have a motorcycle. Uncle Abe wrote off the rent for the flat on St. Urbain, he saw to the doctor's bills, which were considerable, but he would not sanction frivolities.

Joey left home in December 1937 and though the police, the Baron de Hirsch Institute, and finally the seediest of private detectives, one of the Boy Wonder's contacts, tried to find him, he was not heard from again until the autumn of 1938, when he sent Hanna a postcard from Toulouse, France. Europe! Where did he get the money? There were those on St. Urbain who were scathingly quick to point out that a neighborhood garage had been held up a day before Joey disappeared. Others (remembering Baruch, perhaps) felt that he had most likely signed on a ship. There was another postcard in the summer of 1939 and this one had a Mexico City postmark on it.

"He's not so dumb," Sugarman said. "He wasn't going to be called up."

"Fair is fair. Who would take such a sickly boy in the army?" Jake's father said.

From the day of Joey's departure Hanna never doubted that he would come back. In the spring, she assured the neighbors, glaring venomously at them, when the lilac tree in the back yard would be in bloom, but spring came and came again without Joey. Instead in January 1940 there was a tall man with empty gray eyes standing on Hanna's doorstep. "I'm looking," he said, his smile made to chill, "for Joseph Hersh also known as Jesse Hope." The man explained he was an R.C.M.P. inspector.

"What's he done?" Hanna demanded.

"There's no charge against him. Just want to have a little chat."

"You're not the only one."

Hanna squatted on her balcony or stood by the front parlor window every afternoon, rising involuntarily if an unfamiliar car slowed down. When she had to leave the flat empty, Hanna jammed a note in the door, saying which neighbor had the key. Frosty nights she raked the streets for Joey, hawking *Gazettes* downtown, in front of the Loew's, outside Dinty Moore's, at the Forum after a hockey game. "Gzet! Gzet!" Hanna was a knotted bony woman, all jutting angles, her face as creased as old brown wrapping paper, the same color, too, with heated black eyes and a wart turned like a screw in her hooked nose. On blue-cold winter nights she wore a man's leather cap with ear flaps, a woolen scarf wound around and around her skinny chicken's neck, and over all the sweaters she pulled a red Canadiens hockey sweater. A leather purse was strapped to Hanna's waist, the fingers of her woolen gloves scissored out the easier to give change. She wore sheep-lined air force boots. "GZET! GZET!"

Hanna sought out the crazy, discredited Lubiner Rabbi, whose study was crammed with palmistry charts and phrenology tables, and kissed the fringes of his *talith*, offering money, a bundle, beseeching him to contrive prayers for Joey's return. But his Jewish necromancy failed her. So Hanna climbed the concrete steps to St. Joseph's Oratory, taking each one on her knees, imploring Jesus for help, Jesus Christ, but he failed her too, which hardly surprised her. Then Hanna began going to the railroad stations to watch the troop trains come and go, searching among the soldiers for Joey, with the upshot that one Christmas morning a picture that showed Hanna, thrusting through a group of soldiers, seemingly toward a loved one, appeared in a full-page advertisement in the *Star*. There was a luminous cross on top of the page, the picture itself was framed in mistletoe, and below there was a line drawing of a battle-weary soldier reading a letter. The caption read,

KEEP THE HOME FIRES BURNING . . .
With McTaggart's Anthracite

Hanna carried Joey's photograph everywhere and if anybody on St. Urbain or even in Outremont had visitors from New York or Toronto, if on a Sunday night a synagogue's lights were on for a bar mitzvah or a wedding, then Hanna would come to the door, St. Urbain's blight, scuttling from table to table, flashing the photograph, her manner truculent, accusatory. Asked to sit down she would immediately pounce on the whisky and begin to ramble about Joey. She would tell of the time his puny four-year-old body had been rough as sandpaper with ringworm and how it was touch and go for him with the scarlet fever. She recalled how once he had all but choked on a rusty nail. "And who would have thought he'd survive in the first place," she'd say again and again. "God who watches so well over his Chosen People? Spike Jones? The cross-eyed chief rabbi of the London zoo? Dr. Goebbels? He was born in a freezing miner's shanty in Yellowknife, with the help, if you can call it that, of a drunken

Polack midwife while his father was out boozing somewhere. Too weak to cry. Only this big and blue as ink, my Joey. Who would have thought he'd live? Me. Only me."

During the baseball season Hanna advertised in the Personal columns of major league cities and the week of the Kentucky Derby she always ran an ad in the Louisville *Courier*.

REWARD

Anybody with information as
to the whereabouts of Joseph
Hersh, also known as Jesse
Hope, 6 ft. 1 in., black hair.
Write Box . . .

Increasingly hostile, she shoved Joey's photograph under the noses of startled strangers in hotel lobbies or coming out of the air terminal or disembarking from boat trains. Finally she was the subject of a newspaper column, Mel West's What's What, in the *Herald*. "HOPE SPRINGS ETERNAL, as the Bard sez. Missus Hanna Hersh, a longtime character on our Main Stem . . ." Uncle Abe summoned Hanna to his office in the Dominion Square Building, the offending newspaper column on his desk. "Feh," he said.

"It's my first-born son," she said.

But not her only child. Less than a year after Joey disappeared Jenny had to quit Fletcher's Field High to take a job. Jenny was given credit for contributing to the support of the family and raising Arty almost single-handed. People felt it certainly indicated quality that she continued with her studies at Wellington Night School, but they also agreed that Jenny was too sour. For now that her pimples had dried out she was really rather attractive, especially strolling home from work in a sweater on a summer evening, her handbag, groceries, and a Modern Library book in her arms, her bottom snug in its skirt as a watermelon in its skin, but there was not a boy on St. Urbain good enough for her. It was also rumored that Jenny came home disconcertingly late from night school and did not, some neighbors said, treat her mother with the respect to which Hanna was entitled.

Even Hanna.

"Gzet," Hanna hollered on street corners, "Gzet" and without warning she would begin to sob or curse passersby obscenely.

Early one spring morning, when the lilac tree was in bloom, Hanna emptied the coffee tin in the kitchen of all the week's food money, hurried to Rachel Market, and returned with a tongue for pickling, a fat goose, marrow bones, chicken livers, pickles, Bing cherries, imported grapes, and a pineapple. Singing to herself, she lit the stove. Jenny, off to work, was not so much disconcerted by the squandered money as terrified to see Hanna so elated, seemingly untouchable.

"Joey's coming home today," Hanna said.

"You heard from him?"

"Vas you dere, Charlie? A mother knows."

Jenny returned from work to find the kitchen stove laden with simmering pots. A tray of sweet-smelling, crispy raisin buns came out of the oven and in went a honey cake. The dining room table was set, the fruit basket covered with a linen napkin. Arty had been made to put on his High Holidays suit; his shoes had been polished. Hanna sniffed at Jenny. "Her best friends wouldn't tell her," she said, reeling back in a mock faint. "Use Lifebuoy."

Finally Hanna had to go and pick up her *Gazette*'s. "If he comes before I get back," she said, "you and Arty are not to ask any dumb questions, understand? Not why did you go and where have you been? You pour him a snort from the bottle of Chivas Regal and say I'll be home soon." Then, as they both looked frightened, she added, as she tied her change purse to her waist, "Hi-ho Silver!", and pounding herself on the behind, bellowing, she galloped out of the house.

The soup simmered on the stove for two days. The goose dried out and charred. The raisin buns hardened.

"Couldn't we at least rent out his room?" Jenny asked.

"Night school," Hanna said, "you think I don't know what goes on there? You're peddling your ass."

Radio aggravated the bad feeling between Hanna and Jenny. Hanna had always been a fan, but following Joey's departure she and the radio had become inseparable. Hanna's favorite was Bob

Hope. "That Bobby," she'd say, "you can die from him, the things he says." Autographed pictures of Hope, Joe Penner, the Mad Russian, Phil Harris, Edgar Bergen and Charlie McCarthy, and Jack Benny hung on the wall. Sunday night radio was the sore that festered. Jenny, on what was often her one free night, wanted to listen to thought-provoking Canadian Broadcasting Corporation dramas, but Hanna wouldn't hear of it. Especially if on another station W. C. Fields might be visiting Mortimer Snerd. "If you'd only try," Jenny pleaded, "just once."

So Hanna tried. That night, as it happened, there was an up-lifting play on by one of Canada's most liberal-minded writers. It was about a lovely sensitive blind girl, who was being courted by an intelligent man with a basso voice. We know the man throbs with love for the blind girl but we are also led to believe there is something fishy about him. The man raises money for an operation for the girl, but when the surgery is successful and we know she will see again, he is discovered packing in his room. Why? He wants to spare the girl. He's a Negro.

Hanna sighed, rolling her eyes. "Where there's life there's hope, and wherever there's Hope, there's usually Crosby," she said, diving for the dial.

"If you only realized," Jenny said, "what this play has to say about the world today."

"Oh, you, Miss Hotzenklotz. You make me sick. Why don't you go into your room and study up on Walt Disney's dog?"

"For your information it just so happens that Plato was one of the foremost philosophers of all time."

If there was a thorny week between Hanna and Jenny it usually drew first blood when the intractable old lady turned up her radio very, very loud while her daughter, who had com-pleted her high school requirements and immediately gone on to university-level courses, was studying. Jenny would retaliate by stealing a tube and Hanna's next tactic was to crumble matzohs over her daughter's bed sheets. Then Jenny would bring home an unplucked chicken for Friday, necessitating a loathsome job for Hanna, and Hanna would mix Russian oil into Jenny's por-tion of borscht. "Tonight," she'd say, "it's bombs away."

One balmy spring afternoon in 1943, when the lilac tree was in bloom in the back yard, Joey walked right into the house, as casually as if he had only just returned from Tansky's. Hanna melted, moaning, into his arms.

"Well, to what do we owe this honor?" Jenny asked, terrified.

A fire-engine red MG sportscar was parked outside.

Windows whacked open. Neighbors came out to stand on their balconies. Arty, Duddy, Gas, and Jake gathered around the car, overcome with awe. There were stickers on the windshield. FLORIDA, the Citrus State. NEW ORLEANS, Mardi Gras City. GRAND CANYON. COLORADO, LAS VEGAS, TOMBSTONE, CHICAGO, GEORGIA. There was the dust of the desert on the car and the windshield was splattered with bugs and rain. The remains of a dead sparrow were impaled on the grille. The license plate was Californian. Two soft leather suitcases and a kitbag were strapped to a rack mounted on the rear of the car. So was a guitar. The name Jesse Hope was embossed in gold on one of the suitcases and another was plastered with still more stickers, exotic labels from hotels in Spain, France, the United States, and Mexico.

Duddy Kravitz, bolder than the rest, tried to flick open the glove compartment. It was locked. "That's where he keeps his gat," Duddy said.

4

The day Joey returned his fire-engine red MG looked so lithe and incongruous parked right there on St. Urbain, among the fathers' battered Chevies and coal delivery trucks, off-duty taxis, salesmen's Fords and grocery goods vans—the MG could have been a magnificent stallion and Cousin Joey a knight returned from a foreign crusade.

The photograph of Joey that Hanna had flashed in railway stations would not have helped to identify him. Joey had left a skinny boy, sickly, with a rasping cough, and come back a big broad-shouldered man. He had style, Jake recalled, such style. Striding down St. Urbain bronzed as a lifeguard, eyes concealed behind sunglasses, trousers buckled tight against a flat hard stomach, he did not seem to be of St. Urbain any more. There was no suggestion in his gait that a creditor might be lurking around the corner or that a bailiff was waiting to pounce. Joey wasn't going to be tapped on the shoulder by a *goy* bigger than he was. People on the street took pleasure in him, but they feared him, too. When he drifted past Best Grade Fruit on the day after his return, for instance, Lou waved tentatively, beckoning him inside, but he was grateful when Joey merely acknowledged the invitation and strode on. Tansky's regulars, equally wary, immediately recognized that Joey was a drinker. He didn't reel, he was never actually violent, but occasionally there was an underwater slowness to all his gestures and a distinct menace in his manner. Joey wasn't a happy, mischievous drinker, like Jake saw at bar mitzvahs. His state wasn't born of a quick burning little schnapps with honey cake, head tossed back and eyes instantly tearing. Joey drunk was a threatening man.

The afternoon of his return he summoned Jenny and Arty into the parlor. "Our father is alive in Toronto," he said. "He's living with an Irish woman. A widow. She owns a candy store."

That was all; but another day Arty overheard Joey and Jenny quarreling.

"Where did you go when you left here?" she demanded.

"Europe."

"Did you get to Paris?"

"Yes. I was in Hollywood, you know. I made a bad marriage. With a starlet."

"And I'm the Queen of Siam. Now tell me why you came home. Were you in prison?"

He laughed.

"You son-of-a-bitch. I can't even afford Toronto. If you only knew how I hate it here."

"Go, then."

"What about Arty?"

"Hanna's his mother. Not you."

The next morning Joey went shopping and then the parcels began to come. Exquisite white shirts and black silk socks from the Saville Row Shoppe on Sherbrooke Street. A sterling silver cigarette case from Birks. A suit not from Morrie Gold & Son, with padded shoulders, a two-button roll, and slightly zoot trousers, but from a tailor with an authentic British accent. Joey's taste was alien to St. Urbain. He did not favor gaily colored ties or two-tone shoes; neither did he go in for a camel hair coat. Joey dressed as cold and correct as a Westmount lawyer.

He soon discovered that Arty and Jake, prodded by Duddy Kravitz, were shoplifting at Eaton's on Saturday mornings, and he bawled them out for it, which baffled Duddy, who assumed that Joey was a mobster.

Duddy, Arty, and Jake were even further confused after the blackjack game the next rainy afternoon. Joey, his manner solemn, intimidating, didn't take long to clean the boys out. Afterwards the boys were flattering, they hung around expectantly, but Joey did not offer to return their winnings. "Come on," Duddy pleaded, "it's only peanuts to you. I thought we were playing for fun."

"Gambling is gambling," Joey said sternly.

Duddy, the heaviest loser ($2.85), burst into tears. "You big dumb prick, robbing innocent kids. My father says you were in on the Lindbergh kidnapping."

Before Joey could even reply, Duddy had scuttered out of the door. Outside, he executed a spiteful little dance. "Hey, syphhead," he shouted up at Joey, "make you a deal. You burp up my ass and I'll fart in your mouth."

Only Goody Perlman was sufficiently intrepid to ask, "Where'd you get all the money, Joey?"

"Well, Goody. Well, well," Joey replied. "Look at it this way, *hombre,* it isn't black market money."

Joey had passed Goody Perlman's clothing factory on the Main and dropped in, for old time's sake. Goody drove a Buick in a year when you could only buy them second-hand for much more than the list price, with ten or fifteen miles on the speedometer; and when Joey got home that evening Goody was waiting for him in his car parked outside the door. He beckoned Joey inside and showed him snapshots of his wife and children and the medical report turning him down for the army. His eyes charged with apprehension, he talked of the good old days. He told jokes. Sweat sliding down his cheeks, he thrust an envelope with two hundred and fifty dollars at Joey. "Please don't make any trouble. We're both Jewish boys. I wish you luck, all the luck in the world, you're such a prince of a fella." And Joey, it was reported, reached for his cigarette lighter, lit the envelope, actually lit the envelope, and did not drop it until the money was engulfed in flames. Then he eased himself out of the car without a word and Goody drove off, grinding the gears, and went right home to bed and asked Molly to send for Dr. Katz.

Joey set up a makeshift gym for himself in the backyard. Punching bag, medicine ball, mats. Occasionally strangers came to spar with him, bringing girls, high-quality girls, who sipped martinis, their legs delicately crossed. Arty and Jake would watch, concealed behind Arty's bedroom curtains, which was how Jake first came to see the fantastic play of scars on Joey's back. A splattering of uneven cuts and holes. One of the girls, lanky and blonde, usually wearing dark glasses and riding clothes, came more often than the rest and stayed longer, rubbing Joey down with a towel after his workout and then waiting in his MG while he changed into riding clothes too, and they drove off together, to the Bagg Street stables, to rent horses. Other times the girl came late at night, just to fetch Joey, or turned up alone in the afternoon. Once, as she was sipping martinis in the backyard with Joey, a tall, elegantly dressed man with gray hair rang the front doorbell. The girl hid in the shed. And Hanna, answering the door, said Joey was out. The man sat in his car waiting for almost two hours before he drove off.

Another woman who came alone usually arrived by taxi. She was dark and extremely attractive, though clearly older than Joey. He seldom seemed pleased to see her and never allowed her to rub him down after one of his workouts. Once, as she began to sob in the backyard, pleading with him, he flicked her with his towel, making her cry out. Other times, though, he drove off with her, not returning until the next morning, laden down with parcels from the Saville Row Shoppe.

The elegantly dressed man with gray hair returned to the house on St. Urbain again and again, and once he sat in the backyard to watch Joey at his morning workout. Jake and Arty couldn't hear what he was saying, but it was evident that it inflamed Joey; he hit the bag harder and harder, his eyes shooting hatred. When Joey finally quit, the man offered him a long brown envelope, his smile ingratiating. Instead of taking it, Joey made as if to punch him playfully. The man laughed, flashing a

big smile, and all at once Joey struck him so ferociously in the
stomach that the man remained doubled over and gasping, unable
to catch his breath, for a worrying time. When the man left,
Jake and Arty raced around to the front balcony to watch him
walk stiffly to his car. Hanna was sitting on the balcony. She
watched with the boys as another man, younger but equally tall,
opened the front door for the man. The two tall men began to
talk earnestly even before the car had driven off. Hanna spit over
her left shoulder and retired to the house, leaving Jake and Arty
behind to speculate.

One day Joey piled all the boys into Max Kravitz's taxi, took
them to Delormier Downs, and led them to the box seats on the
first base line. The first baseman waved. "Hi, Joey."

Joey nodded and waved back lazily.

"You know him?"

"We were in the Dodger chain together for a season."

"You mean you played professional baseball?"

"For a spell."

On the ride home, Joey said: "How come Jenny gets back
from night school so late on certain nights?"

Arty didn't know, neither did Jake.

"Chev-or-let?" Duddy asked. "Snatcherly," he answered. And
for one frightening instant it seemed like Joey was going to hit
him. Instead he said, "Tell Jenny what a good time you had
with me today. Tell her you like me."

But Jenny had spent the day typing invoices in the sticky,
sweltering offices of Laurel Knitwear.

"There's something wrong with taking them for a treat?"
Hanna asked.

"The polio's going around. They shouldn't be in public
places."

Hanna groaned, crossing her eyes.

"Why can't he go out and work in this heat?" Jenny protested.

Yet when Joey offered to contribute two crisp one hundred
dollar bills toward household expenses, Jenny scorned the
money, saying, "Where did you steal it?"

"You shouldn't leave your bra and panties hanging over the tub in the bathroom," Joey said softly. "Arty's a growing boy."

"Don't tell me you're going to start making the laws around here?"

"I've got dem blues," Hanna sang, spinning, the broom clutched to her cheek, "I've got dem Kotex, rag-time . . . blues . . ." coming to an abrupt stop immediately before Jenny. "Is that the kind of manners you learned from Jimmy Durante's brother?"

"His name happens to be Durant. And he's an outstanding author."

The neighbors were astonished to learn that not only could Joey ride horses but he had a commercial pilot's license. He could actually fly an airplane. They were eager to fill Joey in on all he had missed in his six years' absence. Zalman Freed, they told him, was an artillery officer. Cooperman's boy had joined the navy and was serving on a corvette in the North Atlantic. Marv Bloom had been shot down over Malta and his story was broadcast repeatedly in radio spots to promote the sale of Victory Bonds. ("Hey, mister," the announcer said, "remember Marv Bloom, the fresh, freckled kid who used to deliver your morning newspaper . . .") To all these stories, Joey responded with a bemused smile. "And meanwhile," he would say, "you're all making money, hand over foot."

Joey had only been back a week when he began to cough and wheeze, waking in the middle of the night. And so whenever he left the house, Hanna waited up until he returned, which was not until one, sometimes two, o'clock, and Jenny would be wakened by their voices.

"It's going to be a mild winter, Joey. Everybody says so. Honestly, the winters here aren't what they used to be."

Roused by the aroma of spicy food and the clanging of cutlery, Jenny would attempt to join them in the kitchen, where a variety of pots simmered on the stove.

"It's nothing," Hanna would say, her smile forbiddingly sweet. "An old bone. A soup. You wouldn't go for it."

"I'm not even hungry," Jenny would reply, aloof.

"Good. Have a nice sleep."

It was Sugarman, albeit inadvertently, who lit the bomb. He told Joey that the windows in Jewish shops were being broken and swastikas had been painted on the pavement outside the *shul* on Fairmount Street. French Canadian followers of Adrien Arcand were to blame.

"What are you going to do about it?" Joey asked.

What are we going to do? The children are forbidden to play softball on Fletcher's Field because of roaming gangs of French Canadian toughs.

The next afternoon Joey collected Arty, Duddy, Jake, Gas, and the rest of the boys and took them to play ball on Fletcher's Field. He accompanied them the following afternoon and the one after that. Now if the French Canadians got any ideas they sneaked one look at Joey, lolling on the grass behind the batter's cage, and faded away.

Duddy Kravitz, taking heart in Joey's presence, shouted obscenities in French after the retreating toughs. When the boys whirled around, Duddy, clutching his genitals, shouted, "*Votre soeur, combien?*"

One of the French Canadians hurled a stone.

"*Yoshka in drerd arein,*" Duddy yelled.

Another stone bounced in the dirt. Duddy bent over, pulled down his trousers, and wiggled his pale narrow white ass in the air. "For Pope Pius," he hollered.

Unwillingly, the French Canadians started back. Joey rose, scooping up a bat, and took a few slices at an imaginary softball. The French Canadians dispersed.

Duddy, Jake, Arty, and the others brought glowing, exaggerated reports of the incident back to St. Urbain, but their parents were not pleased. There was already enough trouble. Street incidents caused by roaming gangs of truculent French Canadians were constantly increasing. Premier Duplessis's Union Nationale Party circulated a pamphlet that showed a coarse old Jew, nose long and misshapen as a carrot, retreating into the night with bags of gold. Laurent Barré, a minister in the Duplessis cabinet, told the legislature that his son, on entering the army, had been exposed to the insult of a medical examination by a Jewish doctor. "Infamous Jewish examiners," he said, "are regaling themselves on naked Canadian flesh." The next morning Uncle Abe, driving to his cottage in the mountains, was astonished to see "*À bas les Juifs*" painted on the highway. He met with other community leaders who contributed heavily to the Union Nationale election fund and they went to chat with a minister and were photographed together shaking hands and smiling benignly on the steps outside the Château Frontenac in Quebec City. The following day a junior minister issued a statement to the press. "Anti-semitism," he said, "is grossly exaggerated. Speaking for myself, my accountant is a Jew and I always buy my cars from Sonny Fish."

Joey burst into the cigar stores, he visited the barber shops, exhorting the men, mocking them, asking them what they intended to do about such insults.

That was Wednesday. On Friday, a St. Urbain Street boy who had gone to the Palais d'Or dance hall to look over the *shiksas* made off with a girl whose husband was overseas with the Van Doos. The boy was beaten up and left bleeding on the sidewalk outside his house and the story was printed in all the newspapers. On Saturday morning Joey went from one cigar store to another, this time carrying the newspaper with him, upsetting the men, hectoring, goading, and in the evening a group of twelve embarrassed men, armed, it was reported, with baseball bats and lengths of lead pipe, set out in four cars for the Palais d'Or. French Canadian boys who came out with girls were separated from them and taken into the alley. When the police finally turned up the St. Urbain Street boys had already fled, leaving a French Canadian boy unconscious in the alley. The story made page one perhaps because the boy, who had not been involved in the previous brawl, happened to be a nephew of an advocate who was prominent in the Ste. Jean Baptiste Society. The boy was a student at the University of Montreal. The Palais d'Or was boarded up and the next night and the night after that police patrol cars cruised slowly up and down St. Urbain. Store owners and pool room proprietors were fined for infractions of city by-laws that had not been enforced for years. Huberman, stopped for doing no more than thirty miles an hour, offered the traffic cop the traditional five-dollar bill with his license and found himself charged with attempting to bribe an officer. Leaders of the community sent a contrite letter to the French Canadian boy's family and another letter to the *Star*. No stone, the letter said, would be left unturned. A delegation, Uncle Abe among them, went to see the French Canadian advocate and promised that whoever had injured the boy would be uncovered by the community and turned over to the proper authorities for punishment.

On St. Urbain, stores shut down early and hardly anybody went out after dark. A special prayer was said at the Galicianer *shul*. People sat by their windows, waiting. The next morning, before anyone else in the house was up, Joey, who had been back home for all of five weeks, packed his bags and was gone again. Two days later, Jake remembered, they found Joey's fire-engine red MG overturned in the woods off the highway. The rest was rumor.

Joey's car was discovered upended and gutted, burned out, alongside the road to New York, some ten miles out of town. Some said there had been two cars parked down the street from Joey's house all night and that six men had huddled there, smoking, passing a bottle, until Joey had emerged and they took off after him. Others argued, no, it was an accident. Not bloody likely, Jake thought, because one of Joey's suitcases had been found ripped open, the contents strewn in the woods. The lid had been torn off another suitcase and somebody had defecated inside. Among other items discovered in the vicinity there had been a photographic sheet with four studies of JESSIE HOPE, exclusively represented by Nate Herman, Wiltshire Blvd., Hollywood. There was a profile and a full-face study, a photograph of Joey in boxing trunks and another showing him in a cowboy's outfit, drawing a gun menacingly.

Joey's wrecked MG was found on a Wednesday. The following Monday the cops visited Brotsky, the city councillor, as usual, for the weekly pay-off, and there were no more surprise

visits from Wartime Prices & Trade Board inspectors to neighborhood stores and wholesalers. The case against Huberman, who
had been arrested for speeding and charged with bribing an officer, was dropped for lack of sufficient evidence.

A month later Jenny quit the house on St. Urbain, whisking
Hanna and Arty off to Toronto. Escaping, escaping. "From now
on this family takes no more money from Uncle Abe," she proclaimed. "Sweet, fucking Uncle Abe."

5

Jenny.

How Jake had revered her, how she had once excited him! Jenny, with her Modern Library books, her map of the Paris metro and line drawings of Keats tacked to her bedroom wall. Jenny, who devoured the *Saturday Review of Literature* from cover to cover and subscribed to every "Y" lecture series. Who read Havelock Ellis. Who wrote impassioned letters to writers she admired, especially the CBC radio playwrights, Douglas Fraser among them. Who visualized herself not as just another *yenta*, but as a delectable olive-skinned Jewess waiting for some behemoth of a Thomas Wolfe to pluck her off suffocating St. Urbain and set her down in a Manhattan penthouse, a voluptuary, where she would become, she once confided to Jake, his *raison d'être*.

Vibrant, full-breasted Jenny, St. Urbain's bursting bud, who was anathema to all the awkward, unprepossessing Hersh girls, that abrasive gaggle of pimply faces, shrill voices, and flat chests. Cousins Sandra and Helen, Uncle Abe's daughter Doris, and Jake's sister Rifka, all of whom, tricked out in kiss curls and muslin, pearls and silvery pumps, lost their boyfriends to Jenny in a sweater at family bar mitzvahs and weddings, and were abandoned to pout on the sidelines as she glided across the dance floor, glued to Dickstein's boy or thrusting against Morty Cohen.

"She gives them what they want," Rifka explained.

Jenny, in the old days, had certainly given Jake reason to envy Arty. Jake's big sister, Rifka, would never bathe him, giving him a chance to contemplate her ballooning breasts as she bent over him in the tub. Neither would Rifka ever wrestle with them on long unwinding Saturday afternoons as Jenny did—occasionally —memorably—unworried about flying skirts, trapping Arty in a headlock or Jake's struggling head against her marvelously firm bosom, sinking to the floor as Duddy Kravitz locked her in a rubbing rhythmic bearhold; and not complaining when the match, inevitably, slowed down and Duddy's hands no longer pretended to find secret places in error. Instead she would rise briskly but good-naturedly, saying, "That's as far as we go with the peanut gallery. Enough, *shmendricks*," and then she would make them chopped liver sandwiches before going out to a movie. Or to the mountain. "To walk among the falling autumn leaves," she said.

To which Duddy's unfailing response was, "Can I come? No pun intended."

But only Jake, who fetched her books from the "Y" library, was ever allowed to accompany her to Mount Royal.

In the autumn, Jake recalled. When the trees on the mountain went crimson and yellow and curling brown and all at once the streets were strewn with swirling leaves. When the sports pages would be charged with speculation and photographs of youngsters with broken front teeth who were trying out at the Canadiens' hockey training camp. When the synagogues advertised that there were still seats available for the High Holidays.

Jenny saying, "You won't catch me growing old selling raffle tickets for Hadassah, my bloated husband snoring on the sofa after dinner."

Telling him about the drama group she had joined. With Kenny Pendleton, who, Montreal being what it was, had to earn his living dressing Eaton's windows, but acted—professionally, Jenny emphasized—in CBC radio plays and Montreal Repertory

Theater productions. And who, when his flat mate Ross Evans was away, cooked her steaks, which they ate by candlelight in the basement apartment on Tupper Street. Which apartment, no *nouveau riche* Outremont showcase, was not overstuffed with sofas and lamps, each shade shielded by plastic, but was artistically furnished. With a blown-up photograph of Michelangelo's David in the dining room. *New Yorker* cartoons in what Kenny called the throne room. And posters by Jean Cocteau. And Henri Matisse.

"At Kenny's parties, we sit on the floor and drink French wines. We don't talk about gall bladder operations or linen sales or the almighty dollar."

In the golden autumn, lying together on a slope, everywhere you looked, couples necking.

Jenny saying, "I don't want you to have anything more to do with Duddy Kravitz."

"Why?"

"Never mind."

But Arty, she swore, would study at McGill. Even if she had to work overtime. And Jake, her acolyte, mustn't settle for hateful Outremont. Another money-grubbing, complacent Hersh.

"This is nowhere, St. Urbain. We're nothing here. We have to leave."

Jenny, who wept for Abélard and Héloïse, lent him *Nana*, and kept *The Shropshire Lad*, a gift from Kenny, under her pillow, was, to Jake's mind, altogether too rare a creature for St. Urbain. So on those evenings when he would contrive to cycle up and down outside Laurel Knitwear at closing time, he would be heartsick to see her emerge, looking as coarse as the other factory girls, her face drawn, sullen, her forehead greasy, until she saw him and would laugh, delighted, allowing him to cycle home beside her.

"Well, well," she'd say, yanking his hair, "picking up girls outside a factory. What would your Uncle Abe say?"

"Aw."

One evening she announced he could be her date; she would take him to the movies next Saturday afternoon.

"On *shabus?*" he whispered.

"You think you'll be struck by lightning?"

"I'm not even scared."

Instead of starting out together they met furtively on a street corner and did not go to a downtown movie, where they might run into neighbors, but to a movie in an unfamiliar *goyische* district. Afterwards Jenny took him to a soda bar and lectured him about Emily Dickinson and Kenneth Patchen. They agreed to meet again the following Saturday. Jenny, amused with herself, dressed up for these occasions, but out of consideration for Jake she never, after the first time, wore high heels or her hair in an upsweep, so that Jake, straining (and, though she didn't know it, with wads of newspaper stuffed under his socks), seemed almost as tall as she was.

On the first Saturday they did no more than hold hands stickily, but just as the main feature came on the second time out Jenny lifted Jake's arm over her shoulders and snuggled up against him. It was the same the next Saturday and the one after that. Then, one Saturday afternoon, as Jake put his arm around her his hand fell accidentally over her breast, dangling, the little finger barely grazing the softness there. He froze, not bold enough to go further but not willing to retreat either, until Jenny whispered impatiently, "It's all right. Honestly, it isn't a crime," and Jake, swallowing hard, squeezed her breast with such sudden and pent-up savagery that she had to grit her teeth to save herself from crying out in pain. Then Jenny took his hand and showed him how and he began to stroke and squeeze her gently and as soon as he seemed less frantic, Jenny (Oh my God, he thought) unbuttoned her dress, unsnapped her bra, and stroking his hand reassuringly led it over her bare breast and amazingly stiff nipple. Time passed achingly, deliriously slow, until, sweating with fresh alarm, he felt her hand undoing his fly buttons, groping inside, freeing him, and then caressing him and pulling him briefly, too briefly, before he shot off, humiliated, into her hand. "I'm sorry," he whispered, but Jenny shushed him and reached into her purse for a handkerchief and wiped them both. Afterwards they went to a soda shop. Jenny lit a cork-tipped cigarette. "Want one?" she asked, her eyes taunting him.

"Sure," he said, but the cigarette made him cough.

"Do you pull off at night? Like Arty. With pictures?"

"*You crazy?*"

"I thought so," she said, her smile venomous as she reached for her coat.

"You going?"

"Yes. And no more movies. Come back when you're old enough."

Old enough. How they longed to be old enough, Jake remembered. In the afternoons they studied for their bar mitzvahs at the Young Israel synagogue and at night they locked the door to Arty's room, dropped their trousers to their ankles, and studied themselves for bush growth. Pathetic, miserable little hairs, wouldn't they ever proliferate? Duddy Kravitz taught them how to encourage hair growth by shaving, a sometimes stinging process. "One slip of the razor, you shmock, and you'll grow up a hairdresser. Like Gordie Shapiro." Duddy also told them how Japanese girls were able to diddle themselves in hammocks. Of course Duddy was the bushiest, with the longest, most menacingly veined, thickest cock of all. He won so regularly when they masturbated against the clock, first to come picks up all the quarters, that before long they would not compete unless he accepted a sixty-second handicap.

Oh God! Oh Montreal!

Today's TV

2:30 p.m. (12) Medicine and the Bible. Modern endo-
crinology used to interpret the scriptural events. Could
Esau have been suffering from low blood sugar and that's
why he sold his birthright? Could Goliath have had a
pituitary gland imbalance? Dr. Robert Greenblatt, author
of *Search the Scriptures,* offers some of his theories.

Stranded. Some three weeks after his abortive trip to New
York, Jake was still stuck in Montreal. Unemployed, without
prospects. Jenny had made good her escape eight long years ago,
in 1943, but not me, he thought, coming out of the System,
having survived another triple bill. Abysmally depressed, with
nothing to do and nowhere to go, when he saw Gas. Towering,
plump Gas Berger, of all people, sailing purposefully down St.
Catherine Street, shoulders dug manfully into the wind, carrying
a pigskin briefcase.

"Knock, knock," Jake said.

"Who's there?" Gas replied, heaving with laughter.

Gas bounced a punch off Jake's shoulder and Jake reached up

and yanked Gas's buttercup ears rapturously, and they retired
to the Tour Eiffel to drink together. Emerging from the dark
two hours later to squint into the unsparing autumn sunlight,
they bought a bottle of whisky, some delicatessen, and took a
taxi to Arty's rooming house near McGill University.

Arty, who was being put through dentistry school by Uncle
Abe, had returned to Montreal years ago. "Well," he exclaimed,
"will you look who's here!"

Jake, Gas, and Arty settled down on the carpet with their
smoked meat sandwiches and curling French fried potatoes and
whisky. It was an absolutely marvelous afternoon, maybe one
of the most enjoyable of Jake's life. No longer boys they were
but, mercifully, not yet full-grown men either, envy-ridden,
harassed by mortgages and calorie intake and child education.
Everything was still possible. Nobody had yet looked at himself
maturely and settled for the workable marriage or the tolerable
job. In the years to come expectations would contract, success
or failure would divide them. But that glorious afternoon in
Arty's rooming house they were overcome with regard for
each other. They talked about the incomparable time and place
they had shared. They argued about John Foster Dulles, tartar,
Jackie Robinson, sharp practices in real estate, foreign cars,
Johnny Greco's second fight with Beau Jack, the claims made in
toothpaste advertisements, Duddy Kravitz, St. Urbain Street,
and, ultimately, Joey.

"Was he in the rackets," Gas asked, "or was that horseshit?"

"I never found out for sure, but I'll tell you one thing. Last
year, you know, in New York, I was watching an old Western
on TV, Randolph Scott rounding up a posse, and who in the
hell jumps on one of the horses but Joey. My big brother Joey
riding with Randolph Scott, for Chrissake!"

"Where is he now?" Jake asked.

Arty's gaiety faltered, he put down his sandwich. "I don't
know. You'd have to ask Jenny."

Who had married a radio writer in Toronto, her dreams fulfilled, and was presently visiting Montreal in her office as CBC
script editor.

"How is she?"

"The same. Difficult."

If Jake hadn't seen Jenny for years, it was only because once she had put Montreal behind her she had resolutely proclaimed she wanted nothing further to do with the Hershes, even Jake, which was not exactly true. For Jenny flaunted her Gentile husband at visitors to Toronto and demanded to know what the bigoted Hershes were saying of her marriage. And as she began to circulate among the anointed, suddenly on first-name terms with Toronto's conclave of writers, directors, and actors, she relayed messages to Montreal, aimed like poisoned arrows at the Hershes, to signal the celebrated company she kept. Alas, Uncle Abe was not impressed. Neither was Uncle Jack. All Jenny's vengeful attempts to dazzle were unavailing. Her world was alien to the Hershes.

"Of course I'll see you," she said when Jake phoned. "If you're not scared of being contaminated?"

"What?" Jake demanded, irritated.

"I should have thought I was *verboten* to any Hersh. A fallen woman."

So the next afternoon, he sat in Jenny's room at the Laurentian Hotel, where she poured him what she called a gin-and-It.

Wearing too much eye shadow, her wet glistening lips too jarringly red, Jenny remained an immensely attractive woman, volatile as ever, her black eyes smoldering. She told Jake that she was bitterly disappointed in how Arty had turned out. Studying dentistry. "The predictable ghetto syndrome. Anyway I suppose he's . . . *content.*"

"And you?" Jake asked, surprised to find himself annoyed for Arty's sake.

"Well, at least I haven't been sucked into the gilded ghetto. Working out my sexual frustrations by organizing bazaars. Like your precious cousin Sandra. I'm doing *meaningful* work. And how's dear Doris?"

"The same, I suppose. I hardly ever see her."

"She's frigid, you know. Her husband phones me when he's in Toronto. I suppose he's heard about the important people who come to our parties. Or that I'm hot stuff. Anyway I told him it's a call girl he needed. I don't service B'nai B'rith brothers out of town. Especially, I told him, somebody who looked to me like he was no good at it. 'I'm sorry, darling, if I came too quickly.' You should have seen his face. I thought he'd turn gray on the spot."

They sat together stiffly, Jake uneasy because he could hear somebody, a man, singing in the shower.

> "Take me back to Mandalay,
> where the flying fishes play . . ."

"You're a puritan," Jenny said. "A real Hersh. And you weren't supposed to be here for another half hour."

Leaping up, Jake said, "I'll come back later."

"Come tomorrow. We'll have breakfast together."

Jake sat seething in a leather armchair in the lobby until Duddy emerged from the elevator. "You son-of-a-bitch," he said.

"Jealous?" Duddy asked, smirking.

"Duddy, do me a favor. Lay off her."

Duddy smiled spitefully, reaching up to remove an imaginary hair from between his teeth, wiggled his eyebrows, released the hair delicately and watched it drift to the carpet. "Her husband," he said pityingly, "can only go seven innings."

Jake discovered what Duddy was after when he joined Jenny for breakfast the following morning and she declared that she was willing to rescue him from the Hershes. She would buy him an air ticket and help him get into television in Toronto. They traveled on the same flight.

"Duddy feels he's stagnating," Jenny said, "and so he's thinking of making a fresh start in Toronto."

"Don't get entangled with him. He only wants to use you."

"And you?" Jenny asked.

7

Jenny's husband was waiting for them in the living room.

"And here he is," was how Jenny thrust Jake on him, "my little Jake, who used to feel me up in the movies. Would you believe it?"

"She's quite a gal," Doug said, contemplating his suede shoes with a pinched smile.

Doug Fraser, one of Canada's most uncompromising and prolific problem playwrights, wrote for stage and radio, adaptations and originals, as many as thirty plays a year. He had a streak of irony in him. In one of his plays, for instance, a self-made businessman sets himself single-mindedly to making . . . THE FIRST MILLION. He has only just acquired it, consummating the biggest deal of his life, and is now preparing to get to know his family, as it were, when the doctor tells him it isn't an ulcer —it's stomach cancer! ! ! Which made for a somewhat downbeat ending. This didn't put off Canada's highbrow CBC, but it was clearly not the sort of stuff American TV networks would tackle, especially, as Doug said, in the Aspirin Age. Jenny and Doug had no children. Their way, they said, of facing up to the Fact of the Bomb. Doug maintained an office with filing cabinets labeled IDEAS, CHARACTERS, and CONTRACTS. "I'm just not the longhair, live-in-a-garret type," he said.

Jake asked eagerly after Hanna.

"Luke was here earlier. He took her to the movies. The new Tarzan," Doug said, shaking his head.

"Oh, great," Jenny said tightly, "just great.· They're bound to be late getting back. And drunk."

No sooner had drinks been poured than Jake inquired about Joey.

"After all these years," Jenny admitted, laughing at herself, "I've inherited Hanna's disease. You know I sometimes think I've seen him on the street. I'll jump off a bus, rush up to a stranger with a familiar back and shout, Joey! Only it's never him."

Joey, she said, drank prodigiously during his five-week stay on St. Urbain. He was able to sit in the gloom of the living room for hours, a bottle of Chivas Regal beside him, engrossed in dark reveries of his own. She had often asked him why he had come home after six years, but he only deigned to answer once. "I'm waiting for a long-distance call. It could come at any time." He went out most afternoons and, unfailingly, his first question on coming home was, "Any phone calls for me?" Joey was also the first one up in the house to scan the morning mail. If one morning there was a letter for Jenny—a notice for a new concert series, perhaps, or something from her night school—he would open the bedroom door, waking her. "Of course," Jenny said, "he was well aware that I didn't wear pajamas." Then she inveighed against Joey's drinking again. "A bottle a day was nothing for him." So, Jenny said, if she wakened in the early morning hours to hear a chair being knocked over, cursing, or somebody breathing heavily immediately outside her bedroom door, she knew that Joey, like his father before him, was drunk again. Next she would hear him retching in the toilet or he would start to make phone calls, dropping the receiver, shouting at the operator. In the morning Hanna was the one who would strip his bed, wash the sheets, mop the toilet, and take his suit to the cleaners. "Hanna," Jenny said, "who would never so much as dust my room."

"But why do you think he came home after so many years?"

"You mean you don't know? Joey wanted to fuck me."

Jake's cheeks burned stinging red.

"Come, come now. How parochial can we get? Surely you don't think incest is peculiar to *goyische* people?"

"Certainly not," Jake said, feeling foolish.

"Sorry to cut in," Doug said, looking intense, "but that is a form of prejudice Jews are prone to."

"You're very perceptive," Jake said. Then he turned to Jenny. "Was Joey a communist?"

"That line of questioning," Doug interrupted, his boyish face throbbing with concern, "leaves a bad taste in the mouth."

"I'm not here for the Un-American Activities Committee. I'm merely asking a question about my cousin."

Jenny rose uncertainly. "I'm going to have a bath. We're having one of our parties tonight, Jake. Everybody will be here."

"And we're glad to have you too," Doug said. "You see, it isn't often I get a chance to kick the conversational ball around with someone of your generation." He tugged his hassock closer to Jake. "Do you guys care, I mean really care?"

Jenny's party was characterized by a free flow of liquor and food. Not fortifying, over-rich Jewish food, as Jake had longed for, but instead ghetto-emancipated canapés and hors d'oeuvres. Transparent slivers of Italian salami on crackers. Assimilated anchovies curled like worms on white bread. Little liberated pork sausages. Jenny's Toronto people were very, very sophisticated, everybody a nonconformist, seeing right through *Time* and the frame-up of Alger Hiss, and against war-mongering in Korea. They spoke admiringly of Rod Serling, Horton Foote, and other Philco Theater playwrights. Paddy Chayevsky was compared to O'Casey.

"Yes, yes," a television writer agreed, "but exciting things are beginning to happen right here in Toronto, you know."

"Like what?" a tall, bespectacled young man demanded belligerently.

"If Toronto isn't good enough for you, Luke, why don't you leave?"

"Look at it this way. Until the very day of Pearl Harbor, the Japanese kept an ambassador in Washington."

Jake laughed appreciatively.

"And who in the hell are you?" the writer asked, turning on Jake.

"Call me Ishmael. And should I know your name?"

"Damn right you should," he replied stoutly, "if you're the least bit interested in Canadian culture."

"Don't tell me. You're Mazo de la Roche."

Luke grinned.

"I don't have to put up with this sort of crap from a couple of kids."

"Don't, then."

As Doug bore down on them, smiling, Luke slid away. Jake did not catch up with him again until he retreated to the garden, where he was delighted to discover Hanna drinking beer and laughing with him.

"Yankel," she exclaimed, and they embraced.

The years had turned Hanna to mahogany; her hair was white.

"Meet my boyfriend, Luke Scott. He takes me to all the hockey games. And the wrestling matches."

Jake and Luke shook hands.

"Jenny tells me you may be staying in town," Luke said. "I've got an apartment. I'd be glad to put you up, while you look around. We could share expenses."

"Are you sure?" Jake asked.

"He's sure," Hanna said, and she made a place for Jake beside them on the bench. "Do you know what it is a week tomorrow?"

"No."

"Yom Kippur. Do you fast?"

"Sorry, Hanna. No."

"Last year she wouldn't let me."

"At her age, Hanna's not taking any chances."

"Shettup, Luke. She stood over me, shouting, you eat non-kosher food all year and today you want to fast? Not in this house. O.K., so next week I'm pretending to visit a sick friend. Well, what do you think of him, Yankel?"

"Who?"

"Her little shmock of a husband."

"Our Ibsen," Luke pitched in.

"Come on, Hanna. Jenny's looked after you all these years, hasn't she?"

"Well, at least we don't fight any more. We've made a truce. I pretend to Mr. Nothing and Nobody she's out with me when she's really banging somebody else, she was born with round heels, that one, and she gives me movie money. My reward."

Jenny's little shmock was holding forth in the living room, explaining his play-in-progress, *Accident*. "I've been doing research on the subject with a doctor, we checked the records of bus and truck companies and two hundred ordinary motorists, and you'd be amazed at the things we uncovered. There is a small minority of drivers who are extremely susceptible to accidents, and these accident repeaters seem to suffer from the same problem. *An inability to adjust to the codes of society*."

Descending on the group, Jake slapped his cheek, he whistled.

"But it's all based on fact, Jake. We made a study of forty taxi drivers, twenty of them with long-standing safety records and the other half of the sampling clearly accident prone. The safe drivers tended to be quiet, reserved men, almost a bit dull. They came from stable family backgrounds, were faithful to their wives, didn't gamble much, and were courteous to passengers. But the accident repeaters tended to be social misfits. Thirteen had drinking fathers or domineering mothers. Twelve were school dropouts with frequent appearances at juvenile court. Eight owned up to sexual promiscuity. Thirteen drifted in and out of jobs. Fourteen bootlegged liquor. We classify these accident repeaters as 'mild psychopathic' personalities."

"I see," Jake said, rubbing his chin. "I see."

"Interestingly enough they share certain characteristics. They tend to be intelligent, but impulsive, they hate discipline, abhor routine, and want to be their own boss. They are good conversationalists, but bad listeners. They don't relate. They always want to be the center of the stage. Furthermore, we have noted that the rash drivers have one trait in common. *An underlying aggressiveness directed against authority*. While the safe driver deals with frustration in a socially acceptable form, the accident repeater uses his car as a means of acting out hostility. Our studies have satisfied us that accident repeaters are directing animosity against authority figures—the police or their employers. Then they blame other drivers, particularly women. You can narrow down the focus of their anger to their wives and ultimately the mothers who have dominated them. In extreme cases it would be fair to say they were using their cars . . . to prove their manhood. Trying to assert their masculinity, they climb into souped-up cars and wreak vengeance on the whole female sex."

"But the child they knock down," Jake said, "could be yours."

"Right you are, Jake. You see, in our culture, it is a major problem that a man is too often measured by his risk-taking."

Which was when Jake finally managed to corner Doug alone.

"I'm sure you've heard this often before, but I did want to tell you how very much I've always admired your work."

"Well thanks, Jake. Glad to have you in the fan club."

Prick. "There's always real red meat in your stuff. It's challenging."

"Now you tell me where *you're* going. What are *your* dreams?"

"I'm glad you asked me that. You see, I'm dying to get into TV, now that it's finally starting in Canada. I'd like to direct, but, you know, I lack your connections. I'm sure nobody at the CBC would even have time to see me."

"When you say 'direct,' do you see it as a job or a vocation?"

"A vocation, naturally. No riding the American money mill for this boy. I want to stay in Canada and make my statement here. One day, maybe, I could direct plays as good as yours."

"With content?"

"Yessiree. It's getting started that's got me stymied."

"Mnn. I'm dead set against nepotism, you know."

"Me too, Doug."

"Take Yugoslavia, for instance. It can even corrupt a socialist-structured society."

"I couldn't agree more. But I'm a working-class boy, you know. I'm not seeking favors. I'd be willing to start as a stage hand, if only somebody could get the door opened for me—just a crack."

"Let me think about it."

"Don't put yourself out, Doug. The important thing for you is to write. Your time is valuable, but—well, I certainly would appreciate your expert help."

Jenny caught up with Jake in the hall.

"Do you hate me?"

"Oh, Jenny, please."

"You love me, then?"

"Yes. Sure."

"I tried so hard. I applied myself to learning and literature with a kind of hatred for it, so that if I ever fell in with what I think of as the blessed, talented people, I could fit in. I would understand the references . . . And so what happens? You know how I can tell the people of real quality who come to this house? The few who aren't phonies? They spend all their time talking to Hanna. Hanna, that bitch, what did she ever do to deserve such attention? They avoid me. And they poke fun at Doug. Unless they're on the make."

"Is that so?" Jake said stiffly.

"Your fly buttons are done up, kid, but your ambition is showing. You never used to be calculating."

"I'm growing up," Jake said, and he led Jenny upstairs to her bedroom. "Now tell me about Joey. Was he a communist or not?"

"Who knows what he was, or is, he was such a liar."

The first phone bill to come after Joey's return was for a staggering sum. Long-distance calls to New York, San Francisco, and Hollywood, some of them lasting twenty minutes. "He paid the phone bill with cash," Jenny said.

"Didn't you ask him what he did in those six years away from home?"

"O.K. One night—he was pissed at the time, mind you—one night he told me that he was in Spain in 1938. Madrid."

"Oh, my God, the scars on his back."

"Sure. Only they could have been made by lots of things."

"What else did he tell you?"

"From Spain he went to Mexico. Coyocán."

Where Trotsky was living. Jake's heart hammered. He told Jenny how he had been mistaken for Joey and stopped at the American border.

"So. Does that have to be political? You think he fought in Spain. I'm convinced he was running away from trouble with gangsters. He came home to lick his wounds, then he found he was attracted to me, and left again for my sake."

"Oh, come off it, Jenny."

"Come off it. You think I'm telling you everything?"

There was a sudden upshot of laughter from downstairs. Shrieks of delight. "There she goes again," Jenny said, pounding her fist against the arm of her chair, rising abruptly, Jake trailing after.

"Gzet! Gzet!" Hanna, her old Canadiens sweater pulled over her head, loped drunkenly from group to group. "Gzet! Gzet!"

Luke Scott, looking perturbed, bore down on Hanna, but Jenny intercepted him, seizing his arm. All at once her manner softened. "Meet Luke Scott," she said to Jake, nuzzling his cheek, "a would-be writer in need of succor."

"Pardon?" Jake pleaded over the party din.

"You heard me right the first time," Jenny called back, "and you're still too young for me anyway."

Jake watched them whirl off together, Luke obviously embarrassed, keeping an eye out for Hanna.

Over a group of bobbing heads Jake caught Hanna accosting another bunch.

"In Yellowknife," she said, "you couldn't bury people in the winter. The ground freezes hard as rock. And so every autumn, the undertaker, Formaldehyde Smith, used to size us up before he figured out how many graves to dig in advance. He looked at my Joey, my four-year-old Joey, nobody expected him to live, he was so sickly, and he dug a pint-size grave for him. With my own eyes, I saw it. His momma. Mr. Smith, I said, you fill that hole in immediately or I'll cut your balls off and fry them for dog food . . ."

8

Duddy Kravitz descended on Toronto within a month and, by way of establishing his name, was soon having himself paged at the cocktail hour in those bars that were most frequented by ad agency and CBC types, including those insufferable scoffers, Jake Hersh and Luke Scott.

Reactivating an old company of his, Dudley Kane Productions, Duddy sent out letters of introduction. But the going wasn't good. Without connections, an interloper, he had one door after another shut in his face. Only Jenny was helpful. They lunched together once a week and then retired to his apartment on Avenue Road, where he mounted her absently, eliciting an orgasm in time to shower before his next appointment. The CBC would not buy Duddy's idea for a television quiz game and no ad agency required his services as a self-styled troubleshooter. On a frenzied trip to New York, he bid for, but failed to win, the Canadian distribution rights for the hula-hoop. Instead he returned with the rights to a reducing pill. Take one a day, eat all you want, and shed twenty pounds within two weeks. But, at the time, Duddy was dubious and also lacked sufficient funds for promotion and advertising. He was stripped down to his last thousand dollars, stacks of unpaid bills, and a bleeding stomach ulcer when he opened the *Star* one afternoon and read that somebody was going to publish a Canadian Social Register and, lo and behold, according to the newspaper's most outspoken columnist, there would be no Jews in it. Which was what inspired Duddy to break into publishing, simultaneously doing something for his people and laying the cornerstone of his Toronto fortune.

The Canadian Jewish Who's Who (published by Mount Sinai Press, president, Dudley Kane) was, for a year, no more than an obsession, the all-consuming dream Duddy laid himself to bed with in his increasingly squalid apartment, the fervent hope he tramped the winter streets on, driving himself to concoct schemes that would yield a quick turnover. Stake money. Blessed stake money. Where? How? What, he thought, about Jake Hersh, the sentimental prick?

Jake, risen from stagehand to studio floor manager, had little time for him. He had little time for anybody in fact except well-born Luke Scott, who had yet to have a script accepted anywhere. They shared an apartment, competing for girls, their appetite prodigious, but otherwise intensely loyal to each other, inseparable, professional abominators, dragging nutty old Hanna everywhere with them, bursting in on parties only to insult people. Equally disliked, Duddy discovered, by older established directors and writers whom they denigrated without mercy. The small talents for whom, they said, endearing themselves to no one, Canada was a necessary shelter.

Who would never sell out, Luke taunted, because no invitation was likely to be proffered.

For whom integrity was not a virtue, Jake pitched in, but a habit born of necessity. Like his Aunt Sophie not being a courtesan.

Arriving at their apartment, Duddy was relieved to find Jake alone. "You guys live in style here," Duddy said. "I envy you."

Tricked out in his shabbiest suit, spitting into a ketchup-stained handkerchief, owning up to an ulcer he couldn't afford to treat, hinting the bailiffs were breathing on his back, Duddy skewered his old schoolmate by reminding him that they had been kids together, St. Urbain's shining morning faces, and even as Jake struggled, anticipating a touch, Duddy nailed him with a sweetener, promising not to service Jenny any more, and he managed to wring a check for five hundred dollars out of Jake as well as the promise of his signature on a twenty-five hundred dollar bank loan.

None too soon, as it happened, for a moment later Luke whacked open the door, ushering in Hanna ahead of him. "Well," he exclaimed with appetite, "look who's here."

Hanna, sensing trouble, disappeared into the kitchen to unload her shopping bag and prepare supper.

"I was just going, Mr. Scott, sir," Duddy said, fleeing.

Jake was infuriated. "Look here, Luke, there are many of your friends whom I cannot abide, but I don't behave like that."

"You behave worse."

Hanna stepped between them. "You know what you sound like, the two of you? A couple of fairies. Jarvis Street rough trade."

After supper, Hanna, in rare high spirits, her black eyes sparkling, suddenly fell on a deck of cards and shuffled them as Luke had never seen them handled before. Jake shook with laughter as she dealt a hole card to Luke, another to him, and one to herself. Then she turned over hers, revealing an ace. "You know who taught me that?"

"Joey," Jake said, beaming.

Hanna nodded, reaching for her bottle of Carlings. Then she began to tell them about her husband. "He was a born bummer, my Baruch, an animal. He used to go for the beer, he could guzzle it all day, and at night it was a whore for him or the wrestling matches. He stole from your grandfather, Yankel. As a youngster, he was in and out of prison for disturbing the peace. Years before I met him, ask your father if you don't believe me, your family didn't see Baruch for three, maybe four months, and then my man would turn up at two in the morning, banging on the door with his fists, drunk, his head bloody and stinking of vomit, shouting curses at your grandfather. Jews, he would holler, I'm here! Jews, it's Baruch, your brother is home!"

She continued to reminisce about her husband in the car.

"Once he gave Yosele Altman such a beating he had to go into the hospital for stitches. He didn't care for your paw, you know that, don't you, Yankel? Once he said to him, hey, you know what you are, Issy? No, what? Your father's mistake. Or he would shove a finger under his nose and say, that's the one that went through the paper, Issy. Oh, he was a walking garbage can, my Baruch, a brawler. A crook. And a nut case! I should drop dead if he didn't once travel as a strongman for six months with a French Canadian carnival bunch, chewing razor blades and bending bars in Chicoutimi and Trois Pistoles and Tadoussac. In the old days in Montreal, when there were no sidewalks on St. Urbain, just mud everywhere, and whorehouses, he used to hang out in the taverns on the docks with sailors and naturally one day he signed up for a ship himself. Either he was drunk or kidnapped. Who knows?"

Hanna insisted they come into the house with her, and led them by the hand into the basement, through the playroom, into her own bedroom, where she stood on a chair, stretched her dry twig of a body, and brought a hat box out of her cupboard.

"You know what this is," she said, gently easing a black-felt, broad-brimmed fedora out of its tissue paper, "it's a genuine Borsalino, my friends. One of the very first to be seen in western Canada. My Baruch used to wear it in Winnipeg," Hanna said, wiping tears from her eyes, "strutting down Portage Street, and the hunky women would come in their pants, they'd never seen the likes. The Métis, who were afraid of nobody when they had the liquor in them, would step down into the gutter to let a man pass."

Jake and Luke drove back to their apartment in silence, each unwilling to speak, but neither of them could sleep, so they broke open a bottle of brandy and opened the window to the summery breeze.

There was such a spill of Hershes, Jake explained, second

cousins by the bushel and a clamor of aunts, short, red-haired cousins by Shmul Leib's spiteful second marriage and fiercely corseted great-aunts from Motke's side, such a world of Hershes, Jake said, that as a simple-minded boy he had simply accepted the fact that Hanna, yet another Hersh by marriage, had materialized out of the heat haze one day with three children and no husband. But of course there was a husband.

Baruch.

In 1901 Jake's paternal grandfather and great-uncle abandoned Lódź to come to Montreal, where they both begat enormous families (Jake's grandfather, fourteen children; his great-uncle, twelve) and this, Jake went on to say, he had assumed as a boy, made for the sum total of their Hershes. He had been mistaken. There was a third brother. Baruch. Jake's grandfather and his brother sent money to Poland so that Baruch, the youngest of the three, could join them. Only a week off the boat in Montreal, Baruch cut loose, he was transmogrified. He proclaimed himself a *shoimar-shabus* no more. Defiantly, he ate non-kosher food and was prepared to work on the sabbath. His elder brothers disowned him.

Eventually, Baruch either signed on a ship or, as Hanna suggested, was kidnapped. In any event, he sailed as a stoker to Argentina. He swung around the Cape on an oiler and served for a season as a longshoreman in Australia. He ventured to Japan and peddled slot machines in China. He lived in Tahiti and prospected for gold in the Yukon before he finally settled in Winnipeg, where he married Hanna, had a daughter, and knew brief but gaudy affluence as a whisky runner during prohibition. Baruch was shot up in a gun battle on the Montana border and following that, as far as Jake knew, his luck soured. A leg wound never healed properly, he developed gangrene, and the leg had to be amputated above the knee.

Luke rose shakily, staggered into the kitchen, and boiled some water for instant coffee. "Hey, it's getting brighter," he said, "or they've just polished off Etobicoke with the Bomb."

In the distance, the sky was on fire. Bleeding red.

"Let's call some girls," Luke suggested. "Gorgeous girls, eh, with long legs and filigreed undies." But it was 5:30 a.m. "It must be spiffy," Luke mused, "to have your own breasts. To get up in the morning, you know, and not have to send out." Then he sat in the window sill, glaring into the gathering traffic below, and began to excoriate all things peculiar to Toronto. "I hate this city. It's ugly. It's provincial."

"It's the farm club, Luke. We are permitted its minor league facilities so long as we don't linger."

England, England, Jake thought, and, though he had yet to direct his first TV play, he declared he would settle for nothing less than becoming a film director of international importance. "If I'm thirty and still in TV, I quit."

Luke swore his first stage play would have to be good enough to open in London or New York. Or not at all.

They had only just fallen asleep, it seemed, when the door bell rang, Luke taking it.

"It's not you I want, Mr. Scott, sir."

Duddy went to Jake's room, shaking him awake, and, resentfully, Jake struggled into his clothes and accompanied him to the bank to sign for the twenty-five hundred dollar loan.

With which, after shaking salt over his left shoulder, slipping into a synagogue to kiss a *sefer torah*, touching the first cripple he encountered on Jarvis Street, Duddy registered Dr. McCoy's Real Wate-Loss as a limited company, cajoling an acquaintance he had already softened up, the corner druggist's son, a dense but greedy Bavarian, to serve as vice-president and mail drop for a cut of the gross. It was more than a dumb hunch. Two weeks earlier, brooding over a midnight coffee at Fran's, kidding the obese waitress, Duddy had doled out one of his pills, promising it would help. To his amazement, when he popped in again ten days later, the fat Polack bitch had actually lost eighteen pounds. Even though, as she swore, she was still eating prodigiously. More than ever, with insatiable appetite.

Dr. McCoy's Real Wate-Loss pills, its mail order advertising limited, sales ultimately dependent on word of mouth, caught on surprisingly well from the beginning, especially in rural areas and mining towns, like Sudbury and Elliot Lake. Duddy, his projected profits huge, luxuriated in Jake's apartment, foolishly impervious to Luke's withering presence, saying he would soon cut out his New York supplier and manufacture the pill himself, going Canada-wide with a splash, and maybe even dropping the Bavarian punk.

"Probably, he's a Nazi anyway," Luke said.

"Well, you'd know, wouldn't you? That's your line."

Luke cursed, he lashed out impatiently. Again and again they went at each other with knives, with a penchant for evoking the worst in each other.

Luke, burdened by his acquired liberal baggage, and possibly a shade too proud of it, castigated Duddy because he felt that it was just this manner of unprincipled operator who undermined his impassioned defense of Jews to his father and his bemused cronies at the Granite Club.

Duddy feared Luke. He didn't trust him.

"You know, Jake, when I want something, I grab it. I fight, no holds barred. That bastard, he's a cool one, he sits back and waits for it to drop in his lap. Because it's coming to him, like everything else in this country. What's the world? It's the inheritance of Lucas Robin Scott, Esq. But underneath that self-mocking tone, and that cool, there's a heart of stone. He takes care of number one just like you and me, Yankel, but he was raised to coat it with sugar."

Instinct, albeit based on a distressing incident, saved Duddy from going Canada-wide, as he had bragged. Ensconced in Fran's one night, sipping coffee as he scrutinized the market pages in the *Globe*, he inquired solicitously after his once corpulent waitress. Maria was in the hospital, wasting away, they said. God knows, he thought, it could be an abortion. Or the clap. But all the same, on his next trip to Montreal, Duddy sought out a French Canadian druggist, somebody unlikely to ask questions, and had the pill analyzed, saying it was something his overweight wife had been given on their Mexican holiday. When he discovered the pill's crucial component, he drove all through the night back to Toronto, where the enraptured Bavarian boy, his

proud father burbling blessings over both of them, greeted him
with more orders.

"George," Duddy said, "this has to be a small gold mine, right?
I mean, projecting conservatively, there has to be ten thousand
dollars a year net in this with hardly any work or capital outlay,
and that's only the beginning?"

George beamed, his father clucked gleefully.

"But I'm in bad trouble."

Gravely, the old man brought out a bottle, pouring Scotch
into beakers.

"I've got a real estate problem in the Laurentians. A tax headache. I need ten thousand dollars. Like yesterday. I hate doing
this to you, fella, because we're buddies, but I've found a
buyer—"

"We're partners," George brayed.

"—and the shrewd bastard, he wants it all."

"You are partners, Mr. Kane. My son and you—"

"I don't want to be unpleasant, but if you study our letter of
agreement, you will see I have the right to buy you out at any
time."

Father and son consulted heatedly in German.

"Ten thousand lousy dollars. It's a steal. But what am I to do?
I'm cornered."

"What if my father was to raise the money?"

"Naturally, I'd rather sell to you, but, fellas, let's be realistic.
Where can you raise ten thousand dollars"—Duddy paused—
"within ten days"—and paused again—"in cash?"

Which simultaneously provided Duddy with a stake and
washed him clean of Dr. McCoy's Real Wate-Loss. None too
soon, either. For a week later the first ambiguous news story
trickled out of Elliot Lake. Two uranium miners had been admitted to the hospital in an emaciated condition. Duddy, joyously
laying the *Star* aside, called his broker, overriding his objections
to put in a hefty order for uranium stock shorts, and then wrote
letters to three of the most radical socialist M.P.'s in Ottawa,
enclosing the *Star* clipping. Only three days passed before one
of them rose indignantly in the House to ask a leading question

about the inherent dangers of radiation to miners and, just as Duddy had anticipated, the stocks began to tumble.

Hoo haw, Duddy thought, singing in the shower, dancing into his suit, as he prepared to attend the party in honor of the first television play to be directed by Jacob Hersh. His schoolmate, little Jake, with his name up there on the trans-Canada network screen. "General Motors Theater presents . . ."

Doug Fraser was there, so was Jenny, all the girls from the cast, the crew, and, naturally, loping, straw-haired Lucas Scott, Esq., still a zero, up to his neck in rejected scripts.

"How goes it, Shakespeare?" Duddy asked, beaming.

"Don't ever make the mistake of trying to match witticisms with me, Kravitz. You haven't a hope."

Retreating, Duddy joined the circle on the floor around Hanna, who was telling tales of Joey. "He was born in a freezing miner's shanty in Yellowknife, with the help, if you can call it that, of a Polack midwife . . ."

Because Jake, caught up with his goysy set, Scott's rich bunch, seemed to have no time for him, Duddy left early, hoping to buy a *Globe* and check the latest uranium market figures. Which were beautiful.

Go-ahead money, Duddy thought. Real and desperately needed go-ahead money.

For all the while Duddy had not rested from his labors on his Canadian Jewish Who's Who, the work slow and increasingly frustrating, as he had urgently required a presentable office, sizable bank credit, a printer, and a sales staff, all of which would now be available to him. And so he would at last be free to concentrate on the pursuit of fat cat sponsors, whom he hoped to secure by his promise of turning over ten per cent of his profits to Jewish charities.

Working in secrecy, Duddy pored over Canadian telephone directories from coast to coast, the social pages in newspapers and Jewish weeklies, extracting the names of Jewish professionals and businessmen. On Jake's advice, he commissioned a shnook in Winnipeg, one of those poetry-writing professors, to compose a stirring ten thousand-word history of Jewish achievement in Canada, beginning with the first settlers who came over in 1759 with General Amherst, conspicuous among them Reb Aaron Hart, the commissary officer (buying cheap, selling dear even then, Duddy mused) and many more, who took one quick look around and leaped into the fur trade. "Bringing," Duddy wrote into the margin, "modern marketing knowhow and sales savvy to hitherto underdeveloped but colorful *coureurs-de-bois*."

The history led off with a quotation from none other than the Right Honorable Vincent Massey, Canada's first Canadian governor-general, who allowed that the Jews were "a fruitful and fertilizing stream" in Canadian life (which is to say, we're horse manure, Duddy thought) and it skimmed over any reference to prohibition whisky running, the Jewish Navy Gang of the twenties, or latter-day Montreal bookies and gaming house barons. Another professor was hired to write a eulogy on medicine, from Maimonides to Leonard Hyman Jacobson, Toronto's outspoken child psychologist. This, and specimen pages from further essays, Duddy had reproduced, under headings in Old English print, on the most luxuriant paper he could get without paying, by writing off to England for sample rolls, ostensibly soliciting a Canadian franchise for the sheets.

Meanwhile, after riding the fall in uranium shares, as scare stories proliferated, Duddy called his baffled broker again, took his profit in shorts, and then flew to troubled Ottawa to seek out the appropriate minister, waylaying him in the snow outside the Rideau Club. "I must have a word in confidence with you, sir."

"What's that?"

"Kravitz's the name. I'm a personal friend of Senator Scott's son. You know, the budding playwright," Duddy added, enjoying himself.

"Yes."

"I am able to impart to you the true reason behind the miners' illness at Elliot Lake. I wish to offer you this information as a long-standing admirer and lifelong anti-communist."

Back in Toronto, Duddy called his broker yet again, reversing his investment gears by ordering him to buy uranium shares heavily on option, his reward coming when the self-satisfied minister rose to speak at question time in Ottawa the next afternoon.

The *Globe* ran the story on the front page the following morning and, reading it, Luke whistled with astonishment, and passed it to Jake.

Minister Reveals Mail Order Scandal
INSTANT REDUCING PILLS
CONTAIN TAPEWORM

"Well, now," Luke said, "I'm moved to pity. For they are bound to lock Duddy up and throw away the key, and I certainly never wished that on him."

"Would you like to bet on it?"

"But he'll never wiggle out of this one, Jake."

"Say, twenty dollars?"

"Right."

As Duddy expected, George and his father, quaking with anger, were waiting in the outer office when he arrived, emboldened by the presence of an over-eager young man drumming his fingers on an attaché case.

"You their legal-eagle?" Duddy asked, waving them into his office.

"I am their lawyer, if that's what you mean to say in what I take to be show-business parlance."

"*Azoi.*"

"I beg your pardon?"

"George, we could have talked this over together. I'm surprised at you. You've got a lawyer, so now I get a lawyer. And what happens, the letters fly, threats, we get nowhere, and they coin it in hand over foot."

"It is perhaps the oldest and most pernicious trick in the books," the young man said, springing out of his chair, "to try to separate a client from his attorney."

"You'd better read this, Perry Mason," and Duddy heaved a file at him.

There was a letter to George imploring him not to buy Dr. McCoy's Real Wate-Loss, at best a risky venture, and another letter, to the New York manufacturer, saying Duddy no longer wished to lend his name to a product, whatever its sensational initial benefits, which he feared might ultimately not be in the best interest of users health-wise.

"Why, you sharp Jewish bastard, you haven't heard the end of us."

Duddy flicked on his intercom. "Miss Greenberg," he said, glaring at the lawyer's card, "would you please get me Seligman, at the Anti-Defamation League, and ask him who we've got on the bar council? Thank you." Then, turning on his visitors, he said, "My secretary will give you my lawyer's name on your way out."

Duddy stayed home that evening to watch Jake's production of Luke's first television play, having decided that he would settle for nothing less than a brilliant production of the shittiest play ever written. But, before the first act was over, he realized that Lucas Scott, Esq., could write rings around anybody in Toronto. It seemed unjust, even perverse, that having been born into everything, he should also be abundantly talented. Well, maybe he'll die young. There's always hope. But Duddy, his mood sour, did not attend the party that was to follow the production.

After the party, Jake and Luke drank in the dawn together, embarrassed to be waiting for the reviews. For if they were bad, it would be humiliating, and if they were good, it wouldn't be satisfying either, because this was merely Toronto. So when the reporters started to phone, Luke was withering and Jake did his utmost to give offense.

There were more plays, larger triumphs, and other post-production mornings, unwinding with girlfriends until dawn, then deprecating the reviews no matter what they said, for both men continued to take Toronto's approval as a stigma. England was what filled their thoughts more and more. England, England, as soon as the time was ripe.

Duddy, envious of their shared celebrity, sulking as he felt

Jake had thrown him over, retreated from both of them, increasingly absorbed in his own dreams.

The Canadian Jewish Who's Who.

After all, it was time for Duddy to bait the hook.

A test mailing of one thousand forms was dispatched across the country to doctors, dentists, lawyers, and businessmen, who were asked to return photographs and biographies, under no obligation to themselves. Their names, they were informed, had been selected as community leaders by an exacting and distinguished committee, for it was not possible to buy your way into an epoch-making compendium that was destined to become part and parcel of our incomparable Jewish heritage. An order form was enclosed in each envelope, in case the recipient wished to reserve a numbered, gold-embossed copy of the limited first printing (*bound to double in value as a collector's item*) of the Canadian Jewish Who's Who. Or the Jew's Who, as it came to be known in the inner sanctum of the Mount Sinai Press.

One hundred and twenty-two people enclosed checks for twenty-five dollars, of which only eighteen bounced, and Duddy hurried over to his bank, threatening to switch elsewhere unless more credit was instantly forthcoming.

Duddy Kravitz cleared fifty thousand dollars in legitimate profit on the Jew's Who, entering Jake free of charge, for old time's sake, as the noted up-and-coming television director, who would soon move on to bigger and better things, directing on the other side of the pond.

Luke had already left for the Eastern Townships, to spend his last week in Canada on the lake with his family. Jake was taking Hanna to dinner on his final night in Toronto, but Duddy, he said, was welcome to join them.

Join them he did, enormously depressed to see Jake go, and leaving them early to sit in his own apartment and ruminate.

Certainly on the high road to his first million, Duddy nevertheless felt something lacking in his life. His handsomely-appointed apartment with a built-in bar backed by a mural of can-can dancers lit from behind, equipped with hi-fi and a bathside telephone, was forever in a mess. Smelly socks and soiled shirts strewn everywhere. Pots and pans riding the sink. Salami butts shriveling in corners. And, most distressing of all, he still had to make do with restaurant food or something sent up from the delicatessen. He longed for home-cooked food (chicken soup, flanken, knishes) and something nifty yet *haimeshe* in a wife. What good was a million, he reflected, if you had to eat *dreck* alone every night and then either pulled yourself off to sleep or sent out for a hundred-dollar call girl, still damp from the last customer. Syph-bringers. The girls he relieved himself with were just the thing for a weekend in Buffalo, but not the sort he could take to the Pine Valley Country Club.

> The girl that I marry will have to be
> as soft and as pink as a nursery.
> The girl I call my own will wear satins
> and laces and smell of cologne.

Hanna, in a melancholy mood, was tearful throughout dinner, even though Jake assured her he would send her the fare to come to London on a visit, maybe for the opening night of his first film, he joked.

"Everybody leaves this cold country. Joey; now you," and she told him a story that Baruch had brought back from his travels, a tale told to him by a Spanish sailor. "You know how this country got its name? It was written on a map by the Conquistadors in Peru. On their map of the Americas, one of them wrote on the uncharted space over the Great Lakes, '*Aquí está nada.*' It was shortened to *aquí nada.* Or Canada."

Baruch, Baruch.

"When he was in agony," she said, "after they cut off his leg, what kept him going was his hatred for his brothers. They'll bury themselves with twigs, he said, so that when the Messiah comes they can dig their way to him. Fat chance. I'll see them rotting six feet under, he swore, those crazy sons of bitches, and if any of you ever take anything from them, it's good riddance and an old man's curse on you."

After his leg had been amputated, Baruch returned to Yellow-knife, the mining town where Joey had been born, bought a diner, lost it and everything else speculating on claims.

"He might not come home to sleep for maybe a week and I wouldn't stop sobbing or cursing. And when he'd come home, finally, with bottles and his *goyische* ruffians, he would smack me on the ass, push a bloody parcel into my hands, and send me still crying into the kitchen to cook him *traifes*, sweetbreads, and pork chops . . . and he'd pull Joey out of bed, and Jenny too, kissing and pinching them, passing them from hand to hand. He'd pull down Joey's pajama bottoms, grab him, and shout, There's a cock for you, a Jewish cock, when he grows up, watch out for your daughters. He would give Jenny beer to drink and laugh when she spit it out and he would put a cigar in Joey's mouth and light it . . . and we would have to stay there, drinking and eating with his cronies, until he started a fight with one of them. There isn't one of you here, he'd boast, who can pin this one-legged Jew to the floor. Or maybe he'd pass out cold and the other men, ashamed for me, would file out of the house, saying polite things, telling me that Baruch had forced them to come to the house and that he was one hell of a fellow."

Baruch moved the family to Toronto, where Arty was born, and squeezed out a fitful living hustling worthless claims and penny mining stocks. He acquired a mistress and began to drink heavily again. Joey was taken over by the Baron de Hirsch Institute and placed in an orphanage. He fled, ending up on the Boys' Farm. Hanna ran to Montreal, where she literally threw herself at the feet of Jake's grandmother and Uncle Abe.

So Hanna and her three children, Jake recalled, as he brooded on the train to Montreal, were whisked into a cold-water flat on St. Urbain and put on an allowance.

Jake said goodbye to his mother, promising to write regularly from London. He went to see his father and his uncles, inform-ing them, not that they had asked, that Hanna was well, and bringing the conversation around to Baruch, who, once abandoned by his mistress, had settled into a rooming house in Toronto's Cabbagetown.

"Whatever money he needed for beer and beans, that one," Jake's father said, laughing, shaking his head, "he made selling newspapers outside office buildings and washing up in restaurants. He kicked the bucket in 1946, you know."

"Yes," Jake said sharply, "I am very well aware of that."

Uncle Abe, recently made a Q.C., with larger triumphs hinted at in the future, smiled, amused. "You've got a lot to learn, Jake." He patted Irwin's ten-year-old head and added, "You should get to know my boy here. His teachers are amazed. They've never seen anything like him. Irwin can recite the names of all the forty-eight states of America."

Which set Jake off. He scolded his uncles for being smug, he accused them of abandoning a broken old man to a lonely death in a squalid rooming house and of treating Cousin Joey, the only Hersh to have actually fought in the Spanish Civil War, even more shabbily. His uncles guffawed; they retorted heatedly, but justifiably, that any (or almost any) Hersh could get work with one or another of them, which only fired Jake's anger more. He warned them that he was bound to come across Joey somewhere, in England, where he was last heard from, or Israel, possibly. He would never abandon him, as his uncles had Baruch. On the contrary, he would do everything he could to help him.

Without realizing it, Jake had become Cousin Joey's advocate.

Three

Neighing, the stallion rears, obliging the Horseman to dig his stirrups in. Eventually he slows. Still in the highlands, emerging from the dense forest to scan the scrub below, he strains to find the unmarked road that winds into the jungle, between Puerto San Vincente and the border fortress of Carlos Antonio López.

In Frankfurt, the Horseman sits in the court presided over by Judge Hofmeyer.

A witness remembers Mengele.

"Exactly the way he stood there with his thumbs in his pistol belt. I also remember Dr. König, and to his credit I must say that he always got very drunk beforehand, as did Dr. Rohde. Mengele didn't; he didn't have to, he did it sober."

Dr. Mengele was concerned about the women's block.

". . . The women often lapped up their food like dogs; the only source of water was right next to the latrine, and this thin stream also served to wash away the excrement. There the women stood and drank or tried to take a little water with them in some container while next to them their fellow sufferers sat on the latrines. And throughout it all the female guards hit them with clubs. And while this was going on the S.S. walked up and down and watched."

Bodies were gnawed by rats, as were unconscious women. The women were plagued by lice.

"Then Mengele came. He was the first one to rid the entire women's camp of lice. He simply had an entire block gassed. Then he disinfected the block."

Mengele's pitch, his most cherished place, was on the ramp with the Canada detail. The Canada men unloaded prison transports and collected the baggage of new arrivals. Watches, pocketbooks, blankets, jars of jam, sausages, bread, coats. These valuables were lugged to storehouses with the collective name Canada, so called because of the country's reputation as a land of immense riches.

"Mengele cannot have been there all the time."

"In my opinion, always. Night and day."

2

Surfacing from a dream of the Horseman, only a week after
Ingrid had formally filed charges against him and Harry, he
thought—no fear, Jake—soon Ormsby-Fletcher will arrive. Ormsby-Fletcher, his consolation. To remark on the weather and clap
his bowler down on the monk's bench in the outer hall. Then
the two of them would retire to the study to mull over the
day's defeats and plan tomorrow's campaign.

Ormsby-Fletcher.

When it became obvious, even to Jake, that there would be
no stopping Ingrid's complaint and that the case would actually
go to court, his first embarrassed thought was he did not want
a Jewish lawyer, no twisting, eloquent point scorer who would
outwit judge and prosecutor, eat witnesses, alienate the jury,
shine so foxily in court in fact as to ultimately lose him the
case. No. Say what you like about the *goyim*, they had their
uses. For his defense Jake required an upright plodding WASP;
and, in his mind's eye, swishing cognac around in his glass night
after night, Jake methodically fabricated his identi-kit champion.
He would be unaggressively handsome, after the fashion of the
British upper classes, that is to say, somewhat wanting, like an
underdeveloped photograph. Without salt. He would commute,

Jake imagined, from a detached in an unspoiled village in Surrey (nr. Guildford, 40 min. Waterloo), where on weekends he tended to the rose bushes and fought off encroaching crabgrass with his toothy wife. (If it isn't too much to hope for, Jake thought, fighting down the tears, we'll swap cuttings, my *goy* and I.) *England worries him.* Raised on the King James version, lemon squash, *Tom Brown's Schooldays*, hamsters from Harrod's pet shop, Daddy's Ceylon tea shares, Kaffirs, debentures, chocolate digestives, and duty, he would find today's swingers perplexing. He would approve of the court's decision on *Lady Chatterley's Lover*, but would argue—Jake hoped—that issuing the novel in paperback, thereby making it available to untutored minds, was going too far, rather, like MBE's for the Beatles. He would have been to a good but minor public school, doing his national service with a decent regiment, going on from there to Pembroke, Cambridge (his father's college) before being articled to a solicitor. He would not have crammed at university because his nagging parents had never had the chance *oy* and were doing without *oy oy*: he would have muddled through to a degree. He was a Tory, but no Blimp. While he felt, for instance, that black Africans were not quite ready for self-government, he could jolly well understand their point of view. His wife—"The vicar's daughter," Jake decided aloud—ordered a joint (tenderized) for Sunday and cleverly made do (color supplement shepherd's pie, not-*too*-hot curry) until Tuesday. Waste not, want not. Instead of dinner on Wednesday they got by with high tea, cucumber and fishpaste sandwiches, bread and jam, while he helped his son with his Latin prep and she read *Mary Poppins* aloud to their little girl. Mnnn . . . I know, Jake added, clapping his hands, there is no central heating because they both agreed it was unhealthy. When she was having her menstrual period he was not so boorishly selfish as to hint at alternative forms of gratification: instead he came home bearing boxes of chocolates.

My *goy's* wife, Jake thought, once the most feared left-winger on the Girton hockey field, twice mentioned in Jennifer's Diary, drives him to his commuters' train each morning, both of them fastened into their seat belts, and—Jake added—if he makes a telephone call from my house he will offer me four pence. If she has stunning breasts she would keep them decently bound and cashmered: similarly, if her bottom was ravishingly round it would be squared into a tweed skirt.

We'll chat about politics, Jake thought, my *goy* and I, agreeing that while Harold Wilson was too clever by half and George Brown wasn't the sort of chap you'd send to see the Queen, they were, after all, entitled to their innings. Jake's solicitor would no more fiddle the tax inspector than cheat his mother at bezique; and what about the *Times* crossword? Yes, yes, of course he does it. Faithfully.

Perfect!

But where oh where, Jake wondered, consumed with ardor for his image, will I find such a limp prick? And then he remembered Ormsby-Fletcher. Stiff-collared, cherub-mouthed Ormsby-Fletcher, whom he had met at one of Luke's parties, finding him as abandoned as an empty beer bottle in a corner of the living room. "I daresay," Ormsby-Fletcher said, "I'm the only one here not connected with the arts. I'm Adele's cousin, you see."

So Jake located Ormsby-Fletcher and phoned him at his office. "Mr. Ormsby-Fletcher," he said, "I'm afraid you won't remember me. This is Jacob Hersh—"

"Indeed I do."

"I'm in trouble."

"I'm afraid I don't handle divorces myself, but I'd be glad to refer—"

"What about, um, criminal law?"

"I see," Ormsby-Fletcher said, faltering, retreating, already contriving excuses, Jake thought.

"Couldn't we meet," Jake cut in. "Informally, if you like."

They met at a pub, Jake arriving first, showily carrying a *Times* and *Punch*. "I fancy a long drink myself," Jake said, already tight. "What about you?" A gin, he said; and then Jake suffered chit-chat and fortified himself with uncounted doubles before he risked saying, "This is probably not your cup of tea, Mr. Ormsby-Fletcher. I shouldn't have troubled you. You see, it's a sex charge."

The blood went from Ormsby-Fletcher's strawberry-colored cheeks and he drew his long legs in from under the table tight as he could to his chair.

"Hold on. I'm not queer. It's—"

"Perhaps if you began at the beginning."

Brilliant. So Jake started to talk, circling close to repellent details, backpedaling furiously, hemming, hawing, hinting obliquely, retreating from the excruciating moment he would have to get down to concrete details, the crux, which would oblige him, just for openers, to use words such as penis and penetration . . . or, Jake wondered, hesitating again, was he expected to lapse into a gruffer idiom, something more forthrightly colonial? And then Ormsby-Fletcher, permanently endearing himself to Jake, volunteered, "I see. So then he led her into your room and, on her own initiative, she took hold of your roger . . ."

My roger of course. "Yes," Jake said, igniting with drunken delight, "then the bitch took my roger in her hand . . ."

"But if that's the case, Mr. Hersh—"

Jake clapped his hand on Ormsby-Fletcher's shoulder and locked him in a manful heartfelt look. "Jake," he said.

"Edward," Ormsby-Fletcher responded without hesitation.

Unburdening himself now, Jake released the sewer gates. Careful not to incriminate Harry, he told all. Well, almost.

"I see."

"Well, Edward?"

"Can't promise anything, you understand, but I'll see what I can do."

"That's good enough for me," Jake said, compromising him, he hoped.

"I suggest you come to our offices first thing tomorrow morning," Ormsby-Fletcher said, and he called for a round-for-the-road.

"Sorry. No more for me," Jake said, immensely pleased with himself. "I'm driving, you see."

It was, as it turned out, the first of a seemingly endless run of conferences at offices, with ruinously expensive barristers, and at Jake's house.

Jake, doting on Ormsby-Fletcher, came to anticipate his needs.
Five sugars and milk heated hot enough to make a fatty skin for
his coffee. Brandy, yes, but not an ostentatiously sloshed three
fingersful into a snifter: rather, a splash, British style, sufficient
to dampen the bottom of the glass. Ormsby-Fletcher liked to
relax with a cigar and natter about this island now. "I daresay,
to your way of looking, we *are* hopelessly inefficient . . ."

"But living here," Jake protested, looking deep, "is so much
more civilized than it is in America. After all, man doesn't live
by time-motion studies alone, does he?"

Encouraged, Ormsby-Fletcher asked, "Is it really true that
corporations interview and grade executives' wives?"

"It's ghastly. Diabolical," Jake said, shaking his head. "I simply
wouldn't know where to begin . . ."

Ormsby-Fletcher enjoyed sucking Smarties as he pondered his
brief. Hooked on glitter, he liked to think Jake was on intimate
terms with the stars, and Jake, lying outrageously, cribbing gossip
from *Variety*, more than obliged. "Bloody Marlon," Jake began
one evening, unaware that Nancy had just entered the room,
"has done it again. He—"

"Marlon who?" Nancy asked.

"The baby's crying."

Suddenly Ormsby-Fletcher said, "If it doesn't sound too
dreary, I wonder, well, Pamela thought if you had nothing better
on, perhaps you'd both drive out to our place for dinner on
Saturday night?"

"Why, that would be absolutely super," Jake said.

But he wakened ill-tempered, dubious, and he phoned Ormsby-
Fletcher at his office. "Edward, about Saturday night—"

"You needn't explain. Something's come up."

"No. Not at all. It's, well—your wife—Pamela—does she know
what I'm charged with?" Would I disgust her, he wanted to say.

"You mustn't even think like that, Jake. We'll expect you at
eight."

Wednesday morning a postcard came, written in the most
ornate hand and signed Pamela Ormsby-Fletcher. Were there
any foods that didn't agree with either of them? Now there's

breeding for you, Jake thought, and he wrote back to say all foods agreed with them. The next morning Ormsby-Fletcher phoned. "It's just, ah, well, are there any dietary laws . . .?" No, no, Jake said. Not to worry. But swinging out onto the Kingston by-pass on Saturday night, Nancy in the car beside him, he began to worry more than a little himself. "Let's not have that smart-assed argument about pantos and homosexuality tonight, the principal boy being a girl . . ."

The Ormsby-Fletchers' cottage, overlooking the common in an unspoiled village in Surrey, exceeded Jake's fondest fantasies. It was Georgian, with magnificent windows and climbing red roses. Pulling into the driveway Jake braked immediately behind a black Humber with the license plate EOF 1, grateful that Nancy hadn't noticed the plate, because he did not want to admit to her that Edward's father, who had bought the original, had been called Ernest, and that Edward was so called because no other anything-OF 1 plate was available.

"Hullo, hullo," Ormsby-Fletcher said, and he led them through the house into the garden.

Floribunda roses. Immense pink hydrangeas. Luscious dahlias . . . Pamela, a streaky blonde and very nice to look at, wore a Mary Quant sheath cut high above the knees and white crocheted stockings. There was another guest, a plump rumpled sybarite called Desmond—something in the City he was—waiting on the terrace, where drinks were served with cheese sticks and potato crisps. Suddenly a pale stammering boy called Edward was thrusting a book and pen at Jake. "What?" Jake asked, startled.

"It's the guest book," Nancy said. "You sign your name and birth date."

The *au pair* girl fetched Ormsby-Fletcher's other son, an unpleasant three-year-old called Eliot, to be kissed good night. This done, Pamela began to chat about the theater: she was mad keen.

"But how do actors do it," Desmond asked Jake, "going on night after night, doing the same bloody thing . . . ?"

"They're children, inspired children," Jake said triumphantly.

Pamela jumped up. "Would anybody like to wash their hands?" she asked.

"What?"

Nancy kicked Jake in the ankle.

"Oh, yes. Sure."

Pamela led Nancy to the downstairs toilet and Jake was directed upstairs. Passing Eliot's bedroom, he discovered the boy squatting on his potty, whining. The *au pair* girl was with him. "Anything wrong?" Jake asked.

The *au pair* girl looked up, alarmed. Obviously, she had seen Jake's picture in the newspapers. She knew the story. "He won't go to sleep without his golliwog," she said, "but he won't tell me where he put it."

Jake locked himself in the bathroom and immediately reached into his jacket pocket for the salami on rye Nancy had thoughtfully prepared for him. Munching his sandwich, he opened the medicine cabinet, but it yielded no secrets. Next he tried the laundry hamper. Shirts, socks, then at last, Pamela's smalls. Intricately laced black panties, no more than a peekaboo web. A spidery black bra, almost all filigree. You naughty thing, he thought.

Dinner commenced with hard-boiled eggs, sliced in half. Paprika had been sprinkled over the eggs and then they had been heated under the grill to suck out whatever moisture they still retained. Pamela flitted from place to place, proffering damp, curling white bread toast to go with the eggs. Jake washed down his egg with a glass of warm, sickeningly sweet, white Yugoslav wine, watching gloomily as Pamela brought in three platters. One contained a gluey substance in which toenail-size chunks of meat and walnuts and bloated onions floated; the next, a heap of dry lukewarm potatoes; and the third, frozen peas, the color running. Pamela doled out the meat with two ice cream scoops of potatoes and an enormous spoonful of peas and then passed around the toast again.

"You *are* a clever thing," Desmond said, tucking in.

Next the cheese board came out, a slab of British Railways cheddar, which looked uncannily like a cake of floor soap. There was dessert too. A running pink blob called raspberry fool.

Desmond did most of the talking. The Tories, he admitted,

seemed all played out at the moment, but one of these days another leader with fire in his belly would emerge and then we should see the last of that faceless little man in Number 10.

"We'll leave the men to their port now, shall we?" Pamela said, and, to Jake's astonishment, she led Nancy out of the dining room.

There actually was port. And cigars. Desmond apologized for the absence of his wife. She was in the hospital, he said, adding, "It's nothing. Just a plumbing job."

Ormsby-Fletcher recalled that when he had done his national service with the Guards on the Rhine he had occasionally gone to Hamburg on leave. "A chance to dip the wick, don't you know?"

Jake leaned back in his chair, aghast; Ormsby-Fletcher, he thought, you saucy fellow, dipping the wick on the Reeperbahn; and just as he was searching himself for an appropriate off-color story, Desmond rode to the rescue with the one about the Duchess of Newbury. "On her wedding night," he said, "the Duke naturally decided to have a bash. The Duchess, it turned out, couldn't get enough. 'Is this what they call fucking?' she asked at last. 'Yes,' the Duke said. 'Well then,' she said, 'it's too good for the working classes.' "

Ho ho ho. Time to join the ladies. Jake excused himself, going to the upstairs toilet, his stomach rumbling, but when he finally rose to pull the chain nothing happened. This didn't surprise him at first, knowing British plumbing as well as he did, but again and again he pulled, and still nothing happened. Oh my God, Jake thought, a big fat stool staring him in the face. What to do? Ah, he thought, opening the toilet door softly. There was nobody in the hall. Jake slipped into the adjoining bathroom, found a plastic pail, filled it with water, tiptoed back to the toilet, and poured it into the bowl. Now the stool floated level with the toilet seat. Flood tide. Pig, Jake thought. Sensualist. Hirsute Jew.

Wait. Don't panic, Jake thought, opening the toilet window wide. There's a simple solution. Wrap the stool quickly in your underwear, lean back and heave it into the rose bushes. *Yes, yes,* Jake agreed, *but how do I pick it up?* It's yours, isn't it? Your very own bodily waste. Disgust for it is bourgeois. *Yes, yes, but how do I pick it up?* Sunshine soldier! Social democrat! Middlebrow! Unable to face life fully. Everything is holy, Jake. Holy holy. *Yes, but how do I pick it up?* With your underwear. Quickly. Zip, zoom. Then lean back and heave. The Hersh garbage ball, remember? Inimitable, unhitable. In an instant Jake stood resolutely over his stool, jockey shorts in hand, counting down: ten-nine-eight-seven-six-five-four —— three —— two —— one-and-a-half——one!——three-quarters——whooa! *Voices in the garden.* Jake tottered backwards, relieved. I'm no bourgeois chicken, though, he thought. Another second and I would have done it.

Jake lit a cigarillo. So, they're all outside on the terrace again. Good, good, he thought, stepping into his underwear, sneaking out of the toilet, swiftly down the stairs, and then into the downstairs toilet. *Baruch ato Adonoi,* he said twice, before he pulled the chain. It flushed. Should I go upstairs again, fetch the stool, and . . .? No. Exhilarated, Jake flushed the toilet again, noisily, and then he began to pound on the door. Finally Ormsby-Fletcher came. "I seem to be locked in," Jake shouted.

"Oh, dear." Ormsby-Fletcher told Jake how to unlock the door and then he led him into the garden, where Pamela was exhibiting paintings. A landscape. A boat in the harbor. A portrait. All reminiscent of the jigsaw puzzles of Jake's childhood. He made loud appreciative noises.

"Now nobody tell him." Then Pamela, bursting with mischief, turned to Jake. "Would you say these pictures showed talent?"

"Absolutely."

"But amateur?" she asked enticingly.

Jake glanced imploringly at Nancy but her face showed nothing. Bitch. He stepped closer to the picture on display. "Mn," he said, gratefully accepting a brandy from Ormsby-Fletcher. "Professional. The brushwork," he added. "Oh, yes. Professional, I'd say."

Desmond clapped a pink hand to his mouth, stifling a laugh.

They're hers, Jake thought. Afternoons, wearing her spidery black bra and nearly nothing panties, she—

"Oh, for heaven's sake," Ormsby-Fletcher said. "Tell him."

Pamela waited, savoring the expectant silence. Finally, breathlessly, bosom heaving, she exclaimed, "All these pictures were executed by mouth and foot painting artists!"

Jake gaped; he turned pale.

"Didn't guess," Pamela said, shaking a finger at him, "did you?"

"... no ..."

Ormsby-Fletcher explained with a certain pride that Pamela was a director of the Society for Mouth and Foot Painting Artists.

"And still finds time to make such sumptuous meals," Desmond said. "Oh, you are clever."

"This picture," Pamela said, holding up a seascape, "was done by a boy of seventeen, *holding the brush between his teeth.*"

With trembling hand, Jake held out his brandy glass to Ormsby-Fletcher.

"He has been paralyzed for eight years."

"Amazing," Jake said weakly.

Desmond felt the group's work should be publicized in America. Swinging London, decadence, and all that tosh. Here was a bunch of disabled people who refused to cadge on the welfare state. An example to all of us, especially the run-down-Britain brigade.

"This one," Pamela said, holding up a portrait of General Montgomery, "is a foot painting. It's one of a series done by a veteran of El Alamein." Next she showed another mouth painting, a still life, done by a street accident victim.

Shamelessly holding out his glass for yet another brandy, Jake shouted, "I'll buy it."

Pamela's mouth formed an enormous reproachful O. "Now you'll go away thinking I'm frightful," she said.

"But it's for such a good cause," Jake said.

Pamela's enthusiasm ebbed. "You may only buy one if you really, really think it's good."

"Oh, but I do. I do."

"You mustn't condescend to disabled people," she said sulkily.

Jake pleaded and Pamela, all forgiveness now, allowed him to have the Montgomery portrait for twenty-five guineas. Then, bosom heaving again, she added, "And I'll tell you what I'm going to do for you. I'm going to take you to see the artist in his studio."

Jake shook his head, he waved his hands imploringly, no, but he didn't know what to say.

"It would be so encouraging for him to know," Pamela continued, "that somebody in your position admired his talents."

"Couldn't I just write him a letter?"

"But you'd adore Archie. He has such a wonderful sense of humor."

"He has?" Jake's voice quivered.

"And courage. Buckets of courage." Then Pamela started into what Jake figured must be her set piece for women's club luncheons. "If a man has the talent and urge to paint," she said, "he will paint. He will paint even if it means living in a back street garret on a near starvation diet. If he has no arms he will paint with the canvas on the floor and a brush between his toes. If both arms and feet are lost he will grip the brush between his teeth."

The upstairs light went on. Jake gripped his brandy glass tighter and hastily lit a cigarillo.

"Speaking as a creative person, wouldn't you say, Jake," Pamela asked heatedly, "that art thrives on difficulty?"

Another upstairs light was turned on. "You're goddam right," Jake said.

The *au pair* girl raised her voice, a pause, then Eliot began to shriek. Ormsby-Fletcher leaped to his feet. "I'll see what it is, darling."

"It seems to me," Pamela said, "the sterner the trials of creation, the finer that which is created."

"My wife isn't feeling well," Jake said, shooting Nancy a fierce look.

"Pardon?"

"I must take Nancy home immediately."

In the house again they ran into a flushed ill-tempered Ormsby-Fletcher; he was coming from the kitchen, carrying a pump.

"What is it?" Pamela asked.

Eliot sat at the top of the stairs, tears running down his cheeks. "Didn't do it," he wailed. "Didn't do it."

"He's been naughty," Ormsby-Fletcher said tightly.

"Don't be too hard on him," Jake pleaded compulsively.

Ormsby-Fletcher seemed to notice Jake for the first time. "Not going so soon, are you?"

"It's Nancy. She's unwell."

"Just an upset stomach," Nancy said, trying to be helpful.

"*No. Not a—*" Jake stopped himself. "What I mean is . . . she's being brave. Good night, everybody." He assured the Ormsby-Fletchers that they had had an absolutely super evening and, clutching his Montgomery portrait, he hurried Nancy to the car. Eliot's howling pursued him.

"What in the hell's got into you?" Nancy asked.

But Jake wouldn't talk until they reached the highway. "I've got a splitting headache, that's all."

"What do you think the child did?"

"Stuffed his bloody golliwog down the toilet, that's what."

While Nancy got ready for bed, Jake poured himself a stiff drink and sat down to contemplate his Montgomery portrait. What am I doing in this country, he thought? What have I got to say to these nutty, depraved people?

Well, Yankel?

3

If. If, if. If only I had never left Toronto for London.

London, Why, in God's name, had he come to London in the first place? Because, thanks to the Horseman (and his own big mouth), New York wouldn't have him.

As a boy England had signified many things to him, but he had never been drawn toward it. He was a Labor-Zionist. He had despised the British because they stood between him and his homeland. He used to sit by the radio with the rest of the family when Churchill spoke. ". . . some chicken, some neck . . ." He could recall toothy photographs of Elizabeth and Margaret in their Brownie uniforms. The blitz. "The King," his mother said one night, "only pours one inch of hot water into his bath now. It's to set an example to the people."

"Who knows what he does when he's alone in the toilet," his father said.

They played commandos in the alley behind the synagogue, pelting Narvik with frozen horse buns. He read books by G. A. Henty and H. G. Wells. Crunching through the snow, bundled against the wind, on his way to Fletcher's Field High each morning, he passed the armory of the Canadian Grenadier Guards and outside, under a funny fur hat, there always stood some tall unblinking *goy*. "If they were ordered to do it," he was told, "they'd march over a cliff. There's discipline for you." He helped collect money for Bundles-for-Britain and later, from the same houses, more money to buy arms for Hagana. A British Ferry Command pilot with a handlebar mustache came to sell his father a Victory Bond. "The Russians aren't such a bad lot, actually," he said. "You have to look at it this way. They never had an industrial revolution. They're squeezing a hundred years of progress into a generation."

He had been misinformed. Not everyone on St. Urbain Street was a red.

"In Finland," his father said, "they had to chain them to their guns. That sort of thing is bad for morale."

England was George Formby, Tommy Farr, and fog. "Elementary, my dear Watson." Big Ben. His mother coming home with puffy eyes from *Mrs. Miniver*. On Empire Day, in Shawbridge, the ghetto's summer swimming hole, a young girl drowned after eating too many *latkas*. Over the mountain, where there was a real lake, the Gentiles swam. England was where they drank tea all the time. Without lemon. They were the finest craftsmen in the world. Once, one of ours had been their prime minister. England was the fox hunt. G.B.S. Bulldog Drummond. Charles Laughton tossing a chicken leg over his shoulder. Ed Murrow. A Nightingale Singing in Berkeley Square. It also meant his own Scots schoolmaster making them memorize Tennyson: "Break, break, break/ At the foot of thy crags, O sea!" and Scott: "The stag at eve had drunk its fill/ As danced the moon on Monan's Rill." They felt no attachment.

At college, where they began to borrow from a different set of ideas, England came into another, equally distorted focus. A literary experience. The exquisite novels of Jane Austen. Decency, wit, political maturity.

England, England. He and Luke set out to conquer.

Standing by the ship's rail, as they slid out of Quebec City into the broadening St. Lawrence, impossibly exhilarated, Jake demanded of Luke, "I say! I say! I say! What's beginning to happen in Toronto?"

"Exciting things."

"And Montreal?"

"It's changing."

Their first contact with England was sooty Liverpool. On the boat train they were amazed by the enormous dessert spoons, grit in your luke-warm tea, and a notice that read, "Gentlemen will please lift the seat." Trundling into London in a taxi, they experienced only a moment's self-doubt when they espied all those bow windows on either side of the road, dressing tables shoved against them from within to shut out the obtrusive sun. Should it appear.

They froze.

Jake remembered the first weeks in London as an unending fight against the bone-chilling damp. A spill of shillings down the gas meter because parsimonious Luke insisted on the cheapest hotel available while they looked for a flat. They made the required, wearying pilgrimages to the British Museum, the Tate, and Westminster, scornfully avoiding (though they were both desperate to see it) the changing of the guard.

Earlier, in Montreal, Jake had earnestly assured his troubled relatives that their city was a cultural desert, a colonial pimple, and he was off to nourish himself at the imperial fountainhead, but once he was there and rid of them, all he thought about was girls. *Where were the girls?* Take me, have me. Oh my God, the ones he saw in the pubs were so depressingly lumpy, all those years of bread-and-dripping and sweets and fishpaste sandwiches having entered their young bodies like poison, coming out here as a mustache, there as a chilblain, and like lead through the teeth. And the elegant *shiksas* of Belgravia, the ones he ravished with his eyes, who for generations had packed their tomato-faced husbands (C. Aubrey Smith, Ralph Richardson) off to take India, Canada, and Rhodesia (or come back, God forbid, to get four white feathers in the mail); those insufferably arrogant-looking women, he thought, would see him only as a boy late with the avocado delivery from Harrod's.

Within weeks, Jake was miserable. London, he came to believe, was no more than a gum-gray, depressing city. Where the workers were short with black teeth and the others were long and pallid as forced asparagus with a tendency to stammer.

Goysville. Tasteless white bread. Sawdust bangers at the local. Brussels sprouts floating in tepid greasy water. At the Windmill Theater, he and Luke watched an aging stripper with jellied thighs. No sooner had the febrile comics bounced on stage—

"Do you know we've got a plane bigger than any plane the Yanks ever built?"

"No."

"Yes, we have. Salisbury Plain."

—than the countrymen in tweed caps, who filled the first two rows, lit matches and bent over their girlie books.

"I've been to Brighton to watch the football matches under the sea."

"Ruddy fool. There are no football matches under the sea."

"Haven't you heard? There are Twenty Thousand Leagues Under the Sea."

The very day of Jake's arrival, as the pavement continued to heave up at him like the deck of a Cunarder, he went to Canada House, in Trafalgar Square, to inquire about mail.

"Anything for Hersh?"

"What initial?"

"J."

"You're not J. Hersh."

Affronted, Jake slapped his passport down on the counter.

"Oh, I see. There must be two of you, then."

"Can you give me this other J. Hersh's address?" Jake asked, excited.

"I don't think he's in London any more. He hasn't been around in months."

"Has he left a forwarding address?"

"Are you a relation?"

"Yes."

"Well, he knew better than to leave an address." The girl pulled out a wad of letters bound with an elastic. "Overdue bills. Registered letters from his bank. Final notices. Summonses. It's shameful."

"I'd like to leave my address for him, then. Just in case he shows up."

The girl watched, tapping her pencil, as Jake wrote it out. "Have you just come over from Canada?" she asked.

Jake nodded.

"Travelers abroad should think of themselves as good-will ambassadors for our country. We're well-liked here."

"Like Willy Loman. I know. But you see," Jake said, "I'm a drug addict. I came over to register with the National Health." And scooping up his parcel, he retreated to the reading room.

The parcel was from Jake's father. A Jewish calendar, listing the holidays to be observed, a skullcap, and a prayer book. There was a message tucked into the skullcap: WRITE WEEKLY, NOT WEAKLY.

Jake and Luke arrived in London riding the crest of a TV play which Luke had written and Jake directed, in Toronto, that was to be repeated on British commercial television.

It was, as it turned out, a most propitious time for Canadians, however callow, to descend on the United Kingdom. Commercial television was burgeoning, but desperate for skilled hands. Whereas Americans, who required work permits, were prohibited, overeager colonials, like Jake, like Luke, were elected to fill that office. In those frenetic, halcyon days of live television drama, when plays were usually rehearsed for two weeks with two additional days of camera rehearsal, the Canadians bullied the indolent native camera crews, cajoling in the morning, proffering baksheesh in the evening, into actually moving their hitherto static cameras, zooming in here, dollying out there, imitating film everywhere, improvising from the control room when camera three blew out during transmission and waiting exhausted by the telephone all the next day for the summons from on high that didn't come. From the Holy Trinity: M-G-M, Columbia, Twentieth. The chance to break into film.

Until Jake became entangled with the girl who was his production assistant, moving into a flat of his own, he and Luke shared a place in Highgate. In the semi-detached houses around them, wherever there flourished a salesman or shopkeeper, who had only yesterday slipped in under the middle-class wire, there bloomed not an aspidistra but a Tory poster in the window, the badge of breathless arrival, as Sir Anthony Eden led his party into an election. Jake, convinced it was time he entered fully into the life of his adopted country, scooted round to the local Labor Party office to volunteer for work, secretly expecting that considering his rising reputation his name would be instantly recognized by the dreamiest deb in the place, unfortunately sex-crazed (Yes, I'm *the* Hersh), and that he would be prevailed upon to direct a party political piece for the telly, sweeping Hugh into office, and creating totally unexpected conundrums for himself when he emerged as the cynosure of the Hampstead set. "Yes, I do appreciate it's a safe seat. I'm not ungrateful, Hugh. But . . ."

The flaking Labor Party office, a bankrupt laundromat on short lease, was empty except for a stout middle-aged lady in a tweed suit. "Yes," she asked sharply, "what is it?"

Disheartened, Jake nevertheless inquired whether there was any work he could do.

"Do you know my son?" she demanded. "Do you know him personally?"

Her son was the candidate. "No," he confessed.

"Then why do you want to work for us?"

"I'm a Labor supporter," Jake said, retreating.

"I see. Well, I really don't know . . ." She flapped about, a startled hen, finally perching on a pile of pamphlets. "I guess there'd be no harm in your putting these through letter boxes . . ."

Gradually Jake climbed from roistering bottle parties to invitations to dinner, cards left out on his mantelpiece to be scanned by lesser types, the uninvited. He directed, Luke wrote. Within a year they had become the darlings of Armchair Theater and, to fill the time, began work on their parody script, *The Good Britons.*

Jake regularly took his lunch at the Partisan Coffee Bar, on Carlisle Street, though his revanchist stomach rumbled against the militant Irish stew. With Luke, he stood in blinking attendance, on Easter morning, 1957, when Canon Collins led CND marchers into Trafalgar Square one more time.

When the summons from on high finally came it wasn't from Columbia, M-G-M, or Twentieth Century-Fox. Neither was it Jake they wanted, but Luke. A play he had submitted to the Royal Court, rewritten since Jake had first directed it for Canadian television, had been accepted for production. It was then that the two friends, seemingly inseparable partners, came unstuck through a variant of an affliction that was peculiar to Canadian artists of their generation: a suspension of belief in each other's real rather than national trading stamp value. They had emerged, *pace* Auden, from *tiefste Provinz*, a place that had produced no art and had exalted self-deprecation above all. They were the progeny of a twice-rejected land. From the beginning, Canada's two founding races, the English and the French, had outbid each other in scornfully disinheriting them. A few arpents of snow, Voltaire wrote contemptuously, and Dr. Johnson dismissed the dominion as "a region from which nothing but furs and fish were to be had."

Jake, Luke, and others of their generation were reared to believe in the cultural thinness of their own blood. Anemia was their heritage. As certain homosexuals pander to others by telling the most vicious anti-queer jokes, so Jake, so Luke, shielded themselves from ridicule by anticipating with derisive tales of their own. Their only certitude was that all indigenous cultural standards they had been raised on were a shared joke. No national reputation could be bandied abroad without apology.

Adrift in a cosmopolitan sea of conflicting mythologies, only they had none. Moving among discontented commonwealth types in London, they were inclined to envy them their real grievances. South Africans and Rhodesians, *bona fide* refugees from tyranny, who had come to raise a humanitarian banner in exile; Australians, who could allude to forebears transported

in convict ships; and West Indians, armed with the most obscene outrage of all, the memory of their grandfathers sold in
marketplaces. What they failed to grasp was the ironic truth
in Sir Wilfred Laurier's boast that the twentieth century would
belong to Canada. For amid so many exiles from nineteenth-
century tyranny, heirs to injustices that could actually be set
right politically, thereby lending themselves to constructive
angers, only the Canadians, surprisingly, were true children of
their times. Only they had packed their bags and left home to
escape the hell of boredom. And find it everywhere.

When the summons from on high finally came, Jake's girlfriend cooked a dinner to celebrate. After she retired, the two
friends became uneasy with one another. Luke was in a turmoil.
He was reconciled to Jake's directing his play at the Royal Court,
if he insisted, a most unlikely prospect, but he wasn't going to
ask. Luke had faith in Jake's talent, even though it was forged
in Canada; he had a deeper rapport with him than he could possibly enjoy with another director, and yet—and yet—given his
first big chance for a breakthrough, unsettled by enormous self-
doubts, he yearned for the reassurance of somebody unknown
to him. A reputation. Somebody real, somebody British. Jake, on
his side, was already casting the play in his mind's eye, worrying
about the second act, when he realized with a heavy heart that
Luke, his manner surreptitiously pleading, would be happier
with somebody else.

Initially, Jake was not inclined to let Luke off the hook.
Dangle, baby. Suffer. Flitting about the periphery, but never
confronting the problem, the two friends waited each other out.
One didn't ask, the other didn't volunteer. Desperately, they retreated into reminiscences, surprisingly finding no restorative
warmth there, but, instead, unsuspected resentments. Finally,
Jake had had enough.

"I should have said as much earlier, Luke, but much as I'd
like to do your play, I'm not going to be free."

"I see."

"It's a terrific play. I always thought so. But I've got to think
of my own career, don't you think?"

Luke recoiled warily.

"I've already done the play in Toronto. I'd only be repeating myself."

So big, skinny, straw-haired Luke, fumbling with his glasses, was able to quit the flat not churning with guilt, as he had entered it, but bracingly angry, for he had already begun to convince himself that the play had been Jake's for the asking, only he didn't want to do it. He was sad, he was incensed, but he was also immensely relieved. He believed he had a better shot at success with a British director, his new and risky venture unencumbered by a cherished friend who even so was merely another Canadian and therefore a reminder of his picayune beginnings. Even so, anger failed to sustain Luke all the way home. He crawled into bed feeling lousy, dismayed by his own cunning.

Jake continued to drink alone, hurt and indignant, for his best friend had judged his talent and found it wanting, and yet—and yet—he grudgingly had to admit, in some dark and secret place, that he was astonished the Royal Court had considered a Canadian play, even one of Luke's, good enough to be produced. He was also relieved that his own first effort on the British stage would not be a Canadian play. He assumed, based on his education and sour experience, that nothing Canadian was quite good enough. His conjecture was poor old Luke's play wouldn't fail, but neither would it succeed. It would open to end-of-the-column notices, uniformly solicitous, play to half-filled houses for six weeks and then fade into the middle distance, condemned as a promising first effort.

Within the Canadian colony, there was more skepticism than envy when Luke revealed his play had been sent to Timothy Nash, a young director only two years down from Cambridge but already a fabled name.

"Don't count on anything," another writer cautioned him with appetite. Somebody else ventured, "It's very encouraging. Even if your play isn't ready and Nash is overrated . . ."

Nash, to Luke's amazement, read the play within a fortnight and summoned him to a meeting. The only friend Luke wanted to consult beforehand was Jake, but he knew that would be improper, especially considering his own unbridled enthusiasm. So Luke spent the evening alone, unfortunately re-reading his play. It struck him as windy, adolescent, and embarrassing, as if he were not sufficiently fearful of tomorrow's meeting with Nash.

"Your p-p-play's a swinger, m-m-man. I d-d-dig it. I haven't been so h-h-hung up on anything for years."

Grab your play and run now, Luke thought—go—but he didn't. He couldn't. He was far too bedazzled by Timothy and Lady Samantha, and more than somewhat grateful for Jake's absence, which enabled him to flatter the Nashes with impunity.

But if not then, Luke thought, he certainly should have broken it off once Nash pranced into rehearsal and it became sickeningly clear that his reputation was unearned. He was a fraud, albeit a delightful one. But Luke was astute enough to grasp that Nash's presence festooned his play with glitter. What might have been merely another opening was acquiring the dimensions of an event. Nash not only attracted classy actors, otherwise prohibitively expensive, but with a wave of his wand he drew Fleet Street columnists out of El Vino's and the promise of the most desirable West End theater, should the play transfer.

Transfer? Luke, increasingly depressed by the shape of rehearsals, soon wished his play would never open. He took his fears to Jake, as well as implied remorse, and, without ever asking him directly, cajoled him into coming to a rehearsal, slumping in the back row with him, as in Toronto days. Jake made copious notes, he sat up all night with Luke, raking through the script again and again, and he was back the following night and the next. Then Luke bundled Nash into his sheepskin-lined suede coat, took him to Étoile for lunch, inflating him with extravagant flatteries before he punctured him with some hard points. His hammer, Jake's nails.

Opening night, Jake went to the Royal Court to commiserate, armed with rehearsed responses of singular generosity, but was obliged to stay on to celebrate Luke's unmistakable success. Sullen and envy-ridden, but simulating pleasure, he stood well apart from Luke backstage, unwilling to claim him like other old associates, callow TV types, discontented Canadians, equally flattering in Luke's presence, but once expelled to skitter on the periphery, inclined to carp.

"Derivative, don't you think?"

"Tynan will like it, because it's left-wing. Otherwise . . ."

Flushed and chain-smoking, noticeably swaying, but in fine form for all that, Luke was hemmed in by the sort of people who, on being introduced to either of them at parties hitherto, immediately began to formulate apologies, retreating, excusing themselves to serve whatever celebrities were holding forth that night. Producers and agents, journalists, and breathless, silken girls. Graciously Luke broke free, abandoning everybody to seek out Jake.

"You're coming to the party. Right?"

"Sure."

The play's producer bore down on Luke and began to tug at his arm. "Wait for me," Luke called back.

But Jake left immediately and was in fact the first to arrive at the Nashes' place.

The address in Fulham, he figured, retracing his steps to peer at the street sign again, must be wrong. This had to be a joke. The grubby, flaking row of sinking terrace houses, a slippered old crone drifting down the street, a MacFisheries, an ABC, a butcher shop, its window choked with Argentine beef, bespoke poverty practiced for generations. In each garden, a center-piece of grit-encrusted hydrangeas. And through the smog held at the bottom of the hill, the rising gas works.

But it was a willowy, toreador-trousered girl, her big feet bare, who opened the door. "You must be Jacob Hersh," she said, her accent grindingly South Ken.

One living room wall was lined in dark-brown cork and an-other was dominated by an enormous John Bratby painting of a fat woman squatting on a toilet bowl. A kitchen-sink school epiphany.

"Would you care for a drink?"

"Thank you, Lady Samantha."

"Sam, if you please."

Elegant leather pouffes, white here, black there, drifted on islands of Tibetan lamb rugs. Within minutes the house was overflowing with well-wishers and Timothy Nash, a slender slip of a chorus boy, descended on Jake. A lick of black hair curled over Nash's forehead. He wore a T-shirt under his corduroy jacket, faded jeans, and canvas sneakers, but the attaché case he sent sliding across the floor was a Gucci. "Luke goes on and on about you," Nash said. "I'm *m-m-meshgugga* for the things you've done on the telly."

"*Meshugga*," Jake said.

Ultimately, a car was dispatched to Fleet Street to fetch batches of the morning newspapers. The reviews were resoundingly good. "O.K., we can cut now," Luke said, seemingly satiated.

So they quit Lady Samantha's flat, armed with bottles of champagne and smoked salmon sandwiches liberated from her kitchen. Five a.m. and still dark, the wintry air tingling. Crocus sprouts poking through the frost here and there. An articulated lorry, its muzzled headlights glowing, trundled down the Fulham Road. Outside a butcher shop, a man in a bloody white smock bent under the burden of a side of beef. Inside the news agent's shop next door, a fat lady, squinting against the cigarette burning between her lips, was sorting out the morning newspapers. Luke's head began to bob, drifting lower. Jake nudged him, passing the bottle. They were rounding Hyde Park Corner now and the water trucks were out, washing down the black streets.

"In summer," Jake said, "when we were kids in Montreal, we used to run after them, leaping in the spray."

"Montreal, P.Q. That stood for Piss Quick in Toronto."

"What's P.L.P. stand for?"

"Public Leaning Post. And what about W.H.D.?"

"Wandering Hand Disease."

"Oh Gertie McCormick, of the cotton panties, where are you now?"

Finally, they reached Luke's flat in Swiss Cottage, lighting all the gas heaters and rubbing their hands.

"What are we doing in this ridiculous country?" Luke asked.

"Acquiring culture."

"Quite so, Hersh."

"Bang on, Scott. Now be a good chap and let's have some more champers, what?"

Luke read the reviews again, aloud this time, savoring each recalled Toronto insult he had endured, not forgetting his most cherished enemies in London, imagining them one by one, as they wakened to the same newspapers, their day irretrievably soured.

"You're going to be a thingee now," Jake said.

"It's *m-m-meshgg-g-gugga*. Damn it. I'm going to bring Hanna over. I'm going to fly her in to London."

"Why, that's a great idea," Jake said, seething inwardly. For that was his dream. He was going to bring Hanna over on the day of his triumph.

Jake sat on the window sill. Outside, an ill-tempered mother passed, dragging a sniveling five-year-old boy after her. The boy tumbled to the pavement and she reprimanded him loudly. He began to wail. Impulsively, Jake whacked open the window. "Leave him alone," he hollered.

The mother looked up, startled.

"Let him be," Jake said, lowering the window. Then he turned to Luke, "You know, I'm going to be thirty soon. In two months I'm going to be thirty years old."

They sat down to breakfast. Luke added vodka to Jake's orange juice, stirring it with a fork handle before handing it to him.

"Not all the candidates pass," Jake said.

"What?"

"Auden."

When the phone rang it was Tanfield's Diary. *The Daily Mail.* "Yes," Luke said. "I see."

He glanced at Jake, all at once a crumpled, disconsolate figure, and, for old time's sake, he decided to pay the toll once more, reverting to what had once been their iconoclastic rule. Their shared boyish hatred of phonies. "I usually write wearing my Hardy Amies dressing gown," he told Tanfield's Diary. "Eccentricities? Oh, I adore walking in the rain. I'm also mad keen to drive in my bare feet."

Jake sensed Luke was trying to please him, but he could also see his friend's glee was simulated. No sooner had he hung up than he was regretting his gesture, which was impractical. When the phone rang again, the *Evening Standard* this time, Jake suggested that Luke take it in the other room.

Next it was the Canadian Press, which hardly mattered. "Just one moment, please," Luke said, and before passing the phone to Jake, he added, "It's for you, Mr. Scott."

"No," Jake said. "I don't feel like playing."

Jake's head pounded, his throat was raw. Luke's eyes burned, he itched everywhere.

"Do you realize," Luke said, "the hockey season's almost half done and we haven't made our bets yet?"

"Maybe we'll skip it this year."

Luke's agent phoned to say he had arranged a meeting with a firm of accountants for tomorrow morning and then called again to say they were having lunch at the Mirabelle on Tuesday, with Columbia, and that there was a book United Artists wanted him to read immediately.

On Wednesday, Luke flew to New York, first class, all expenses paid, to enter into negotiations for a Broadway production of his play and to deal with other offers.

Alone, Jake sobered up. There were scripts he had to read, appointments to be kept, but instead he slept in late each morning, made lists, read magazines.

The reviews of the play in the posh Sundays unsettled him even more. He was prepared for Luke's accolade, but not for the praise that was accorded Timothy Nash's production. Nash, of whom one critic wrote, that with this play he had taken a big leap forward, a sometimes showy talent soaring with inner confidence for the first time. On wings of Hersh, Jake thought.

In a way it was gratifying, very gratifying, this necessarily surreptitious triumph of Jake's, especially considering Luke's initial lack of confidence in him, but he could not make the rounds, an ancient mariner, protesting the best touches were his, not Nash's. Jake had always abominated those seedy retailers of inside tales who were endemic to the trade. The unknown myopic film editor who had saved the name director's picture; the publisher's reader, laboring through the night in his Camden Town bed-sitter, who had stitched together the best seller from an unjustly celebrated author's endless, inchoate manuscript; the talented but naïve young collaborator who had been swindled out of his screen credit. The real makers, if only the truth were known. The industrious little Clem Attlees behind all your swaggering Churchills.

Not for the first time, Jake recalled the rumpled sports writer he was so fond of drinking with at the Montreal Men's Press Club; the man who told him about a former Montreal Royals pitcher, a farmhand of rare promise, who, once granted his major league shot with the Brooklyn Dodgers, had failed, through no fault of his own, to work his way into the starting rotation. Unaccountably, the team couldn't knock in runs for him. When he was on the mound they tripped over themselves on the field. The pitcher, returned to the Royals, refused to yield to bitterness. "In this game," he told the sports writer, "either you do or you don't."

Yes, Jake thought. Yes, indeed. Or a farmhand you remaineth forever.

After an absence of eight days, Luke returned from New York, bedazzled.

"You've got to hear this, Jake. It's crazy. They sent a limo to meet me at the airport, a black cad with a phone inside. All I could think of is I've got to make a call, but who would believe me if I said I was phoning from a car crawling down Madison Avenue. They booked me into the Essex, a suite overlooking the park, and before I've even got time to pee the place is filled with guys from the agency. Flick my cigarette and there's a Yaley under me with an ashtray. Hold out a hand and Miss Colgate shoves a martini into it. Everybody's talking cockamamy—"

"Talking what?" Jake interrupted meanly, for in fact the word was familiar to him. He had heard it from a Hollywood agent.

Luke explained, then continued: "Anyway, my very first night in town he sets up this lavish dinner party. He lives in one of those East Side co-ops, naturally. Truman Capote's in it, and a clutch of Kennedys. It's choked with antiques, pieces of Chinese jade, and first editions, the bastard doesn't read anything but synopses. There's a Chagall hanging in the living room and a Giacometti piece standing by the window. I no sooner step in the door than he whispers in my ear, you see that girl over there? Do I see her? Man, she's the first thing I do see. Undulating on the arm of the sofa. Well, he says, she's here for you to fuck. Bloody crude, don't you think?"

"Yes," Jake agreed, bitten with envy.

"And me, I'm dead beat. Anyway, all through dinner he's trying to get me to say yes to writing an original screenplay for —" and here he named the star the producer had under contract. "He's bulldozing me, honestly, but with everybody there. We're eight at the table. Look, I said, I don't write for actresses. I'm not that kind of writer. If I do something and it happens to fit, well, lucky me, but I can't start with the actress. Are you crazy, he says, and all through dinner he keeps drumming away at me. Finally, come the brandies, everybody still at the table, he says what do you want? You want me to double the fee, I'll double it. That's not the point, I say feebly. Wouldn't you like to dance in the White House on Kennedy's inauguration night, he says?"

You bastard, Jake thought.

"Not particularly. It's a game now. I keep saying no, and trying to change the subject, and he keeps sweetening the offer. Finally, I say I'm going, I've simply got to get some sleep and, wham, the girl pops up, can you drop me off, she asks? The producer gives me the big nudge. Well, I think, poor kid, she'll only get into trouble if I don't drop her off. Maybe there's a big part at stake for her. So I say, O.K., the taxi stops, and I'm too tired to get out. Won't you come in for a nightcap, she says."

"What did you do?"

"What do you think? The flesh is weak. Jake, they've seen your TV work and like it. If you want, I'll write the script. We can do the picture together."

"If you want to do it, why use me as an excuse?"

"A week in New York, Jake, and you'll wonder what you're doing in this city. In the end, we're Americans you know. You wouldn't feel like a foreigner there."

"I can't get into the States, remember?"

"The climate's changed. I'm sure you can clear it up with the proper lawyers." Luke paused. "I'll lend you the money."

"You'll what?"

"I said I'll lend you the money."

But Jake said no, and they parted abruptly outside Chez Luba, walking to their cars, Luke suddenly hollering back, "I'm having some people in on Tuesday night. Can you make it?"

"I think so. Sure, why not? Poker?"

"Nancy Croft's coming."

"Who?"

"Didn't you meet her in Toronto? Naw, if you had, you'd remember. She's gorgeous. Oh Christ, hold on a second. Almost forgot. I've got a registered letter for you. It arrived at my flat yesterday."

Jake ripped open the envelope in his car.

The letter, from Canada House, wasn't even for him, it was for Cousin Joey, signed by an official in the Consular Section. The detailed voucher attached was for "financial assistance rendered to you by the Canadian Embassy in Madrid, Spain."

Dear Mr. Hersh,
    We have just been requested by our Department to send you the enclosed Account Receivable Voucher, 248c, dated

Jan 27, 1959, in the amount of 132.67 (£47.2.6) We would be grateful if you would pay this sum at your early convenience.

You should return to us as soon as possible the emergency certificate issued to you by the Canadian Embassy in Madrid.

Mistaken for the Horseman again.

4

Jake was wakened by the phone before nine the next morning.

"So, shmock, your big friend finally gets a play on in London, why don't you direct it?"

"Who in the hell is this?"

"Can you use a smoked brisket? Direct from Levitt's."

"Duddy, what are you doing in London?"

"Launching a star. I've got to speak to you."

"All right, then. What are you doing right now?"

"Masturbating. And you?"

Within the hour, Duddy was at Jake's flat insisting that he read the play he had brought with him—read it immediately—before they talk—and Jake's protests were unavailing. Grudgingly, he retired to his bedroom and when he emerged, having skimmed through the play, Duddy leaped up from the sofa. "So, big expert, what do you think?"

"I hope you're not putting any money into it. It's a disaster."

"Atta boy. I'll buy that dream," Duddy said, and then he unburdened himself.

He and Marlene Tyler, née Malke Tannenbaum, showstopper of the Mount Carmel Temple's production of *My Fair Zeyda*, and occasionally seen on CBC-TV, were wed, or as the rabbi put it, joined hands for nuptial flight, within two months of their first meeting. Something of a show biz celebrity by this time, often seen around Toronto with local lovelies, Duddy was interviewed by the *Telegram*. "When it comes to wedlock," he said, "there was never any doubt in my mind that I would marry one of our own brethren. I've seen too many mixed marriages. It just can't work." And Marlene said, "It may sound silly, but we won't have milk after meat in our house for hygienic reasons germane to our faith."

The house Duddy built in Forest Hill, the letter K woven into the aluminum storm door, antique coach lamps riding either side, double garage doors electronically controlled, was sumptuously furnished for Marlene Tyler, the girl of his dreams, pink and white, like a nursery. But he had assumed that after their marriage, she would give up stage and television, as she was only an adequate performer and could see for herself that they were rich and there was no need. After the lonely years of struggle and bachelorhood, gulping meals in restaurants and sleeping with *shiksas*, he had yearned for home-cooked meals, an orderly home life, and screwing on demand. "Like on drippy Saturday afternoons after you come home loaded from a bar mitzvah *kiddush*. Or like on Saturday night after the hockey game and there's only Juliette on TV. I even had a TV set put in the bedroom with remote control, so that we could watch from the bed and get in the mood before they picked the three stars. Foreplay, that's the word I want."

Duddy had anticipated nights on the town together, marvelous dinner parties, and, in the fullness of time, children. A son. "After all, what's the struggle for? It's a hard world, you know, everybody in business is rotten to the core." Somebody who would not know his early hardships, but would have a first-class education. The Harvard Business School. And ease the pressure on him at Dudley Kane Enterprises, because who could you trust if not your own? Nobody. "But instead, damn it, I was fool enough, for a wedding gift, to buy the Toronto rights on an off-Broadway musical. I backed the production on the condition that Marlene would star in it. Well, you know she wasn't ab-

solutely awful. Some reviewers liked her. And next thing I
know she's beginning to get work here and there. TV variety
shows, theater reviews, dances. And one, two, three, I'm a
bachelor again. Only worse. Dinner at home? Sure, why not?
The maid defrosts a TV dinner for me in the oven. Or I eat out
and spend the night playing poker with pals. And then what?
Me, I'm too tired to stand. I drive down to the theater or TV
studios to pick her up. She's standing outside in her furs, giggling
with the rest of the cast. Most of them are fags, all right, but
the others? Who knows what they do in the dressing rooms?
You haven't met Marlene yet. *Oy.* For a Jewish girl she likes it,
let me tell you. Now I'm a man of some sexual experience, you
know. Not to brag, I'm well-hung. It's a big one. Masturbating
helps, can you beat that? I mean, remember on St. Urbain we
were told it would give us pimples or stunt growth? Bullshit.
Scientifically speaking, what's a cock? Tissue and veins. You pull
it, it stretches. You don't use it, it shrivels. Where was I? Oh,
I've had a hundred and ninety-two girls, not counting Marlene,
and more than one has pleaded for me to stop. Enough, Kravitz,
you insatiable monster. Big Dick, one of the girls used to call
me. Nice, huh? I liked that. Big Dick Kravitz. The girls tell me
I'm a very virile guy and I don't come quick as a sneeze either,
like lots of *shmecks* today. Or need to be spanked, no shit, you'd
be shocked what some *goyim* go in for. Those girls are expensive
but an education, the things they can tell you. Would you believe that in Toronto, Ontario, there is a genius of a broker
sitting on Bay Street who forks out a hundred dollars every
Friday night to have a girl stand on him in her high heels, that's
all she's wearing, and pee all over him? Goddammit, Jake, that
bastard is one broker in a thousand, he's one of the greats. I'd
get into high heels and piss on him for nothing every day and
twice on Saturday if only he'd handle my portfolio. Anyway, in
Marlene I met my match. She can take it and come back for
more, pumping away for dear life. So what goes on there at
rehearsal, they're always grabbing each other in those dance
numbers, hands everywhere, and everybody in tights and getting
worked up? She's a good Jewish girl, it's true, but the way I look

at it they're only human. So I pick her up at midnight, I'm pooped, let me tell you, and I have to be at the office at eight thirty or they'll steal me blind. And she, she's rarin' to go. Let's have a drink at the Celebrity Club, don't be an old square, she says to me, and all the fags trail along with us, giggling like high school girls. And who pays each time? Daddy Warbucks, you can count on it. They're all squealing with laughter at jokes I don't get, I'm half asleep in my chair, and when we finally get home, she wants to eat. Who can wake up the maid? She'd leave us. So me, *me*, I make her scrambled eggs. I'm sleepwalking and what does she say, thank you, darling? No. She says you never talk to me, you sit there like a lump. Yawning in my face. It's two o'clock, I say, I'm all talked out, what do you want from me? You can sleep in until noon. Me, I'm out at eight. And quiet. I mustn't wake her, poor thing."

So, Duddy went on to explain, he had made a deal with Marlene. He agreed to bring her to London, where he had some business to transact in any case, and try to get the play produced. He would let her do it, with the proviso that if it failed she would renounce the theater and have a child. "So," Duddy asked, "do you think anybody would be crazy enough to put it on here?"

"No. In Toronto, maybe. Who wrote it, incidentally?"

The author's name had been xxx'd over on the title page.

"Doug Fraser."

"Oh, my God, I should have known as much."

"Geez, I didn't realize the time," Duddy said, leaping up. "Would you have dinner with us tonight. I promised Marlene . . ."

"Not tonight. I'm busy. Tomorrow, if you like."

"Done. Oh, one thing. If Marlene asks, we had lunch together today. Dig?"

"Look here, Big Dick, I thought you were in love with her."

"Sure I am. But she's bound to be unfaithful to me sooner or later. It's in the cards. Why should I be the one to look like a fool? This way I get my licks in first. Tomorrow at seven. Right?"

. . .

Plump, bejeweled Marlene Tyler, resplendent in a dress of glittering blue sequins, her massive helmet of spun hair bleached blond, false eyelashes heavy and flickering, a beauty patch dabbed on her chin, a gold Star of David plunging between her squeezed bosoms to fend off the evil eye, floated across the lobby of the Dorchester to join Duddy and Jake. "You know where I trod this afternoon," she said. "I trod where Dickens trod. You're so lucky to live here, Jake. It reeks with atmosphere."

At dinner, Duddy started to tell Jake how he had missed the Hersh social event of the year, his Cousin Irwin's bar mitzvah. "Your Uncle Abe spent enough money on it to float a battleship. He adores the kid. He thinks he's a genius."

But Marlene could not be diverted from talk of the play. "Do you think we'll have trouble finding backers here?" she asked.

"Why doesn't your rich husband put up the nut?"

"How would it look?" Duddy demanded, glaring at Jake. "I wish the play every success, but if it was only put on because of my money, we could become a laughing stock. Like Randolph Hearst and Marion Davies."

Eventually Marlene sailed off to the ladies' room.

"Duddy, why are you leading her on? She loves you."

"What are you talking, she loves me?" he charged, exasperated. "Who in the hell could love Duddy Kravitz?"

5

"Marriage is a rotten bourgeois institution," Jake allowed in Paris. "It stinks. I keep up with the times, you know. But, Nancy, ours would be something special. A rock."

Jake's father saw it differently. A week before Jake stood up for Nancy, with Luke in attendance, at the Hampstead Registry Office, he sent him an airmail letter, special delivery, with a clipping from the Montreal *Midnight* enclosed.

MIXED MARRIAGES STINK!

Most mixed marriages misfire!

This sad conclusion was reached by *Midnight* after careful probing into the status quo of this important question as an ever-increasing number of young couples are crossing religious and racial barriers in teaming up with a mate "for life."

Dear son, his father's letter began.

You take it for granted that I will bless this unholy marriage and seal it with a gift check, but I must disappoint you. In the past I have had to defend your character on many occasions, but how can I defend you for this disgraceful deed that you are planning?

I was beginning to be proud of you when your first television play came out in Toronto, and hoped that some day you might direct a good and successful one, and find yourself a proper lifemate, and I would be able to come to your home without shame. Oh, not you. You had to go to England to direct plays there. You made a nice salary in Toronto, more than I make. But Canada wasn't big enough for you. YOU COULD GET ALL OF EUROPE INTO IT EASY, I told you that, but what does the old man know? He is only good for a touch.

In your letter you state that you are not marrying a Jewess or a Gentile, but a woman, THE WOMAN YOU LOVE. Now tell me did you ever see young couples marry for hate? No, it's always for love, or even better, love at first sight. That's lafs (LAFS is the first letters of love at first sight).

And what about her family, if she has any? Do they want to accept a Jew in their midst? *Goyim* are such bigots, as we all know. And what happens when you have directed a bad play, or had a job refusal, and there is no money to pay the bills? You get mad and knowing you, you go to the bottle. Words, arguments, your fault, no it's your fault, and so forth, and perhaps a third party mixes in, then what, the first thing you'll be told off in these words, the dirty Jew, the good for nothing, the boozer, the shmock—

"Shmock," on reflection, had been xxx'd over by his typewriter.

—and you'll come back with words said in anger, and knowing you I AM SURE they won't be nice words, the plays you direct are full of nasty words, you are saturated with them, it will come naturally to you.

You have been present in the time of a breakup of what was once believed to be the IDEAL MARRIAGE, but hard times, moneyless days, interferences, and third parties turned love into hatred. Now what can YOU expect? LIVE spelled backwards is EVIL, and the way you are starting out I can only see a doomed and disastrous marriage, without a happy ending.

THINK THINK THINK hard before you take the fatal step. From after Aug. 20, your fatal day, my door and all that goes with it will be closed to you. The doors of all the Hersh family will not welcome you. Not being married according to the Jewish laws your children, if any, will be considered illegitimate.

So now it is up to YOU to choose between—

A. Your father who has tried to do the best for you.

B. An unwelcome woman that has come into your life.

If you choose B, I see no alternative but to ask you to forget my address, and not to try to see me. And so, with the utmost regrets I close this letter, which might be the last.

IT IS UP TO YOU NOW. "TO BE OR NOT TO B, THAT IS THE QUESTION."

A for Dad

But, alas, for what had seemed like the longest, most excruciating time, actually no more than two months, it had not been up to Jake, whose mind was irrevocably resolved. It had been for Nancy—unreservedly loving one day, withdrawn and sullen the next—to pronounce. Nancy, who did not say no in Paris, but would not say yes either. Who declined, though she knew it stung him, his persistent attempts to literally wrap her from head to toe in gifts, as she feared this would only certify possession.

Stamp her Jake's. Irretrievably Jake's.

Even on their return to London, she vacillated, delighting in his presence most of the time, but on her despairing days enormously resentful of the manner in which he overwhelmed her, after the first week no longer phoning to ask if she was free tonight, but instead turning up after work every evening as a matter of course, sinking to the sofa, putting his legs up on the coffee table, knocking off his shoes, and pouring himself a drink. He was suffocating her, she feared, and yet—and yet—she anxiously awaited his arrival each evening, fretful if he was late, embracing him at the door, and yielding to him in bed before dinner. He excited her, he made her laugh. She had never experienced such tenderness from a man. But there were days, abysmally depressing days, when she felt like a prize, one Jake desired only because Luke had sought it first, and when she would have been gratified not to see him, however marvelous their evenings together. Days when she would have been happier not to bathe and oil and perfume and powder herself, make up, and dress from the inside out, all to arouse Jake, to give Jake pleasure, but, instead, could do her own things. However modest. Like wash her lingerie, mooch about the flat in an old sweater and jeans, read, listen to records, and nibble cheese and crackers when she felt like it instead of preparing an elaborate dinner for the two of them. Which dinners, another growing resentment, were increasingly consummated not by their inherent succulence, for she was a first-rate cook, but only when the master rubbed his hands gleefully over the plate, smacked his lips, and dug in with a vengeance. And there were evenings when she would have been grateful to indulge her own fancies, however despicable, rather than be obliged to rise and respond to his moods. His hopes. His work. His burgeoning ego.

He was of course impatient of her attempts to find work.

"Publishers here don't pay a living wage," he said. "They hire debs for a pittance."

Stealthily, pretending all the while there had been no change in their relationship—admitting, in principle, she was free to see other men—he began to move into her flat by calculated inches. One night he came with fresh asparagus from Harrod's, a thoughtful gift, and the next he arrived with steaks as well—and a teak salad bowl—and a machine for grinding coffee beans— and when she protested heatedly that they would either eat what she could afford or he could visit after dinner, he seemed so hurt, even ill-used, that she surpassed herself in bed, flattering the bejesus out of him, and this he took as license, on the weekend, to turn up with a carful of groceries and liquor, cartons of his favorite food and drink.

To begin with, he lingered in her bed until three in the morning and then, because she insisted on her independence, which meant separate flats, he rose groggily, overcome with self-pity, to drive off in the cold and flop on his own bed. But having once been allowed to stay overnight, it seemed no more than sensible to keep a toothbrush at her place, his shaving things, clean shirts and underwear. And, come to think of it, scripts he had to read, his bedside lamp, the morning papers *he* wanted, and matzohs

which he munched absently in bed. Her bed. Phone calls began
to come for him at the flat. Indignantly, she took messages. Like
his secretary. Or mistress. *But you are his mistress now, aren't
you, Nancy, dear, and your day doesn't truly begin until he
comes through the door. You sleep better with him beside you.*
Which only heightened her self-disgust. For why should she be
dependent on another for her happiness? Who knows if he could
be trusted? If she hadn't already begun to pall on him? Then one
morning, scratching himself on her sheets, he was foolish enough
to wonder aloud, "Why don't we stop kidding ourselves and
move in together?"

Which made her spring out of bed, "No, no, no. This is my
place," and hastily stack his things in the middle of the living
room. His shirts. His underwear. His coffee-grinding machine.
His scripts. His bedside lamp. His jar of pickled herring. He disappeared into the bathroom, taking a suspiciously long time to
collect the rest of his stuff, and then with an, oh well, if that's
the way you want it, scooped up his things, a salami riding the
top of the heap. She stood by the window, tears sliding down
her face, as she watched him descend the outside stairs, chin dug
into his mound of possessions, his bedside lamp cord trailing after
him, the plug bouncing on the steps.

Typically childish, he didn't phone the next morning, and she
wept copiously, humiliated because she didn't dare leave the flat
in the afternoon, just in case he did phone. He didn't come by
in the evening, either, and she was incensed. Suddenly, the flat
seemed empty. Without excitement or promise. Such was her
rage at what she had to admit was her dependence that when he
did condescend to phone the next morning, she informed him,
with all the frostiness she could muster, that no, sorry, she had a
date tonight.

Nancy bathed and oiled and powdered herself, she put on the
garter belt that had made him whoop, beating the pillow for
joy, and the bra with the clasp he couldn't solve. She slithered
into her dress, undoing the top two buttons, then doing them up
again contritely, feeling wretched, fearful she couldn't yield to
another man. *And why not? She was hers to give, wasn't she?*

So she defiantly opened her medicine cabinet to make sure—just in case, as it were—that she was not without vaginal jelly. She was still searching for the tube and her cap, incredulous that he would actually have the gall, cursing him, when the doorbell rang and, running to answer it, she undid first two, then three, buttons of her dress, blushing at her own boldness.

Tall, tanned, solicitous Derek Burton, the literary agent who had phoned her every morning for a week, wore a Westminster Old Boy's tie, carried a furled umbrella, and did not instantly sink to the sofa, kicking off his shoes, but remained standing until she had sat down, and lit her cigarette with a slender lighter he kept in a chamois pouch, and raised his glass to say, cheers. He didn't have to be asked how she looked, grudgingly pronouncing her all right, and taking it as an invitation to send his hand flying up her skirts, but immediately volunteered that she looked absolutely fantastic. Outside, he opened his umbrella, and held it over her. Derek drove an Austin-Healey with a leather steering wheel and what seemed, at first glance, like six headlights and a dozen badges riding the grille. There were no apple cores in the ashtray. Or stale bagels in the glove compartment. Instead, there were scented face tissues mounted in a suede container. There was also a coin dispenser, cleverly concealed, filled with sixpences for parking meters. As well as a small, elegant flashlight and a leatherbound log book. Once at the restaurant, Derek tucked the car into the smallest imaginable space, managing it brilliantly, without cursing the car ahead of him, or behind, in Yiddish. Then she waited as he fixed a complicated burglar-proof lock to the steering column. Jake would absolutely hate him, she thought, which made her smile most enticingly and say, "How well you drive."

"One does try," he allowed, and he asked if she had ever competed in a car rally.

Alas, no.

Could she read maps, then?

No.

A pity, that, because he had hoped they might compete together.

Somehow or other, mostly by encouraging him to tell her about his military service in Nigeria, they struggled through dinner without too many embarrassing silences, but she was hard put to conceal her boredom, and would certainly not have invited him into her flat for a drink had she not espied a familiar car parked across the road, the lights out.

Fortunately, Derek was easily managed and when, breathing quickly, his cheeks flushed, he did lunge at her, squeezing her breasts like klaxons, murmuring all the while that she was super, a smashing girl, the phone began to ring. Ring and ring.

"Shouldn't one answer it?" he asked.

"Would you mind taking it, please?"

He did. Listened, blanched. And hung up.

"Don't let it worry you," Nancy said. "It's a local pervert. He usually gives me a tinkle at this hour."

Which was when he began to pull insistently at her dress, his expectations seemingly fired by the phone call, and, pleading fatigue, she handed him his umbrella and saw him out. Once he had driven off, she crossed the street, swinging her hips, and stopped in front of Jake's car to hike her dress and adjust her garter.

Sliding out of the car, he shrugged, shame-faced.

"Ooo," Nancy exclaimed, "I never dreamed it would be you. I was hoping to turn over a quick fiver."

"All right," he said. "All right," and he trailed after her into the flat, contemplating the dents in the sofa.

"Come," she said, opening the bedroom door, "don't you want to see if the sheets are mussed?"

"O.K.," he protested, "O.K.," but he did peer into the bedroom.

"Bastard. What did you say to him on the phone?"

"I don't know what you're talking about," he said, fleeing into the bathroom, and emerging to demand, "Have fun?"

"Super fun. Would you care for a drink?"

But he was already pouring himself one.

"I have been invited for a weekend in the country," she announced, curtsying. "With the Burtons. The Berks. Burtons, don't you know?"

"Well now, I never suspected you of social climbing."

"And can you give me one good reason, Jacob Hersh, why I shouldn't go?"

"Go," he said.

"Oh. Oh. Go to hell! And what if we were to marry and I was to bore you after ten years. What then? Would you trade me in for a younger model, like your fine friends?" His film friends.

"I love you. You could never bore me."

"How can you be sure?"

"Oh, Nancy, please!"

"You can't know. How can you know? And maybe you'd bore me after ten years?"

"I've got it. Let's get a divorce right now."

She had to laugh.

"Look here, if we continue to anticipate, without venturing, we can suck all the pleasure out of it."

"Yes. I know. May I have a drink too, please?"

Instead, he kissed her and, undoing her buttons, led her to the bed, where suddenly she didn't respond, explaining she couldn't, not tonight, because her equipment had mysteriously disappeared.

"How could that be?" Jake asked, his voice quivering.

"You tell me."

"Maybe if you looked again . . ."

"Oh, Jake. Darling Jake. I suppose I will have to marry you."

"When?"

"Tomorrow, if you like."

"Christ Almighty!"

6

Oscar Hoffman considered the tangled and confused carton of accounts, receipts, and statements Jake had brought him, and then a bony little man, a bantam with steel-rimmed glasses, gathered them together, his smile servile, and retreated from Hoffman's office as unobtrusively as he had entered.

Returning to his cell. The tiny cell where he consumed his days, increasingly busy and acrimonious days, vengeful days, sipping lukewarm milky tea with his chocolate digestives. The cell where he squinted over the fanciful expense accounts of film types (producers, directors, writers, and the very stars themselves), ostensibly the most nondescript and obsequious underling in the offices of Oscar Hoffman & Co., Accountants.

Harry Stein, he mused, easily the most servile of bookkeepers, a treasure, a fiddler *ne plus ultra*, even more effusive than the embarrassing Sister Pinsky, ready with his autograph book whenever one of the anointed was paraded down the hall to Father Hoffman's sanctuary, to cogitate over the virtues of a company in the Isle of Man as opposed to selling ten years' future earnings to Galaxy, taking shares in the Trust in lieu of salary. Or founding something new on the rock of the Bahamas. Or Luxembourg. Obliging Harry, first to offer a star a magazine or a cuppa, a clean ashtray, perhaps, if she had to wait in her (deductible) furs and obligatory dark glasses before being ushered into Father Hoffman's confessional, petulantly settling her lubricant cunt into an unaccustomed hard chair, squeezing her clever little accountant between an assignation and a visit with her osteopath. "I don't know what I'd do without you, Oscar. I simply don't understand anything about money."

Harry instantly at the star's side to chirp, "I must take this opportunity to tell you how marvelous you were in . . . ," picking out the picture the critics had damned.

"Why, thank you," she'd say, not even bothering to look at him, a blatant nonentity. His praise after all as inevitable as rain.

Particularly enjoyable to Harry were the left-wingers, those staunch heroes of the Hampstead barricades, who signed letters to the *Times* protesting the latest American obloquy. Who refused to hold shares in Dow Chemical. Who defied the "establishment" on television interviews and were unfailingly on first-name terms with their chauffeurs. And yet—and yet—had need of Father Hoffman's intercession with the Almighty to save them from surtax on earth and the avarice everlasting of used wives.

"I must say," Harry would enthuse, "I am looking forward to your latest . . ."

"Why, that's very good of you, Mr. . . . ?"

"Stein."

"Yes. Say there, Stein, how would you like to come to the opening?"

"Ooooo . . ."

Two tickets to the first night of the latest epiphany, albeit in the second balcony, where the grips and electricians squatted with their wives, old cows tricked out in garish finery, who arrived earliest and lingered longest in the lobby, craning their seamed necks, oohing, aaahing, at a glimpse of the fabled as they emerged from big black cars, the men in evening dress trailing starlets who rivaled each other in cleavage, bitches acknowledging the roped off but bedazzled plebs with a teensy wave, pausing, tits outthrust for the bothersome photographers from the *Mail* and the *Express*. Harry delighted in treating one of the models from the Graphic Arts Academy to such displays, saying, "Not to worry, dear," as she swelled to a legendary presence, "she's as much of a whore as you are."

In his ill-ventilated cell, heated by two electricity bars and hatred, it was Harry's special chore to sift through a client's bills, a year's debaucheries, and calculate expenses, inventing here, fabricating there, any one restaurant bill, from the Mirabelle or Les Ambassadeurs, possibly exceeding his own weekly salary. Indispensable he was. Father Hoffman's most cherished novitiate . . . but lately an ominous cloud had gathered over the once blessed spires of Oscar Hoffman & Co., Accountants. Increasingly the angel fallen from Inland Revenue contemplated the sacrifices on the altar and pronounced them lacking in sufficient faith, for his Chancellor was a jealous one and would tolerate no other havens before him. Where hitherto the anointed and the fabled had passed out of Father Hoffman's sanctuary, overcome with beatitude and astonishment, for his prayers were always heard, some of them now barged in red-faced and even in tears, voices were raised, threats made, and they strode out in obvious fear and trembling of the angel fallen from Inland Revenue and the judgment to come.

Father Hoffman looked poorly. He shook his head, he pulled his hair. Come noon, he forswore The White E. to partake of cottage cheese salad and yogurt at his desk, nodding over his ledgers. Consulting the books of law as they had been handed down.

"There's a serpent in our midst, Harry. Keep your eyes open, will you?"

There were afternoons now when Father Hoffman paused by the water cooler, contemplating his flock, counting the blessings he had showered on them, loans and luncheon vouchers, bonuses, paid holidays, pension schemes, and the annual party; afternoons when he wondered who had denied him more than thrice. Which was Iscariot?

Once Harry remained in his cell for lunch, unknown to Hoffman, and came out to find him scurrying hither and thither, stooping over wastepaper baskets, riffling through briefcases and rummaging through desk drawers. "Harry, people come to us with their confidences. We are trusted. There's a sewer rat in this office, a bastard without equal, and when I find him I'm going to break his bones."

Sprung from his office for the day now, Harry Stein, the amateur photographer, footloose in Soho, did the bookshops, not reduced to perusing the cellophane-wrapped magazines hanging on bulldog clips from the walls or comparison-shopping the strip films, but immediately beckoned into the back room to sift through the boxes on the trestle table. Bondage, Unusual Positions, Rubber Garments, Flagellation. Then, with an hour still to kill before classes, he took a pint at the Yorkminster and then, for a lark, put in a 'umble 'arry appearance at the Trattoria Terrazza, asking the haughty girl at the desk for a table for eight at nine p.m.

Impossible, she replied sniffily, and Harry, perplexed and stammering, produced a piece of notepaper and asked if this was *the* Trattoria Terrazza.

Yes, certainly.

Mr. Sean Connery sent me. I'm his driver.

Ah, well, then . . .

Still feigning to read from his notepaper, he added, garbling his French, that he wanted four bottles of Château Margaux opened to breathe at eight forty-five and a *gâteau*, yes, with thirty-eight candles. Would that be too much trouble?

Then Harry patiently sought out a functioning call box, extracted his little black book and selected the ex-directory number of a star who had sent him out of the office and into the rain earlier in the day—

"Aren't you a sweetie?"

—to fetch a pair of theater tickets while she waited, long shaven legs crossed, for an audience with His Holiness Father Hoffman.

"Hullo, my little darlin'."

"I'm so glad to hear from you again." Icily delivered this, but fearful. "The police are intercepting all my calls now, you see."

"Well, I'll tell you why I called then. How would you like me to pop over right now and lick it for you? I mean lick it like it's never been licked before. Lick it bone dry."

"I'm not hanging up. You just go ahead. They're listening to every filthy word."

"That is to say, if you're up to it. After the abortion, like. Because I wouldn't want to be spitting out stitches, would I now?" and laughing, he slammed down the receiver.

For it was time for night school and, gathering together his photographic equipment, Harry proceeded to the basement studios of the Graphic Arts Society, of which he was a long-standing associate fellow.

7

Sammy.

Jake imagined once the doctor had pronounced her pregnant beyond doubt, anointing her, so to speak, she would become ethereal, a stranger to lust, and he, attentive, solicitous, not to say self-sacrificing—

"Don't worry, darling. It will go down by itself."

—would demonstrate the magnitude of his love by approaching her with tenderness in lieu of passion, taking her as an object of adoration rather than a love vessel.

Fat chance.

Instead of maternal content, Nancy's swelling belly unleashed the wanton in her. Not so much the Holy Mother as Our Lady of the Orifices. A sexual acrobat. So, heedless of her condition, even as her rock-hard breasts began to yield a sugary substance, making him an even more recalcitrant lover, she, abandoned to pleasure, came clawing after him nightly. With teasing fingers. Breasts that brushed him erect. A tongue that licked him alive. And self-denying Jake, roused beyond any possible concern for the unborn, rode her to a climax, a shared and soaring release, anxious only afterwards for the creature swimming within her.

Some introduction to my son, he'd think, lighting up, asking if she was all right, if he hadn't been too brutish. Some how-do-you-do, ramming him like a crazed billygoat. He was tormented by a vision of the boy, his *kaddish*, born with a depression in his skull, bearing into manhood the imprint of Jake's cockshead in his scalp. An unanswerable reproach. In another nightmare, even as he stooped to lick her nether lips, teasing, biting—lo and behold, a nose protrudes. *Hello, hello.* Or a tiny, unspeakably delicate hand reaches out to stick him in the eye. *Hello, hello.* Or the waters break, drowning him. Deservedly, you satyr. Or trembling, quaking to a climax, she actually expels the baby, squirting him across the bedroom in a sea of placenta and blood. And me, he thought, I wouldn't even know how to tie the cord. I'd fail her, fainting.

Nancy did nothing to alleviate his anxiety when, her passion spent, she would suddenly say, "Give me your hand!"

"What now?"

"Can you feel the movement?"

Yes, he'd say, snatching it away, scorched.

"He's some kicker, isn't he?"

Kicker? The poor bastard is choking on my semen. "Maybe we should lay off, well, until afterwards . . ."

Nancy was well into her eighth month when Jenny and Doug passed through London on their way to an international conference in Tangiers: Television and the Developing Countries.

"We haven't seen you since Duddy staged your play in Toronto," Jake said. "I'm sorry about that. I do think it deserved better notices."

"I wasn't the least bit surprised. After all, nothing offends like *gravitas*. But I will say this for Kravitz, he resisted every commercial pressure, the director's, Marlene, he wouldn't let them change a word."

"He respected your integrity as a writer."

Doug nodded. Jenny, eager to change the subject, asked Jake if he remembered Jane Watson, a Toronto actress.

"Yes."

"She had a boy. It was a normal birth—"

"You see," Jake said to Nancy.

"—and three months later she developed this growth in her womb. When they removed it they found it was a tumor with teeth and a little beard."

"Charming. And how come," Jake charged, surfacing nasty, "you've never been pregnant, Jenny? Do you take the pill?"

"I don't take Doug," she said.

Eventually, Jake was able to have a word alone with Jenny. He told her how he had been mistaken for Joey twice. On arrival in London and when a registered letter from Canada House had come to him in error. "I wonder where he is now?"

"Israel maybe. Or Germany."

"Germany?"

"Hanna gets postcards from time to time."

Hanna, who had still to take up Luke's invitation and come to London.

"What's the last address you have for him?"

"Joey never sends addresses. But he was in Israel in forty-eight. During the so-called War of Independence. Hanna still gets letters from a woman there who claims to be his wife."

"What does she say?"

"She asks for money, what do you think? She claims Joey deserted her."

The next morning Jake read in the *Times*,

TIRED MEN WITH LIVES
IN THEIR HANDS
Surgeons on duty for 48 hours
Because of shortages of staff, surgeons in some hospitals
are carrying out emergency operations, including brain
surgery, after being on duty for up to 48 hours, often
with as little as two or three hours' snatched sleep.

Oh, Nancy. Nancy, my darling.

Nancy's water broke at three a.m., on a Thursday morning, and the baby was delivered without mishap. Sammy had no dent in his head and appeared, on first count, to have the prescribed number of everything. Reassuringly, he wore a bracelet with his name on it, but all the same Jake committed distinguishing features to memory. After all, this was his *kaddish*.

Luke, in spite of everything, was invited to become Sammy's godfather. "Why, if you hadn't leaped at the chance of getting me to pay for your dinners at Chez Luba, Nancy and I might never have gotten together in the first place."

"What do you think of her now?" Luke asked.

"Not much. You?"

Once having married, letting herself go, such was Nancy's bliss, her pleasure in Jake, the baby, looking for a house, that she could not understand why she had hesitated. But she soon grasped that her husband was not all of a piece, as she had hoped. On the contrary. Jake was charged with contradictions. Ostensibly consumed by overweening ambition, he was, on black days, filled with self-hatred and debilitating doubts, largely because he took himself to be an impostor and his work, given its fragile nature, a con. She began to wonder why he had chosen to become a director in the first place and feared, in agonizingly lucid moments, that if he did not rise as far as he hoped, he might yet diminish into bitterness.

Swaying gently as she nursed Sammy in the kitchen at three in the morning, she searched for a way of assuring him that he did not have to become famous for her sake. Or Sammy's. But such was his drive, there seemed no way she could say as much without wounding him and, rather than that, she said nothing.

If, on rare occasions, he eked some satisfaction out of his work, he was, for the most part, laden with contempt for his peers, too many of whom, he felt, presented with a script, knew instinctively what would play well, and that's all. Almost everybody in television was a lightweight, he complained to her, and a cliché monger. Such was his scorn for actors that, watching him on the set one day, she wondered why they endured him. For, unlike the others, he would not flatter and cajole those he needed, arousing them to surpassing performances. Instead he mocked, he teased, he laid low with pointed jokes. He flayed them for their vanity. Even he could not understand why they tolerated him. "When I directed my first play in Toronto," he once said to her, "telling the writer what had to be rewritten again and again, not that a hack could ever get it right, and keeping the actors late and making them go through a scene for the umpteenth time, I had to retreat to the toilet more than once, overcome by giggles—incredulous—because they had listened."

He seldom took one of his leading actors to dinner, he never sent flowers to a leading lady. The only companions he sought out on any production, those he fooled and played poker with, were the cameramen, the grips, the stagehands, and that company of failed actors, the bit players of whom no wrong could be uttered, who were jokingly referred to as Jacob Hersh's Continuing Rep. Largely drunks, has beens, never beens, itinerant wrestlers, wretched drag queens, superannuated variety artists, decrepit Yiddish actors, befuddled old prize fighters, and more than one junkie, all of whom not only counted on Jake for work and handouts but, in a suicidal mood or awakened in a hospital after a bender, could summon him in the middle of the night.

All of this, however endearing, would only have been acceptable, Nancy felt, had Jake been blessed with a talent of the first order, but, she sadly allowed, this was not the case, and so she was fearful for his sake. Fearful, touched, and apprehensive. For it made her heartsick to see how ferociously he threw himself into each play he did, however ephemeral, often going sleepless for nights while he blocked it, and afterwards, drained and becalmed, waiting for the telephone that didn't ring with the offer of a film. Then besieging his agent's office, quarreling with him, demanding to know how he got lesser directors film assignments.

Adding to his troubles, Jake had begun to insult the writers available to him in television. Those he longed to work with were either not the type to accept a commission or, though they liked him personally, were chary of committing a screenplay to a director unproven in film.

The less satisfaction his work gave him, even as he drifted on the crest of the television plateau, having done everything he could there and beginning to repeat himself, the more he began to talk about his cousin Joey, speculating about his whereabouts, wondering what he was really like, oddly convinced that somehow Joey had answers for him.

Once, there was a telephone call.

"May I speak with Joseph Hersh, please?" a man asked.

"He doesn't live here. This is Jacob Hersh's house. Why do you want to speak to him?"

"Do you know where I can reach him tonight? It's important."

"No, but—"

"Are you a relation, then?"

"Yes."

"Tell him Hannon called. I know everything. If he comes within a mile of here again, I'll kill him."

"Why?"

"You just give him the message; he'll understand."

Another time, a bill that wasn't theirs was stapled to their monthly statement from Harrod's. It was for cigars and brandy, some thirty-five pounds, and it was signed "J. Hersh."

"Why should he do this to me?" Jake protested. "If he needs money, why doesn't he come to me? Why doesn't he come to see us anyway? I don't understand."

He told Nancy how Hanna used to advertise for Joey in the Personal column of the Louisville *Courier* during Kentucky Derby Week. Maybe, he joked, he should run an ad in the *Times* now that the Grand National was coming up. Then there was Ascot. He also told her that in the days when he had shared a flat with Luke, he sometimes rushed home from wherever he was, convinced the Horseman was waiting at his door. When he had lived alone there had been nights when he had held imaginary dialogues with his cousin, saying it was the family, not Jake, who had betrayed him and allowed Baruch to die in squalor. Offering to put things right, however he could. "He's got a commercial pilot's license, you know. He's played pro baseball. Once, he was in the movies. He actually rode with Randolph Scott."

Jake was not entirely without film offers. Again and again he was sent scripts to mull over and asked to consider the sort of production that required an instant decision. Either the subjects were deplorable or the deal he celebrated on Monday, yielding to euphoria, dissolved on Wednesday. After the second film Luke had written won a prize at Cannes, the three of them went to dinner at Chez Luba, but it didn't work. Luke asked Jake to read his latest work, an original screenplay.

"I'd be glad to read it and give you an opinion," Jake said, "but if you're looking for a director, why not try Tim Nash? He's gone into films now, you know."

Out of necessity, Jake met most often with fringe producers, inept dreamers whose fantasies he submitted to after lunch.

It was after one such engagement that he came home to discover Nancy was pregnant again. He ought to have guessed, because only a month earlier, Nancy was suddenly inclined to drift off to sleep, a book in her hand, after lunch, and she was, come nightfall, uncommonly lecherous in bed.

Molly, born in May, came easily. Nancy had only been home for a month when Herky and Rifka descended on them breathlessly, having already done Copenhagen, Paris, Rome, and Venice. Their first European tour.

"Did you enjoy Venice?" Jake asked.

"It was really something."

"What was Copenhagen like?"

"Very, very clean."

"And Paris?"

"It was a real experience."

Herky and Rifka had not come without a tribute for the first-born Hersh, but Nancy, unwrapping the gift, a tangle of wires and pads, was obviously baffled.

"You see, Rifka, I told you. They haven't even seen it here yet. It's an anti-bedwetting device. Early Warning System."

"Just what we wanted," Jake said.

You lay it into his crib, Herky explained, plug it in, and no sooner does he pee than, whamo! he gets an electric shock. "It's sure-fire. We're doing very well with it."

Jake hastily removed them from the bedroom, taking his sister and brother-in-law to a Jewish restaurant in Soho. Riding two whiskies, Herky began to enthuse about his grand tour.

Each according to his trade. American neophyte painters coming over for the first time hasten to the Tate, Jeu de Paume, the Uffizi, the Prado. Beginning writers seek out Dr. Johnson's chambers, Oxford, Cambridge, Jane Austen's Bath, and in Paris hope for a glimpse of Sartre at Les Deux Magots and take a meal where James Joyce did, not forgetting the Ritz bar, Hemingway and Fitzgerald. Too many times to count, Jake had taken sentimental visitors to Marx's grave and past old Sig Freud's flat, he had pointed out the Café Royal, Bloomsbury, the bookshop in Hampstead where Orwell had served, and other sanctified places, forever ours. But Herky Soloway was a special case. In London, above all, he wished to pay obeisances at the shrine of the incomparable Thomas Crapper, repository of stools immortal, where the Cascade had first been successfully flushed and the Niagara had been invented. Herky, warming to his subject, told Jake of the sparkling enamel toilets of Copenhagen, each bowl a joy to behold, and how he had bought a bidet (a fun thing for his showroom) in Rome, and descended into the sewers of Paris, winding through the very bowels of the city, and in a smelly café in Montmartre actually squatted on the craziest thing, no seat, only imprints for your feet, and a light switch that went on and off as you locked or unlocked the door. What misers, eh? But a good precaution against the syph. In St. Germain and Étoile he had tried the pissoirs. Amazing, right out there on the streets, stinking to high heaven, and he had read in Henry Miller, there's a hot writer for you, that perverts left bread there in the morning to eat at night after everyone had peed on it. Europe, *oy veh iz mir*. But *c'est la vie, n'est-ce pas?* And in Versailles, you've heard of it, I suppose, would you believe that they used to do it in corners and the tapestries—excuse me, Rifka, I know you haven't finished your dessert yet, but I must tell him—were for wiping themselves. The nobility yet.

Once Rifka had been dropped off at the Dorchester, Herky rubbed his hands together, he clapped Jake on the back (Now we can have us a ball, Yankel), and Jake took Herky out to savor the delights of London, swinging London, after dark. Beginning with the fabled cottages of Hyde Park Corner.

"Now, Herky, before we go down, let me tell you they have blinkers on all the urinals and for a good reason. Don't start up conversations or stick your nose in everywhere. Provocateurs are not uncommon in there."

"What do you mean?"

"Cops looking for importuning fags, if you must have it spelled out."

"Listen here, my pockets are full of credit cards. I've got a personal letter of recommendation from my bank manager."

"Do me a favor, Herky. In and out."

They also took in the public conveniences of Piccadilly at its finest hour, shortly after midnight, when the acid and shitheads and pushers joined together to turn the place into a junkies' bazaar. Herky pushed open a door to discover a young man sprawled on the floor, mainlining it. Herky retreated, whistling. "Thank God we haven't got any national health plan in Canada."

Finally, they returned to Herky's suite, and Jake's brother-in-law, in an expansive mood commingled with gratitude, poured them each large brandies. "I don't know about you, Yankel, but I had a ball. We didn't do the tourist bit, did we? Not many people see the London I'm seeing."

Jake agreed, and the next afternoon, by arrangement, he took Herky to Raymond's Revue Bar and then to shop for gifts, while Rifka went to a matinée of *The Sound of Music*. Harnessed with photographic equipment, including a movie camera, Herky tramped happily through Hamley's and Liberty's, he had Jake shoot some film of him feeding the pigeons in Trafalgar Square, grinning and blowing kisses on the steps of Canada House, and then continued to Harrod's, where he immediately asked for the toilets.

Oh, Harrods, her toilets perceived.

In all of his grand tour, Herky had seen nothing to rival the Gentlemen's Toilet adjoining the men's hairdressing salon on the lower ground floor of Harrod's. Bug-eyed, he exclaimed, "This is quality, Yankel. This I call class." The floors were marble. So were the sinks. The door to each closet was oak. "This is something. This is really something. Damn it, you could eat off the floor here."

Overriding Jake's protests, he began to take photographs. Endless snaps of the fabulous appointments. A gentleman, emerging from a closet, stared at Herky, dumbfounded. "Good heavens!"

Somebody else heatedly demanded Herky's film. Harsh words were spoken.

"Buggers," another man shouted, banging his cane. "Filthy buggers!"

Barbers descended on the toilet. Somebody seized Herky's camera. "It's insured," Herky assured Jake, just before he was driven against the wall, sweaty and stammering, desperately dealing out business cards. A store detective appeared, taking charge. Which led to their being marched to an office on the fourth floor, where Jake, biting back his laughter, began to explain.

8

In the morning Harry was dispatched to the Dorchester to deliberate over a star's newly acquired mass of bills; an affair's detritus. The star, internationally known, obscenely overpaid, was attended in his suite by a bitch-mother private secretary, a soothing queer architect to keep everybody's glasses filled with chilled Chevalier Montrachet, and, kneeling by the hassock on which his big bare feet rested, a chiropodist. The chiropodist, black leather toolbox open before him, scissors-filled drawers protruding, black bowler lying alongside on the rug, was kneading the star's feet, pausing to snip a nail reverently or caress a big toe, lingering whenever he provoked an involuntary little yelp of pleasure.

"I am ever so worried," the chiropodist said, "about your returning to Hollywood, sir."

"Mmmnnnn." This delivered with eyes squeezed ecstatically shut.

"Who will look after your feet there?"

Harry, riding too much wine at an unaccustomed hour, contrived to leave in company with the chiropodist, inviting him to the pub.

"Do you get to do many of the stars?"

"Oh, yes. Yes, indeed. They all send for me."

"The women too?"

"You'd be surprised some of the things I've seen," he burbled. "You learn to knock on the door first."

"And to keep your eyes down when you're on the job, what?"

"Now look here, they're all good types. All of them."

"And the bigger they are," Harry said, ordering another round over the chiropodist's objections, "the nicer to deal with."

"Just so."

Harry motioned the portly pink-faced man closer. Lowering his voice, he asked, "What about the bloody toe jam?"

"What's that?"

"Do you think it smells better than yours? Or mine?"

The chiropodist laughed, "Oh, I say. I say," his eyes darting, "you're a salty one."

"Keep it. You could sell it, don't you think? If you were doing Elizabeth Taylor, for instance, there'd have to be a lot of money in her toe jam."

"Why that's nasty. That's very nasty, indeed, sir."

"Then there's the toenails. Think of the toenails. You could store them. Do you know that Christie used to pluck the pubic hairs from his victims and keep them in a tobacco tin?"

"I've had enough. Quite enough."

"Or their farts. Did you ever think of that," Harry persisted, driving him into a corner. "Their bloody farts are totally wasted. If you had an airtight bag in that case of yours and were quick enough to trap their farts, why there'd be a bloody fortune in it. Take Marilyn Monroe, now that she's dead. Why, if you had one of her farts trapped in an airtight container—"

"I refuse to listen to any more. I'm not listening."

"You're a servile little turd," Harry said, knocking his bowler off. "Do you hear me? A servile little turd."

9

Summer.

Drifting through Soho in the early evening, Jake stopped at the Nosh Bar for a sustaining salt beef sandwich. He had only managed one squirting mouthful and a glance at the unit trust quotations in the *Standard* (S&P Capital was steady, but Pan Australian had dipped again) when he was distracted by a bulging-bellied American in a Dacron suit. The American's wife, unsuccessfully shoehorned into a mini-skirt, clutched a *London A to Z* to her bosom. The American opened a fat credit-card-filled wallet, briefly exposing an international medical passport which listed his blood type; he extracted a pound note and slapped it into the waiter's hand. "I suppose," he said, winking, "I get twenty-four shillings change for this?"

The waiter shot him a sour look.

"Tell your boss," the American continued, unperturbed, "that I'm a Gallicianer, just like him."

"Oh, Morty," his wife said, bubbling.

And the juicy salt beef sandwich turned to leather in Jake's mouth. It's here again, he realized, heart sinking, the season.

Come summer, American and Canadian show business pleni-potentiaries domiciled in London had more than the usual hardships to contend with. The usual hardships being the income tax tangle, scheming and incompetent natives, uppity *au pairs* or nannies, wives overspending at the bazaar (Harrod's, Fortnum's, Asprey's), choosing suitable prep schools for the kids, doing without real pastrami and pickled tomatoes, fighting decorators and smog, and of course keeping warm. But come summer, tourist liners and jets began to disgorge demanding hordes of relatives and friends of friends, long (and best) forgotten schoolmates and army buddies, on London, thereby transmogrifying the telephone, charmingly inefficient all winter, into an instrument of terror. For there was not a stranger who phoned and did not exude warmth and expect help in procuring theater tickets and a night on the town ("What we're really dying for is a pub crawl. The swinging pubs. Waddiya say, old chap?") or an invitation to dinner at home. ("Well, Yankel, did you tell the Queen your Uncle Labish was coming? Did she bake a cake?")

The tourist season's dialogue, the observations, the complaints, was a recurring hazard to be endured. You agreed, oh how many times you agreed, the taxis were cute, the bobbies polite, and the pace slower than New York or, in Jake's case, Montreal. "People still know how to enjoy life here. I can see that." Yes. On the other hand, you've got to admit . . . the bowler hats are a scream, hotel service is lousy, there's nowhere you can get a suit pressed in a hurry, the British have snobby British accents and hate all Americans. Jealousy. "Look at it this way, it isn't home." Yes, a thousand times yes. All the same, everybody was glad to have made the trip, it was expensive but broadening, the world was getting smaller all the time, a global village, only next time they wouldn't try to squeeze so many countries into twenty-one days. "Mind you, the American Express was very, very nice everywhere. No complaints in that department."

Summer was charged with menace, with schnorrers and greenhorns from the New Country. So how glorious, how utterly delightful, it was for the hard-core show biz expatriates (those who weren't in Juan-les-Pins or Dubrovnik) to come together on a Sunday morning for a sweet and soothing game of softball, just as the Raj of another dynasty had used to meet on the cricket pitch in Malabar.

Sunday morning softball on Hampstead Heath in summer was unquestionably the fun thing to do. It was a ritual.

Manny Gordon tooled in all the way from Richmond, stowing a fielder's mitt and a thermos of martinis in the boot, clapping a sporty tweed cap over his bald head and strapping himself and his starlet of the night before into his Aston-Martin at nine a.m. C. Bernard Farber started out from Ham Common, picking up Al Levine, Bob Cohen, Jimmy Grief and Myer Gross outside Mary Quant's on the King's Road. Moey Hanover had once startled the staff at the Connaught by tripping down the stairs on a Sunday morning, wearing a peak cap and T-shirt and blue jeans, carrying his personal Babe Ruth bat in one hand and a softball in the other. Another Sunday Ziggy Alter had flown in from Rome, just for the sake of a restorative nine innings.

Frankie Demaine drove in from Marlow-on-Thames in his Maserati. Lou Caplan, Morty Calman, and Cy Levi usually brought their wives and children. Monty Talman, ever mindful of his latest twenty-one-year-old girlfriend, always cycled to the Heath from St. John's Wood. Wearing a maroon track suit, he usually lapped the field eight or nine times before anyone else turned up.

Jake generally strolled to the Heath, his tattered fielder's mitt and three enervating bagels filled with smoked salmon concealed under the *Observer* in his shopping bag. Some Sundays, like this one, possibly his last for a while, Nancy brought the kids along to watch.

The starting line-up on Sunday, June 28, 1963 was:

AL LEVINE'S TEAM	LOU CAPLAN'S BUNCH
Manny Gordon, ss.	Bob Cohen, 3b.
C. Bernard Farber, 2b.	Myer Gross, ss.
Jimmy Grief, 3b.	Frankie Demaine, lf.
Al Levine, cf.	Morty Calman, rf.

Monty Talman, 1b.	Cy Levi, 2b.
Ziggy Alter, lf.	Moey Hanover, c.
Jack Monroe, rf.	Johnny Roper, cf.
Sean Fielding, c.	Jason Storm, 1b.
Alfie Roberts, p.	Lou Caplan, p.

Jake, like five or six others who had arrived late and hung over (or who were unusually inept players), was a sub. A utility fielder, Jake sat on the bench with Lou Caplan's Bunch. It was a fine, all but cloudless morning, but looking around Jake felt there were too many wives, children, and kibitzers about. Even more ominous, the Filmmakers' First Wives Club or, as Ziggy Alter put it, the Alimony Gallery, was forming, seemingly relaxed but actually fulminating, on the grass behind home plate.

First Al Levine's Team and then Lou Caplan's Bunch, both sides made up mostly of men in their forties, trotted out, sunken bellies quaking, discs suddenly tender, hemorrhoids smarting, to take a turn at fielding and batting practice.

Nate Sugarman, once a classy shortstop, but since his coronary the regular umpire, bit into a digitalis pill, strode onto the field, and called, "Play ball!"

"Let's go, boychick."

"We need a hit," Monty Talman, the producer, hollered.

"*You* certainly do," Bob Cohen, who only yesterday had winced through a rough cut of Talman's latest fiasco, shouted back snidely from the opposite bench.

Manny, hunched over the plate cat-like, trying to look menacing, was knotted with more than his usual fill of anxiety. If he struck out, his own team would not be too upset because it was early in the game, but Lou Caplan, pitching for the first time since his Mexican divorce, would be grateful, and flattering Lou was a good idea because he was rumored to be ready to go with a three-picture deal for Twentieth; and Manny had not been asked to direct a big-budget film since *Chase. Ball one, inside.* If, Manny thought, I hit a single I will be obliged to pass the time of day with that stomach-turning queen Jason Storm, 1b., who was in London to make a TV pilot film for Ziggy Alter. *Strike one, called.* He had never hit a homer, so that was out, but if come a miracle he connected for a triple, what then? He would be stuck on third sack with Bob Cohen, strictly second featuresville, a born loser, and Manny didn't want to be seen with Bob, even for an inning, especially with so many producers and agents about. K-NACK! *Goddammit, it's a hit! A double, for Chrissake!*

As the players on Al Levine's bench rose to a man, shouting encouragement—

"Go, man. Go."

"Shake the lead out, Manny. Run!"

—Manny, conscious only of Lou Caplan glaring at him ("It's not my fault, Lou."), scampered past first base and took myopic, round-shouldered aim on second, wondering should he say something shitty to Cy Levi, 2b., who he suspected was responsible for getting his name on the blacklist years ago.

Next man up to the plate, C. Bernie Farber, who had signed to write Lou Caplan's first picture for Twentieth, struck out gracefully, which brought up Jimmy Grief. Jimmy swung on the first pitch, lifting it high and foul, and Moey Hanover, c., called for it, feeling guilty because next Saturday Jimmy was flying to Rome and Moey had already arranged to have lunch with Jimmy's wife on Sunday. Moey made the catch, which brought up Al Levine, who homered, bringing in Manny Gordon ahead of him. Monty Talman grounded out to Gross, ss., retiring the side.

Al Levine's Team, first inning: two hits, no errors, two runs.

Leading off for Lou Caplan's Bunch, Bob Cohen smashed a burner to center for a single and Myer Gross fanned, bringing up Frankie Demaine and sending all the outfielders back, back, back. Frankie whacked the third pitch long and high, an easy fly had Al Levine been playing him deep left instead of inside right, where he was able to flirt hopefully with Manny Gordon's starlet, who was sprawled on the grass there in the shortest of possible Pucci prints. Al Levine was the only man on either team who always played wearing shorts—shorts revealing an elastic bandage which began at his left kneecap and ran almost as low as the ankle.

"Oh, you poor darling," the starlet said, making a face at Levine's knee.

Levine, sucking in his stomach, replied, "Spain," as if he were tossing the girl a rare coin.

"Don't tell me," she squealed. "The beach at Torremolinos. Ugh!"

"No, no," Levine protested. "The civil war, for Chrissake. Shrapnel. Defense of Madrid."

Demaine's fly fell for a homer, driving in a panting Bob Cohen.

Lou Caplan's Bunch, first inning: one hit, one error, two runs.

Neither side scored in the next two innings, which were noteworthy only because Moey Hanover's game began to slip badly. In the second Moey muffed an easy pop fly and actually let C. Bernie Farber, still weak on his legs after a cleansing, all but foodless, week at Forest Mere Hydro, steal a base on him. The problem was clearly Sean Fielding, the young RADA graduate whom Columbia had put under contract because, in profile, he looked like Peter O'Toole. The game had only just started when Moey Hanover's wife, Lilian, had ambled over to Al Levine's bench and stretched herself out on the grass, an offering, beside Fielding, and the two of them had been giggling together and nudging each other ever since, which was making Moey nervy. Moey, however, had not spent his young manhood at a yeshiva to no avail. Not only had he plundered the Old Testament for most of his winning *Rawhide* and *Bonanza* plots, but now that his Lilian was obviously in heat again, his hard-bought Jewish education, which his father had always assured him was priceless, served him splendidly once more. Moey remembered his *David ha'Melech: And it came to pass in the morning, that David wrote a letter to Joab, and sent it by the hand of Uriah. And he wrote in the letter, saying, Set Uriah in the forefront of the hottest*

battle, and retire ye from him, that he may be smitten, and die.
Amen.

Lou Caplan yielded two successive hits in the third and Moey
Hanover took off his catcher's mask, called for time, and strode
to the mound, rubbing the ball in his hands.

"I'm all right," Lou said. "Don't worry. I'm going to settle
down now."

"It's not that. Listen, when do you start shooting in Rome?"

"Three weeks tomorrow. You heard something bad?"

"No."

"You're a friend now, remember. No secrets."

"No. It's just that I've had second thoughts about Sean Fielding. I think he's very exciting. He's got lots of appeal. He'd be a
natural to play Domingo."

As the two men began to whisper together, players on Al
Levine's bench hollered, "Let's go, gang."

"Come on. Break it up, Moey."

Moey returned to the plate, satisfied that Fielding was as good
as in Rome already. May he do his own stunts, he thought.

"Play ball," Nate Sugarman called.

Alfie Roberts, the director, ordinarily expected soft pitches
from Lou, as he did the same for him, but today he wasn't so
sure, because on Wednesday his agent had sent him one of Lou's
properties to read and—Lou's first pitch made Alfie hit the dirt.
That settles it, he thought, my agent already told him it doesn't
grab me. Alfie struck out as quickly as he could. Better be put
down for a rally-stopper than suffer a head fracture.

Which brought up Manny Gordon again, with one out and
runners on first and third. Manny dribbled into a double play, retiring the side.

Multi-colored kites bounced in the skies over the Heath. Lovers
strolled on the tow paths and locked together on the grass. Old
people sat on benches, sucking in the sun. Nannies passed, wheeling toddlers with titles. The odd baffled Englishman stopped to
watch the Americans at play.

"Are they air force chaps?"

"Filmmakers, actually. It's their version of rounders."

"Whatever is that enormous thing that woman is slicing?"

"Salami."

"*On the Heath?*"

"Afraid so. One Sunday they actually set up a bloody folding table, right over there, with cold cuts and herrings and mounds of black bread and a whole bloody side of smoked salmon. *Scotch. Ten and six a quarter, don't you know?*"

"On the Heath?"

"Champagne *in paper cups*. Mumm's. One of them had won some sort of award."

Going into the bottom of the fifth, Al Levine's Team led 6–3, and Tom Hunt came in to play second base for Lou Caplan's Bunch. Hunt, a Negro actor, was in town shooting *Othello X* for Bob Cohen.

Moey Hanover lifted a lazy fly into left field, which Ziggy Alter trapped rolling over and over on the grass until—just before getting up—he was well placed to look up Natalie Calman's skirt. Something he saw there so unnerved him that he dropped the ball, turning pale and allowing Hanover to pull up safely at second.

Johnny Roper walked. Which brought up Jason Storm, to the delight of a pride of British fairies who stood with their dogs on the first base line, squealing and jumping. Jason poked a bouncer through the infield and floated to second, obliging the fairies and their dogs to move up a base.

With two out and the score tied 7–7 in the bottom half of the sixth, Alfie Roberts was unwillingly retired and a new pitcher came in for Al Levine's Team. It was Gordie Kaufman, a writer blacklisted for years, who now divided his time between Madrid and Rome, asking a hundred thousand dollars a spectacular. Gordie came in to pitch with the go-ahead run on third and Tom Hunt stepping up to the plate for the first time. Big black Tom Hunt, who had once played semi-pro ball in Florida, was a militant. If he homered, Hunt felt he would be put down for another buck nigger, good at games, but if he struck out, which would call for rather more acting skill than was required of him on the set of *Othello X,* what then? He would enable a bunch of fat, foxy, sexually worried Jews to feel big, goysy. Screw them, Hunt thought.

Gordie Kaufman had his problems too. His stunning villa on Mallorca was run by Spanish servants, his two boys were boarding at a reputable British public school, and Gordie himself was president, sole stockholder, and the only employee of a company that was a plaque in Liechtenstein. And yet—and yet—Gordie still subscribed to the *Nation;* he filled his Roman slaves with anti-apartheid dialogue and sagacious Talmudic sayings; and whenever the left-wing *pushke* was passed around he came through with a nice check. I must bear down on Hunt, Gordie thought, because if he touches me for even a scratch single I'll come off a patronizing ofay. If he homers, God forbid, I'm a shitty liberal. And so with the count 3 and 2, and a walk, the typical social-democrat's compromise, seemingly the easiest way out for both men, Gordie gritted his teeth, his proud Trotskyite past getting the best of him, and threw a fast ball right at Hunt, bouncing it off his head. Hunt threw away his bat and started for the mound, fist clenched, but not so fast that players from both sides couldn't rush in to separate the two men, both of whom felt vindicated, proud, because they had triumphed over impersonal racial prejudice to hit each other as individuals on a fun Sunday on Hampstead Heath.

Come the crucial seventh, the Filmmakers' First Wives Club grew restive, no longer content to belittle their former husbands from afar, and moved in on the baselines and benches, undermining confidence with their heckling. When Myer Gross, for instance, came to bat with two men on base and his teammates shouted, "Go, man. Go," one familiar grating voice floated out over the others. "Hit, Myer. Make your son proud of you, *just this once.*"

What a reproach the first wives were. How steadfast! How unchanging! Still Waiting For Lefty after all these years. Today maybe hair had grayed and chins doubled, necks had gone pruney, breasts drooped and stomachs dropped, but let no man say these crones had aged in spirit. Where once they had petitioned for the Scotsboro Boys, broken with their families over mixed marriages, sent their boy friends off to defend Madrid, split with old comrades over the Stalin-Hitler Pact, fought for Henry Wallace, demonstrated for the Rosenbergs, and never, never yielded to McCarthy . . . today they clapped hands at China Friendship Clubs, petitioned for others to keep hands off Cuba and Vietnam, and made their sons chopped liver sandwiches and sent them off to march to Aldermaston.

The wives, alimonied but abandoned, had known the early struggling years with their husbands, the self-doubts, the humiliations, the rejections, the cold-water flats, and the blacklist, but they had always remained loyal. They hadn't altered, their husbands had.

Each marriage had shattered in the eye of its own self-made hurricane, but essentially the men felt, as Ziggy Alter had once put it so succinctly at the poker table, "Right, wrong, don't be silly, it's really a question of who wants to grow old with Anna Pauker when there are so many juicy little things we can now afford."

So there they were, out on the grass chasing fly balls on a Sunday morning, short men, overpaid and unprincipled, all well within the coronary and lung cancer belt, allowing themselves to look ridiculous in the hope of pleasing their new young wives and girlfriends. There was Ziggy Alter, who had once written a play "with content" for the Group Theater. Here was Al Levine, who had used to throw marbles under horses' legs at demonstrations and now raced two horses of his own at Epsom. On the pitcher's mound stood Gordie Kaufman, who had once carried a banner that read *No Pasarán* through the streets of Manhattan and now employed a man especially to keep Spaniards off the beach at his villa on Mallorca. And sweating under a catcher's mask there was Moey Hanover, who had studied at a yeshiva, stood up to the committee, and was now on a sabbatical from Desilu.

Usually the husbands were able to avoid their used-up wives. They didn't see them in the gaming rooms at the White Elephant or in the Mirabelle or Les Ambassadeurs. But come Brecht to Shaftesbury Avenue and without looking up from the second row center they could feel them squatting in their cotton bloomers in the second balcony, burning holes in their necks.

And count on them to turn up on a Sunday morning in summer on Hampstead Heath just to ruin a game of fun baseball. Even homering, as Al Levine did, was no answer to the drones.

"It's nice for him, I suppose," a voice behind Levine on the bench observed, "that on the playing field, with an audience, if you know what I mean, he actually appears virile."

The game dragged on. In the eighth inning Jack Monroe had to retire to his Mercedes-Benz for his insulin injection and Jake Hersh, until now an embarrassed sub, finally trotted onto the field. Hersh, thirty-three, one-time relief pitcher for Room 41, Fletcher's Field High (2–7), moved into right field, mindful of his disc condition and hoping he would not be called on to make a tricksy catch. He assumed a loose-limbed stance on the grass, waving at his wife, grinning at his children, when without warning a sizzling line drive came right at him. Jake, startled, did the only sensible thing: he ducked. Outraged shouts and moans from the bench reminded Jake where he was, in a softball game, and he started after the ball.

"Fishfingers."

"*Putz!*"

Runners on first and third started for home as Jake, breathless, finally caught up with the ball. It had rolled to a stop under a bench where a nanny sat watching over an elegant perambulator.

"Excuse me," Jake said.

"Americans," the nurse said.

"I'm a Canadian," Jake protested automatically, fishing the ball out from under the bench.

Three runs scored. Jake caught a glimpse of Nancy, unable to contain her laughter. The children looked ashamed of him.

In the ninth inning with the score tied again, 11–11, Sol Peters, another sub, stepped cautiously to the plate for Lou Caplan's Bunch. The go-ahead run was on second and there was only one out. Gordie Kaufman, trying to prevent a bunt, threw right at him and Sol, forgetting he was wearing his contact lenses, held the bat in front of him to protect his glasses. The ball hit the bat and rebounded for a perfectly laid down bunt.

"Run, you shmock."

"Go, man."

Sol, terrified, ran, carrying the bat with him.

Monty Talman phoned home.

"Who won?" his wife asked.

"We did. 13–12. But that's not the point. We had lots of fun."

"How many you bringing back for lunch?"

"Eight."

"*Eight?*"

"I couldn't get out of inviting Johnny Roper. He knows Jack Monroe is coming."

"I see."

"A little warning. Don't, for Chrissake, ask Cy how Marsha is. They're separating. And I'm afraid Manny Gordon is coming with a girl. I want you to be nice to her."

"*Anything else?*"

"If Gershon phones from Rome while the guys are there please remember I'm taking the call upstairs. And please don't start collecting glasses and emptying ashtrays at four o'clock. It's embarrassing. Bloody Jake Hersh is coming and it's just the sort of incident he'd pick on and joke about for months."

"I never coll—"

"All right, all right. Oh, shit, something else. Tom Hunt is coming."

"The actor?"

"Yeah. Now listen, he's very touchy, so will you please put away Sheila's doll."

"Sheila's doll?"

"If she comes in carrying that bloody golliwog I'll die. Hide it. Burn it. Hunt gets script approval these days, you know."

"All right, dear."

"See you soon."

10

Lou Caplan, who had a three-picture deal with Twentieth Century-Fox, beckoned to Jake at Talman's house, and led him out into the garden. "You know what all these fucking flowers are called?" he demanded, irritated, his gesture sweeping.

"Certainly."

"Ptsssh," Caplan hissed, appreciative, and he suddenly thrust his finger out. "This one, then."

"Why, that's a tea rose. Unmistakably an Ena Harkness."

"And this?"

"Phlox."

"Bluffers I don't care for. Sit down here. Why haven't you made a picture yet? I caught your last play on TV. You're a genius, Jake."

"*What?*"

"That's exactly how I would have directed it."

"Oh. Oh, I see."

"You've got style. You're fast. You're good with cameras. But I also hear you're poison ivy with actors. A real *grobber yung*. There's something I want you to read. If it excites you, I'll talk to your agent. If not, who needs him. Right?"

So yet again Jake read until two o'clock in the morning, cogitating, running through the novel twice.

"It's only a thriller, Nancy. But I could do things with it. I'm going to say yes."

"Where's it set?"

"Israel." Then, sensing Nancy's concern, he smiled and added, "I won't get overexcited, don't worry. For all I know five other directors are considering the project right now. At best, I'm third choice."

But, unbelievably, Caplan had lunch with his agent on Wednesday and they agreed on terms immediately. Naturally, Caplan would not allow him casting approval, but he said he could hire his own writer. "Maybe," he ventured, "your hotshot friend Luke Scott wouldn't ask for a million dollars to do the script if he knew you were directing it . . ."

"No," Jake said sharply. "Luke's absolutely out."

A letter of agreement was signed and delivered by hand on Monday, just as Caplan had promised. Only one hitch remained, Twentieth Century-Fox, but after ten endless, nerve-wracking days, Jake was approved by their New York office.

"That does it," Jake said to Nancy, "now we celebrate," which they did, and, afterwards, lying in bed together, he confessed, "I had begun to believe I'd never get my chance."

A fortnight later, still incredulous, Jake flew to Israel to search for locations and, he hoped, find out more about the Horseman, maybe even unearth his Israeli wife, who was supposed to be on a kibbutz somewhere.

On arrival, it was balmy, marvelously bright and blue; and what with London's wet gummy skies only six hours behind him, Jake began to feel elated. After all, this was Eretz Yisroel. Zion. He checked into the Garden Hotel, in Ramat-Aviv, stopping by a poolside table for a drink. Foot-weary, middle-aged tourists were sunning themselves everywhere. Among them, Mr. Cooper. Shooing flies away with a rolled newspaper, pondering his toes as he curled and uncurled them, the portly, bronzed Mr. Cooper, his eyes shaded by a baseball cap, basked in a deck chair, his

manner proprietorial. "And where are you from?" he asked Jake.
Jake told him.

"Ah ha. And how long you here for?"

"A week. Ten days maybe."

"Longer you couldn't stay. This is Israel, it's a miracle. So, Mr. Hersh, what line of business you in?"

"The junk business."

Early the next morning a bellboy rapped on Jake's bungalow door; a Colonel Elan, Lou Caplan's Israeli partner, was waiting for him. Squat and sinewy, his solemn face hardened by the wind, Elan was casually dressed. "*Shalom*," he said.

Mr. Cooper passed with his wife, who was wearing flower-print pedal pushers. "So, Mr. Hersh, have you decided to settle here yet?"

"What about you?"

"Me, I'm too old. So I come here to spend."

Elan shrugged, his gray eyes scornful. No sooner had Jake climbed into his Ford station wagon than Elan said, "I wonder what that man's name was before it was Cooper?"

"And what," Jake asked, surprised at his own indignation, "was yours before it was Elan?"

"You'll find that we're a new kind of Jew here. We have restored Jewish pride."

The other side of Ramla, the car began the slow winding rise and fall, rise and fall, through the bony, densely cultivated mountains. Arab villages jutted natural and ravaged as rock out of the hills. The gutted shells of armored trucks lay overturned around the bends in the narrow steepening road. Here a dried wreath hung on a charred chassis; elsewhere mounds of stone marked where a driver, trapped in the cab of his burning truck, had died an excruciating death. These ruins, spilled along the roadside, were a memorial to those who had died running the blockade into Jerusalem during the Arab-Israeli War, at a time when the Arab Legion had held the vital heights of Bab el Wad and Kastel, an ancient Roman encampment and crusaders' castle which dominate the closest approaches to the city.

"Look here, Elan," Jake said, suddenly uncomfortable, his embarrassment rising, "have you read the thriller the film is to be based on?"

"Yes."

"The script's not going to be like that at all. I want you to know I'm not coming all this way to make a vulgar film."

"We need the foreign currency," Elan said ambiguously.

Jake told Elan that a cousin of his, Joey Hersh, sometimes known as Jesse Hope, had fought in the first Arab-Israeli War, and might even be in Israel again now, but Jake did not know where.

"It's a small country, but I don't know everybody. Try the Association of Americans and Canadians in Israel."

But Jake couldn't get anywhere with the man at the Association.

"Half the Anglo-Saxon Jews who come here," he said, "leave after two or three years. Why do they quit? Let's face it, most of them come from middle-class homes and settling here means a big drop in their standard of living. Many others miss their close family ties. Momma."

That, Jake replied pointedly, would not have been the problem with Joey Hersh, but the Association had no record of him. Or a wife.

On Tuesday Jake drove to Acre with Elan, to look at possible locations. Old sacks had been stretched across the narrow stinking streets of the Arab marketplace, offering shade to vendors and buyers alike. Donkeys, chickens, and goats wandered somnolently through the maze of stalls. The wares on display were pathetic. Rusty keys for ancient locks, faded cotton dresses, split boots. Barefoot boys scampered through the muck. Flies were everywhere. "They don't have to live like that," Elan said, anticipating Jake. "A lot of them own property. They bury their money in jars. Actually, there's no such thing as an 'Arab.' What, for instance, has an Arab in Cairo in common with a Bedouin from Iraq?"

"Jerusalem?" Jake dared.

"All the Arabs have in common is the fact that they're Moslem. We must teach them that it is not such a bad thing to be an Arab in Israel."

"Possibly," Jake said, "the trouble is they have loyalties outside their own country. Like my friend Mr. Cooper."

The Canadian Embassy had no knowledge of Joseph Hersh.

Wednesday morning Jake drove to Beersheba with Elan to look at the Arabian Nights Hotel, then still under construction. About a half hour out of Tel Aviv, the station wagon wheeled into a lush cultivated belt. Then, quite suddenly, they were streaking across the desert. "We are seventy miles wide here," Elan said. "One day this will be our bread basket."

Finally, the station wagon rocked to a stop on the outskirts of Beersheba. Squinting against the windblown sand, Jake saw an enormous roadhouse rising abruptly out of the desert. The proprietor, a Mr. Hod, hurried toward them. "I'm putting up the finest hotel in Israel," he said. "We're going to have a golf course, hot springs—the works. Soon we'll have the biggest neon sign in the country. THE ARABIAN NIGHTS HOTEL. I'm even organizing a society to be called Sons of the Arabian Nights."

After lunch Hod began to knock back one snifter of brandy after another. "One day," he said to Jake, "I met a Spaniard in Beersheba. A rich man. He told me that in Madrid he was an antisemite. He said he didn't believe these Jews would ever build a country so he thought he'd go and see for himself. Well, I've seen the country, he said, and it's marvelous. But you're not Jews here, you're different. The Jews in Spain would only fight for their families and their businesses. You're different here, he said."

"If you run into him again," Jake replied tightly, "tell him some of the Jews in Canada not only fought for their country and this one, they also fought for Spain. Like my cousin."

On the long drive back to Tel Aviv, Jake feigned sleep. Finally, Elan dropped him outside the Garden Hotel.

"You're the fastidious one, aren't you, Hersh? You wonder why we have vulgar hotels and would finance exploitation films to be made by second-rate people. It's because we need the currency. We need it to survive."

"Yes," Jake said feebly, "I'm sure you're right," and retiring to his bungalow, he combed through the thriller yet again and decided that with the help of a decent script, the right cast, it would be a good film, he would make it meaningful, and he wasn't taking it on merely because he was no longer a boy, as time and pride dictated he had to direct a film now.

Jake wakened resolved, even cheerful. Then Elan telephoned. "Your cousin," he said, "went by the name of Yosef Ben Baruch here. He was a proper son-of-a-bitch, which shouldn't surprise me. His wife is on the kibbutz of Gesher Haaziv."

Immediately after lunch, Jake hired a taxi and bounced across the coastal plain, through Haifa, and into the Upper Galilee to Gesher Haaziv, a kibbutz lodged in the hills hard by the Lebanese border, untroubled at the time except for smugglers bound for Acre with pork or hashish. He discovered Chava in the dining hall, a burly lady with frizzy black hair, lachrymose black eyes, and hairy legs. A two-gallon tin of pickles hooked under her broad arm, she shuffled from table to table, depositing exactly six pickles in each center plate for the evening's feast. The Passover *seder*.

"I'm your husband's cousin. I'd like to talk to you, if you don't mind."

"Is he dead?"

"Not that I know of. But why do you say that?"

"Because I never hear from his family. I thought when he died there might be papers maybe. Something for our son."

Zev was ten years old.

"Why would you need money on a kibbutz?"

"It's no life any more. I want to leave for the boy's sake."

"Are you from . . . America?"

"Before Theresienstadt, I don't know where from," she said, drifting off to another table with her pickles.

"The family sent money. They asked me to give it to you."

"How much?"

Jake scratched his head. He cogitated. "A thousand dollars."

"A thousand dollars?" She shrugged. "But they're so rich."

"And a hundred dollars a month to help with support for the boy."

"Would they give more?"

"No."

"You try. You talk to them. I'll give you pictures of Zev to take back."

They strolled to her cabin, which comprised three rooms, including a bedroom for Zev. On Gesher Haaziv, the children were no longer brought up communally but lived with their parents. "We had hoped this generation would be different. They would be saved the curse of a Yiddish momma, but it didn't work. Parents kept slipping off to the children's house with candies for their own. If one of them caught cold, the mother was immediately there. Jews," she said plaintively.

There was a photograph of the Horseman on the mantelpiece, circa 1948. Cousin Joey was in uniform, astride a white stallion.

"He won the horse from the *mukhtar*'s son. After a fight."

Had she known him at the time, he asked.

"No, but I was familiar with the stories. He was one of those mixed up with Deir Yassin, a disaster for us. Some say he was even a ring leader, but who knows, he wouldn't talk about it."

In April 1948, units of Etzel and the Stern Gang mounted an unprovoked attack on the quiescent Arab village of Deir Yassin, on the western fringe of Jerusalem. It was a calculated act of terrorism, meant to serve as a lesson. The Jewish Agency repudiated the massacre, but the Arabs were able to use it to justify their own atrocities.

"He turned up again in the third convoy into Jerusalem, the one that took such a battering at Bab el Wad. Some of the burned-out chassis have been left by the roadside, a reminder."

"I've seen them."

"It was the last convoy to get through. They brought chickens, eggs, and matzohs for Passover, but there was no hope of getting out of Jerusalem again. Yosef joined a unit fighting in the Old City. More trouble. This time with Neturei Karta. The orthodox from the orthodox, you know. They still don't recognize the state, it's an intrusion, they're waiting for the Messiah. One of their graybeards came to him, and said it was too much for the women and children, the shelling was awful. He wished to arrange a special truce with the Arabs to exclude their quarter from the fighting. Yosef said if the old bastard raised a white flag, he would shoot him. Just like that. There were maybe eight hundred orthodox women and children sheltering in the Yohanan ben Zakkai synagogue, with the Arabs just across the street. When the rabbis tottered out, carrying a white sheet between two poles, somebody shot from the Jewish lines, wounding one of them."

The Horseman, who drank prodigiously, was disliked on Gesher Haaziv. He would disappear for three days at a time, sometimes even a week, on a bender in Acre, where he was thick with the Arabs in the marketplace. Afterwards, there was no doubt that he was involved with the hashish smugglers.

"What do you mean, afterwards?"

After the Kastner business, she meant.

Early in April 1944, Dr. Rudolph Kastner, a leader of the Hungarian Jewish community, established contact with *Hauptsturmführer* Wislicency of the *Sondereinsatzkommando* Eichmann and, under conditions unimaginably chilling and gruesome, negotiated to purchase the freedom of some 1,700 Jews for 1,600,000 dollars. Those ransomed had to be selected from 750,000 who were consequently not warned that they were bound for the ovens and so had no opportunity to resist or flee to the woods. Among the 1,700 saved were Kastner's relatives. Jews of substance and social importance were in preponderance.

After the war, Kastner settled in Israel. Years later an obsessed man took to the street corners of Jerusalem, brandishing a broadside that claimed Kastner was in fact a collaborator and his machinations had meant 750,000 Jews went unknowingly to their doom. And the Horseman, drunk in the dining hall of Gesher Haaziv, taunted the men, asking them what are you going to do about it, as if it was their affair. As if, like everyone else in the country, they were not torn by the accusations and the trial that ensued. Some taking Kastner to epitomize all that was corrupt in the *Judenräte* of Europe, others arguing that in an appalling time he saved as many as he could, and still others saying we can no longer comprehend what moved men to action then and it was time for silence.

Kastner won a Pyrrhic victory in the libel trial held in 1953, his name not so much cleared as clouded, and the Horseman, rising the next morning, ostensibly to drive a truck to the turkey farm, did not stop there. The truck was discovered abandoned in Acre and the Horseman was not seen in Gesher Haaziv again.

Kastner was completely cleared in another trial, held in 1957, but one night a few months later he was shot dead in the street by a Hungarian Jew.

"Now one minute," Jake said. "You mean you have not seen or heard from him in all these years?"

"He comes to Israel from time to time, but never here. He left us for a year even before fifty-three, you know. He was in France for all of fifty-one."

At Maison-Lafite, where, being a foreigner, he was not allowed a license as a horse trainer, and so worked illegally, as it were, his papers classifying him as a gentleman's jockey.

"Did. he ever talk to you about the family? About Montreal?"

"When he was drunk. He said they were responsible for his father's death and his, almost."

"*He said that?*"

She nodded.

"Were those his exact words? They were responsible for his death, almost?"

"It was so long ago. He was drunk. We were quarreling. Listen, people quarrel. Yosef would not allow me to apply for my German reparations money. Oh, he was a purist, that one! Such a purist! About some things . . ."

"What do you mean, some things?"

"Oh, taking money from the Germans, who did they rob it from in the first place if not us, this was not right, but collecting from his women . . ." she broke off, laughing dryly, sunken in bitterness.

"Why would women give him money?"

"Women. Husbands, fathers. Nobody has reason to be afraid any more. I burned every single letter. He hated your family, you know, and he was also a liar."

"What letters did you burn?"

"Who are you snooping for, you have to know everything?"

"Nobody."

"I have nothing against the Hershes and I'm very, very grateful for their help, if only it were more."

"Yes, I understand. But did he say anything else? Please, it's frightfully important to me."

"He was fond of saying that if the Hershes had been in the Old City, in forty-eight, they would have been the first to wave the white flag."

"That's hardly fair."

"Did I say it was fair? Fair. How old are you?"

"Thirty-three."

"Tell me something you know in this life that's fair. Come. Go ahead."

"Do you ever hear from him?"

"Postcards. Mostly on Zev's birthdays."

She went on to say how when he was on one of his benders, more often than not he was washed up at the Kibbutz of the Survivors of the Warsaw Ghetto, near Haifa, where they knew how to drink, and there was a museum and archives on the holocaust. Then Chava opened a dressing drawer, digging out a file. Among the postcards, Jake discovered yellowing newspaper and magazine photographs. Rosy-cheeked *gemütlich* Frau Goering going about her shopping on the Theatinerstrasse. The austere Von Papen family, the eldest boy named Adolph, posing on a leather chesterfield. "Sepp" Dietrich looking severe. There were also well-worn pages from a journal, describing the activities of Josef Mengele, philosophy student and chief doctor at Auschwitz, who lived quietly in Munich until 1951, when he fled over the Reschenpass-Merano route to Italy, with the help of ODESSA, and from there to Spain, then Buenos Aires, and when the Perón regime collapsed in 1955, to Paraguay.

DECLARATION. *I, the undersigned, Dr. Nyiskizli Miklos, former prisoner of the KZ. Number 8450, declare that this work was drawn up by me in strict accordance with reality, and without the slightest exaggeration, in my capacity as eyewitness and involuntary participant in the work at Auschwitz.*

As chief physician of the Auschwitz crematoriums I drafted numerous affidavits of dissection and forensic medicine findings which I signed with my tattoo number. I sent these documents by mail, countersigned by my superior, Dr. Mengele, to the Berlin-Dahlem address of the Institut für rassenbiologische anthropologische Forschungen . . .

As Chava droned on, complaining about the cost of finding even a modest apartment in Tel-Aviv, he read:

Dr. Mengele—the medical selector—makes a sign. They line up again in two groups. The column on the left includes the aged, the crippled, the feeble, and women and children under fourteen. The column on the right is made up of able-bodied men and women . . .

Chava brewed tea. She poured it.

Everybody is inside. A hoarse command rings out: S.S. and Sonderkommando leave the room. They obey and count off. The doors swing shut and without the lights are switched off. At that very instant the sound of a car is heard. It is a de luxe model furnished by the International Red Cross. An S.S. officer and a S.D.G. (Sanitätsdienstgefreiter) hold four green sheet-iron canisters. He advances across the grass, where, every thirty yards, short concrete pipes jut out above the ground. Having donned his gas mask . . .

"Look," Chava said, "here it is. A postcard that came only six weeks ago."

From Munich.

"He's a big singer, didn't you know?" She laughed for the first time. "Jesse Hope, Western Music & Folk Songs."

11

Horseman, Horseman.

Unable to sleep, thrashing in bed, Jake saw him, in his mind's eye, cantering on a magnificent Pleven stallion. Galloping, thundering. Yosef Ben Baruch. Son of Baruch the longshoreman, slot-machine peddler, backwoods strongman, sailor of the China Seas, prospector and whisky runner. Baruch who dared to hurl curses at the *zeyda*. "Jews, I'm here. Jews, it's Baruch, your brother's home." Who bred Joey in a miner's shack in Yellowknife. Joey, who demanded in the dining hall of Gesher Haaziv as he had once asked on St. Urbain, What are you going to do about it?

Jake contacted Elan early the next morning. "I'm leaving today," he said.

"But I have things laid out for you. I thought you were staying at least for another week."

"I've decided not to do the film."

"What?"

"It's a long story and you wouldn't understand anyway."

Instead of flying directly to London, Jake caught a plane to Rome, and continued on to Munich from there. Nancy, to his astonishment, was more relieved than upset. When he phoned her from the airport, she said, "I never thought you'd go through with it. Something better will come along, don't worry."

He doubted it.

"But what are you doing in Munich?"

Jake explained.

"How on earth will you ever find him?" she asked.

"I've got to give it a try."

The bodies are not lying scattered here and there throughout the room, but piled in a mass to the ceiling. This is explained by the fact that the gas first inundates the lower layers of air and rises but slowly to the ceiling. That forces them to trample and clamber over one another. At the bottom of the pile are the babies, children, women and aged; at the top, the strongest. Their bodies, which bear numerous scratches occasioned by the struggle which set them against one another, are often intertwined. The noses and mouths are bleeding, the faces bloated and blue.

Jake scoured the *jazzkellers* of Schwabing and then the clubs closer to the Maximilianstrasse. From the Märzenkeller he carried on to the Schuhplattler, from there to the Lola Montes, the Moulin Rouge, the Bongo, and other cellars, until jerky accordion music reverberated in his ears, even on the black night streets. You're in Gehenna, Jake. The lowest regions. Shouldn't he raise fires? Shout at passersby? Murderers, murderers. But he continued to walk. One foot, then another. Once he bumped into a middle-aged lady wrapped in a silver fox and hastily said, "*Entschuldig mir*," hoping she would take it for German, not Yiddish, instead of following through with his shoulder and stamping on her. Hatred was a discipline. He would have to train harder, that's all.

Nobody had ever heard of the Canadian folk singer called Jesse Hope, but the doorman at the Bongo recommended he look in at the American Way Club, formerly Hitler's Haus der Kunst. Sure, why not? When in hell, see the sights.

Explore.

On entry, Jake was confronted by the cardboard figure of a hillbilly. Pappy Burns' Tune Twisters, the poster promised,

would entertain on Friday night. Heartened, Jake joined the
queue before the information desk.

"Where you coming from?" the soldier ahead of him asked.

"Jerusalem," Jake said on impulse.

"No kidding? What's the gash like there?"

"Crazy for it."

Over the desk a poster advertised:

DACHAU
Bus Leaves Every Saturday at 1400
VISIT THE CASTLE
AND THE CREMATORIUM

"Hope. Jesse Hope," the deskman pondered the name, his smile
sly. "Are you from the military police?"

"No. Why?"

He tittered.

"You know him?"

"He was playing at the Bürgerbraukeller, but they ran him out
a week ago."

"Why?"

"Ask them."

The Bürgerbraukeller, another American Army Service Club,
was no more, no less, than the hall wherefrom Hitler had led his
abortive march on the Bavarian parliament in 1923. In the Nazi
pantheon, a shrine.

Jake arrived just before closing time, screwing his eyes up
against the smoke, to see big and belligerent soldiers everywhere,
slouching over tables with checkered tablecloths, comatose,
listening to a hillbilly singer on the jukebox.

> am goin' back
> to war ah come from
> war the mockin' bird is singin'
> on the lilac bush

The manager had known Jesse Hope—yes—he had played here —it's true—but he was unwilling to discuss the matter with unauthorized personnel. Even a relative. Perhaps, if Mr. Hersh would return in the morning, the rabbi—

"*The what?*" Jake demanded, astounded.

"Captain Meltzer. He conducts services here on Saturday mornings. And he knew Jesse Hope."

Gehenna, yes, the very lowest regions. The innermost circle. Fifteen kilometers to Dachau, no more. Bring your Rolleiflex. Yet Jake slept very well indeed at his hotel and wakened with salubrious appetite. The rolls were delicious. So was the ham, so were the eggs. The coffee, the very best. The service, impeccable. Should he eat lunch at Humplmayr's, trying their fabled goose livers? Take a stroll in the English Gardens, perhaps? Look in at the Hofbrauhaus? Jake spread the phone book on the bed and looked up "Goering." Four entries. There were no Eichmanns, but plenty of Himmlers.

—Hello, Heinrich, what's cooking?

—Ask a foolish question. The Jews, what else?

Jake was back at the Bürgerbraukeller before ten in the morning, absolutely bewildered, unsure whether to be appalled or moved to see a sad little mouse of an army chaplain in a *talith* raise the holy scrolls aloft, before a makeshift sanctuary, in the very place where Adolph Hitler had fired his first two shots in the air. "Hear O Israel," he sang, "the Lord is our God, the Lord is One."

Jake and Rabbi Irwin Meltzer took coffee together at a café. The captain had once been a rabbi in Georgia. "Quite often," he intoned in a disconcertingly high-pitched voice, "I was wakened in the middle of the night. To rush to the hospital. Accidents. We were on the main highway to Florida, you see, and so many of the collisions involved our people . . ."

He had not been to England yet, but he was coming.

"Ah, London. Oliver Twist. Sherlock Holmes. Liza Doolittle. Centuries of literature. The pageant flashes before my mind."

Jake asked him about the Horseman.

"A very troubled spirit, I thought, looking for answers in the bottle, but not, mind you, without an interest in metaphysics."

"Is that so?"

"Once he actually came to services, smirking all the while, it's true, and red-eyed drunk, and then he cornered me. You know, rabbi, he said, you're right. The Lord is our God, and the Lord is One. But do you know why, rabbi? It is because our Lord has such a tapeworm inside him, such a prodigious appetite, that he can chew up six million Jews in one meal. And if the Lord, our God, were Two. What then? Twelve million. Who had them to spare at the time? So, the Lord our God is One, because Two we couldn't afford."

"And what," Jake asked, "did you say to that?"

"I pointed out to him that there are mysteries within mysteries and even in blasphemy, faith can take root. It was not for me to know everything, I forewarned him, and even in God's ground crew I was no more than a rifleman."

"Which didn't satisfy him?"

"No. It is commonly supposed, rabbi, he said, that in the camps there was no rebellion, our people went like sheep to the slaughter, but in fact survivors testify that among the Jews there was indeed rebellion of the most profound nature. Not against man. For what can be expected of other men? Venality, depravity, murder. Against God. The Holy Name. It is reported that in Auschwitz on Yom Kippur among the orthodox Jews there were those who did not fast for the first time in their lives. This much was for once denied the Lord, our God, who is One."

The rabbi ordered more coffee.

"My good man, I said, do not question the Almighty, or He might call you up for an answer."

"Now tell me what kind of trouble Joey ran into here."

"Trafficking in hashish, they said, but there was no positive proof, and in fact no formal charges were brought against him. He was, however, not very well liked. Either by our own men or the local folk. He was always bothering people, asking them questions. He was particularly interested in the affairs of the

Mengele family, who have a factory not far from here, in Günz-
berg. In a word, he wasn't the type to let sleeping dogs lie."

Joey, he added, had continued on to Baden-Soellingen, where
he had been booked to perform on the R.C.A.F. base.

R.C.A.F. 4 Wing, at Baden-Soellingen, lay in the green and
restful Schwarzwald, ringed by mountains that were rich in cool
pine trees and crumbling castles, and only fifteen minutes' drive
from the elegant spa of Baden-Baden. Spring, Jake had to allow,
suited the province splendidly. In the foothills and valleys, the
apple and pear and plum trees blossomed.

Jake talked his way past the sentry at the gate, flashing his
Canadian passport and old CBC identification papers, saying he
had come to look into the possibility of doing a TV documentary, and asking to see the PRO. He was directed to a sequence
of concrete apartment blocks, Permanent Married Quarters, just
outside the base proper. A sign in the hallway read:

ACTION ON FALLOUT WARNING

Go To Basement, At Time Told You

Do Not Eat, Drink, Smoke or Chew Until

Assured Food, Water, Etc. is Safe

Amiable, apple-cheeked F/O Jim Hanley wore a black disc
around his neck, a Dosimeter, so that in the event of fallout his
radiation level exposure could be measured. His companion, F/L
Robert Waterman, also wore one.

"Say, I wasn't expecting you until next week."

"You weren't?" Jake asked.

"Aren't you from the unit shooting *Freedom's Defenders?*"

"That's the ticket. But, like I'm an advance man. The rest of
the guys won't be out for a week or so."

"Let's go to the mess," Hanley said.

The school teachers attached to the base were in the midst of
a cocktail party and Jake mingled with them briefly. Small-town
Ontario gigglies. Lamely, Jake asked the first girl he brushed
against, "Like it here?"

"The Germans are a *fantastic* people," she replied. "*This* is the country for me."

Jake beamed. "We have a lot to learn from them, don't you think?" Then he slid away to the bar and the serious drinkers, settling on a stool under a sign that declared SECURITY IS ALWAYS IN SEASON.

"Your money's no good here," Jim Hanley bubbled. "Just tell me what brand of poison you prefer."

An American air force major, suggesting a failed insurance agent more strongly than Steve Canyon, bore down on them, eliciting hoots. The major, clutching his stomach, pretended to totter and, after a good deal of horseplay, finally agreed to a hair of the dog that bit him.

"How goes the battle?" Hanley asked.

"Fuck." The American major was attached to a combined NATO maneuver at a nearby French base. "It's a lousy war."

"What's wrong? Is it only a paper war?"

"Naw. We got refugees and all sorts of shit. The refugees are blocking the fucking roads. By the time the real fun starts, you're dead beat. I'd rather be back out there fighting the fucking gooks."

Their circle widened to include a tall, obdurate flying officer with an unusually thick neck and, ordering another drink, Jake regarded him with appetite.

"He's from security," Waterman said to Jake.

"Security?" Gravely, Jake asked the flying officer if he had any real fucking security problems on the fucking base. "With the mother-fucking commies."

"That's classified."

Waterman explained that Jake was from the CBC and clapping Jake on the back, he said, "I suppose you know you can't get to look at one of the CF-104's—that's classified too. But if you care to park outside the gates with high-powered binoculars you can copy down the serial numbers as the planes take off and land. In fact you can easily figure out how many planes we've got here and how often they fly."

"What about that?" Jake asked the security officer.

"No comment."

"Want to know how to build one," Waterman continued, "buy a copy of Model Airplane News. Hey, here comes our nuclear defense man. If the bomb falls his job is to tell everyone to fucking relax."

Jake detached the security officer from the rest. "If it isn't classified, can you tell me what you do for entertainment out here?"

"We've got a bowling alley. Movies. There's a hockey rink—"

"Ever have a singer called Jesse Hope play here?"

"Why?"

"I ran into him in Munich a couple of weeks back."

"A poker game?" the security man asked.

"Yeah."

"Son-of-a-bitch ran a game here that started on Friday night and ran right into Sunday afternoon. I figure he cleared out of here with something like three thousand fucking dollars."

Slowly, evenly, Jake replied: "Glad to hear it."

"Lookit, fella, you're drunk."

"Not yet. Waterman, what about another one for me?"

"Can do."

"Jesse Hope is my cousin."

"I wouldn't fucking brag about it."

"But I do, see," Jake said. "Because he's a real soldier, not a toy one. Not merely another dumb crud hanging his ass on a pension. He fought on the Ebro. Any idea where that is?"

"You tell us, buddy boy."

"It's classified."

"Hey, he *is* drunk."

"You believe it."

"It's in Spain. 'On that arid square, that fragment nipped off from hot Africa, soldered so crudely to inventive Europe . . .' He also fought in Israel in forty-eight. For Jerusalem," and leaning closer, Jake demanded, "any idea where that is?"

"You're a beaut."

"This joker says he's a cousin of the card sharp," the security officer announced. "Jesse Hope."

"You know why he left Israel? I've got it right here on a post-card he sent his wife. I quote, gentlemen. When Rubashov is in prison, as they march him up and down the yard for afternoon exercise, the crazed man behind him, another old Bolshevik, repeats over and over again, 'This could never happen in a socialist country.' Rubashov hasn't the heart to tell him they're actually in Russia. Unquote. Would you know who wrote that?"

No answer.

"Well, it wasn't Mazo de la Roche. It was Flying Officer Arty Koestler. *Chaver* Waterman, I require another drink."

"Why don't we push on?" Hanley asked, perturbed.

"Were you in the war?" Jake asked.

The security officer nodded.

"How does it feel having the Nazis for allies now?"

"Boy, you must be Hope's cousin. You got the same muscles in your shit."

Waterman intervened. "There might have been some Germans who once thought the Nazi Party was a good thing, but I never met any."

"They want to leave their past behind them," Hanley said.

"And you know something, taking the long view," Jake said, "they weren't such a bad lot. Let's say they murdered six million Jews, say five. Who wanted them? Joel Brand offered Lord Moyne a million of them in forty-four for some trucks and, as his Lordship put it so succinctly in Cairo, what shall I do with a million Jews? Where shall I put them? Right. And what, gentlemen, are our biggest problems today? Overpopulation and the mother-fucking commies. Six million Jews would have bred at least another six by this time and, let's face it, they would have voted communist in sufficient numbers to have put the reds in power in France and Italy after the war. And then what? Big trouble. You guys would still be based in Trenton, Ontario. Mosquito country. No PX. No maids. No supplementary gash."

"It doesn't surprise me that this Jesse Hope bird is your cousin," the security officer said.

"Sir, I should have thought anything beyond a Dr. Seuss Beginning Reader would surprise you, but never mind. Skip it."

"You're a beaut. You really are."

"Fetch me another one, Waterman."

"Tomorrow's another day. I think we'd better get you back to your hotel now."

"Yeah. Maybe."

But, once in Baden-Baden, Jake embraced Waterman and insisted he join him for a nightcap.

"Waterman, I like you. You've got wit. Intelligence. Style."

Waterman grinned good-naturedly. "Say, is Hope really your cousin?"

"No. I have figured out who he is. Finally. Jesse Hope, also known as Yosef Ben Baruch and Joey Hersh, is the Golem. Surely that surprises you?"

"What's the, um, Golem?"

"A sort of Jewish Batman."

"Oh."

"The Golem, for your information, is the body without a soul. He was made out of clay by Rabbi Judah Ben Bezalel in the sixteenth century to defend the Jews of Prague from a pogrom and, to my mind, still wanders the world, turning up wherever a defender is most needed. You lose much in the game, Waterman?"

"A couple of hundred maybe."

"Where was he going from here?"

"Frankfurt."

"Waterman, because you're such an original mind, and lovable, I'm going to let you in on something, a confidence, but you are not to say anything to the security officer."

"Sure thing."

"The CBC unit coming out here next week is only pretending to be shooting something called *Freedom's Defenders*. How many air women have you got stationed on the base?"

Waterman appeared perplexed.

"Is it classified?"

"Maybe a hundred."

"When the CBC unit arrives you keep close tabs on them. The

truth is they're really putting together a film on lesbians in the armed services. You'd better believe it, Waterman."

Frankfurt could only mean the Horseman was attending the proceedings against Robert Karl Ludwig Mulka, Friedrich Wilhelm Boger, Dr. Victor Capesius, and others of Auschwitz-Birkenau.

"Mengele cannot have been there all the time."

"In my opinion always. Night and day."

Dr. Mengele, Jake learned, sitting in the press section, was concerned about the women's block.

". . . The women often lapped up their food like dogs; the only source of water was right next to the latrine, and this thin stream also served to wash away the excrement. There the women stood and drank or tried to take a little water with them in some container while next to them their fellow sufferers sat on the latrines. And while this was going on the S.S. walked up and down and watched."

Bodies were gnawed by rats, as were unconscious women. The women were plagued by lice.

"Then Mengele came. He was the first one to rid the entire women's camp of lice. He simply had the entire block gassed. Then he disinfected the block."

As Hanna, St. Urbain's blight, had once scuttled from table to table at bar mitzvahs, flashing Joey's picture, stopping strangers in railway stations and shoving the photograph under the noses of startled arrivals in the air terminal, so Jake besieged reporters outside the court house, in bars and restaurants, asking whether they had seen the Horseman at any of the hearings.

"Sometimes when members of the special detail removed the bodies, they would find that the hearts of some of the children were still beating. That was reported and the children were shot."

"Were there also other methods of killing children?"

". . . I saw them take a child from its mother, carry it over to Crematory IV, which had two big pits, and throw the child into the seething human fat . . ."

Nobody at the court house, nobody in the bars, nobody in the restaurants had seen Joey. Neither was he performing in any of the nightclubs or cellars Jake sought out.

"Mengele cannot have been there all the time."

"In my opinion, always. Night and day."

If God weren't dead, it would be necessary to hang Him.

12

Jake directed his first film in 1965 and another the following year. The year Luke won a prize at Venice, not a word was heard of the Horseman, Molly fractured her ankle, Hanna suffered a mild stroke, and he bought the sprawling house Nancy had found for them in Hampstead. In the autumn, Nancy discovered she was pregnant again. She was well into her eighth month, in April 1967, when Jake had to fly to Montreal. Cancer, which had lodged in Issy Hersh's kidney three years earlier, had been cut out, flared again and been trimmed with a knife again, taken root, and spread tentacles throughout his body.

"What can be done?" Jake asked his father's doctor.

"Nothing. He's filled with it from here to here."

Dragging himself unwillingly back to Issy Hersh's sweltering apartment, which overlooked an Esso service station, Jake sat by the bedside telling his shriveled father how once he was well again they would take in Expo together, with VIP treatment laid on, and they would drive to the Catskills, just the two of them, all roads leading to Grossinger's, but Issy Hersh continued to stare at him with large vacant eyes. Jake told him how his own son, Sammy (bound to outlive both of us, the little snot-nose) often asked about the *zeyda*, but this elicited no response from the head lolling on the crushed pillow. He assured his father that he was happily married. Yes, yes, the old man's eyes responded, but to a *shiksa*.

MIXED MARRIAGES STINK!

Jake sat by his father's bedside and invited him to come to London and stay with them. They would take in the strip shows in Soho together, hornier than anything the old Gayety had ever dared to offer. But Issy Hersh did not react. So Jake began to ramble on about the old days, trying Tansky's Cigar & Soda for size, evoking the summer shack in Shawbridge, but his father, his eyes turned inward, did not smile. Jake promised to buy him a cane, he offered him a new dressing gown. He reminded his father about Saturday mornings at the Young Israel synagogue, he chattered about *seders* past, the first time they had been to the steam baths together, but he could bring no spark to his father's eyes. Finally, he helped Issy Hersh into his dressing gown, trying not to stare at the wasted body, his father's hitherto ballooning belly reduced to an empty flap overhanging surgical cuts that circled him like a belt. Supporting him on his paralyzed side, Jake led him into the stuffy, cluttered living room, and the TV set, where father and son watched the Jackie Gleason show together, Issy Hersh wheezing with laughter, his eyes suddenly sparkling.

"Oh, boy, that Gleason, the crazy fool, the spots he gets into . . . Do you get the show in London?"

"No," Jake snarled, and he dared to ask his father a direct question about his mother and the year of their divorce.

"Water over the dam," his father replied, smiling again, his pleasure-filled eyes claimed by Gleason.

"I know him," Jake put in angrily.

"You know Jackie Gleason . . . personally?"

Jake basked in his father's awe.

"In real life is he . . . such a boozer?"

"Yes."

Issy Hersh smiled, satisfied, and did not speak again until the commercial break. "Do you get *Bonanza* in London?"

"Yes."

"He's a Canadian, you know, Lorne Green. A Jewish boy."
Then, as if it was too much to hope for, he added, "Do you
know him?"

"In the old days," Jake said, "I would never use him."

"You mean to say you could have had . . . Lorne Green . . .
for a part . . . and you didn't . . . ?"

"Absolutely."

Liar, the old man's eyes replied. "He's a millionaire now, you
know. He really made it."

On screen, Bobby Hull tooled down the sun-dappled 401 in a
Ford Meteor. Coming on strong.

"You wouldn't know James Bond. What's his name?"

"Yes I do."

"In real life, what's he like?"

"Natural," Jake said vengefully. Then, just as his father's gaze
was reverting to the TV screen, Jake retrieved him. "He's after
me to direct his next picture."

"Hey, there's a lot of money in that."

"Would you be proud of me?"

"James Bond. Boy."

Jake, embarrassed by his lie, said nothing more, and once
Gleason was done he supported his father back to the bed he
would never quit again. "The trouble is we never talk," Jake
said, "never really talk to each other."

"Who needs quarrels?"

Jake helped his father out of his dressing gown and eased him
on to the bed, where he lay briefly uncovered, an old man in a
sweat-soiled vest and shorts, smiling dependently. Reaching for
his blanket, Jake caught a glimpse of his father's penis curling
out of his jockey shorts. A spent worm. Jake's mouth opened, a
cry of rage dying in his throat. Years and years ago, he and
Rifka used to listen by their bedroom door on Friday nights,
hands clasped to their mouths to suppress giggles, as Issy Hersh
padded to the kitchen stove in his long Penman's underwear,
flung the used condom into the sabbath fire, where it sizzled
briefly, and then retreated to his bed. Matching singles they had,
each with a red chenille bedspread. In another bedroom, Jake

remembered, a different time, this cock was my maker. He stooped to kiss his father good night.

"Everybody kisses me these days," Issy Hersh said, bemused.

"You're popular."

"Those James Bond pictures are big hits, real money-makers. You should have seen the lineups here for the last one."

"Yes," Jake said at the door. "I'm sure."

"Oh, Yankel?"

"Yes."

"You get the *Playboy* magazine?"

"Yes."

"When you're through with them, you could send them on to me. I wouldn't mind."

Issy Hersh's wife, Fanny, risen from the basement with a basket of laundry, waylaid Jake in the hall.

"I love your father, he's been a wonderful husband to me, I'm taking excellent care of him."

"I'm grateful. So is Rifka."

"They wanted to put him in an incurable hospital, they said it would be too much work for me, but I said no, he's not going to die there."

"For Chrissake, he isn't deaf. He can hear us."

"It's good you came here. You must be doing very well."

"What?"

"Well, the trip from England is expensive. I'm so glad you're doing well and that we've grown fond of each other. You and your wife will always be welcome here. I'm not one of your aunts, a snob. I don't look down my nose." Now she paused, a hedge-shy horse before the big leap. "Being Jewish isn't everything."

"I'll tell Nancy you said that. See you tomorrow."

The next evening, the first night of Passover, Rifka came with Herky and their two rowdy overfed boys. Lenny was twelve, Melvin only five years old. Fanny had set up a bridge table in the bedroom for the *seder* and Jake, a skullcap balanced on his head, rose to ask the four questions falteringly. Turning to his father on the bed he recited, "Why is this night different from all other nights? For on all other nights we eat either bread or matzoh, but tonight only matzoh. For on all other nights we eat any vegetable, but tonight—bitter herbs."

The old man's eyes were glazed; he made no response.

Years ago, Jake recalled, when the time had come to pass around the hard-boiled eggs, his father had unfailingly grinned and asked, "Do you know why the hebes dip their eggs in salt water on *Pesach?*"

"No, Daddy. Why?"

"Because when they crossed the Red Sea, the men got their eggs soaked in salt water."

Jake continued: "For on all other nights we do not dip our vegetables even once, but tonight—"

It was the doorbell; Elijah the Prophet come early to claim his cup.

"The doctor!" Fanny exclaimed. The long-awaited specialist. A Gentile.

Let me take your hat, sir. This way, sir. Thank you, sir.

They all waited in the living room while the specialist examined Issy Hersh, his unnervingly cheery voice carrying clearly through the wall.

"Well, well. You don't look that bad. How old are you?"

"Sixty-five, sir . . ."

"When were you born?"

Issy Hersh surfaced with a date. Another century's wintry morning in a Galician *shtetl*.

"What's today? Can you tell me?"

"Wednesday . . . no, no . . . Tuesday . . ."

"Can't always get out just the word you want. Is that right?"

A muffled acquiescence.

"Would you play a game with me, Mr. Hersh?"

"Yes, sir."

"Name off the months of the year for me."

"January . . . February . . . March . . ."

Sapient Herky fixed Jake with a knowing look. "He's testing the old man's reactions."

Jake glowered and scooped up his bottle of Passover wine,

which he had prudently filled with forbidden Remy Martin.

"Difficulty swallowing?" the specialist inquired.

"Yes, sir."

Fanny Hersh's foolish eyes glowed with pleasure. "When Bronfman was sick, with all his millions, he had the same specialist. He's world-renowned."

"Daddy's made it at last," Jake announced, turning on Rifka. "The hands that have probed Bronfman orifices are actually touching him."

Rifka bounded from the sofa to hurry her boys out to buy ice cream sundaes.

"If we can just turn you . . . that's it," the specialist said. "Are you related to Jacob Hersh?"

"He's my son."

"Is that so?"

". . . come all the way from London to see me. He's going to direct the next James Bond film."

"Hey," Herky said, suddenly alert. "Congrats."

"He's doing very, very well."

"Need any help on the casting couch?"

As Rifka was about to reclaim her place beside Herky on the sofa, her spreading bottom threatening the flattened pillow, Herky slid his hand under, the thumb protruding like a spike. "Gotcha."

Rifka sprang forward, giggling.

"You goddam fools," Jake hissed.

"I'm using psychology, you shmock. If we go back into that bedroom wringing our hands will it do him any good?"

No sooner did the specialist emerge from the bedroom than Jake hustled him into the outside hall.

"We haven't met yet, doctor. My name's Jacob Hersh."

"I've always admired your work on television."

"Thank you. Now look, I know my father's filled with cancer . . . but, well, what happens next?"

"Cerebral hemorrhage, possibly. Maybe a heart attack. Or his lungs."

"He thinks he's recuperating. He'd like to have exercises, therapy."

"If you want, I can arrange it. But they don't like working on terminal cases. It's depressing for them."

"It's depressing for my father." He wasn't, Jake discovered, on morphine yet. "How long has he got?"

"He won't last the summer."

Jake waited.

"Six weeks maybe."

13

And what of me, Jake thought, flying back to London, what of me and my house? Nancy, Sammy, Molly, and the baby to come. Only a week before Molly was born, he remembered, Mrs. Hersh had insisted on coming over to stay with them.

Upstairs, Nancy put Sammy to bed, singing.

"On the first day of Christmas,
my true love gave to me,
a partridge in a pear tree."

Downstairs, Mrs. Hersh kept Sammy busy, helping him make a Lego building.

"Do you know what this building is called, precious one? It's a synagogue."

Sammy continued to add to his structure.

"Where we pray," Mrs. Hersh said.

"Church."

"No, synagogue. Now say it after grandmaw. Synagogue."

"Synahog."

"Oh, my precious lamb. Yes. Synagogue."

They were a new breed, these mixed-marriage kids. With a Christmas tree in December and matzohs in April. Instead of being unwanted, hounded here for being Christ-killers, mocked there for being bland WASPS, they belonged everywhere. With a stake in Jehovah and a claim on Christ. A taste for hot cross buns and bagels.

Bloody Rifka, on first being presented with Sammy, had instantly rummaged through his nappy. "I see you've had him done, Jake. That's something."

Then the squealing infant Molly had been brought in for her and Herky to comparison-shop.

"A blondie," Rifka said, pursing her lips.

"So was I," Jake protested pointedly, "when I was a kid, remember?"

"And all babies have blue eyes," Herky added placatingly, "isn't that a fact?"

Many brandies later, back at their suite in Grosvenor House, Herky sat down beside Jake, his manner suddenly conspiratorial yet benevolent, and whispered, "I want to talk to you, kiddo."

"Go ahead, then."

Herky rose to listen by the bedroom door, satisfying himself that Rifka was asleep. "There's something you ought to know."

Rifka shoplifts. "Yes," Jake said warily.

"It's all right now. Everything's A-O.K."

"Good."

"You can come home." Herky patted Jake's cheek, tears welling in his eyes. "Time heals. You read me?"

"Speak plainly, will you?"

"You married a *shiksa*. The family didn't exactly flip with joy. So you did the decent thing, not to embarrass us within the community, and you didn't move to Montreal with her. You stayed on here."

"*What?*"

"Well, some of us have more modern ideas now and in any case she obviously keeps a clean house for you and you've got kids now and, well, I've had a talk with your father. To make a long story short, it's O.K." Beaming magnanimously, he said: "You can come home, Yankel."

"But, Herky, I live in London out of choice."

"What's pride? Pride is foolishness. What are you handing me a bill of goods? It's Herky here, your brudder-in-law."

Desperately Jake grabbed the brandy bottle and poured himself another one.

"Do you mean to say," Herky demanded, "you'd actually prefer living here than in Montreal?"

"Yes."

"But they're such cold fish. Even the Jews you meet here speak with a la-di-da accent. Aw, you're kidding me."

"I'm not kidding you. Honestly."

"But everything is so broken and old in Europe. At home, we're really going places. Do you know you can drive to Ste. Agathe these days in an hour flat? It's the new highway. *Six lanes.*"

The children's mixed heritage, and Jake's faltering attempts to imbue them with a sense of social justice, all came together or, rather, temporarily unstuck, over the garden problem, which culminated in Jake's humiliation two days before Christmas.

When Nancy finally bought a house for them in Hampstead, in April 1966, Jake drove in from Pinewood, where he was shooting, to look it over; he pushed open the French doors in the rear and, lo and behold, there was this seemingly endless unfilled green space. Thick with overgrown and prickly bushes. A stagnant pond buzzing with mosquitoes in the middle, and an Anderson shelter crumbling at the far end.

Immediately, Nancy's goysy Ontario childhood came to the fore, aglow with the memory of granny churning her own ice cream—raspberry picking—homemade jam—old grandad pricking out beds in the greenhouse. "Lookit, Nancy, it's such a big sky." *Ontari-ari-ario.* Toronto-liberated mother enthralled to be shoveling pig shit again, singing, Hi, Neighbor, as some Mennonite freak moseys past. And, lookee yonder, it's the Ford V-8, Dad come out for the weekend, escaping the incomprehensible city, where Jewboys own the shoe factories and try, try, try, he couldn't sell enough to please Mr. Goldstein. Goldarn it.

"Henry," mother calls, "the fish sure are jumpin' in the creek."

"Yippee!"

Nancy licked Jake's ear, she hugged him, and initiated him to the splendors of their cabala, confounding him with talk of herbaceous and mixed borders, biennials and autumn stalwarts.

Appalled, confused, Jake gruffly reminded her that this was alien to him, he had been raised on urban backyards, wherein you dumped punctured tires and watermelon husks and cracked sinks and rotting mattresses. Within weeks, however, it was Jake who emerged as the household's most perfervid gardener, taking it as his directorial duty to impose order on such an unseemly mess. He came out of John Barnes with a two-stroke lawn mower, pruners, shears, tubs, rakes, insidious sprays, seeds, and secateurs. The following afternoon, as soon as Nancy had gone out shopping, he set to work with Sammy and Molly, burning masses of autumn leaves and clearing his spread, his Hampstead holding as it were, just like Van Heflin in *Shane*. He uprooted one barren-looking bush after another, trimmed the rhododendrons and, forking over the soil, stabbed into some seemingly cancerous-type growths, all of which he unearthed and stacked in the barrow.

Nancy was not pleased. "Oh God," she exclaimed.

Autumn leaves, properly rotted, she pointed out delicately, could be of enormous value. The scraggly things he had uprooted were in fact mature rose bushes and the cancerous growths he had dug out were not only nonmalignant, they were peony tubers. Bloody *shiksa*, he thought, seething inwardly, Ontario hick, you don't know the Holy One's Secret Name, the sayings of Rabbi Akiba, or how to exorcise a dybbuk, but you would know that sort of crap, and he retreated to the living room to sulk and study his newly acquired gardening manuals. The Orangeman's Talmud.

It was no use. He lacked the touch. So Jake shiftily argued that what with the need to decorate and furnish a newly acquired house, as well as there being the children to attend to, they ought to hire a jobbing gardener to come in twice a week. They're hopeless, Nancy warned. Overriding her objections, he insisted. Largely because he wanted control, and the hired hand was bound to be responsible to him in his office as guv'ner. But beery old Tom, the gardener, a Scots countryman cunning as he was leathery, with a hound's nose for class distinctions, immediately sniffed out an urban rat in Jake, somebody who didn't know leaf curl from mildew and, from the first, he merely tolerated him, his smile small. Nancy was something else again. Nancy, poised and knowledgeable, the beautiful countrywoman fallen into the hairy Jew's grasp, he truly revered and constantly deferred to. Standing by the window, outraged, Jake watched them stroll together through his garden, two bores out of a Thomas Hardy novel, delighting in rustic trivia, exchanging their Gentile secrets, the text derived from the Protocols of the Elders of the Compost Heap.

Determined to eke at least a splinter of satisfaction out of Tom's presence, Jake tried to use him as a case in point to further Sammy's sense of social justice. As his son, home early from prep school, raced across the garden to him, shouting they had won the cricket match for once, Jake suddenly said: "Tom's grandchildren won't go to a private school, but you're not better than they are."

Sammy stared, startled.

"What I mean is your grandfather is a poor Jew," Jake continued defensively.

Only the evening before, at the school concert, Jake had sat, the only glowering man among as many beaming parents, as Sammy sang with the others:

"Away in a manger, no crib for a bed,
The little Lord Jesus laid down his sweet head:
The stars in the bright sky looked down where he lay,
The little Lord Jesus asleep on the hay."

The next afternoon, after a hard day's editing at Pinewood, Jake poured himself a gin and tonic and thought to seek solace in his garden. There, lying in wait, shedding his sweat-stained fedora to mop his brow, was the cunning old *goy*. Jake felt obliged to return to the kitchen and fetch his hired man a gin as well, which made him resentful. He couldn't fob Tom off with a beer as that went against his egalitarian ideas. It was also a bad example for Sammy. But even sharing his liquor with Tom, he was made to feel an intruder in his own garden. For Jake had only to sink into a deck chair in the shade for old Tom to begin to dig with maniacal drive. He thinks I only sit out here to demand my pound of flesh, Jake thought, and he dismissed Tom abruptly, doing the old man out of two afternoons' work a week rather than continue to subject both of them to embittering class conflict.

"Why doesn't Tom come any more?" Sammy asked.

"I fired him. He was lazy," Jake blurted out, remembering too late that only the night before, tucking in Sammy, he had explained to him that it was unforgivably rotten to complain, as other parents did, about how lazy the working man was. "Men like old Tom," he had said, "and others, who work on factory assembly lines, have to do jobs they hate in order to earn their daily bread. So, naturally, they're resentful and do their jobs grudgingly. Really, there's nothing worse for a grown man than to have to go to a job he hates day after day. You're getting a good education and when you grow up you will be able to choose. You won't be forced into soul-destroying work. So you must always be especially considerate to those who weren't so lucky."

And now, not surprisingly, Sammy looked at his father quizzically. All eyes.

"He wasn't lazy. He annoyed me."

Tom continued to labor for others on Jake's road. In the evening, Jake would step up to the saloon bar in his local, ordering a large gin; and, in the public bar, rolling a cigarette with a shaky hand as he contemplated his pint, sat Tom, his smile malevolent.

Come autumn, Tom was seen less and less often on the road. Nobody needed him. But only two days before Christmas, he surfaced again.

Yuletide was, in any event, an uneasy season for Jake, the tree in the living room an affront no matter how rationally he explained it away to himself. As a fertility symbol. As a pagan ritual. As Nancy's birthright, and the children's, for after all they did spring from both traditions, and in Hersh's half-breed house they did not festoon the tree with anything but interfaith baubles. Which is to say, there was no haloed *Yoshka* riding over all. And yet—and yet—hang it with chocolate Santas, spray it with silver, drape it with colored balls, even rub it down with chicken fat, if you like, and, by God, it was still a Christmas tree. His forebears hadn't fled the *shtetl*, surviving the Czar, so that the windows of the second generation should glitter on Christmas Eve like those of the Black Hundreds of accursed memory. Old Hanna, for one, would have said, feh, Yankel. Yes, yes, he argued with her, but this was Nancy's home too. Sammy's and Molly's maternal *zeyda* was merely a *goy.* Untroubled by Spinoza, not perplexed by the enigmas of the Zohar, he was, to be fair, nourished by the intellectual illuminations common to his breed. He perceived, for instance, that wrestling matches were fixed, and having allowed him as much, Jake was so pleased with himself that he slapped his knee and laughed out loud.

Typically, this Christmas as last, he put the offending tree out of mind to lose himself in the pleasures of shopping with Nancy. After all, looked at objectively the holiday was no more than an excuse for gift-giving and overeating with loved ones. They plunged into Harrod's, demanding Norfolk-bred turkey and a Yorkshire ham; and in Fortnum's, they splurged on caviar and vintage wines. The smoked salmon, an ecumenical concession, came from Cohen's; and once more, Jake insisted on chopped liver as well, preparing it himself, lustily singing *Adon Olam* in the kitchen as he wielded his chopper. His gesture to Jehovah.

It was after just such a shopping expedition, only two days before Christmas, that Jake answered the door in his slippers to discover the long stooping cop with the correct face standing there.

"I'm sorry to trouble you, sir. But were you robbed last night?"

"No. Certainly not," Jake protested, and peering over the bobby's shoulder Jake noticed a plainclothesman sitting in the rear of the car. Beside him, his smile small under his battered and discolored fedora, was old and leathery Tom. "Hey, that's my old gardener."

"Ah, well, that explains it." He would not have bothered Jake, the bobby went on to say, had the man not been able to accurately describe the interior of his house. "This is the season for them," he allowed, grinning, "isn't it?"

"What do you mean, it's the season for them?"

"Suddenly, it's winter. The weather turns nasty. There's no work. Their minds turn to the problem of bread and board for the coming months. So they come to the station in droves, claiming to have robbed somebody's house, hoping the state will tide them over until the spring."

"Wait, officer. Maybe I'm mistaken. He could have stolen something, you know. Something small maybe," Jake ventured.

The sergeant was impassive.

"Come in, won't you? I'll just run upstairs to check things out."

But Nancy said there was nothing Jake could do for Tom now. Unconvinced, he raced down the stairs to confront the sergeant again. "Well now, officer," he asked, beaming, "I wonder if you could enlighten me on a point of law?"

"Possibly, sir."

"How much would the old man have to take to get three months?"

"If you are missing anything, you must swear out a complaint against him," he replied, taking out his pad.

"Oh," Jake said, retreating.

"It would be your duty."

"Duty? The old bastard's got nowhere to sleep. Do you want him to die of exposure?"

"That, sir, is hardly my affair."

"What is your affair, then," Jake suddenly charged, exploding. "Breaking up demonstrations? Beating up West Indians?"

"Steady on."

Nancy appeared at the top of the stairs, aghast.

"British justice," Jake scoffed.

"You an American, then?" the sergeant inquired, bemused.

"No. I'm a Canadian. What's your name?" Jake demanded hotly.

He told him.

"Oh ho," Jake chortled. "Ah ha," he said, rubbing his hands and looking up at a horrified Nancy. "Well then, that fits, doesn't it, mate?"

"Why?" he asked, baffled.

"How do you spell it?"

"H-O-A-R-E."

Hours passed before a rueful Jake emerged from his aerie.

"We're all becoming our fathers, you know," he said to Nancy. "Luke's joined the Garrick Club and I'm turning out a fool. How could I behave like that?"

Gathering his photographic equipment together, Harry decided, what the hell, he would treat himself to a taxi tonight, and hailing one, he gave the driver the address of the Graphic Arts Society in Fulham.

Bloody ridiculous, he thought, descending into the basement, more than usually standoffish with the others waiting about. Bowler hat bunch tonight, mostly. Commuters. Laden down with cameras, light meters, tripods, and, in some cases, props for the girls.

Eventually, the professor's assistant, a massive but good-natured capon, made his appearance. "Hello, hello, hello. The model we've selected for you tonight, at no regard for expense, is Miss Angela, star of more than one Harrison Marks flick. 39-23-38. Yes, my darlings, 39. So stand back. Make room. We'll be expecting more than one bright idea from you tonight. Angela will submit to active type poses, but—but—with this proviso. Nothing on the kinky side, duckies, that's what her boy friend says, and you wouldn't want to mess with him. Would you now, you naughty things?"

Miss Angela, adorned in a diaphanous blue negligée, a frilly suspender belt, and black stockings, drifted into the studio, sat herself on a stool, and contemplated the men with indifference. Refusing cigarettes, scorning chitchat. Allowing only Harry a small wave of recognition.

"Enjoy the flick?" Harry asked.

"Smashing. Ta."

The professor, wearing a blue beret, a foulard knotted around his neck, black velvet shirt, levis, and sandals, skipped onstage to initiate the proceedings with a lecture illustrated with slides from his classical studies. As his assistant doused the lights and projected the first slide, he began. "You will note here that it is the forward surge of the human figure that tautens the model's locomotor muscles and gives such a sense of irresistible movement. Next, please . . . Ah, Stella. Here again you will observe that it is the extension of the figure, giving suspension to full breasts, that so enhances the suggestion of pride and dignity. But in this case you can also plainly see that it is the confluence of the most effective lines into a central void, a visual balance carefully maintained between centrifugal and centripedal forces, supplemented by the dispersion of irregular and interlocking triangular shapes, that renders such opportunity for an appreciation of the angular qualities of the figure."

Finally, the professor did his bit for those who were, perhaps, visiting the academy for the first time, relating his troubles past and present, with the censors, and warning them that the price of artistic freedom was eternal vigilance. He speculated on what a foolish and hypocritical world they lived in, a world wherein anybody might walk into a British post office, purchase a money order, and send off to liberated Denmark for absolutely anything, whereas prize-winning British photographers, such as himself, were unable to compete by supplying a domestic market, not to mention contributing to export trade that would, incidentally, bolster the Back Britain campaign. Allowing that signed copies of his own book were available for five guineas, he concluded, "Just as graphic artists, from time immemorial, have found the unadorned nude an ideal subject for stereographic, that is to say, solid, drawing, so does today's photographic artist discover in the nude his only possible medium for the proper understanding of the play of light on irregular morphic masses."

Then the men surged forward, lugging their cameras and tripods and props, jostling for position in the queue, and Miss Angela descended from her high stool to stand under the lights.

"Would you be a dear and hold this cane? Ta. Now threaten me with it."

Click.

"And again."

Click.

"And once more. Bless you."

Then the next man edged forward, crouching behind his camera. "Stick your tongue out. Jiggling it."

Click.

"Yes. Bless you."

Click.

"And could you drop your nightie now? Leaning forward a bit more. Super."

Click.

"Yes. Hold it."

And the next man.

"Give me a filthy look. Stronger. As if I've suggested something absolutely unspeakable. Lovely, dear. Lovely."

Harry's turn at last.

"Last two chaps didn't have any film in their cameras."

Which earned a knowing giggle from Angela, who then extended her hands for Harry to slip on the cuffs, and shook her blue negligée off her shoulders, letting it float to the floor. "Shall I look scared, luv?"

"Absolutely terrified, because," and Harry leaned forward to whisper in her ear, demonstrating just one of his special privileges, "it's bleeding Neville Heath coming after you. It's Ian Brady come calling."

"Oooo," she sang out, shuddering.

15

Jake had waited forever, it seemed, for the opportunity to make a film, and so long as he had actually been immersed in its production, agonizing over the script with the writer, casting, shooting, and, most enjoyable, editing, he had been able to believe his labors had point, but once the film was finished and it had opened, he could see all too clearly that what he had brought forth was neither splendid nor odious, but merely good. Another interesting film for the circuit. The energy he and others had expended, the one million two hundred thousand dollars they had consumed, could have been used much more beneficially providing shelter for the homeless, food for the hungry. So much for honor, so much for grace.

Beginning work on his second film, a thriller, in 1966, Jake grasped that he was thirty-six and being young was something past and done with. He was thirty-six and a professional; no more. For the first time in his life, it seemed, susceptible to germs. His teeth had begun to loosen and slide. His bowels burned, cherry-size hemorrhoids blocking the passage.

1 Family in 22
in Britain today
is affected by Heart Disease

THE HEART
What makes it tick
How 60,000 miles
of arterial plumbing
can go wrong.

It was winter, a season Jake abhorred, especially in London, where there was neither sun nor snow, only lowering gray skies. Once winter had been something to endure and spring could not come quickly enough for him. Now he yearned for time to pass at a less febrile pace. Spring was no longer a celebration so much as another season to be counted. Something to be consumed and not to be had again. Something to be filed with a year number and entered in a ledger. "In spring 1967, as my father lay dying, I . . ." Proust put off for so many seasons would now have to be read or discarded. If he did not see Athens this year, next he might be too busy. Or ill.

Lying in bed with Nancy, their bodies entwined, his hands clasping her breasts, had once filled him with such content that he had taken it for a fuller expression of their love than the passion of other nights, so quickly spent. Now death muzzled him here as everywhere else. Lying together, he could think only of the obtruding bones beneath the wasting flesh. When she turned to kiss him, heavy with sleep, he sometimes caught a whiff of sour breath. The rot eating into the walls of her stomach and, most assuredly, his. DEATH, SIGNS OF. *Hippocratic countenance*, discoloration of the skin, failure of ligature, *Hypostasis*, loss of heat, rigidity. "Putrefaction is a certain sign, and begins in two or three days, as a greenish tint over the abdomen."

For Nancy. For Sammy, for Molly. The baby to come. For me too.

What compounded Jake's sense of oppression was an inner conviction that it was all so unspeakably banal; after all, fear of aging and death was something he shared with all men approaching middle age inexorably. Even so, there was at least one extraordinary circumstance. He was happily married. Oh, he sometimes thought, if only his union with Nancy was oppressive, stale, charged with resentments and acrimony, he could then, like most of his film acquaintances, seek solace with vacuous girls, indulging in sex without love, punishing himself, as it were. Like Myer Gross.

"Listen here, Jake, you think I enjoy deceiving Sylvia? I like her. I'm genuinely fond of her. Every time I have it off with a new secretary it's anguish for me. I'm so guilt-ridden, I suffer palpitations, and that's not good for me, you know."

"And so, Myer, why do you . . . ?"

"Well, once it was every night, even twice a night, but now we make it, let's say, once a week, going at it like dray horses, it's an effort for me to keep it up and I don't even think she comes any more. It's only the sound effects now. But if you could see me in the sack with an enthusiastic new puppy. Young. Firm. I'm a youngster again. A bull . . . Maybe I'm doing the wrong thing. But if that's the case, Jake, I'm the one who will pay for it in the end."

Dr. O'Brien pumped Myer Gross's rump full of hormones, Bob Cohen swore by an evil-smelling concoction he mashed into a glass each morning, and C. Bernard Farber mainlined a Hungarian recipe, made of crushed bumblebees. Ziggy Alter was irrigated regularly at Forest Mere. With me, Monty Talman confessed to Jake, it isn't a question of sex. "To tell you the truth, I'm a bigger talker than a doer. If I'm unfaithful, it's fundamentally because I know I bore her. Shit, we've been together eighteen years, there isn't a story of mine she doesn't know and couldn't tell better than me. Picture this. We've got new people coming to dinner, I start to tell a story and right off I can see her eyes glaze over. Or, if she's really in a rotten mood, out she comes with the punch line. Jake, I never drove women crazy with my sexual prowess, but I like to make them laugh. It gives me a real charge to make their eyes light up, and when I walk into the White Elephant I like to be seen with a chick that makes the others burn with envy. My God, you don't know what a pleasure it is to take a girl out now, a stranger, and to have her hang on my stories, exploding when I reach the climax.

The truth is there's a flaw in my makeup. I like to impress people. It's my Achilles' Heel. But how could I impress Zelda any more. I fart in bed. I start into an anecdote and buzz, buzz, I hear her thoughts cutting me down like a saw. Liar, she's thinking, exaggerator, bullshit artist. O.K., it's true, all of it, but I'm making good money, the years are flying, did I need someone in the house to remind me of it day in and day out?"

Jake's trouble was that more than any other woman, he wanted Nancy. After ten years, she still excited him in bed. Worse news. He enjoyed talking to her. Fortunately, the others were tolerant. They grasped that if Jake didn't philander it wasn't because he was a miser, like the legendary Otto Gelber, a producer who had married a tiny woman only because it meant fewer skins for the mink coat and, hiring a secretary, didn't demand sexiness above all but sought a girl who cut her nails short and could actually type. Rather than trade his wife in after her menopause, Gelber wasn't ashamed to drive the same model year in and year out. Instead of keeping a mistress, he jerked off in his office every afternoon. "Using a paperback," C. Bernard Farber swore.

Lou Caplan, Al Levine, Talman, and the rest of the film crowd Jake played baseball and poker with were mostly ten years older than he was; he agreed with Nancy that they were corrupt, their wives hard, and understood when she preferred to read in bed rather than endure another of their parties. But Jake forgave them everything for their wit, their appetite, and their ability to rub hope together with *chutzpah* to evoke a film. And from time to time he was touched, as when he discovered the usually ebullient Fiedler drinking alone at Tiberio's at one in the morning, disconsolate, gray in the face and chewing pills. "I can't take these parties any more. They're killing me."

"Why did you go, then?"

"But I left early," he protested. "Here I am. What am I doing here? Dropped in for a nightcap. I should be home in bed."

"Go, then."

"If I hadn't gone to the party, I'd feel I was missing something. Or there are bastards who'd say I haven't been invited. Like I didn't count any more. I have to put in an appearance, you know." He shrugged. "Wherever I go, Jake, I feel I'm missing something. Other guys are having a better time somewhere else and, shit, if I go there, it still seems like the wrong place. It's only the next morning I discover the action was somewhere else altogether. I'm under pressure. My pulse rate makes the doctor turn pale. How about that?"

"Go home, Harry. Get some sleep."

"Yeah. You're right," and he gulped down his drink. "Hey, wait. Come with me to Annabel's. There are going to be a couple of girls there."

As usual, Jake declined. Which is not to say he wasn't tempted from time to time, that after a bad day he couldn't have coped very nicely with a little something on the side. A dalliance, a diversion. Like Cy Levi, who approached all women with ardor, dizzy with desire at parties and in restaurants.

"You see that one over there? No, at the next table. She's got just the kind of ears you like to pull when she's going down on you, don't you think?"

Cy had grieved, he had pulled his hair, he had wept and switched to a Reichian lay analyst before he had been able to divorce his wife. All because of their eleven-year-old boy, whom he adored.

"You tell him, she kept saying. It's your decision. You tell him. So finally, you know, I took him into the living room and shut the door. Biting back the tears, I said, Mark, there are some things you are too young to understand. Brace yourself, boy. And taking his hand in mine, stroking it, I said, I'm leaving your mother, but this does not mean I don't love you. I adore you. I will see you every weekend. Saturday and Sunday, yours. I make no other plans. I am at your service. Now, your mother is a splendid woman. But adults, well, they're difficult, and to be honest we don't get along any more. It's not her fault, it's not mine. We decided it would be best for you if we parted and you were not raised in a bad atmosphere, like I was, for my parents, God bless them, abominated each other and made my childhood miserable. They weren't honest, as I'm trying to be with you. So I'm leaving, son. I will take care of your mother and you. I don't expect you to understand now, but I beg of you not to judge. Love me, Mark, as I love you. Later, understanding will come . . . And blowing my nose, searching his baby-blues for reaction—emotion—anything—I said, that's it, kid. Now what do you say? You know what he said? He said is it all right if I stay up to watch Bonanza tonight?"

Jake was sufficiently tolerant of himself to understand it wouldn't mean anything if he strayed, but given the opportunity he simply liked Nancy too much to humiliate her. He could not abide the idea of her being introduced to another woman at a party, his afternoon's vagary, the other woman throbbing with secret knowledge. He lacked the reckless style of Manny Gordon, for instance, who exulted in watching his wife and mistress of the moment trade niceties at a dinner table, only to nab Jake afterwards, "Oh, am I ever a bastard! But, you know, I live with it now. *That's* where analysis pays off."

Jake also lacked the subtlety, not to say the rich background, of Moey Hanover.

Years and years ago, reading the *Gemara* with his *zeyda*, sharing a glass bowl of pistachios, pinging shells together into a saucer, Moey had learned that if a man holds a sword out of a third-floor window and flying past comes another man, and he stabs him, is the man guilty of murder? Not so simple, says Reb Gamaliel. Was the flying man, for example, going to his death anyhow? Did he jump, asked Rabbi Eleazar, son of Azariah, or was he pushed? Were they related, inquired the sagacious Raschi?

Seemingly, this was a futile exercise in arcane law, with no possible future applications, but it had in fact enabled Moey to grasp at an early age that truth was a many-splendored thing; it had its nuances. So when his wife charged that he had been seen leaving the Paramount Hotel at four in the afternoon, arm in arm with an obvious tart, he had been able to swear to Lilian, hand over his boy's head, that, appearances notwithstanding, he had not been unfaithful to her.

For, he argued with himself, to be unfaithful is to commit adultery, it is to have carnal knowledge of another woman, but to lie on a bed in the afternoon in the Paramount Hotel and have your toes sucked one by one is no such thing, even if he did moan with pleasure, for, as Reb Gamaliel would be the first to ask, could his big toe ejaculate? No. Could his little toe, even nibbled to distraction, impregnate another woman? No. Could it bring home the clap, as Rabbi Azariah might ask? No. These were not even his private parts.

Verily, he argued, even to allow his cock to be licked clean as a lollipop stick was not to be unfaithful, for this, as Raschi would perceive, was oral and not vaginal knowledge of another man's woman and, oh bliss, required no exertion on his part, and therefore, he made a mental footnote, did not even violate the sabbath.

There was also a sneaky side to Jake's constancy. He felt that as long as he was true to Nancy, she could not be unfaithful to him. But—but—if only she could be made to appreciate how onerous it sometimes was, what a burden of responsibility it could be, to enjoy, as they did, a singularly happy marriage. The serious books they read, the films and plays they sat through, all celebrated delicious *angst*. Empty sex in the afternoon with strangers. Existential couplings in parked cars. 'Now' people lonely even at the most crowded orgies. Only the bores and the baddies, the dopes, the characters given all the bad lines, continued to stay together.

Furthermore, to love your wife was to be denied a reprobate's license. Nancy, everybody agreed, was no *yenta* but a rare pearl. For Jake, fortunate Jake, to have strayed would have been to raise disapproving eyebrows. Meanwhile, his film friends, happily unhappy, were permitted everything.

One by one their abandoned wives trooped into Jake's living room to bewail their condition. The children, the children. Betty Levi wept at the dining room table. "Suddenly he's a bed-wetter. He has nightmares. He's doing nothing at school."

Crap, Cy assured them. "The kid's thriving. If only she would stop poisoning his mind against us. Would you believe she put him up to asking me, how come they have to do with a black-and-white and we get color on our set?"

Television rang changes unsuspected by McLuhan on at least two lapsed marriages. Every Thursday evening, Leah Demaine had friends in to watch the girl Frankie was living with sing on her own show. "Have you ever seen such a fat cow?" But Bobby Fiedler had to miss six weeks of *Dr. Who* because Daddy's whore was playing in it.

Frankie Demaine, whose children were grown up, felt that to his own self he could now be true. "Oh, sure, to *outsiders* it appeared we were happy. Eighteen years I suffered. Why? Because I hate scenes. There were the kids to consider. But what was she to me all that time. *My mother.* Why, they even have the same name. Rebecca. Oh, I know what people are saying. Don't worry. When he was sick she took excellent care of him. Never a complaint. But the truth is she *enjoyed* my being ill, it made her feel *indispensable.* Since I began a new life with Sandra I haven't had a day's trouble with my back. It was psychosomatic all these years."

One evening Jake came home to find Ida Roberts weeping in the living room.

"I don't mind his leaving me. It's his life, after all. But it's the indignity of it that makes me hate him. To think that all the time he was pretending to be such an attentive father, driving off to Brighton at the drop of a hat, my own daughter was letting him use her flat."

Alfie Roberts had been bewitched by a student at the University of Sussex, his daughter's roomie.

"Did I tell you he smokes pot now? You should see him, the fool, he even wants me to take it up. He says it's easier on the liver than gin. Oh, no. This time, I'm not taking him back. You know he always leaves his hi-fi equipment behind, and when the girl he runs off with discovers that what she took for a young ram is really an old billy goat, he's suddenly coming around to borrow records or to take some cigars from his humidor. Well this time I threw him out with the hi-fi equipment and the cigars after him, and I warned him, hey, swinger, travelin' man, don't forget your hormone injections. *Or it will be very embarrassing for you, won't it?"*

C. Bernard Farber, his foulard, his suede vest and trousers from Mr. Fish, the pendant bouncing on his belly made for him by one of his girl friends, and his Aston-Martin suddenly blooming with flower decals, insisted Jake make the scene at his newly acquired pad, a mews flat in Belgravia, the Rolling Stones blaring from speakers everywhere. "You don't know what a blessing it is just not to have her sitting behind me in the projection room any more. Print that one, I'd say, and she sighs. *Oy.* What's wrong, I'd say, you prefer a different take? It's your picture, she says. I'm a new man. I wake up in the morning, I bounce out of bed singing. Letting the sunshine in. I simply can't believe my luck she's no longer lying beside me. Moaning, bellyaching. Any morning you ask it's either after her period. Or before her period. Or it is her period. I think she's better off too, you know. We never related. We made bad vibrations. The kids have the right idea, Jake, you've got to go with the flow."

Yes, yes, possibly, but Cy Levi soon began to find dieting a severe punishment. Lou Caplan was suddenly embarrassed that he snored and slept with his mouth open. Farber was ashamed of being seen in his truss yet frightened of going without it. Undressing, Bob Cohen hastily stuffed his underwear into his trouser pocket, just in case there was a brown stain, which would offend a young girl. Al Levine, ever mindful to take a digitalis pill before, pretended he was popping something groovy. Myer Gross confessed, "It's embarrassing at my age to get up in the morning and lock the bathroom door before I rinse my dental plate. But I don't dare let her see me without my teeth."

All agreed they envied Jake.

"What have you done to deserve Nancy? What a girl!"

But, gradually, their fulsomely declared envy was overtaken by disapprobation, even sneers. "You know, Jake's a bore," Talman said. Lou Caplan pronounced him square. And C. Bernard Farber, putting him beyond the pale, declared to the poker table that he gave off bad vibes.

And what, Jake thought, if they have a point?

"HAPPY" MARRIAGES MAY BE JUST DULL,
PSYCHOLOGIST SAYS

Washington—A lot of "happy" marriages may be merely dull, says a psychologist at the National Institute of Mental Health.

Dr. Robert Ryder, who directed an institute research project involving 200 young, middle-class couples, warned about the "unexamined idea that compatibility is a good thing."

Jake feared that a felicitous marriage not only reflected poorly on Nancy and him, stamping them superficial, tin-like, but it was also bad for the kids. Everybody he admired, his most imaginative and resourceful friends, had emerged from afflicted homes. Dad a zero, mum a carnivore. Parents so embittered that they wrote off their own lives and toiled only for the children's sake. Divorced parents, vying shamelessly for the kids' affections. Quarreling, lying, but, inadvertently, shaping rebels. Hammering out artists. Whereas in their home there was only symmetry, affection, parents who took pleasure in each other's company.

What are we spawning here, Jake wondered? Surely from such a well-adjusted and cozy childhood only ciphers could spring. Cocooned and soft-minded dolts, who would grow up totally unprepared for life. Sammy would never shoplift. Molly wouldn't have hysterics. In a drug culture, they were already tranquillized.

England, England.

London was almost Jake's home now, but he had mixed feelings about the place. For if the city he had come to know was no longer Big Ben, Bulldog Drummond, and the anti-Zionist fox hunters of his childhood dreams, neither could it be counted the cultural fountainhead he had sought so earnestly as a young man. Slowly, inexorably, he was being forced to pay the price of the colonial come to the capital. In the provinces, he had been able to revere London and its offerings with impunity. Fulminating in Montreal, he could agree with Auden that the dominions were *tiefste Provinz*. Scornful of all things home-baked, he was at one with Dr. Johnson, finding his country a cold and uninviting region. As his father had blamed the *goyim* for his own inadequacies, mentally billing them for the sum of his misfortunes, so Jake had foolishly held Canada culpable for all his discontents. Coming to London, finding it considerably less than excellent, he was at once deprived of this security blanket. The more he achieved, feeding the tapeworm of his outer ambitions, the larger his inner hunger. He would have preferred, for instance, that the highly regarded Timothy Nash had been worthy of his reputation and that it was utterly impossible for Jacob Hersh to be as good. He would have been happiest had the capital's standards not been so readily attainable and that it were still possible for him to have icons.

Ruminating in his study, Jake grasped it wasn't only London or Canada that was exasperating him, but also the books, films, and plays he had consumed. Years and years ago, he recalled, another Jake, ponderously searching for a better way than St. Urbain's, had started out on his intellectual trek immensely heartened to discover, through the books that shaped him, that he wasn't a freak. There were others who thought and felt as he did. Now the same liberated bunch dissatisfied, even bored, him. The novels he devoured so hopefully, conned by overexcited reviews, were sometimes diverting, but told him nothing he had not already known. On the contrary, they only served to reaffirm, albeit on occasion with style, his own feelings. In a word, they were self-regarding. As he was, as his friends were. If it had given the callow Canadian boy who had once been Jake reassurance and pleasure to see his own dilemmas endorsed, rendered real in print, now the further prospect of others torn by his own concerns, more malcontent and swollen egos, filled him with ennui.

Literature, once his consolation, was no longer enough. To read of meanness in others, promiscuity well observed or greed understood, to discover his own inadequacies shared no longer licensed them, any more than all the deaths that had come before could begin to make his own endurable.

Oh, Horseman, Horseman, where are you?

Jake craved answers, a revelation, something out there, a certitude, like the Bomb before it was discovered. Meanwhile, he was choked with self-disgust. Given his *curriculum vitae*, orthodox Jewish background, emergent working class, urban Canadian, his life until now read to him like any Jewish intellectual journeyman's case history. To begin with, his *zeyda* was a cliché. A gentle Jew. A chess player. His childhood street fights, the stuff of everybody's protest novel, lacked only one trite detail. Nobody had ever said to him, "You killed Christ." On the other hand, his mother actually said, "Eat, eat." She was aggressive, a culture snob, and his father was henpecked. As they were divorced, he could also qualify as the product of a broken home. At fifteen he had been sufficiently puerile to tell his father, "The synagogue is full of hypocrites," and two years later he had the originality to describe himself as . . . ghetto-liberated.

If, rather than a code of unspoken nonconformities, there was a battery of written tests for intellectual novices, then Jake felt he would have passed top of the latter-day yeshiva class. He had done all the right wrong things, even to marrying a *shiksa*, voting for the better candidate to this day and, squeezed in a vise between the moral values of two generations, worrying about Arab civil rights in Israel, on the one hand, and kids having to make do with impurities in their pot, on the other.

Luke still swam into focus from time to time. Back from Rome, on his way to Hollywood, between trips to New York. On his return from Malibu, they went out to dinner together, not talking to begin with, but instead replaying their friendship like an old movie. Exchanging anecdotes like bubble-gum cards.

"You must understand I'm not exaggerating," Luke said, "this is exactly how they go about it. Before they sit down to the poker table, they remove their trousers. All the men, six of them. There's a girl under the table and she blows them, one by one, as the game goes on . . ."

"Oh, God, Luke, what's to become of us?"

"Look here, baby. We're on the *Titanic*. It's going down. Everything, everybody. Me, I've decided to travel first class."

"Is that all?"

"Before you turn around, you're dead." Luke fiddled with his glasses, embarrassed. "All right, then, what do you believe in?"

"Praising those who were truly great, those who came nearest the sun. I believe in theirs and ours. Dr. Johnson, yes, Dr. Leary, no."

I'm a liberal, Jake thought, driving home. If only he labored for Dow Chemical, yielding napalm, and so was utterly committed to evil, or if, conversely, he practiced medicine among the Bantu, death's enemy . . . As it was, he was merely another ranks contributor to the arts. Like most of what he read or saw on stage or screen, only to deprecate it fiercely afterwards, he felt his own work had no importance other than the intermittent pleasure it gave him. The time it filled, the social office it provided. After all the posturing, the assumed moral stance, he was, like his mindless uncles, no more than a provider. Worse. A provider with pretensions. Applying Norman Mailer's stricture as a rule, he could not honestly claim that he was adding an inch to the house.

Which is not to say on some mornings, for no ostensible reason whatsoever, Jake did not wake ineffably happy. Nancy stretching beside him. Sammy and Molly romping on the bed. Waken to descend into the kitchen, prepare a delicious breakfast, and drive them into the country. Then, cavorting in a meadow, savoring the sun and his family, he would all at once be riddled with anxiety. *Why am I being allowed to enjoy myself?* The Gods raise you, only the better to strike you down. So look sharp, Yankel, there's something lousy in store.

His glee only simulated as he chased Sammy now, Jake would scrutinize the surrounding woods for advancing Nazi troops. Search the grass for poisonous snakes. Rake the skies for falling planets. Stealthily maneuvering his giggly, frolicking brood closer to the car, he would assure himself that his jack handle was within reach in case they were suddenly set upon by Black Panthers zonked out of their minds on speed. Remember, immediately before Oswald took aim, John Kennedy seemed the most blessed of princes. Malcolm X had further speaking engagements. Even Albert Camus must have had plans for when he reached Paris.

Still playing, but hard put to conceal his apprehensions, Jake would try to outwit the avenging Gods by trying to conjure up the most appalling things that could befall him, forearming himself as it were.

Nancy discovers a lump on her breast. Molly's heart springs a leak. Sammy, a sex maniac's meal. For him, lung cancer.

Whenever Jake flew anywhere, he arrived untimely early to loiter by the insurance machine, just to make sure nobody was investing too heavily. Among the credit cards in his wallet, there was a card that read: "This is to declare that in the event of my death in a street accident, I, the undersigned, wish to be buried intact. None of my organs are available for transplants under any conditions whatsoever."

                                                    DISSOLVE TO:
EXT. DAY. GOLDERS GREEN. THE NONDENOMINATIONAL
CREMATORIUM
Rain. Wind in the sorrowing trees. No birds sing. As a black limousine pulls up . . .
INT. DAY. GOLDERS GREEN CREMATORIUM
Mourners include NANCY, LORD and LADY SAMUEL HERSH, MOLLY and GAYLORD X (her husband, the Black Panther), and LUKE SCOTT. The others are mostly CREDITORS.
TRACKING IN ON CASKET
Made of cheap plywood, just thick enough to contain its vicious smells. Some wilting, scraggly flowers here and there. But atop the casket, as a last request of the deceased, there is a PLACARD that reads:

　　　EENY, MEENY, MINEY, MOE,
　　WHICH OF YOU IS NEXT TO GO?

ANOTHER ANGLE
As LUKE SCOTT mounts the podium. He's in his sixties, wearing stitched-on shoulder-length hair, earrings,

grandmaw glasses, and a medallion hanging from his wizened neck.

LUKE

(reciting)

He disappeared in the dead of winter:

The brooks were frozen, the airports almost deserted,

And snow disfigured the public statues;

The mercury sank in the mouth of the dying day.

O all the instruments agree

The day of his death was a dark cold day.

ANOTHER ANGLE

As the CASKET begins to slide into the flames, stage curtains part to reveal . . . THE ANDREWS SISTERS

ANDREWS SISTERS

(singing)

Bei Mir Bist Du Shayn

DISSOLVE TO:

INT. LORD SAMUEL HERSH'S BELGRAVIA MANSION. DRAWING ROOM. ALL of YANKEL HERSH'S PROGENY gathered together. Drinking. Eating.

LORD HERSH

I say, what shall we do with the old fart's ashes?

MOLLY

What about mother?

LORD HERSH

That would never do. It would put Luigi off his love-making, don't you think?

MOLLY

Well, I won't have them. It's morbid for the children. Besides, I haven't told them that they're one quarter kikes.

(pause)

You keep them. At least you've got a cat.

LORD HERSH

Capital idea!

As NANCY enters, her see-through dress half-unzipped, bite marks everywhere, pursued by a slavering, hirsute ITALIAN BUS BOY

NANCY

Say hello, Luigi, baby.

LUIGI

Chow.

INT. DAY. STUDY. LORD HERSH'S MANSION

LORD HERSH seated behind the desk, mounds of papers before him. The others gathered around, drooling with greed. As LORD HERSH bangs the desk for silence.

LORD HERSH

For form's sake, we should dispense with his last wishes first. There's only one.

(reading)

He wanted his son to say . . .

(difficulty reading)

kaddish for him. Anybody know what that is?

MOLLY

Isn't that the greasy stuff he used to make in the kitchen? With chopped onions and—

LORD HERSH

No, that's chopped liver.

(opening a folio)

Let's get on with the balance sheets, what? First of all, the best bid for his heart came from St. George's Hospital. £1,000. They said it was an especially big heart . . .

PAN BRIEFLY OVER FAMILY. An instant's flicker of guilt.

LORD HERSH

The kidneys fetched another £100, but the lungs and liver were no good at all. A dead loss.

NANCY

What about his roger?

LORD HERSH

Was just coming to that. We finally flogged it to a children's hospital. Wouldn't fit anyone but a twelve-year-old, don't you know?

• • •

Unknown to Nancy, or so Jake assumed, he kept a baseball bat under his bed. He had joined a shooting club, which entitled him to keep a rifle. He had even planned, before retiring, to distribute plates on the stairs leading to their bedroom, so that when the vandals came he could be roused from his sleep in time to defend his family. But he could think of no satisfactory explanation for Nancy.

Nancy, his love. Seized unawares by a joyous mood in the evening, taking Nancy to dinner on impulse, ordering succulent dishes and wines too splendid for him to appreciate, except by price, following it with brandies and protestations of love, he would suddenly, unexpectedly, clamor for the bill. *Gas leak.*

"Why do we have to run?" Nancy would ask, irritated, believing him to be bored with her.

GAS LEAK! My God, can't she see them? Sammy and Molly. Sprawled lifeless on their beds.

Gone, gone.

When it wasn't the children's safety, death, or the Germans' second coming that plagued him, it was the fact that he felt his generation was unjustly squeezed between two raging and carnivorous ones. The old establishment and the young hipsters. The shits and the shit-heads. Unwillingly, without justice, they had been cast in Kerensky's role. Neither as obscene as the Czar, nor as bloodthirsty as Lenin. Even as Jews, they did not fit a mythology. Not having gone like sheep to the slaughterhouse, but also too fastidious to punish Arab villages with napalm. What Jake stood for would not fire the countryside: decency, tolerance, honor. With E. M. Forster, he wearily offered two cheers for democracy. After George Orwell, he was for a closer look at anybody's panacea.

Jake was a liberal.

He would have been willing to vote for the legalization of pot, but he couldn't feel that a sixteen-year-old was deprived if he lacked for a pack of Acapulco Gold. He was *against* puritan repression, *for* fucking, but not necessarily on stage. A born cophater, he still wouldn't offer one a sandwich with shit spread between the bread. Though he felt the university was too intricately involved with the military-industrial complex he didn't think it was a blow struck for universal love when students tore a professor's work of twenty years to shreds. Admittedly, Hollywood had lied, so had the *Satevepost*, but he didn't want Molly to feel a wallflower if at fourteen she didn't submit to a gang bang. When Reb Allen Ginsberg preached to the unformed that all history was bunk, what first sprang to mind was Goering reaching for his gun when he heard the word culture. Increasingly, wherever he turned, Jake felt his generation was being crushed by two hysterical forces, the outraged work-oriented old and the spitefully playful young, each heaving half truths at one another. Not that his own bunch filled him with jubilance. For one day, Jake feared, they would be dismissed as trivial, a peripheral generation. Crazy about bad old movies, nostalgic for comic books. Their Gods and mine, he allowed, don't fail. At worst, they grow infirm. They suffer pinched nerves, like Paul Hornung. Or arthritic arms, like Sandy Koufax.

But, above all, it was the injustice collectors Jake feared. The concentration camp survivors. The hungry millions of India. The starvelings of Africa. Months after his first film had been released, a letter reached him from Canada.

DEAR DIRECTOR (OF LIFE, ITS STRUGGLES)

　　MY ADVISE TO YOU AS AN ARTIST IS TO SET YOUR GOAL CLOSE TO THE PEOPLE, AS G.B.S. HAS DONE IN HIS HUMBLE BEGINNING. WHICH NOW GIVES RAISE TO THE MASSAS. THE UNIMPLOYED. THE DEFEATED ON THE SKID ROADS OF NORTH AMERICA. INCLUDING THE SLEEPING GIANTS OF CANADA. OUR FISHERMAN AND LOGGERS. AND THE POOR FARMERS NOTWITHSTANDING.

　　TO RAISE THE SPIRIT, READ, THE LOGGERS. THE CIRCUS BY THE TALENTED HOBO, JIM TULLEY. THE BEGGERS OF LIFE HE PUT ON THE SCRENE OUT OF HOLLEYWOOD.

　　ALSO READ THOSE BOOKS THAT MADE UPTON SINCLAIR FAMOUS. THE BRASS CHECK, THE JUNGEL, ETC. AS WELL AS THE IRION HEAL BY LONDON.

　　THE BEST ON RELIGIONS IS THE GOLDEN BOUGH BY FRAZER. ON PSYCHOLOGY RIEK, MYTH AND GUILT. AND FOR A MAGAZINE, FATE, SHOULD BE READ WITH AN OPEN MIND.

　　SHOULD YOU CONSIDER A JOB TO OPEN NEW AVENUES IN MOD-

ERN THOUGHT. HERE'S A BIG TIP. GO TO A REAL ESTATE COMPANY
IN YOUR CITY OR CHICAGO, N.Y.C. OR NEWARK, N.J. SHOULD BE A
LARGE OUTFIT THAT CONTROLS SLUM PROPERTY. SUCH WORK
WOULD BRING YOU CLOSE TO LIFE.

LOAN OFFICES ARE ALSO GOOD WHEN SEARCHING FOR JEWELS
TO MAKE YOUR DIRECTION BRILLENT.

ALL I NEED IS A TAPE RECORDER AND YOU: FOR THAT HIT MOVIE
I STRIVE FOR.

I HAVE SHORT STORIES, VERSE, ADVENTURE, ETC. I FEAL I AM A
NATURAL. I KNOW VERY LITTLE IN SUCH ART. UNIVERSITIES ARE
KNOWN TO DIM DIAMONDS. S.B. BURNS. BUT I LIVE IN CHI.
TWENTY FIVE YEARS, AND SLAVED IN BUILDING TRADES. WITH A
THIRD GRADE SCHOOLING. IN THE YEARS OF THE GREAT PANIC I
TRAVELLED THOUSANDS OF MILES BY ACCIDENT. AND LARNED IN
THE STRUGGLE.

MY YEARS ARE THOSE FROM 1893, AUGEST. I WORK IN ENGLE-
WOOD, B.C.

I WISH YOU LUCK KID,
SINCEARLY YOURS,
STUART MCCALLUM

He feared the Red Guards of China and the black fanatics, for
he knew they would knock on his door one day and ask Jacob
Hersh, husband, father, house owner, investor, sybarite, and film
fantasy-spinner, for an accounting.

The more he brooded on it, the more time he spent in his
aerie, sifting through the Horseman's papers.

The pages from *Doktor* Mengele's journal.

More than once, in his mind's eye, Jake saw the Horseman
Entre Ríos, where Argentina meets the Paraná River. He saw
him cantering on a magnificent Pleven stallion. Galloping, thundering. Planning fresh campaigns, more daring maneuvers.

One night, as he was tucking Sammy into bed, the boy said to
him, "Tibbett believes in God. We don't, do we?"

"I don't, but—"

"Me too," Molly sang out from the bottom bunk bed.

"—you'll have to decide for yourself, Sammy."

"What do you believe in, then?"

He was about to say the Horseman, it was on the tip of his tongue, but, fortunately, he stopped himself. "It's late. We'll talk tomorrow."

Retreating from their bedroom, troubled, he grasped that for years now he had begun to insinuate tales of St. Urbain's Horseman between his bedtime stories about Rabbi Akiba, the Thirty-six Just Men, Maimonides, the Golem, Trumpeldor, and Leon Trotsky. His Jewish allsorts bag. Pouring himself a drink, he realized that ever since he had turned down the film in Israel because, to his mind, it was an offense against everything his cousin stood for, the Horseman had become his moral editor. Considering a script, deliberating for days as was his habit, consulting Nancy, arguing with himself, vacillating, reading and rereading, he knew that in the final analysis he said yes or no based on what he imagined to be the Horseman's exacting standard. Going into production, whether in television or film, he tried above all to please the Horseman. For somewhere he was watching, judging.

Once Cousin Joey's advocate, he was now his acolyte.

Four

1

Jake heard from Ruthy for the first time the morning after he was fired from the production of his third film, the phone ringing just as he sat down to breakfast.

"Is this Jacob Hersh?"

"Yes."

"Can you tell me where your cousin Joseph is, please?"

"Who's speaking?"

"Never mind."

"No. I'm sorry. I have no idea—"

The woman laughed scathingly, as if this was exactly the sort of duplicity she had expected of a Hersh.

"But, honestly, I haven't seen him in years."

"You are his cousin, aren't you?"

"Yes."

"Then tell me one thing. Do you come from an old French Jewish family called de la Hirsch?"

Jake had to laugh. Immediately, he regretted it. The woman had begun to weep.

"We're from Galicia," he said, feeling foolish.

"Well, to take the bull by the horns, I'm in trouble. Joseph was supposed to marry me. He's disappeared. Can you see me?"

"Certainly."

"I finish work at five-thirty. Do you know the King's Arms on Finchley Road?"

"Yes. Sure."

Jake summoned a waitress.

"I'd like an egg and tomato sandwich, please."

"It's not on the menu."

"I know. But could you get me one, please?"

"I'm sorry, sir, we don't serve egg and tomato sandwiches."

"You serve egg sandwiches, don't you?"

"Yes, we do, sir."

"And do you serve tomato sandwiches?"

"Yes, sir."

"Well, then, if it isn't too much trouble, could you please make me an egg and tomato sandwich?"

"But we don't serve—"

"Tell you what. You order me an egg sandwich and a tomato sandwich. I'll pay for both—"

Americans.

"—and you, you clever thing, you make me a combination sandwich of the two."

"But that would be an egg and tomato sandwich."

"Yes, I expect so."

"Egg and tomato sandwiches are definitely not on the menu. If you would like to see the manager—"

"Forget it. Just bring me a large gin, please. And a tonic."

Jake didn't know what, exactly, to expect. But he was certainly not prepared for Ruthy. A Rubenesque lady, big as she was dark, with a plump bosom, clearly in her forties, but managing a miniskirt with élan. Her soft brown eyes were watery, she plucked her eyebrows, and there were minuscule pocks on her chin where facial hairs had been clumsily removed. Ruthy settled into her chair, sighing, her bulging imitation leather handbag landing on the table with a clunk. She worked in a neighboring dress shop, she said.

"Joseph's a good man. I know he is. But he's in psychological trouble and that's why he lies. My brother never should have interfered."

"Couldn't I get you something?" Jake asked.

"A Pepsi-Cola, please."

Ruthy was a widow with two children. Her husband had died five years ago, a heart attack. "Where can anybody my age meet a decent, compatible man?" Ruthy had formed a Reading and Discussion Circle and Joey had seen the advert in the *Jewish Chronicle* and drifted into the first meeting. "There were several women there and he made an impression on all of them. One immediately asked if he was married, isn't it disgusting how some people are? But you could tell from Joseph's manner that he did not wish to give any information about his private life."

I'll buy that.

"He stayed on after the others had left and we talked. He's very interested in construction, but I suppose you know that, and he warned me about the damp in the kitchen wall. I should speak to the landlord, he said. Well, that's me, I said, and we had a giggle together. He came to visit me again during the week."

The somnolent waitress handed Jake his large gin and poured Ruthy's Pepsi into a glass. She was about to remove the empty bottle when Ruthy seized it, jolting the girl awake. "Oh, well," the waitress said sniffily.

"Before the evening was over he told me he was a bachelor and asked me to marry him," Ruthy said, peeling the label off the Pepsi bottle. "Well worse accidents happen at sea, I suppose. I told him it was too soon to know what he was like, but he told me that when two people meet who can be well mated it was a waste of time at our age to let even one day pass and not be together. I thought to myself," she continued, slipping the label into her handbag, "here is a man who is forthright. I had also observed that he was quick-witted, quiet, and sincere. Joseph said I would have to give him an answer within a week because it was beneath his dignity to beg a woman. Well I fancied him very much, he certainly attracted me physically. I also must say that I could tell he was well versed in philosophy and Greek mythology. But how could I tell he didn't have a wife somewhere? I shouldn't have asked him. It made him terribly indignant. 'I could hardly be after your money,' he said. 'since it's obvious you have none.' Well not none, I said. Not *quite* none. He told me if we married, I could give up work. He didn't say what he did for a living, but you could see that he was an employer, not an employee.

"I talked to my brother—that was my first mistake—and he said I must try to find out something about the man first. You can't just marry a stranger. Meanwhile, I was afraid of losing Joseph. When he came around again I asked him why he hadn't married until now and he said he was always on the lookout for a clever woman with a great deal of sex and beauty. He said he was certain I possessed all three of these qualities. He seemed to be a great lover of feminine beauty, beauty of the body. And speaking frankly, I didn't know if I could live up to that. I told him that, objectively speaking, I was not beautiful. I had incisions on my body. Also I told him I didn't know if I could satisfy him sexually. But," Ruthy said, twirling her empty glass, "he dispelled these fears."

"Would you care for another Pepsi?"

"Ta."

"We'll have the same again," Jake told the waitress. "No, one moment, please. Make it a large gin and two Pepsis."

"Still I told him no—it takes more than sex to make a fruitful marriage. I had to be reached spiritually, mentally, and *then* sexually. We're not animals, don't you think?"

"Of course not."

"I could not mate with a man who did not give me understanding and companionship. Well, he continued to put up many arguments about sex." Ruthy sucked in a deep breath. "Like *Lady Chatterley's Lover*. He was certainly very well read. But the body-beautiful stuff frightened me. Also his love-making was—well very torrid. I said we should wait, but he said the love-making could proceed while I made up my mind. Well, in for a penny, in for a pound." As the waitress approached with her tray, Ruthy leaned closer to Jake. "Keep your Pepsi bottle," she whispered.

But this time the waitress, her manner haughty, did not even attempt to remove the Pepsi bottles.

"The next thing was I didn't hear from him for a fortnight. Nothing. Not a word. I had a heartache, a bad one let me tell you. I thought my brother had scared him off, but he said he hadn't done a thing. Then suddenly he's at my door again. He said he had had to go away on an unexpected business trip—"

"To Germany?" Jake asked.

"No. But he's very well traveled, you know."

"Yes, I do. Did he tell you that he'd ever been to Germany?"

"For a spell, he said."

"What did he tell you he was doing there?"

"He didn't say. Anyway, he said there was this unexpected business trip and he had felt insulted by me so he hadn't phoned. But the truth was he couldn't stay away from me. He said the time had come to have a serious talk about our future. You should know I'm kosher and Joseph even discussed this matter with me. He said he didn't care for *kashruth* at all, he made no secret of it, but he told me I could keep a kosher home—he wouldn't interfere with it. I think that was very generous of him. Don't you?"

"Yes."

"Well," she mused, absently peeling the labels off the two Pepsi bottles, "actually he's not such a big eater."

"I hadn't thought of that."

"Anyway from the beginning my brother felt there was something fishy about Joseph. My brother's a real-estate agent and property developer. You looking for a house?"

"Not at the moment."

"You don't have to go to him. I'm not the pusher type, you know. If a customer comes into the shop, I don't try to sell her this and sell her that, anything to make a sale, isn't it dreadful? And the way they bargain! Well, my brother's honest too and that's a quality these days. You could say my brother's well known for his honesty. In his line he meets the public and he prides himself on being a judge of character . . ."

Ruthy's brother, the character judge, met Joey only once,

visiting him in his flat, in Earl's Court, and immediately warned Ruthy against him. But when Joey came to her the next day, obviously overwrought, and explained that he needed money urgently to fly to Israel and wind up his tangled business interests there, she dipped into her Building Society account and lent him seven hundred pounds.

"As soon as he came back, we were going to get married. I knew he planned to come back. He even left his riding clothes behind."

Joey, she went on to say, was a superb horseman. He cantered through Richmond Park twice weekly.

"Well, that was more than a month ago, and then I got this letter."

The letter was from a hotel in Galway. Galway, Jake thought, his heart hammering, where Skorzeny has settled on a vast estate. S.S. Colonel Otto Skorzeny, who had landed a Fieseler-Stortch near the hotel in Gran Sasso d'Italia, the highest range in the Abruzzi Apennines, and flown out again with Mussolini. Who on July 20, 1944, after Stauffenberg's bomb had failed at the Wolf's Lair, had rallied the S.D. at the tank formation school and gone to the Bendlerstrasse and put handcuffs on the remaining plotters. Who had slipped through the lines in the Ardennes, his men wearing American MP's uniforms, and spread confusion. Tried and acquitted by a U.S. tribunal at Dachau in 1947. Then to Spain and South America, and from there to Galway, where there were so many of them now. Gentlemen farmers.

Joey's letter said please trust me, I love you, but for personal reasons I can't return to Israel at this moment. I'm going to Argentina to discuss an important position with an internationally known engineering firm and I will send for you in six months' time.

Argentina. *Entre Ríos,* perhaps. Where Argentina meets the Paraná River and Uruguay.

"He's got all my savings. What do you think?"

Jake didn't dare say what he thought.

"I know he loves me. Tell me, is your family renowned for its philanthropic activities in Canada?"

"The Hershes? Well, um, I suppose they do give money. Yes, of course," he added hastily. "UJA, yeshivas, Israel . . . I haven't been home for rather a long while."

"O.K. He lies to glamorize himself. It's not murder, is it? I mean to say, you open a newspaper today and there's the H-Bomb. I'm against it, of course. They are contrary to what George Bernard Shaw called the life force. But do I care you don't come from the French nobility? I want Joseph. I love him. Your family was shocking to him. He says they're very bigoted."

"Well, yes, narrow. You could say that. Now, Ruthy, you tell me something. Obviously, you know I'm Joey's cousin because he said so. Did he ever explain to you why he never comes to see me?"

"Oooo," she said, "now you're having me on, aren't you?"

"Am I?"

"You see each other. And how."

"He told you he was in touch with me, then?"

"Yes."

"Has he ever mentioned my work to you?"

"How do you mean?"

Is he avoiding me, Jake wanted to ask, because he has such a poor opinion of me? "Has he seen my films?"

"I don't know."

"I see."

There was a heavy pause.

"Well now, *if* you see him when he comes back tell him I paid his rent for him and took his riding clothes with me," Ruthy said, rising. "I'm keeping them for him."

"If I see him," Jake said.

2

Bloom licked his pencil and checked over his account sheets for the third time, not that there was any point to the exercise. Count on Harry to find an error, no matter what. Harry, the *momzer*. Recently, Bloom had come to think that Harry altered a figure here, a figure there, himself, for it sometimes seemed that there were more eraser marks when Harry returned the sheets for correction than there had been before. There was nothing Harry wouldn't do for a little giggle. Hadn't he seen him, with his very own eyes, on the day of the office picnic at Brighton, conceal Miss Pinsky's handbag, when he knew she was having her monthlies, and not yield it until she had stained herself, fleeing in embarrassment? He hates me. Why? Because I'm kosher. Bloom had to lock his luncheon sandwiches in the bottom desk drawer ever since Harry, in one of his inspired moods, had substituted *traifes* for his chicken sandwich, not saying anything until Bloom had swallowed it. It made him choke that other Jews believed. Had respect.

"Tell me, Bloom, you're such a devout little Jew, did you know it is written in the Talmud that we are supposed to charge Gentiles a higher interest rate than our brethren?"

"And why not?"

"*And vy not?* Lucky is the born ignoramus.""

"With you around, who needs Nasser? You're no better than me."

Above all, Harry exulted in tormenting Bloom about his daughter Aviva.

"I don't understand you, Bloom, you've had no life at all. For all you've tasted of this world's delights, and I willingly include your experience of *la dolce vita* at Bournemouth, you might as well not have been born. Married to a *yachna*. Pinching pennies all these years and for what, so that you can afford a wedding at the Grosvenor Hotel for Aviva?"

"It offends me to even hear her name from your filthy mouth."

"Don't you know sexy Jewish girls don't marry doctors any more? Or go in for big weddings, with the guest list in the *Jewish Chronicle*? They go for the spades, Bloom—"

"*Go to hell.*"

"—and if they get married at all it's at the registry office, because they've got one in the oven."

"You know what I say? I say you're around the bend. Paying girls so you can take filthy pictures of them. Some man about town. Look out, James Bond! Take care, Rex Harrison! Here comes little Harry Stein, can't make a girl do it with him unless he pays her a fiver."

"How much do you want to bet Aviva is on the pill?"

"Oh, look at him. Red in the face. I've got your number, haven't I? Don Juan? More like Yosel Putz, if you ask me."

Once more Bloom licked his pencil and worried over his account sheets, before Harry opened the door to his cubicle, and called, "Bloom!"

Harry contemplated the sheets, nodding, and suddenly smiled and said: "Congratulations."

"What for?" Bloom asked guardedly.

"I hear Aviva has been accepted at the University of Sussex."

"And Oxford. And Cambridge. Now that you've mentioned it, Mr. Stepney Grammar School."

"But she's going to Sussex."

"Yes."

"Smart kid. It's the swinging university, you know. They screw each other black and blue there."

"You know what I smell? I smell sour grapes."

"You don't believe me? Here," and he passed him the clipping, "it was in the *Sunday Telegraph*. There's plenty of pot smoking at Sussex, you know."

"What?"

"Pot. It's not for brewing tea. I speak of marijuana. Drugs. It makes the girls crazy for it."

Bloom began to shake.

"You know what happened when the police gate-crashed the Rolling Stones party? They found a bloke sucking a chocolate bar out of a girl's cunt. But at Sussex the girls are famous for another specialty. The human sandwich. Girl in the middle. Boys poking into either end."

"One day I'll kill you. I'll pick up a knife and put it through you."

Harry smiled benevolently. "Meanwhile, if you don't mind, I'll see how many mistakes I can find here," and he started into the hall.

Where a man sat chain-smoking outside Father Hoffman's confessional.

"I would like to take this opportunity to tell you," Harry said to him, "how much I enjoyed your first film."

"Oh, thanks," Jake muttered preoccupied, shooting up to disappear through Hoffman's door.

Sister Pinsky, too shy to ask, had left a note on Harry's desk.

> The Reading and Discussion Circle—
> so sweet and arty,
> Fabsolutely for the party,
> Which Sandra, Viv, and Ruthy are giving
> On Saturday the 7th
>
> From 8:30 onwards come join the fray,
> Right through dawn until the next day.
> Shlep a bottle or two, or even more,
> But leave your blues outside our door.

The Langley House is the fixed abode,
You'll find it at 22 Belmont Road,
Add N.W.8 to your R.S.V.P.
Saying oui oui—we hope—for our soiree.
Or fourpence in Bell's bag of tricks,
To let us know at HE 1-0376.

Sandra Pinsky
Vivian Gold
Ruthy Flam

Well, why not, Harry thought.

"So," Oscar asked Jake, "what's the latest?"

"Well, today it looks like they may honor my contract and pay me in full."

"Ah ha."

"If that's the case, Oscar, you've got to tell me how to take the money. I don't want to pick it up in the morning and fork it out in surtax in the afternoon, you know."

"There will be no need," Oscar said, reaching for the phone, "to even bring the money into this country in the first place."

3

In the first place, Jake had even had serious doubts about making the film, but he had been through so many scripts, most of them appalling. He would not consider anything being shot abroad, because of Nancy's pregnancy. He was bored, he was restless. So he had foolishly allowed his agent to talk him into it.

From the start, the project was ill-starred. Before the first day of shooting, Jake had turned against the script. He got off to a horrendous start with the actress, a stunning but vacuous British girl, who was to play the lead. She was on a macrobiotic diet and reading Zen, absolutely convinced that the yellow-brick road to international stardom was paved with trendiness. In her world, things were either swinging or a drag, other people groovy or uptight. She was willing to do a nude scene, she told Jake not once, but twice, as long as it was "artistically necessary."

The first day of shooting, always Jake's shakiest time on a set, the producer loomed over his shoulder as soon as he picked up the viewfinder. It was a grueling day, seemingly endless, and when it was over Jake had only shot a minute, a most unsatisfying minute, he knew, without waiting to see the rushes at noon the following day. Ensconced in the screening room with the producer, the star, her agent and others, indignant and in a sweat. Nobody said a word when the lights went on, fearful of committing themselves before the producer pronounced. The producer, who was already whispering in a far corner, with the lighting cameraman, the star, and her thrusting agent.

Announcing that he expected everyone on the set in twenty minutes, Jake strode out, seeking comfort among Hersh's Continuing Rep, many of whom he had hired for the production.

"Don't let him worry you, Yankel. He's a *grobber*."

During the first set-up of the afternoon, a restaurant scene, it all came down. The star, blinking the false eyelashes which she wore over Jake's objections, turned to him between takes and indicated the group assembled under the hot lights since noon, rehearsed—spun into action—shushed—spun into action and shushed again and again—only so that she, the camera tracking after, might sweep through them, making a poignant exit, and getting her three little lines right, turned to him, her entrancing smile aimed at the crouching still photographer, and said, "Aren't they, like, crazy?"

"What?"

"The faces you chose. Are they real people," she asked, "or only extras?"

"They are my friends," Jake said tightly. "And where are you going?"

"We aren't doing it again?"

Yes. And again, and one more time as the producer seethed. Then again, and twice more, until she fled to her dressing room, the perplexed producer tumbling after.

A letter, hand-delivered, turned up at the office of Jake's agent before six. Jake was barred from the set.

"Tell him not to worry," Jake said. "I quit."

"No, you don't. I'll have you back on the set on Monday. You're making this picture."

"Don't threaten me."

There was a meeting on Tuesday and another, with lawyers, on Wednesday. Thursday a subdued agent took Jake to lunch and revealed that another director had been hired. "I've turned

down their offer of a settlement. I'm holding out for your full
salary."

"That's the stuff."

"If I get it, you won't be able to sign to make another film so
long as you were supposed to be working on theirs. If you do,
you'll forfeit the money."

Jake laughed.

"You think it's funny?"

"Hell, I'm going to be paid more monthly not to work than
I've ever earned in my life."

"Don't let it depress you. I can't think of anyone on our list
it hasn't happened to at least once."

With nowhere to go, and nothing to do, except connive with
Hoffman on how to put his money out of reach of the Inland
Revenue, Jake took to sleeping in late and then meandering down
to Swiss Cottage to pick up the *Herald Tribune* at W. H.
Smith's. Almost daily, he passed the dress shop Ruthy worked in.
Ruthy usually rapped hopefully on the window as he drifted by,
startling him out of his reveries. She waved, he waved back, then
this dumb show no longer satisfied her. She took to summoning
Jake to the door.

"Have you heard from Joseph?"

"No."

"Not to worry. But there's no harm in asking, is there?"

Another day.

"Quick. See her? No. Across the street. The lady getting into
the chauffeured Bentley."

"Yes."

"She's a cousin to Lady Cohen. Whenever she comes into the
shop she asks to be served by me personally. It's a pleasure to
deal with her. She's no Golder's Green *yachna*, if you know what
I mean. Anything new?"

Jake looked baffled.

"I mean Joseph. Have you heard anything?"

"Ruthy, please. I haven't seen him since I was a boy."

4

Only five minutes before the babysitter was expected, just as Ruthy was dabbing perfume behind her ears, she was summoned to the phone in the hall. It was Sandra Pinsky. She couldn't come, after all.

"Why?" Ruthy complained.

"You want to know the truth?" Sandra dissolved into laughter. "I'm all out."

"Oooo," Ruthy moaned. "Come on."

"Me and the boy scouts have the same motto: be prepared."

A lot of good it's done her, being prepared all these years, but Ruthy didn't say it. "Couldn't you phone your doctor to leave a prescription outside? You could still pick it up."

"I phoned earlier, but he was just going off for the weekend. I said to him, oh, doctor, but I'm without pills. What pills, he asked? *The* pills. In that case, luv, he said, I'd keep my knickers up until Monday if I was you." She exploded into laughter again. "Isn't he wicked?"

"But there must be a locum he leaves in the clinic. Ask him for the prescription."

"He's a Pakistani. *Oy*, Ruthy, how could I? I'm too embarrassed."

"Oooo," Ruthy pleaded. "Come on."

"I'm not even dressed. I left an invitation out for Mr. Stein. He's coming on Saturday. Watch out for him, dearie, he doesn't look the type, but he's got only one thing in mind."

"*Are you coming?*"

"Come to my place. *The Avengers* are on tonight. It's a two-part one. I saw the first part last week."

"Oh, I see. The penny's dropped. You," she said, hanging up.

Ruthy decided not to attend the Friendship Club again after all; it would be no fun on her own, the so-called 27's to 45's (yeah, sure), pathetic types, most of the men at least fifty, wanting to know how much you were worth, was there a dowry, and, failing everything else, if you were interested in having a little fun.

A quick glance at the *Jewish Chronicle* revealed there was nothing on at the Ben Uri Gallery; neither was there a lecture that appealed. Across the street, she picked up a quarter of sweets and the *Evening News*.

You Cannot Afford To Miss These Films About
CANADA
—it could mean a new life for YOU

Niagara Falls. Deanna Durbin. Yes, and Joseph Hersh, she thought, thank you very much.

Mrs. Frankel stopped her outside Grodzinski's.

"They took Golda back to the hospital this afternoon. Didn't you see the ambulance outside?"

"No."

"Her uterus is hanging, she can't walk. I don't understand; I thought she had it out."

"I wouldn't know," Ruthy said.

"Listen, it's better to grow old than to die young. And where are you going, all dressed up?"

"To eat *latkes* at Buckingham Palace. Where else?" she asked, running for the bus.

Imagine, she thought, a new life. Without *yentas* everywhere.

You pack your bags, you buy tickets, and off you go. Goodbye Quality Outfitting, so long Sunday afternoon teas in Edgware, her sister-in-law asking, "And did you meet anybody this week?" Australia, Canada, South Africa. Even her brother, and he took the *Financial Times* every day, said there was a better future there. He had been to Toronto, the mayor was Jewish. The government didn't squeeze you like a lemon.

Nelson Eddy and Jeanette MacDonald had made a film in Canada, Ruthy recalled, but the title eluded her. "Give me some men, who are stout-hearted men . . ." One would do.

Takes the RUB out of SCRUB. Brewed, Brood. Earn, Urn. Our WURST is truly the BEST. No WAIT to bake, no WEIGHT to eat . . . Swaying on the Victoria-bound bus, Ruthy unsnapped her bulging, coupon-filled handbag and stuffed her dictionary of homonyms inside, still savoring a couple of the winning ones. A RECKLESS driver is seldom WRECKLESS long and—for a baby's name, this—Prince of WAILS.

It was a rotten night, cold and rainy, but there was no harm in *seeing*, was there, she thought, as she joined the knot of people collapsing their umbrellas outside Caxton Hall. Scanning the notice board, Ruthy noted that a yoga group was meeting on the first floor, so was the Schopenhauer Society, and the Druid Order—brrrrr—was holding *its* monthly meeting. The Canadian thing, as she imagined, was in the main hall and she was lucky to find a seat.

You pack your bags, you go. This is the twentieth century. There were chattering people everywhere, some middle-aged and making no pretense about it, but many more who were young, coddling children on their laps. Settling into her chair with an assumed air of indifference, Ruthy offered a sweet to the taciturn man next to her and nervously inquired, "Why do you want to go to Canada?"

"There's too much waiting for dead men's shoes here."

"And you?" Ruthy sang out to the man on her other side.

"Harold Wilson."

"My family's been here for generations. I'm just looking in for a friend."

Trans-Canada Journey, the color movie they were shown about a trip from Halifax to Vancouver, displayed all of the vast dominion's natural wonders and spoke glowingly of the opportunities available there. No sooner was the film done, its final image an R.C.M.P. corporal mounting the steps to parliament, than the lights went on again and a brisk smiling young man, from the Department of Citizenship and Immigration, bounded onto the platform. "You're an excellent audience. Terrific! I can sense our immigration offices will be jam-packed tomorrow morning."

Which evoked more coughing than huzzahs.

"Canada needs people, the RIGHT kind of people—"

Everywhere you go, Ruthy reflected, anti-semites.

"—We have many, many jobs that are just going begging, with one of the highest standards of living in the world."

The young man summoned three experts to the platform and they also smiled brightly, devouring the audience with their enthusiasm.

"Do you welcome unskilled workers?" a man asked.

"That's a loaded question. If you mean a nineteen-year-old, sure, he'll acquire a skill, but if you mean a man of forty, the kind who is on and off national assistance all the time . . . well you get 'em, you keep 'em, we don't want 'em."

"I'm an engineer myself."

"You certainly look like a professional man to me, sir. I realize your question was of a general nature."

"If things are so rosy in Canada, why do so many immigrants return?"

"I'll field that one," the youngest panel member hollered, winking at the first row. "Homesickness. Unadaptability. If your wife is the kind who has to see her mum once a day and four times on Sunday don't come to Canada unless you bring your mother-in-law."

"What's the unemployment situation like?"

"Three point nine."

Somebody guffawed.

"Oh, I admit it gets higher in winter, but—"

"Didn't you have a recession in 1961?"

"Recession, no, a sort of leveling-off, yes. But right now we're booming. Booming. We want people, the right type. We need British immigrants."

"What about medical bills?"

"That's a very, very good question. We have no national health plan, but we do have private health schemes that cost very little."

"I have four children, you see."

"Look, if you're the kind of guy who runs to the national health doctor and sits in his waiting room all day because it's free, and you have the sniffles . . ."

Finally, Ruthy rose and asked in a small voice, "I'm over forty—"

"Louder, please."

"I'm inquiring for a friend who is over forty and works in a dress shop. What are her chances of employment in Canada?"

"That's a very good question. I'm glad you asked it. Now if you were a man, I'd have to say your chances were not so hot because of pension schemes and such . . . but many shops and offices *prefer* to employ women who are past the marrying age."

"Well, thank you. Thank you *very, very* much."

5

Somewhat ashamed of himself, Jake nevertheless worked out an alternative route to W. H. Smith's, but occasionally lapsed into the habitual one when he was self-absorbed. One day, two weeks later, Ruthy stopped him. Could he meet her at the pub again at five thirty. Yes, why not?

"Pepsi?" Jake asked, intrigued.

"No. I'd like a lemon soda. Canada Dry, if you don't mind?"

A celery protruded from her string shopping bag. There were also two tins tucked inside, both of them shorn of their labels. Jake ordered a large gin and tonic for himself, two Canada Dry lemon sodas, and settled back to watch.

"I'm engaged," Ruthy announced haughtily, "or don't you read the *Times* social page," she added with a giggle.

Jake congratulated her.

"He's a lovely, lovely man. Very well versed in literature and political matters. He reads the *New Statesman* and *Tribune*. As a matter of fact, one week he had a poem in the *Tribune*. That's an accomplishment, isn't it?"

"Yes it is."

"I'm going to need the money, you know."

"What money?" Jake charged, jolted awake.

"The seven hundred pounds. The money Joseph took from me."

"But what in the hell do you expect me to do about it?" he asked, bug-eyed as she peeled the labels off the two Canada Dry lemon sodas.

"Tell him I need it. Harry hasn't had much materialistic success. It doesn't interest him."

"Ruthy, for the last time, it's been years since I've seen him."

"Oh, come off it. Come off it, please."

"I'm afraid you'll just have to take my word for it."

"Maybe you could return the money to me?"

"Why should I?"

"Harry saw your film, but I must say he didn't care for it. He didn't think it rang true to life. He says when you direct something about working-class people it is obviously done for the rich to laugh at. In his estimation you're a self-hater."

"Is your brother having him investigated?"

"Harry has nothing to hide. His life's an open book, it is. You want to know the truth about Joseph, why he did a bunk? The plain truth is I consider myself ever so fortunate. I would not have been able to live with him."

"I wish you and Harry the best of luck. I—"

"Your cousin Joseph was some French nobleman. The truth is he is just this side of being a meths man. He's an inveterate drinker."

"Self-hatred, self-destruction. We're a crazy family."

"I'm sure I don't know what scarred him psychologically in his childhood to make him like that. And he must have suffered torments since he fell in love with me, but—"

"I'm sure he did."

"Oh, that's nice. That's ever so nice and gentlemanly. *What right have you to talk to me like that?*"

"I apologize."

"That's why he went away 'on business' for a fortnight. It was to drink. Well, thank goodness I found out before it was too late. I don't hold grudges. I pity him."

"I'll tell him."

Ruthy leaned back and smiled triumphantly. "Caught you out, didn't I?"

"Oh, my God. If I ever run into him again, I mean."

"I caught you out for a common liar. Why don't you admit it?"

"Damn it, Ruthy, I have not laid eyes on Joey for more than twenty years."

"He certainly led me a merry dance."

"Yes, he did. I'm sorry about that."

"Well, not to worry. Worse accidents happen at sea. Harry's a very desirable man, you know."

"I'm very pleased for you."

"Oh, I'll bet you are. But this time my brother made me swear I wouldn't take a chance. No hurrying into marriage in two weeks. He says I should try the water first, if you know what I mean?"

"I see."

"Cyril says I should try the water first and see if the shoe fits. And he's right. Victorian times are over, aren't they?"

6

Jake had nowhere to go, he had nothing to do, but he was being paid a ransom to endure his idleness. An illicit ransom, he allowed, cunningly banked abroad.

One day you'll be proud of me, he had once told Issy Hersh. I'm going to be a famous film director.

Don't shoot me the crap, his father had protested. You want me to be proud? Earn a living. Stand on your own two feet.

Go know, Daddy. Go know.

Jake read, he took Nancy to the movies in the afternoon, and he awakened to light up in the middle of the night, anticipating the long-distance call that would tell him his father had died. Jake wrote to Hanna, telling her about his trip to Israel, saying how he had also sought the Horseman in Gehenna, admitting that once more he had eluded him. He rearranged his library, he put all his back issues of *Encounter* in chronological order. He bought and labeled a steel filing cabinet and weeded the garden.

Jake was sorting papers when the doorbell rang. The small, sneering stranger introduced himself as Mrs. Flam's fiancé.

"Would you care for a drink?" Jake asked.

"It's too early in the day for me."

Jake poured himself a gin and tonic. Harry Stein blew his nose and looked around stealthily, taking in everything in the living room. The rug from Casa Pupo, the winged armchair from Heal's. The kitchen door was ajar and he could see the large gleaming refrigerator. "Nice," he said. "Very nice."

Jake did not go into the kitchen for ice cubes, but decided to have his drink warm.

"Ruthy would fancy a place like this, but she can't afford it. Between you Yanks and Rachmanism, the rents have been forced up everywhere."

"Are you looking for a house, then?"

Harry smiled.

"You wouldn't like to rent it for the summer? I think we're going to Spain."

"Dollars for Franco," Harry said, jubilant.

Screw you, Jake thought, and he went to fetch some ice cubes after all.

"Do you know how many political prisoners are still rotting in Franco's dungeons?"

"I'm a fascist."

"Don't try to take the micky out of me."

"What do you want, Harry?"

"Hear that plane going over? It's American."

"I'm a Canadian."

"They fly overhead day and night with nuclear bombs in the hatch. One has already gone down in Greenland and another in Spain . . ."

"Do you think NW3 is next?"

"You're a very humorous chap."

"Look, Harry, I read the *New Statesman* too. Now what is it you want?"

Harry lit a cigarette, replacing the spent match in the box. "Are you going to charge your holiday to expenses?"

"Maybe."

"I'm on P.A.Y.E., taxed at source. Make thirty-five a week, take home twenty-six. What about you?"

"None of your business. Now what is it you want?"

"The seven hundred nicker."

"You must be crazy."

"Simply tell your cousin—"

"I've already told Ruthy I haven't seen him in years. I don't know where he is, either."

"I dispute that."

"You what?"

"I could turn this matter over to my solicitors."

"For collection?"

"You realize, I hope, that in this country aiding and abetting a fiddle is as serious as committing one."

"O.K. Sue me."

"On the other hand, if you were prepared to settle the debt—"

"It's no go, Harry. Even if I were willing to pay Joey's debt, I couldn't spare the money at the moment."

"Why not dip into the numbered Swiss account?"

"What if I was broke?"

"We have different standards of being broke. Wouldn't you concur?"

"Yes, I suppose I would."

"Ruthy stands on her feet all day, nine to five. She's getting varicose veins. She's up at seven every morning, don't you know? Washes and feeds the kiddies, dumps 'em in a council nursery, and doesn't see them again until she gets home. Nights she has to drag her things to the laundromat. You own a washing machine here?"

"*Which's* Best Buy. We've also got a housekeeper."

"Nice. Very nice."

"I think so. Well," Jake said, looking at his watch.

"Is that your final word, then? You won't honor your cousin's debt?"

Jake nodded.

"You don't remember having met me before, do you?"

"No. Sorry."

"Not to worry. Very few people notice me. I'm used to it, don't you know?"

But even then Harry hesitated at the door.

"You say you haven't got the money, Mr. Hersh, and that even if you so desired you couldn't spare it. A pity, that. For is it not a fact that at the moment you are being paid more monthly not to work than I take home in a year?"

"Who told you that?"

"I put it to you that you have lied to me."

"Where have we met before, Harry?"

"I take it you are implying that we couldn't possibly move in the same circles."

"Inferring."

Harry's cheeks bled red.

"Now tell me how come you know—or think you know—about my private affairs?"

"If you lied to me about that, I say you are prevaricating about your cousin. You know the present abode of Joseph Hersh. Or de la Hirsch. And you are protecting him."

"You don't know what you're talking about."

It was only after Harry had left that Jake noticed the large round hole burned into the fabric of the new winged armchair from Heal's. Why, the bastard, Jake thought, with sneaking admiration, he did it on purpose.

7

The next morning's mail brought a long and abusive letter. LBJ, the war in Vietnam, Barry Goldwater, the CIA, the murder of Malcolm X, and the John Birch Society were all evoked, as well as earlier, if not more vile, examples of American obloquy. Jake passed the letter to Nancy and opened the *Times*.

MONTHLY TESTS FOR CANCER

Every woman over the age of twenty-four, the Health Council enjoined, should carry out two simple tests for breast cancer each month, as nearly thirty women die from breast cancer every day—a fifth of all cancer deaths.

> A few minutes a month—that's all the time needed to check that nothing is going wrong. We hope that every woman over 24 will make it routine, like turning over the mattress.

Nancy, eight months pregnant, went to bed early. So did Jake. The telephone wakened him at three a.m. *My father*, he thought. But when he said hello, nobody replied. Hello, hello. He could hear breathing at the other end of the line, nothing more.

"Harry, you prick!"

Jake knew better than to try to sleep again. He lit a cigarillo, pulled Johnson's *Lives of the Poets* out from between the magazines and scripts stacked on his bedside table, and waited. Twenty minutes later the phone rang again.

"Aren't you going to answer it?" Nancy asked.

"No. Please go to sleep, dear."

In the morning, Jake received a pamphlet about political conditions in present-day Spain, Vicky having drawn the cartoon for the cover. It compared unfavorably with the material he had picked up at the Spanish tourist office about the delights of Torremolinos, and he suggested half-heartedly to Nancy that maybe they ought to consider the Côte d'Azur instead, once the baby came.

Why? He was worried about the milk there, maybe it wouldn't agree with the baby. But she was going to nurse this baby, just like the others. Well, there was olive oil with everything, and the kids wouldn't like it. But the south of France was far too expensive. Yes, yes, but Spain was only cheap because the workers were on starvation wages. Furthermore, tourism helped to prop up a corrupt dictatorship. Oh, really, and wasn't it a little bit late in the day for him to develop the sort of hypersensitive social conscience he mocked in others. The hell it was.

Nancy quit the kitchen for her bedroom and Jake went out for a walk, Sammy trailing after.

"Hey," Jake said. "Across the street. There's a kid in your school uniform."

Sammy didn't deign to look. "Is he leading an elephant?" he asked.

"Um, no."

"Then it isn't Rogers."

After dinner, Jake settled in for an evening's television. News for the Deaf, which he watched weekly, so that should his hearing fail he would not have to learn lip-reading from scratch, was followed by BORN TO LIVE.

> The walls of Denise Legrix's Paris studio are covered with her paintings; paintings of such power that

few would credit the artist was born without arms or legs.

Denise Legrix is in her early fifties. She has a ready smile and a quick wit, but it is in her eyes that one catches a hint of her strength. As we talked, she telephoned for a taxi, dialing the number with a paper knife held between her shoulder and neck. I met her when I was preparing tonight's program. I had framed several questions to bridge my anticipated embarrassment. I need not have bothered. With a knife held under her right armpit and a fork balanced on her left stump, she ate her food with no more fuss . . .

Harry didn't phone until two in the morning.

"Don't answer it," Nancy said.

But Jake had already grabbed the receiver. "Harry, if you call here once more I'm going to come around to your place and knock your fucking brains out."

No answer. Only breathing.

"What if it isn't him?" Nancy asked.

"Don't be absurd."

Jake dialed Harry's number. The phone rang. Rang and rang. Finally Harry said, "Hullo," his voice thick with sleep.

"Harry, it's Hersh. Jake Hersh."

"Wha . . ."

"If you don't stop calling here at all hours of the night I'm going to report you to the police."

"What's that?"

"You heard me, Harry."

"This is an outrage."

"Harry, I've been thinking. Maybe I live in a house like this, possibly I make so much more money than you do, because I'm intelligent and talented and you're just a mindless little fart."

There was a long and excruciating pause. Finally, Harry said: "I dispute that."

"But it happens to be true all the same," Jake hollered. Then he hung up, agitated and ashamed.

"I don't think you should have said that to him," Nancy said.

"All right. O.K. I already did say it."

The phone began to ring again.

"You see, it's a crank. Somebody who doesn't even know us."

Nancy took the phone off the hook, buried it under a pillow, and said, "Let's go to sleep now."

A policeman, fortunately not Sergeant Hoare, came to call at breakfast time. A Mr. Harry Stein had complained that he had been wakened in the middle of the night by phone calls of a threatening nature. Flushed and overeager, Jake explained that, on the contrary, sir, he had been troubled by nuisance calls at all hours of the night and he had merely warned Mr. Stein to desist.

How did Mr. Hersh know the party in question was Mr. Stein?

I'm glad you asked me that question. Because, Jake said, before meeting Mr. Stein, he had never been troubled with such calls.

Did Mr. Hersh have any further proof?

Certainly. But he would only divulge it at the proper time.

Be that as it may, would Mr. Hersh, in the meantime, promise not to bother Mr. Stein any more.

Yes.

Immediately the bobby had gone, Jake climbed to his attic and phoned Harry.

"Well, now. I say, I say. Aren't you the clever little bastard?"

"Oh. But I thought, in your opinion, I was, quote—a mindless little fart—unquote."

Choke to death on Kotex.

"For your information, Mr. Hersh, I belong, intellectually, *if not materially,* to the top two percent of the population of this country."

"Ha, ha. That's rich. *Says who?*"

"Mensa."

"What's that?"

"You don't know Latin, then?"

"It's a dead language."

"Mensa is Latin for table. It's the name of a round-table society I belong to, the only qualification being that your native intelligence places you in the top two percent."

"After all that sobbing about Spain, you're an élitist. A squalid little fascist."

"Mensa has no political or religious affiliations. It does not discriminate on the basis of race, color, or social class. If we are an élite, it is not by birth, background, or wealth, but on the sole basis of innate intelligence."

"Now hold on there. Wait a minute. Are you trying to tell me, little man, that *you're* one of the intellectual élite?"

"I'm saying it is a scientifically proven fact."

"You're being taken for a ride, Harry."

"Am I?"

"What did you pay to join this nut club? How much did they take you for?"

"I passed a test proving my qualifications."

"If you could, so could my son Sammy. Blindfolded."

"Would you be prepared to submit to the test, then?"

"Well, um, sure. But who has time for such nonsense?"

"I see."

"You see. O.K. Where do I get it?"

"I'll have the test sent to you."

"Right. And I'm willing to put down ten quid to your one that I score higher than you ever did. Intellectual élite, my ass."

"We have a bet then, Mr. Hersh."

"Indeed we do. And meanwhile, no more phone calls in the middle of the night, you understand?"

"I refute such a charge."

"Just remember what I said."

"Have you had any further thoughts about your cousin's debt to Ruthy?"

"No. Goodbye."

At the breakfast table, Nancy decided to say nothing. She poured him more coffee.

"What is it with me," he demanded. "Wherever I put my foot down, it's quicksand."

Underline which of the four numbered figures fits into the empty space.

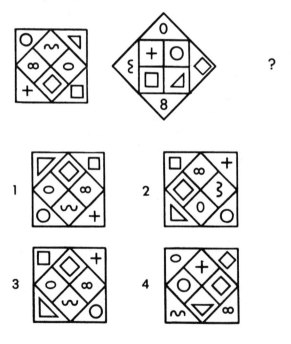

Insert the missing number.

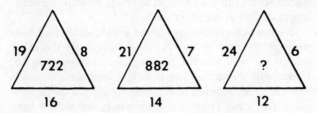

Complete the following.

SCOTLAND 27186453 LOTS 7293 LOAN 8367 AND_____

Underline the odd-man-out.

AZEETRIULOS
OHEELORRUMAELUS
NIVOERINNIURIS
REALOPPOOSILILOO

It's ridiculous. Utterly ridiculous.

While John was at work on the repapering of the hall, Billy and Tony had strict instructions that they should remain in the garden.

Having tired of playing cricket, the boys looked around for something to do. In the course of their wanderings, they came across a pair of snails, so they decided to have a snail-race. The snails were of somewhat different types, and the boys recognized that one of them was a type which preferred climbing, whereas the other was more of a walker. Consequently, some care had to be taken in order to give them both an equal chance.

Both snails were the same size and shape—in fact, the only difference between them was that one preferred to climb rather than to go along the level. The climber found that during his twelve waking hours he could only climb three feet, and during his twelve sleeping hours he slid down a foot. The walker found that he had no bother with sliding, of course, although he slept the same length of time as the other snail.

In consequence, the boys found a wall, and placed both snails at the foot of it. Four feet away from the other side of the wall was the finishing-post, a luscious shrub. If the wall was seven feet in height, and the two snails had sufficient ambition to aim directly for the shrub, how many feet away from the shrub would the walker have to be placed in order to give each snail a fair chance?

A children's game.

Insert the word in the brackets which can be prefixed by any of the letters on the left.

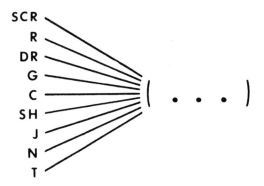

```
SCR
  R
 DR
  G
  C              ( . . . )
 SH
  J
  N
  T
```

Although he is known to posterity on account of his engravings, Albrecht Dürer, who worked during the sixteenth century, would also seem to have had a certain interest in things mathematical.

In his famous picture 'Melancolia,' for instance, astronomy, architecture, and solid geometry all have their place—together with an example of a fourth-order Magic Square, the numbers in the centre of the bottom line of which are reputed to date the picture.

Although, in actual fact, the numbers in the Magic Square are quite clear, consisting of the numbers 1–16 inclusive, suppose that some of them were not, and that the Square gave the appearance shown in Fig. 10.

16			
	10		
		7	
4			

Fig. 10

In what year did Dürer engrave this masterpiece?

And doesn't prove a damn thing, either.

9

The Grand Inquisitor brought Jake to his office by dispatching notices of reassessment for seven years, 1960 through 1966, requiring a total of no less than £7,200 in settlement thereof within thirty-one days.

"What happens now?" Jake demanded of Oscar Hoffman.

"Don't worry about a thing. They'll compromise. They always do."

Hoffman accompanied Jake to the Grand Inquisitor's office, where after an exchange of niceties—

"Ah," Jake exclaimed, espying a copy of *Dance & Dancers* in the out tray, "I see you are a ballet lover too."

"Yes."

"What did you think of Nureyev's Romeo?"

"I'm afraid I'm odd man out there. I thought it was overrated."

"I'm glad you said that, because so did I."

The inspector, who turned out to be a gawky, hesitant clerk in his twenties, contemplated the account sheets for the first trading year of Jacob Hersh Productions Ltd., and read aloud, "On the first annual meeting of Jacob Hersh Productions Ltd., on Oct. 12, 1960, the chairman declared that on a turnover of

£10,000 there was a profit of £841.19.6. It was decided not to declare a dividend. Is that correct?"

"It's so long ago, you know."

Mmmmn, the inspector agreed, tight-lipped.

"To the best of my knowledge, yes, it's correct. As I recall it, I wasted a lot of money taking out foolish options that year."

"It would appear," he said, consulting the sheets before him, "that most of them were paid for in cash, and originated in Canada."

"I know love of country is out of fashion these days," Jake said, "but I'm crazy enough to believe that those Canadians who happen to be sufficiently lucky to live here, where there's such exciting theater and ballet, owe something to writers struggling at home. I keep hoping to develop a good Canadian script, but get my fingers burned again and again."

Oscar Hoffman beamed, recognizing a rank-one scholar.

"I note a payment here of £1,000 advance to one Jean Beliveau, script writer, of the Forum Apartments, St. Catherine St. W., Montreal."

"That loser. I wish I'd never met him. It's a write-off, I'm afraid. Totally unusable."

"I see in the same fiscal year you paid another advance, also of £1,000, to one John A. MacDonald."

"He turned out to be a lush. But I'm still hoping to set that one up."

"You keep a secretary in Canada. Mrs. Laura Secord of 312 Ontario Street, Montreal."

"Yes."

"Are you aware," the inspector asked, loosening the elastic from a wad of restaurant and liquor bills, "that all allowable expenses must be wholly, exclusively, and necessarily incurred for business reasons?"

"Indeed I am."

"In 1960, you claimed £1,750 for entertainment expenses."

"And to think," Jake said, shaking his head, appalled, "if I'd put that money into unit trusts, I'd be sitting pretty today."

"On reflection, how much of this would you claim was actually business expense and how much would you allow was personal?"

"Let's say . . . five percent personal."

The inspector hunched over the wad of bills.

". . . seven per cent *could* be possible. Eight tops."

The statement he produced was from the Victoria Wine Company, February 1960, and came to £81, including an order for one hundred cigarettes.

"How many of these cigarettes would you claim were consumed in the line of business? How many for personal reasons? Given to friends or your wife?"

"There's a very fine line of distinction here. In fact your question is really of a Talmudic nature. So let me answer it, as is the custom, with another question. If I offered you a cigarette right now would it be personal? Or a business expense?"

The inspector did not look up from his accounts, but Hoffman coughed disapprovingly.

"The truth is, I don't remember. But these accounts were accepted in 1960. Why are you coming back to me now?"

"The Commissioners of Inland Revenue never specify the grounds for reassessment. Here's something typical."

It was a restaurant bill. Dinner for four at Chez Luba, £21.

"I took out a producer and his wife. To discuss a project."

"Would you say you brought your wife along for personal pleasure?"

"No. I would not say. She abhors producers. He brought his wife, I had to bring mine. Are we going to consider all these old bills individually?"

No answer.

"I see that, in 1965, Jacob Hersh Productions sub-contracted to World-Wide, of Geneva, Switzerland, leasing the directorial services of Jacob Hersh for an annual fee of £7,500 . . . but previously you were taking in even more."

"It's embarrassing. It's bloody awful. I keep kicking myself. I never should have done it."

"You are aware, I assume, that it is against the law for you to have bank accounts outside the country?"

"Of course I am. Good God, you're not accusing me of . . . tax evasion?"

"We are not specifically charging you with anything."

"What do you want from me, then?"

"I put it to you, that something like ninety-five per cent of these alleged expenses were really of a personal nature."

"Why, that's ridiculous."

The inspector pushed back his desk chair, terminating the interview. "I will consider these accounts further," he said, "and be in touch with you again."

"I think that's best," Hoffman said, speaking for the first time. "My client appreciates that."

"The hell I do. This whole business smacks of the Star Chamber. I do believe you owe it to me to reveal why my accounts have been reopened."

"It is not the policy of the Commissioners of Inland Revenue to specify grounds for reassessment. I will be in touch with you again soon."

10

The next morning's mail brought a letter from Mensa:

Dear Sir,

Thank you for your interesting letter of Apr. 19, 1967.

We do take note of the fact that in your "humble opinion" a society that "discriminates" against 98 per cent of the population can be construed as being "undemocratic," and we note with interest and some sympathy your point that our tests cannot measure talent and originality, but only specific abilities. We do, however, take strong issue with your argument that MENSA fosters delusions of grandeur among "clerks and milkmen, dentists and shop stewards," encouraging them to believe that their ignominy is a reflection of social injustice and not a result of their own ineptitude. Frankly, this sort of thing smacks of sour grapes to us here. Furthermore, if you would not care to be associated with such a "seedy, self-satisfied group," why, then, did you complete our test?

Finally, we would like to make it clear that neither success nor failure in our test is to be taken too seriously. A degree of uncertainty is inherent in any kind of statistical measurement and, as you so strongly suggested, there are theoretical doubts about the measurement of intelligence which can only add to this. . . .

11

"Yes, Harry. What is it?"

"Have you had any further thoughts about your cousin's debt to Ruthy?"

"Screw you."

The minicabs, dispatched to Jake's door at outlandish hours, were a headache, the drivers increasingly truculent. Jake apologized to the firemen, swearing he wasn't the one who had summoned them. He assured the driver from Harrod's that there had been a mistake, he had not ordered a twelve-pound roast. He refused to accept any parcels sent C.O.D. and he returned all books and records mailed to him on approval. Apologizing profusely, he explained to the ambulance driver they were both victims of a hoax.

"Yes, Harry. What is it today?"

"I thought, perhaps, you might have had a change of heart. About the debt, you know."

"I've got nerves of steel, Harry. But if this doesn't stop, I'm going to knock your teeth out."

"If what doesn't stop?"

"Look at it this way. Two can play the same game."

For three days no parcels came. The SPCA didn't call, neither did the man from the Gas Board. The following morning, even as Jake was packing his bag feverishly, the phone rang. It was Harry again.

"What is it *now?*"

"We have a bet. Isn't that right?"

Briefly, Jake was confused.

"I was wondering, Mr. Hersh, if you had heard from Mensa yet?"

"Oh, that. Look, I can't talk now. I've got to be at the airport in forty minutes."

"Where are you going?"

"Cannes. What's it to you?"

"Nice. Very nice."

"It's business, as it so happens. Not pleasure. I'll only be there overnight. Meeting a producer. Phone me tomorrow noon."

Taking off, Jake gripped the arms of his seat and recited the standard litany to himself. Statistics prove it's safer than driving. The Vanguard has an incomparable record. Rolls Royce engines are unsurpassed. It didn't help—it never did—but two double Scotches quelled his stomach, and an hour and a half out of London he was bothered only by his companion, a loquacious American mutual funds salesman. He feigned sleep.

Opening his eyes to order another drink, Jake's heart suddenly began to hammer. The sun, adrift on his righthand side hitherto, was now streaming in through the lefthand window. His ears throbbed. They were losing altitude.

"Didn't want to wake you," the American said, "but we're heading back to little old London, if you ask me."

The loudspeaker spluttered alive. "Ladies and gentlemen, this is the captain speaking. We are experiencing operational difficulties and we have turned to land at Paris. Our expected flying time will be thirty-five minutes."

The stewardess came around with drinks.

"Everything's going to be all right," she sang out serenely. "There's nothing to worry about." But her face was ashen.

I don't believe it, Jake repeated over and over to himself. This sort of meaningless accident only happens to other people.

"My name's Newby," the American said.

"Hersh."

"You believe in God?"

"Of course I do. I always have." You hear?

"Not me. Not any more. I flew B-29's during the war, you know."

"Did you?"

"Twenty-nine missions and never once saw an angel. Neither did any of the other guys."

"Maybe they were elsewhere. Or flying higher."

"Folks won't buy it any more. Not since the space probes. The astronauts haven't seen none either."

"The Russians wouldn't even admit it if they had," Jake countered.

Newby pondered that one.

"Hey," Jake said, trembling, sliding in sweat, "we're still coming down."

"Sure thing. He's taking us down to 10,000 feet, I reckon."

The wings were holding on. Both of them. No engine seemed to be working loose. "Why?" Jake asked.

"If there's an explosion—"

Bite your tongue, Newby.

"—we won't have to use oxygen."

While there was no need for alarm, the captain announced over the PA system, passengers were requested to extinguish their cigarettes and fasten their seat belts.

Immediately, Jake demanded more liquor.

"Everything's going to be all right," the stewardess said.

"I didn't even ask."

"There's nothing to worry about," she replied.

A woman began to sob brokenly. Somebody prayed aloud.

"Ever wonder why we're here?" Newby asked.

Ignoring him, Jake started a letter to Nancy.

"A higher intelligence in another galaxy planted us on earth.

Three sorts. White, yellow, black. We're an experiment. Like in a cosmic greenhouse. They want to know who's sturdiest, which color comes out on top, before they start seeding the other planets."

The plane began to bank, Orly tantalizingly within its grasp.

"We expect to land in Paris in eight minutes," the captain announced.

The stewardess passed from seat to seat, saying it was going to be all right, and asking passengers to remove any sharp objects from their pockets.

"This is it," Newby said, and raising his glass, he added, "Anything flashing before your eyes?"

"Shettup, for Chrissake."

Another stewardess pointed out to Jake that he was sitting beside an emergency exit—

"Am I?"

—and showed him how to open it.

The plane banked again, for a final approach, and touched down with ease, rocking to a stop some distance from the air terminal. There were ambulances waiting on the tarmac, fire trucks too, but they disembarked in the usual manner, everybody euphoric.

"Wasn't it exciting?" the stewardess ventured.

Yes, indeed. Jake asked what the trouble was.

"A hoax," the stewardess replied. "But we can't take chances."

Once the passengers were assembled, a safe distance from the plane, the captain told them, "I had been advised there might be a bomb aboard the aircraft." As the anonymous caller to BEA had given exact information about the flight, airline officials had no choice but to classify the incident as a positive bomb scare. He was sorry for any inconvenience etc., etc. While security officials combed through the aircraft, passengers' baggage was spread out on a field. They were asked to identify their luggage and open it for inspection.

"What's this?" the inspector asked Jake, indicating the unmarked bullet-size pellets in the typewriter ribbon tin he had just opened.

"It's medicinal," Jake replied, flushing.

"What's that?"

Strangers regarded them with interest.

"Could I have a word with you . . . um . . . privately?"

They stepped aside, the inspector maintaining a steel-like grip on his arm.

"They're suppositories."

"Would you speak up, please. The noise . . ."

"I suffer from piles. Like Karl Marx, you know."

The rest of the trip was uneventful, but even more disastrous. The producer Jake was supposed to meet at the Carleton had been unable to wait and had flown to New York. Jake's hotel reservation had been fouled up and he had had to settle for an airless, mosquito-ridden cell in a backstreet pension. Hungover, his nerves frayed, he returned to London in the morning with only one thought in mind. The pleasure it would give him to murder Harry Stein.

Jake sought out Ruthy at the Swiss Cottage dress shop. "I must see your boyfriend urgently. Can you tell me where he works, please?"

Oscar Hoffman, Accountants.

"Oh, no." He doesn't.

"Why not?"

Harry agreed to meet Jake for a drink at noon at the York-minster.

"I'm not going to hit you, Harry. I'm not going to break your teeth. I merely want to warn you that I'm getting a lawyer. I'm going to have you charged with attempting to extort with menaces."

"I don't know what you're talking about."

"What if somebody on that plane had died of a heart attack?"

Harry shook his head, seemingly baffled.

"You twisted little fart," Jake said, grabbing him by the collar.

"Possibly I'm the one who needs a solicitor," Harry said, breaking free, "for it's clear to me what you need is psychological attention."

"You're the mental case, Harry, not me."

"I put it to you, you suffer from paranoid delusions."

"Oh, you are cute," Jake said, ordering another round. "You're not ordinary twisted. I'm beginning to think you're very, very special. And now, my psychotic friend, tell me how long you've been with Oscar Hoffman?"

"Going on ten years."

"That's where we met?"

"Yes."

"You've seen my accounts and you know I'm not broke."

"For the sake of argument, I'll concur with that statement."

"Would you also happen to know I'm now being investigated by the inspectors of Inland Revenue?"

"No," Harry replied, impassive.

"How much did you get for turning me in?"

"You're paranoid, mate."

"Harry, you obscene little auto-didact, there's more to psychology than Penguin paperbacks .. ."

Harry's eyes filled with rancor.

". . . now what are you getting for informing on me? Ten percent?"

"I refute your charges absolutely. If you care to make them formally you shall be hearing from my solicitors."

"Stupid prick!"

"Speaking of intellectual ability, have you heard from Mensa yet?"

Jake fished into his pocket, extracted two fivers, and rammed them into Harry. "Here. Choke."

"Now you only owe me another seven hundred pounds."

"What do you mean, *I owe you?*"

"You're knocking down a thousand a week for doing bleeding nothing—" Harry lowered his voice "—tax-free, my so-called socialist friend."

Jake blanched.

"You're all men of principle, you film types."

"I'm not a film type."

"What are you, then?"

"All right, all right. You know it's blackmail, though."

"I wouldn't call it that."

"The money's not yours, anyway. It's Ruthy's."

Harry ordered a round. "Pay her. Not me."

"What do you want to marry her for? Has she got more?"

"It's your cousin, the fancy-man, who was after her lolly, not me."

"I'm to take it you love her, then?"

"She's an attractive woman," Harry said defensively.

"I should have thought a chap in the top two percent intellectually, one of the élite, as it were, handsome and well-read as you, could have done much better."

"Don't you ever make the mistake of ridiculing me, Hersh. Don't you ever do that."

"Not to worry. If I didn't respect you before, I learned to on the airplane. My God, how could you do such a thing?"

"We're back on that, are we?"

"Come clean, Harry. You phoned BEA."

Harry raised his glass. "Here's looking at you."

"How old are you?"

"Thirty-eight."

"Tell me something else, then. How have you managed to stay out of prison all these years?"

"And who says I have?"

"No kidding," Jake said, regarding him with fresh interest, even respect, "what did they put you away for?"

"I'd better be off now."

"Come to lunch with me. Be my guest."

Harry hesitated.

"We can charge it to expenses. After all, you're one of my financial advisers, aren't you, you bastard?"

"All right, then. If that's the way you put it."

Riding too many large gins, flattered with wine, Harry revealed that he had first become entangled with the law in Lady Docker's England, when there was still rationing and Gilbert Harding, Ealing comedies, Attlee, war in Korea; and Harry Stein, a beginning bookkeeper, read in the *News Chronicle* of the disappearance, possibly a kidnapping, of a particularly coarse and ostentatious lady, the wife of a merchant banker. The police beat the bushes of neighboring Putney Heath, they scoured the abandoned railway sidings, hoping for the best but awaiting a phone call with instructions. Or a ransom note.

Harry obliged.

> If you wish to see your wife alive again, you will deposit £5,000 in used one-pound notes in a small suitcase on Wednesday night, at 7 p.m., beside the gate to the cemetery in Putney Vale. I put it to you that this is no more than you donate to the Conservative Party annually or have indecently earned in a "bad" month out of the honest sweat of the working man. Meanwhile, your wife is safe. I could hardly be sexually aroused by such a spent old bag, but she is cold and frightened. Should you go to the police, she will die, and the same holds true if the money is marked.

Alas for Harry, the lady was discovered in a seaside hotel in Sussex on Wednesday afternoon, none the worse for a postmenopausal fit of amnesia, but Harry didn't know, he couldn't, and as he strolled past the Putney Vale gates on Wednesday evening at seven, the police pounced on him. Harry fervently denied everything, he didn't know what the police were about, but confronted with samples of his own handwriting, undone by stupidity, he then claimed it was all a joke. He had not, after all, kidnapped the lady, which was undeniably true, and he had intended to turn over the money to the defense fund for Julius and Ethel Rosenberg.

Mr. Justice Delaney, at the Old Bailey, took a rather different view. While a family, stricken with anxiety and grief, had waited through seemingly interminable nights by the telephone for news of a loved one, this wretched young man, motivated by malice and greed, had done his utmost to add to the family's considerable torment. Indeed, Mr. Watkins, who had suffered a coronary attack only two years earlier, had had to be put to bed with a sedative on receipt of Stein's abominable note.

"I am asked to take into consideration the accused's hitherto unblemished record, but the case is most repulsive, and all too symbolic of the decadent society in which we live today. Already one tenth of the population of this country is either physically or mentally deficient. It is unfit for citizenship of this great nation. It is, I say, a terrible result of the random output of unrestricted breeding. In my view, young men such as this are treated leniently at society's peril, turned loose only to prey on respectable citizens. This policy is unwise, most unwise. I intend to make an example out of you and my order is that you be sent to prison for three years."

To which Harry, before being escorted below, smiled thinly and replied, "Thank you, my Lord."

Staggering out of the restaurant, the pubs shut, Jake teased Harry into an invitation to his flat, insisting he needed another drink but actually determined to see how he lived.

The cry of birds from Regent's Park Zoo could be heard in Harry's three-room basement flat, comprised of a kitchen, sitting room, and bedroom, photographic equipment lying everywhere, the bathroom also serving as a dark room. The bed was unmade, the sheets unspeakable, a sticky jam jar, bread, and a knife on the bedside table. Stacks of dishes drifted in the kitchen sink. There was a poster of Che in the sitting room, as well as a nude study of Jane Fonda. Harry rinsed a couple of glasses and came up with a half-bottle of Scotch. Encouraged, he read Jake one of his poems:

> *Time-Server*
>
> *The bloke with-*
>   *out*
> *lsd*
>   *or*
>   *fre*
> *edom*
> *doesn't know it.*
> *he's caged*

ineveryfactoryeveryofficeeveryday
but doesn't know it.

docile, obliging
he's a domesticated pussy.
purring at his master's smile.

But when the bloke with-
                                        out
lsd
        or
                fre
edom
shows his teeth or shits on the carpet
the master calls for his riding crop
summons his dogs.
Turned worms must be squashed.

Then he agreed to show him some of the photographs he had taken. Among them, one of an Oriental girl with enormous breasts, her arms upraised, the wrists knotted together by a rope, and hanging chains brushing against her.

"She's got goose pimples," Jake said, finding it easiest to joke as he passed on to the next photograph.

In this one a heavy girl squatted, smirking at the photographer, legs opened wide as she tugged a serpent out from under her and held it to her mouth, her tongue flicking out for a kiss.

"Hershel, Hershel, what's to be done with you?" Jake asked.

Hours later they drained the bottle, sharing the last of the Scotch. Red-eyed drunk, dizzy but exhilarated, Harry talked endlessly. "You know I'm different, see. I'm only telling you this because you understand I'm no cipher. That I've read a book or two and been to a concert. I want you to know what it was like when I was in my twenties. I want you to imagine what I went through. I mean to say, shit, who wouldn't have had a breakdown,

if that's what you want to call it? I had nothing, mate. Sweet fucking nothing and grand expectations of more sweet fucking nothing.
And the years were slipping by. Only I knew it, see, not like
the others. I knew what I was missing and that's always been my
trouble. Not like the others. Terrified of getting the sack. Stor-
ing shillings in the post office account like hamsters. Out of their
minds with joy for a ten-shilling rise. Not Harry. Harry uses
his loaf and that's his trouble, isn't it? One day, listen to this, one
day, this fat old geezer in a Bentley pulls up, he lowers his
window and asks, ever so polite, would you know how I could
get to Battersea Bridge from here? Actually, yes, you old fuck,
I said, but first you tell me how much you'd pay to be my age
again, because you're not long for it, are you, mate, with all
your money. I thought he'd have his stroke right there. I went
to the boat show. Did I tell you that one? About the boat show
at Olympia? I went to the boat show, you see, 1960 it was, you
can look it up in the newspapers if you think I'm lying. I went
thinking I'll buy me a thirtieth birthday present. What a laugh!
I picked one out for me (I've still got the pamphlets, you know),
having the salesman on about the delivery dates. A thousand
nicker all in it was. And I realized if I went without for the
next ten years, I still couldn't afford it. I was never going to
bloody have it. Any of it. No yacht. No MG. No weeks at
Monte. Even though I'm among the top two percent of this
country intellectually, and you've got the proof of it now,
haven't you, mate? Even though I'm scientifically proven more
intelligent than you and certainly any of that lot, I wasn't going
to have anything. Because I'm an insect."

And so, Harry went on to explain, laughing with fond remembrance, he had gone to a call box around the corner, put on
his Latin accent, and warned them there was a bomb set to go
off in thirty minutes as a protest against the government's Cuban
policy.

"They took it seriously, you know. Old Khrushchev waving
his shoe at the U.N. Castro in New York, raising hell. They
didn't take any chances. Police cars. Fire trucks. The lot. And all

those dignified cool bastards and their tarts, you should have seen them move. Spilling out of Olympia very smartly indeed. I watched from across the street, fit to be tied. Do you know they raked that place over from top to bottom. They turned Olympia inside out that night, looking for my time bomb. You look it up, if you don't believe me. Maybe I've still got the press cuttings."

12

The next morning, after driving Sammy to school, Jake sought out Ruthy at the dress shop. But she had not come in to work. Her eldest boy, David, had a temperature of 103.

"Oh, it's you," she said, opening the door to Jake. "I had hoped it was the doctor. I should have known better."

"Why?"

Ruthy explained that she had absolutely refused to bundle up David and take him to Dr. Engel's surgery. She had threatened Engel with a letter of complaint to the National Health Service if he refused to come to the house, and now she was terrified because she knew he would not call for hours, and that when he did finally show up he would be horrid. He was, she said, such a foul-tempered man anyway. Almost as bad as Dr. West. When David had only been a baby, running a temperature of 102 and vomiting, Dr. West had grudgingly come to her flat to look at him. "You're fussing," he had said, "fussing. He's teething, that's all." But twenty-four hours later, with David's temperature still rising, she had bundled him up and taken him to the hospital, where they discovered he had bronchial pneumonia and put him in an oxygen tent.

So Ruthy had demanded her cards back and gone to register

with Dr. Engel. Owl-faced Engel, dribbling cigarette ash, had flicked through the cards, piles of letters from the hospital, and other records, and then said: "You know, there's only one kind of patient who comes to me with a record like this."

"And what kind is that, doctor?"

The neurotic.

"As if," Ruthy protested to Jake, "the NHS comes to us free. We're taxed plenty. If Engel doesn't like being on the NHS, why doesn't he emigrate?"

"And what about you," Jake asked, "have you ever considered it?"

"Certainly not," she replied, affronted. "Harry says you're going to pay me back what your cousin stole from me. Is that true?"

"I've brought you a check."

"Would you care for tea?"

"Oh, thanks. Yes. Ruthy, if you're really that worried about your son, why don't you let me call my doctor. I'm sure he'd come immediately."

"All you have to do is snap your fingers. It must be nice," she mused, "to live your style. With connections everywhere."

"Do you want me to call him or not?"

"Sure, call him. My David is as good as any of yours."

"Where's the phone, then?"

"The second floor maid is using it. You've got six pence?"

"Yes."

"It's in the hall."

O'Brien agreed to look in within an hour. Jake followed Ruthy into the kitchen, where he was astonished to see, as she opened a cupboard in search of tea bags, shelf upon shelf of tins, tins of every conceivable size and shape, all of them shorn of their labels.

"What's going on here?" Jake asked.

"Oh," she giggled, "I'm a competitor from the competitors. Didn't you know?"

Ruthy led him to her "office," the bridge table in the corner of the living room, which was stacked with neatly ordered labels from soups, sardines, soft drinks, biscuits, chocolate bars, crisps, and so forth. There were scissors, paste, envelopes, and entry forms. There was this week's *News of the World* Spot the Ball contest, £5,000 for the outright winner, the competitor who, scrutinizing the action photograph of a football game, made his X exactly where the missing ball was in play. Alongside lay entry forms for the Heinz Golden Opportunity contest, the Opals/Spangles competition, Brooke Bond Name-the-Chimp contest, the Daily Sketch Jackpot, Topcat Win a "Woman" Dream Kitchen, the Great Tetley Treasure Island contest and the £1,000 Pepsi Personality Analysis competition, as well as Horlick's Secret Dream and the Wall's Name-the-Soup contest.

"Would you save your labels for me?" Ruthy asked.

"Well, yes. But which ones?"

"Any with a contest. You don't drink Beefeater's Gin, do you?"

"I could."

"Ooo, they're giving away a Triumph sports car. Would you bring me the labels?"

"Yes. Certainly. But have you ever won anything, Ruthy?"

"You think I'm a dummy. So does my brother. Sure, I've won plenty."

The bridge table. A stainless steel carving set. A dinner service. A carton of Heinz soup. Seven days at Butlin's Holiday Camp. And many, many more prizes.

"I also once won fifty pounds in the pools. So, you think Harry would make a good dad for my boys?"

"He's a rather complex man, Ruthy, isn't he?"

The boys needed a dad. David, her eldest, was too moody and sensitive for exams; he had failed his 11-plus and had to go to a secondary modern school. Sidney, her youngest, still sucked his thumb. Nothing helped. Not tying his arm, not coating his thumb with hot mustard. But her nephew was a boarder at Carmel College, the Jewish public school in Wallingford. "Not bad for a father who was brought up on the Commercial Road and never got any further than the Jewish Free School." On the High Holidays, she said, her brother's family stayed at the Green

Park Hotel in Bournemouth. "Have you ever seen it? It's beautiful. Fantastic. It's just like Versailles."

"Have you been there, then?"

"Are you kidding? Me? 'Let them eat cake.' Do you know
who said that?"

David called and Ruthy excused herself. Their voices were
raised. Ruthy spoke sharply. David began to sob, then she
slammed the door. "He wants to get out of bed. But your doctor's coming; I'd look like a fool."

"What's his temperature now?"

"Only ninety-nine," she admitted glumly.

O'Brien swept in, examined the boy, and emerged from the
bedroom to say, "Mild case of tonsilitis. He should have them
out, you know."

"Don't you think I'm on a waiting list? It's four months already I'm waiting. Maybe, doctor, with your connections . . ."

"Please," Jake said, "Dr. O'Brien is a very busy man."

"You're all busy men," Ruthy said, seeing O'Brien to the door.
Then she picked up Jake's check and scrutinized it again. "As-
suming it's good," she said, giggling, "I've got Harry to thank
for this. He's such a brilliant man, but he's disappointed in himself. If he wasn't Jewish, with his ability, he'd be very rich
today."

"Being Jewish didn't stop Charles Clore."

"It's this country, you know. It's the class system. Harry's got
the wrong accent. There's no old boys' network to take care of
him. If he came from Canada, like you, where quality doesn't
count, he'd be very important. His background wouldn't be
held against him."

"Maybe Harry's trouble is self-pity?"

"You think Prince Charles could get into Mensa?"

"He doesn't need to."

"You said it," she replied triumphantly.

"All right, then, why not emigrate with Harry? Maybe your
kids would have a better chance in Canada?"

"You think I haven't looked into it? Just listen to this, will
you?" She read from the application form. " 'Have you or has

any one of the persons included in this application ever been convicted of, or admit to having committed, any crime or offence?' That takes care of Harry, doesn't it?"

Ruthy opened a dresser drawer and produced a Xerox of the ten-year-old *News of the World* clipping.

HITCHCOCK FILM IDEA
BEHIND BID TO KILL
STARLET

A 25-year-old bookkeeper, inspired by a Hitchcock film, conceived the idea of trying to kill a starlet he had developed a passion for by fiddling with the brakes of her Triumph sports car.

The 24-year-old actress, Carol Lane, who has appeared in *Doctor in the House, The Long Arm,* and other films, managed to change into lower gear and stop the car, said Mr. Godfrey Hale, prosecuting.

And what might have been a tragedy was averted, he added.

The man in the dock, Harry Stein, of Winchester Road, NW3, pleaded not guilty to attempting to murder Miss Lane, who lives in St. John's Wood Road, nearby.

Mr. Hale said this was a pathetic case.

As far as was known, he had never actually met Miss Lane but he had developed a passion for her.

For weeks he had tormented her with obscene phone calls, culminating in a call that stated if he couldn't enjoy her body, nobody else would.

On the evening of May 10, Miss Lane parked her car outside her flat in St. John's Wood Road.

Next morning she drove off in the usual way. On Finchley Road she realized there was something wrong with her brakes. After stopping the car, she called the AA.

When the vehicle was examined the AA inspector came to the conclusion that the braking system had been deliberately interfered with . . .

"He got two years," Ruthy said, "and she went on to bigger and better parts. Only Harry's going to re-open the case now. We're going to clear his name."

"Wouldn't it cost a good deal to appeal the case now?"

"It's not Cyril's money; it's mine," she protested petulantly. "My darling brother convinced my late husband I was a dummy, so my legacy is being held in trust. Harry's read the will. It's full of loopholes, he says. We're going to contest it."

Poor Cyril.

"Oh, one thing, Ruthy. Now that I've settled my cousin's debt, as it were, I would like to have his riding clothes. And the saddle, if I may?"

"Good riddance," she said, going to fetch them.

As Jake entered the house, the saddle slung over his shoulder, riding crop in hand, Nancy clapped her hands, "Look, children, it isn't Daddy. It's Ben Cartwright."

"Ha, ha."

Only then did he notice the packed bag on the hall floor. He froze.

"Don't panic. The contractions are still fairly mild and far apart. But a child can come quickly."

Pilar saw them into the car, sniffling, and Jake drove off with extreme caution. He told her he had given Ruthy the seven hundred pounds.

"I don't understand why you even bother with them," Nancy said.

"Well, we don't stand in queues. And my cousin did take her for a ride, you know."

"Harry gives me the shivers."

"Harry's a street accident and I just happen to be a witness. What should I do, flee without handing in my name?"

"Don't be sharp with me, please."

"I can't stand this enforced idleness any more."

"Look for a film, then. If you find one you want to do, forfeit the balance of the money."

"You make it sound so simple."

"It is, isn't it?"

"Yes," he said, relieved. "You're right."

13

Ben came easily, born squealing and in haste, early the following morning. May 10, 1967. And Jake, jubilant, hurried home to tell Sammy and Molly the news, only to discover that Pilar had taken them to a movie. Luke's secretary informed him the master was in Cannes. On impulse, Jake phoned Hoffman's office and asked for Harry.

"Yes. Stein here."

"Is that the mad bomber himself?"

"Who's this?"

"We at Mensa have decided to disqualify you on the grounds of sexual perversion. You are a disgrace to the rest of the best."

"It's Jacob Hersh, then?"

He invited Harry to lunch, and a half hour later, strolling in the sun through St. James's Park with him, he regretted it. He interrupted one of Harry's diatribes to say, "My God, Hershel, I don't give a shit about the iniquity of the top-hat tax avoidance schemes. Or how Marmaduke's school fees are paid. It's spring. I'm a father again. You and I, we're going to have Scotch salmon together, mouth-watering asparagus, a bottle of hock. Fresh strawberries. I feel good. Don't you ever feel good?"

"Grateful for the treat is what you mean to say. Well, no. I don't fancy being a charity case."

"Harry, you vile thing, what's to be done with you?"

"Right now," he said, "there are lascivious bastards no better than me sunning themselves on the decks of their yachts in the Bay of Cannes, with nubile starlets waiting below, just panting for a chance to suck their cocks. And when I return to the office after lunch, it's to sweat over their accounts."

"Oh, Hershel, Hershel, your idea of the good life and mine are not the same, you know. Leave Ruthy alone, please."

"What?" he said, startled.

"She's not overly bright. Be a *mensh*, Harry. This once."

"I would be ever so grateful if you would not intrude into my personal affairs."

"I thought we were friends now, Harry."

Harry laughed dryly. "Come off it. I amuse you. You enjoy hearing my prison stories. I've got the courage to do things you only dream of."

"Like hell," Jake replied, his anger rising.

"You're not my friend. You'd never invite me to dinner at your house, because I'm not good enough for your wife. Or to be introduced to your real friends. I'm just a thing to you."

"All right, that settles it. As soon as Nancy's up to it, you're invited to dinner."

"Going to make me the household Cockney, are you now?"

"I'm no Old Etonian, you know. I'm a working-class boy too."

"Look, mate, I've never had any friends and I like it that way. You think I'd ever trust you?"

"Why not?"

"Everybody's rotten."

"What if I wasn't?"

"Don't worry. You're rotten."

"*Oy veh.* Did I ever pick somebody to celebrate a birth with. I must be crazy."

But when they reached the White Elephant there was a bottle of champagne drifting in a bucket at Jake's table.

"I ordered it," Harry protested, "and I'm paying for it. It's Veuve Clicquot. Is that good enough?"

"Of course it is. Thank you, Harry. I'm touched. Really I am."

"You've had a bottle or two before, mate. Let's not break into tears over it."

"Cheers, comrade."

"Cheers. Have you put the boy down for a good school yet?"

"Cut it out, Harry. Relax. Let's have a good time."

But Harry was no longer listening. Eyes charged with rancor, he scanned the other tables. Lissome girls in miniskirts laughing at jokes made by men old enough to be their fathers. Harry watched, his silence terrifying, as a tall raven-haired girl in a clinging Pucci shift glided toward the ladies' room, stopping, with the utmost assurance, to pluck a strawberry from the fruit trolley, flicking it on to a darting pink tongue, and then nodding yes, yes, an appreciative hand held to her bosom. "Immediately, madame," the waiter purred.

All at once, Harry seized Jake by the arm. "You don't understand," he cried. "I'm not getting enough of anything, don't you see? And most of the things I want I'm already too old to enjoy."

14

In the end, Nancy and Jake decided Spain was impractical, so was the south of France, and they took a house in Cornwall instead. A week after Nancy came out of the hospital, Jake drove her and the children to the place he had rented near Newquay. Pilar, who had gone on ahead by train, was standing in the door to meet them. Jake stayed the weekend and then returned to London, hopefully for no more than a week, to meet with his lawyers, consult his agent, and discuss the possibility of doing a ninety-minute film for BBC TV.

Night after night, he returned to his house to drink alone in his attic aerie, waiting for the phone call that would say his father was dead. RITA HAYWORTH LEAVES ALY KAHN FOR ISSY HERSH no more. He missed Luke, and wished they were still intimates. Jenny wrote to tell him about Expo, and the possibility of a National Film Development Corporation being formed. "Exciting things are beginning to happen here . . ." Hanna, she added, had begun to suffer dizzy spells. Joey's last postcard, actually the first they'd had in two years, had come from Buenos Aires. Where, Jake noted, consulting his atlas, the Paraná River empties into the Atlantic.

Joey Hersh, Jesse Hope, Yosef ben Baruch, Joseph de la Hirsch, St. Urbain's one and only Horseman, where are you now?

Contemplating the Horseman's journal and his newly acquired effects, the riding habit made for him by Joseph Monaghan, Ltd., Exclusive Tailors to Gentlemen, Dublin, and the Barnaby "International" saddle, Jake tried to grasp how the Horseman could ever have become involved with a woman quite so vacuous as Ruthy. Money, the readiest explanation, was unacceptable to him. And Chava, on reflection, was exceedingly ordinary too. Unlike those elegant girls who had once festooned the backyard on St. Urbain so incongruously, sipping Manhattans as they watched Joey attack the punching bag. Joey, Joey, his back splattered with uneven cuts and holes. Shrapnel? And who, if anybody, had informed on him, and was responsible for the fire-engine red MG turned over and gutted in the woods alongside the highway? Uncle Abe?

Again and again, Jake drifted off to sleep, sliding into dreams of the Horseman, demanding on the kibbutz of Gesher Haaziv as he once had on St. Urbain, "What are you going to do about it?" Sitting in the courthouse in Frankfurt.

Mengele cannot have been there all the time.

In my opinion, always. Night and day.

Dimly, Jake recalled having said to Waterman, "The Golem, for your information, is the body without a soul. He was made out of clay by Rabbi Judah Ben Bezalel in the sixteenth century to defend the Jews of Prague from a pogrom and, to my mind, still wanders the world, turning up whenever a defender is most needed."

Out there, riding even now. St. Urbain's Horseman. Galloping, thundering. Look sharp, Mengele, *Die Juden kommen!* He will extract the gold fillings from the triangular cleft between the upper front teeth with pliers. Slowly, slowly.

Surfacing from a dream of the Horseman, easing himself out of bed, legs leaden and throat raw on Friday morning, June 2, Jake fumbled into his dressing gown and stopped only once to

brace himself against a chair and fart, sighing with relief, before
he reached the front door, where he stooped, instantly overcome
by vertigo, to retrieve the morning newspapers. The *Times*
headline danced before him. Squinting, Jake deciphered it:

MORE EGYPTIAN ARMOR MASSES IN SINAI

The Egyptian Commander-in-Chief, General Mortagi, had issued an order of the day to his soldiers in Sinai, saying, "The
results of this unique moment are of historic importance for our
Arab nation and for the Holy War through which you will
restore the rights of the Arabs which have been stolen in Palestine and reconquer the plundered soil of Palestine . . ." and yet—
and yet—he discovered, reading further, the Israeli forces had
been sent on leave and were disporting themselves on the beaches.

No fighting yet, Jake grasped, baffled, dropping the newspaper
to the floor and starting upstairs again. Where there was more
cheering news to sustain him. Peeing, he scrutinized the stream,
as was his morning habit, hopefully but with critical objectivity.
With *cojones*, he liked to think, as well as a prayer. This morning's urine was a rich bubbly yellow, nice and fleecy with mu-
cous membrane deposits. Spared again. Once more there was no
telltale pink, which would have signified kidney congestion,
stones, or malignancy—his father's fate. Neither was there any
green detectable, which would have meant bile. Or, God help
you, Jake, *black*, signaling intestinal stasis or melanotic sarcoma.

Relieved, almost happy enough to whistle, Jake curled up on
the bed again and began to breathe, heavily, drifting. Wait, wait.
Something was ringing. No, something not in his head this time.
Something outside him. The telephone.

"Yes," Jake said, "who is it?" His voice, thickened by his
stuffed nose, sounded like somebody else's to him.

"If you're going to Cornwall tonight," Harry said, "I was
wondering if I could have the use of your place?"

Cornwall? Oh, yes. Nancy was there. With the kids. "What's
today?"

"Friday."

"Today is Friday. A *guten shabbus* then, Hershel."

"Seen the newspapers yet?"

Yes; and Jake allowed he was extremely concerned about the Israeli situation.

"Take it from me. There's not a thing to worry about."

"Oh," Jake said, tightening. "Why?"

"Oil."

"Knock it off, comrade. I'm in no mood."

"The American Sixth Fleet isn't there for nothing, you know."

"Neither are the Russians."

"Not to worry, the Americans won't let anybody rock the boat. The fixed capital investment necessary to extract one barrel of crude oil daily is a hundred and ninety dollars in the Middle East compared with seven hundred and thirty in Venezuela and fifteen hundred in the United States."

"So what, Hershel?"

"So the CIA, Feisal, and Standard Oil. The—"

"Harry, they've declared a *jihad*—"

"The Middle East is an effing gold mine. The cost of producing a barrel of oil there is only fifteen cents against a dollar sixty-three in the United States."

"—they're planning to exterminate the Jews."

"Not bloody likely. Israel's not a colony suppressed by imperialism, you know, but a *colon*. A settler's citadel. So the Yanks will take care of them. Now can I use your place or not? I wouldn't make a mess or drink your liquor. I'll bring my own."

"Oh, screw off, Harry. I'll call you later. As of now, I don't even see how I can leave for Cornwall earlier than Tuesday morning."

In the bathroom again, Jake removed his bridge, plunked it into a tumbler, added hot water and a Polydent tablet, and bared his teeth to the mirror. More tartar. Increasing drift. Worsening animal erosion. The ravages of PYORRHEA ALVEOLARIS (or Rigg's Disease), now usually known as Periodontal Disease, characterized in the final stages by the promotion of pockets of purulent material around the teeth and loosening of the affected teeth.

Jake brushed his teeth vigorously, spitting pink.

Then he poured himself a shot of Fernet-Branca bitters.

Then he sank to the bed again, raised his knees, spread his legs, peeled the silver foil from a hateful suppository, dipped it in vaseline, and groped for his anus, shoving the pellet home ("Take that, you bitch."), his greasy fingers glancing against a cherry-size hemorrhoid.

Then Jake washed again before inserting the bridge in his mouth.

Then he drank two cups of instant coffee, giving the *Times* a cursory look. A full-page ad followed the editorial page.

> WHILE YOU'RE EATING YOUR DINNER TONIGHT,
> 417 PEOPLE WILL DIE FROM STARVATION
>
> It takes you about an hour to eat a nice, leisurely dinner. From the time you start to the time you finish your dessert, 417 people will die from starvation.
>
> You see, world population has *already* outgrown world food supply. Every 8.6 seconds someone in an under-developed country dies as a result of illness caused by malnutrition. That's 7 deaths every minute. 417 deaths every hour. 10,000 deaths every day. Most of them children.

Jake swept the *Times* off the table and called Nancy in Cornwall. Sammy answered the phone.

"This is the chief of police speaking," Jake said. "We have a report that there's a flying saucer in your garden."

"It's Daddy. Do you wish to speak with Mommy?"

Ben howled as Nancy set him down.

"Hullo."

"Oh, my God, Jake, you sound awful."

"I'm going to quit smoking."

"Where were you so late?"

"I went to dinner with Jimmy Blair and a producer, but I don't want to say anything more at this point because it could all collapse on Monday."

"Was Harry with you?"

Startled, he said, "No," the lie only technical. "Why should you think that?"

"Are you letting him use our house when you come here?"

"No. Yes. What's the difference?"

"I don't want him in our house."

"O.K. O.K., the car's waiting. I'm late. Phone you later from the studio."

Actually, after Jake had parted with Blair and the others at the restaurant, more or less obliged to join them later at C. Bernard Farber's mews flat in Belgravia, he had impulsively made a detour to Regent's Park, having decided that only Harry's malevolent presence could make Farber's brawl tolerable. Harry had to be drummed out of bed.

"Come on, Hershel. I'm taking you to a party. Girls, champers, you name it. We live in swinging London, don't we?"

"You do, maybe."

"Me?" Jake laughed. "Nancy and I read in bed. We hardly ever go to this sort of thing."

"What sort?"

"One of our proconsuls, C. Bernard Farber, has won his laurels. He has found favor in the eyes of a new triumvirate. He's returning to Imperial Hollywood. It's a farewell party."

"What shall I wear?" Harry asked.

"Oh, for Chrissake, anything. As long as you've got dark glasses."

A sea of cars surrounded Farber's flat, spilling out of the mews into the road and beyond. There was a Rolls-Royce painted in psychedelic colors, more than one Ferrari, Aston Martins double-parked and too many E-types to count. Jake's Hillman Minx, a shame for the neighbors, had to be abandoned more than a block's distance away.

Luscious girls festooned the wrought-iron stairwell. They sat on the floor. Driven against the wall, their eyes wandered, seeking out celebrities. And there were many there. A bona fide Hollywood star, and more than one famous director, including the first to show pubic hairs in CinemaScope. A Beatle was rumored to be on his way to Farber's flat, drawing nearer all the time. Already there, real enough to touch, was a man who had once lit a cigarette for Jacqueline Kennedy. Somebody who had told Orson Welles he no longer had it. As well as the first British actress to have her bare nipple tweaked in BCU.

Jake, his mood ebullient, was not seeking trouble when Frankie Demaine accosted him. "Who's your friend," he asked, indicating Harry, "is he important?"

Harry, who had heard, flinched. He couldn't cope with such double-edged jokes. It was not his idiom. Jake flared up. "You're goddam right he is. It's Stein. You know, from . . ." and he succeeded in losing the company's name in the din.

Vindictively, he guided Harry from group to group, introducing him as a producer. He foisted him on girls. "This is Stein," he'd say. "You know, Stein. He's going to be making pictures here now."

Harry, once thrust on the girls he longed for, could not stitch together a coherent sentence. He was either gratuitously coarse without any redeeming wit or stunned into silence. Finally, Jake rescued him. "Let's get the hell out of here," he said.

Outside, Harry protested, "You picked a bad time, mate. I just had a cunt lined up."

"Oh, Harry, please. I don't like women being talked about like that. It offends me."

Harry's face burned with rage.

"All right, then," Jake said, "if you had a girl, where is she?"

"How could I take her back to my place?"

"Go and fetch her. Use my place."

"A fine time to tell me. It's too late now, isn't it?"

Wearily, his smile contrite, Jake invited Harry back to his place for a nightcap.

"Oh, sure," he said snidely. "Only I can't sleep in, mate. That would get me home just in time to shave before going to the office."

"You can stay the night."

"Maid's room is free this week, is it?"

O.K., Harry. Skip it. After dropping him off near Regent's Park, Jake drove on to the White Elephant, where he lost thirty-five pounds at roulette.

Harry's weekly wage.

Remembering, his head still aching, Jake phoned Nancy again, as soon as he reached the studio, to say he could start out for Newquay at six on Saturday morning, but he had to be back in London by noon Monday, which really meant leaving again on Sunday afternoon. More than a little depressed, even sharp with him on the phone, she agreed it would hardly be worth it; all that driving would exhaust him. Satisfied, Jake hung up and hastened to Harrod's, scooting from counter to counter, loading himself down with all manner of meats, cheeses, delicacies, and toys, stuffing the lot into his car and barreling off into the night, bound to join his family in Newquay for the sabbath, just as years and years ago, his father had descended on them in fly-bitten Shawbridge, the ghetto's summer swimming hole, loaded down with watermelons and cherries, kosher meats, bottles of Kik, and pails and sand shovels.

You know what life is, Yankel?

Tell me, you're so smart.

A circle. A little *kikeleh*.

Arriving early on Saturday morning, Jake pounded on the door of their house in Newquay. "Let me in, let me in! It's your husband! Get that buck nigger out of your bed at once!"

Jake slept in until noon and then spent the afternoon on the beach with Sammy and Molly, mindful of sharks, ever-watchful for the periscopes of German submarines.

Nobody on the beach passed an anti-semitic remark.

Not one of the planes circling overhead was a Stuka.

He was close enough to the house to see if it caught fire, and he figured he could get there in time to rescue Nancy and the baby. Pilar too.

In other words, he thought, something really nasty is in the works. Look out, Yankel, any minute now the shit hits the fan.

After the children had gone to bed, he and Nancy ate dinner together, and he told her, though they were certainly not to count on anything, that the picture his agent was striving to set up for him looked extremely promising. He would know more on Monday.

"As girls go," he said, "you're bloody expensive. Look how far I've come, just to make love to you. I nearly turned back at Plymouth, when I realized you are still unable . . ."

"I promise not to send you back to London entirely frustrated."

"Ooo," he said, slapping his cheek, "you filthy thing."

Sunday afternoon he started back for London, promising to use his safety belt and never to exceed seventy miles per hour; and early Monday morning he sat in the projection room at Pinewood, idly probing his scalp for nascent tumors, then placing a hand over his heart to feel for palpitations, as he waited for Jimmy Blair and the others to arrive so that they could screen a film together. He was almost asleep when Sid Patmore whacked the door open to say he had just heard, on the car radio, that the fighting had started. An Israeli spokesman had declared that in response to an Egyptian attack, Israeli armor had gone into action. A fierce tank battle was in progress in Sinai.

Soon there were ten of them in the projection room, chain-smoking and gin-soaked, speculating round a transistor radio. This time, Jake thought, the bloody Egyptians would suck Israeli armor deeper and deeper into Sinai, then Jordan would mount an assault on the Sharon Plain, severing Israel where it was only twelve miles wide. Jake would have to volunteer. He would be obliged to fight. Like the Horseman, he thought.

Along the Ebro.

At Bab el Wad.

Cairo claimed forty-four planes shot down. There was dancing in the streets. The headline in the first edition of the *Evening Standard* announced that Germany was to send Israel twenty thousand gas masks. "Nowadays," Jake hollered at the others, "everybody is a black humorist," and he crushed the *Standard* into a ball.

The Egyptian air force was destroyed on the ground; Jordan undone. Well-meaning acquaintances bought Jake drinks in the bar at Pinewood Studios.

"You've got to hand it to the Israelis," somebody said. "Bloody good show," another man cut in, slapping him on the back.

Israelis swam in the Suez Canal and camped on the banks of the Jordan. Cousin Joey, Jake knew, was there, he had to be, probably in the struggle for Jerusalem. Hoping to find a photograph of him, Jake bought all the newspapers. He screened whatever newsreel footage he could get, stopping the cameras from time to time, to get a closer look at a frame. No Horseman. But in a photograph on the front page of the *Daily Mail*, among the officers conferring with Dayan, stood Elan, Colonel Elan, looking uncommonly handsome and assured.

Jake had never seen Elan again after the day at Beersheba. Neither had he ever run into the Coopers elsewhere. Elan, Jake assumed, had fought bravely, leading his men, not following after. And wherever he was today Mr. Cooper had, Jake felt sure, given generously to support the Israeli war effort. So would all the Coopers everywhere. A man came around to collect from Jake too. Much to his own embarrassment, Jake hesitated. Dayan, melodramatic eyepatch and all, was a hero. Our hero. And yet—and yet—put this arrogant general, this Dayan, into an American uniform, call him MacArthur, call him Westmoreland, and Jake would have despised him. Jake wrote out a check, but unhappily. Being the old kind of Jew, a Diaspora Jew, he was bound to feel guilty either way.

Immediately the fund-raiser quit the house, the telephone rang. It was long distance. Montreal. "Yes," Jake said.

"I've got some bad news for you," Uncle Abe said.

"My father's dead."

"He passed away an hour ago."

"I see."

"Will you come to the funeral?"

"I'll be out on the morning flight. Is my sister there?"

Rifka came to the telephone, sobbing. "He was such a good man," she said. "Such a wonderful father."

All of them would be clustered around the wall-telephone in the kitchen. His aunts, his uncles, nodding their heads, weeping.

"He didn't have an enemy in the world," Rifka continued.

Or a friend. "I'll see you tomorrow," Jake said, hanging up.

He didn't even have to pack. His bags were ready for Newquay. Jake called Air Canada and had only just poured himself a brandy when the telephone startled him again.

"Well, your friend Dayan knows how to take orders, doesn't he?"

Oh, God, Harry.

"You know where he just got back from, don't you?"

"No, Harry. Tell me."

"South Vietnam. He went there to learn about napalm straight from Westmoreland and Marshal Ky. And he got his start working hand in glove with the British army police in 1920, terrorizing Arab villages."

"Harry, you misery, don't you care about the Jewish children?"

"I care about workers' children everywhere and I hate reaction wherever it appears. Israel supported the French in Algeria in 1954 and supplied arms to the Portuguese government in Angola. Do they care about agrarian land revolution or radical land reform? Not on your nelly. Zionism got rid of the Arab fellahs and wants to stay rid of them."

Cutting Harry short, Jake told him he was going to Montreal; he would be gone for a week. Yes, yes, he could have the run of the house, dammit. Jake would leave a key under the mat.

Jake called Nancy to tell her what had happened and promised to call again from Montreal, after the funeral.

After all, Issy Hersh had held on for longer than six weeks. It was two months since Jake had last seen him.

15

A glass of water, with a swab of absorbent cotton resting on the rim, was perched on top of the faulty, whirring air conditioner. Jake's grandmother freshened the water each morning. It was there to slake her first-born son's soul, in the event that it returned thirsty or feverish. The late Issy Hersh's small, modest apartment was stifling. Overflowing. It reeked of Hersh sweat, decaying Hersh bodies, the rumpled men received visitors in the little box of a living room. While Jake's grandmother, Fanny, his sister Rifka, his aunts, accepted mourners like dues in the master bedroom, where cancer, lodging in Issy Hersh's kidney, had taken root and spread tentacles throughout his body.

Earlier, when Jake had emerged from the airplane at Dorval, the worse for six hours of gin, he had discovered Herky pacing up and down in front of the customs barrier.

"Good flight?" Herky barked.

Jake shrugged.

"How's the family?"

"Well."

"And the wife, keeping her looks?"

Fuck you.

"He died peacefully. I want you to know that." Once inside

his air-conditioned Buick, Herky demanded, "That a good tie?"

"*What?*"

"We're going straight to Paperman's." The funeral parlor. "They'll have to cut it with a razor blade. That's the law, you know." Go to hell, Herky.

Jake's big-booted, leathery-faced grandmother, the belly that had swelled for fourteen children hanging useless now, an empty pouch—foolish Fanny determined to outquake Rifka—his dour girdled aunts—all combined to send up a counterpoint of sobs and moans throughout the rabbi's eulogy at the funeral parlor. The solemn menfolk, the brothers and cousins next in line, glared at the coffin, this one tolerating what he had been assured was a stomach ulcer and another awaiting the results of a biopsy.

All his life Issy Hersh had worn forced-to-clear suits and fire sale shoes and now even his casket seemed too large. His last bargain.

The rabbi was brief.

"Words fail me to adequately express the sorrow I share with you. Even as Jewish law limits the topics of discussion for those who mourn, I find my speech curtailed because I mourn with you for Isaac Hersh, who all his years exuded and emanated Jewishness, real *yiddishkeit*, affluent in the rich symbolism of his people, which he readily spread amongst us. May the fond memories we have of a fine, outpouring Jewish soul inspire us to emulate all that was good in him . . ."

The women, subsiding into limousines, caught their second wind at the cemetery and began to lament anew, wailing with abandon. Poor Fanny, whose perch within the family hierarchy was exceedingly rocky now, the tolerated second wife of an under-insured, all but penniless husband, with a stepdaughter who abominated her and a stranger for a stepson, necessarily outbid all the others. Even Aunt Sophie, over whom her son, twenty-two-year-old Irwin, obese, his face florid, held a parasol. Irwin, who wore a straw hat with a tartan band, was staring at Jake. Jake shot him a piercing look, and Irwin, flushing a deeper red, wiggled his eyebrows pleadingly and averted his eyes.

The older generation of Hersh menfolk, brothers and cousins

to Issy, filed past the grave dutifully but truculent, appealingly truculent, each taking up the workman's spade in turn to shovel wet clay onto the coffin. Smack, smack. The Hershes, all of them, seemingly one cherished decomposing body to Jake now. Like him, susceptible to germs. Wasting. Shivering together in spite of the blistering heat. Diminished by one.

Suddenly, the enveloping black birds began to twitter. All manner of rabbis, young and old, blackbearded and cleanshaven, rocked in prayer, heads bobbing, competing in piety. For each Hersh buried paid dividends above ground. Every expired Hersh was bound to be commemorated by a rabbi's study or additional classroom for the yeshiva, a *sefer torah* donated here or an ark paid for there, a parochial-school library or a fully equipped kindergarten. In Everlasting Memory of . . .

"*Oy, oy,*" Rifka wailed.

"Issy! My Issy!" Fanny put in, outreaching her.

Jake couldn't even coax a tear out of himself; he felt altogether too drained and fearful of the wailing to come.

But once back in the widow's apartment, a veritable oven that day, their hands washed and stomachs biting with hunger, the men shed their jackets and loosened their ties and belts, the women unbuckled and unzipped. Everybody was talking at once, positioning themselves by the table, as plates of hardboiled eggs, bagels, and onion rolls were followed by platters of lox, roast chicken, and steaming potato varenikes, apple cake and chocolate chip cookies, peaches and plums, bottles of Tab and diet Pepsi. Once more Jake sensed the immense Irwin gaping at him. Caught out, Irwin wiggled his eyebrows again, blushed, and spit a plum pit into his hand.

Uncle Sam switched on his transistor radio and the sated Hershes gathered around to hear the ram's horn blown at the wailing wall in Jerusalem.

"If only Issy could have lived," Jake's grandmother said, crumpling, "to hear the *shofar* blown in Jerusalem."

An interloping rabbi squeezed the old lady's mottled hand. "You mustn't question the Almighty," he cautioned her, "or He might call you up for an answer."

Exactly what Rabbi Meltzer had told the Horseman. Did they subscribe, Jake wondered, to the same chief rabbi of platitudes? Had they been issued with similar condolence kits on graduation from yeshiva?

Now the men, slippered and unshaven (except for Jake, who scorned that ritual), staked claims, according to their need, to a place on the sofa or a chair by the balcony door, the seat handiest to the kitchen or the one nearest the toilet. As Uncle Jack emerged from the toilet, Irwin asked, "Everything come out all right?" his shoulders heaving with laughter. Then he caught Jake's reproving glance, shrugged, and retreated.

"Did you notice that Sugarman, the *chazer*, wasn't even at Paperman's?"

"It wasn't overcrowded with your in-laws either."

Uncle Abe rubbed his unshaven chin and complained of the first day's stiffness.

"After a few days it gets soft," he was assured.

"That's my trouble too," Uncle Lou said.

Uncle Sam figured the rabbi's speech was a washout, but Uncle Morrie didn't agree. "A rabbi's speech," he said, "should be like a miniskirt. Eh, Yankele?"

Jake saluted the reference to London.

"Long enough to cover the subject, short enough to make it interesting."

Herky, encouraged, pitched in with a convoluted story about a cracker, a Jew, and a Negro, all delivered in an Amos 'n' Andy accent, and culminating with the Negro saying, "I've got foah inches. Is that all? the hebe asks. *Foah inches from the ground, baby.*"

Uncle Morrie laughed and wiped the corners of his eyes with a handkerchief. "You guys," he said.

Jake's ponderous silence was taken for disapprobation.

"Listen here, Yankele," Uncle Lou said, clapping him on the back. "If it was your Uncle Morrie here we had just buried—"

Which earned him a poisonous look.

"—and your father, may he rest in peace, was still with us, he would be leading with the jokes."

"You're absolutely right," Jake said, sorry that they had misunderstood him.

"Then here's one for you, by jove, with a Limey twist. 'Ow do you get six elephants into a Vauxhall?"

"I wouldn't know."

"Blimey, old thing. Three in the front, three in the back."

Jake mustered a smile and raised his glass to Uncle Lou.

"And 'ow would you get six giraffes into the same car?" A pause. "You remove the elephants," Lou exploded.

"Clever."

"Yankel, you should never lose your stench of humor. That's a philosophy that's never failed me."

"I remember," Jake said, and he drifted onto the balcony where Irwin towered over a brood of younger cousins, a transistor clapped to his ear.

"Mays just homered," he said. "They're going to walk McCovey," and seeing Jake, he gulped, and turned his back to him.

Jake decided to seek out Fanny before he had drunk himself into incoherence. She was in the small bedroom.

"Anything I can do for you?" Jake asked.

"Sit."

So he sat.

"You know, one night—after we were married, you understand—your father and I, well . . . ." She blushed. ". . . We were fooling around, you know. You know what I mean?"

"You were what?"

"Well, you know. I got pregnant. But he made me see somebody."

"Why?"

"He thought his brothers would laugh at him. At his age, a baby."

"I'm sorry."

"You're a very thoughtful person. I'd come to visit you in London, if I could afford it."

Which drove Jake back into the hall, where he could see Irwin, alone on the balcony now, waddling over to the railing. He thrust a finger into his nostril, dug fiercely, and slowly,

slowly, extracted a winding worm of snot. Irwin contemplated it, sleepy-eyed, before he wiped it on the railing.

Uncle Jack was holding forth, dribbling cigar ash.

"Hey, did you hear the one about the two Australian fairies? One of them went back to Sydney."

Herky clapped Jake on the back. "Got to talk to you." He ushered Jake into the toilet ahead of him. "How are you fixed money-wise, kid?"

"I'd love to help you, Herky," Jake replied, swaying, "but it's all tied up."

"You don't understand. I don't need your money. You've got kids now. I'm sure you want to invest for the future. You're my one and only brother-in-law and . . . well, I'd like to put you on to something good."

"I read you."

Herky lit up, exuding self-satisfaction. "What do you think is the most valuable thing in the world today?"

"The Jewish tradition."

"Where will boozing get you? Nowhere." Herky plucked Jake's glass out of his hand. "I'm serious, for Chrissake."

"All right, then. Not having cancer."

"I mean a natural resource."

"Gold?"

"Guess again."

"Oil?"

Herky spilled over with secret knowledge. "Give up?"

Don't you know you're going to die, Herky? But he didn't say it.

"Water."

"*What?*"

"H_2O. Watch this." With a flick of the wrist, Herky flushed the toilet. "It's going on everywhere, day and night. Now you take the Fraser River, for instance. More than once a day the untreated contents of one hundred thousand toilet bowls empty into it."

"That's a lot of shit, Herky."

"Flush, flush, flush. Canada's got more clean water than any other country in the Free World, but even so, there's a limit, you know."

Jake retrieved his drink.

"You project ten years ahead and there will be container tankers, fleets of them, carrying not oil or iron ore, but pure Canadian water, to polluted American cities."

"So?"

"Watch closely now." Herky flushed the toilet again. "All over the city, people are doing the same, but—but—this toilet, like any other, *flushes the same amount of water no matter what the need*. You read me?"

"Loud and clear."

"I call them mindless, these toilets, I mean."

"I'm tired, Herky. Come to the point."

"The average person urinates maybe four times a day, but defecates only once, yet this toilet is mindless, it is adjusted to provide enough power to flush a stool down the drain each time. Millions of gallons daily are being wasted in the Montreal area alone. Which is where I come in. We are developing a cistern that will give you all the zoom you need for defecation, but will release only what's necessary to wash urine away. In other words, a toilet with a mind. The biggest breakthrough since Thomas Crapper's Niagara. Once we get costs down and go into production, I expect our unit to become mandatory equipment in all new buildings. I'm offering you a chance to come in on the ground floor. Well?"

"You certainly are thinking big, Herky."

"You've got to move with the times."

"Let me sleep on it, O.K.?"

"O.K., but meanwhile, mum's the word."

A half hour before the first evening star, the rabbis trooped into the insufferably hot apartment in shiny black frock coats. The local yeshiva's Mafia. Ranging from tall spade-bearded men in broad-brimmed black hats to pimply, wispy-bearded boys in oversize Homburgs. Finally, there came the leader, the fragile Rabbi Polsky himself, who led the men in the evening prayer.

Immediately behind Jake, prayerbook in hand, stood flat-footed Irwin, breathing with effort. As Jake stumbled self-consciously through the prayer for the dead, Irwin's troubled breathing quickened — it raced — stopped — and suddenly he sneezed, and sneezed again, pelting Jake's neck with what seemed like shrapnel. As Jake whirled around, Irwin seemed to draw his neck into his body. Bulging eyes and a sweaty red face rising over a succession of chins were all that confronted Jake. But as he resumed his prayers, he was conscious of Irwin, biting back his laughter, threatening to explode. The moment prayers were over, Irwin shot out onto the balcony, heaving, a soggy hand clamped to his nose.

Rabbi Polsky, holy man to the Hershes, was thin and round-shouldered, his skin gray as gum, with watery blue eyes and a scraggly yellow beard. He padded on slippered feet to a place on the sofa. A cunning field mouse. Accusingly impecunious amid Hersh affluence. His shirt collar curling and soiled, his cuffs frayed, Rabbi Polsky came nightly, wiped his mouth with an enormous damp handkerchief, and preached to the Hershes, all of whom virtually glowed in his presence.

"There came to me once a man to ask me to go to the Rebbe in New York to ask him what he should do for his father who was dying. He paid for me the air ticket, I went to Brooklyn, I spoke with the Rebbe, and I came back and said to the man the Rebbe says pray, you must pray every morning. Pray, the man asked? Every morning. So he went away and every morning before going to the office he said his prayers after years of not doing it. Then one morning he had an appointment with a *goy*, a financier, from out of town, at the Mount Royal Hotel. He had to see the *goy* to make a loan for his business. The *goy* said you be here nine o'clock sharp, I'll try to fit you in, I'm very busy. All right. But the man overslept and in the morning he realized if he takes time to say his prayers he will be late. He will lose his loan. All the same he prayed, and when he got to the Mount Royal Hotel and went to the man's room, the *goy* was in a rage, shouting, hollering, *you* keep *me* waiting. You need me and you keep me waiting? So the man said his father was dying and his rabbi had told him he must pray every morning, and that's why he was late. You mean to say, the *goy* asked, even though if I deny you this loan your business is ruined, you were late so as not to miss one morning's prayers for your father? Yes. In that case, the *goy* said, let me shake your hand, put it there, you are a fella I can trust. To lend money to such a man will be a genuine pleasure."

Euphoria filled the Hershes. Only Jake protested, nudging Uncle Lou. "We now know that praying is good for credit, but what happened to the man's father?"

"You know what your trouble is? You don't believe in anything."

Rabbi Polsky, possibly with Jake in mind, continued:

"Sometimes young people question the law. There's no reason for this . . . that's a superstition . . . You know the type, I'm sure. Why, for example, they ask, should we not eat seafood?"

Uncle Lou poked Jake. "Your sister Rifka is on a seafood diet."

"What?"

"Every time she sees food she wants it."

"Why," the rabbi asked, "shouldn't we eat crab or lobster? To which I would answer you with the question why is there such madness among the *goyim*, they run to the psychiatrist every morning? Why? It is now scientifically revealed in an article in *Time* magazine that eating seafood can drive you crazy. It promotes insanity."

"Jake, it's for you," Uncle Jack said, holding out the kitchen phone.

"Who is it?"

"The boss," he replied with a big wink.

"Would you mind shutting the door after you, please?" Jake asked, before taking the call.

It was Nancy, enormously concerned for his sake. "I thought you would phone last night."

"Honestly, I'm all right."

"There's no need to pretend."

"The embarrassing thing is," Jake said, "it's like a family party. I'm not grieving. I'm having a wonderful time."

Sitting with the Hershes, day and night, a bottle of Remy Martin parked between his feet, such was Jake's astonishment, commingled with pleasure, in their responses, that he could not properly mourn for his father. He felt cradled, not deprived. He also felt like Rip Van Winkle returned to an innocent and ordered world he had mistakenly believed long extinct. Where God watched over all, doing His sums. Where everything fit. Even the holocaust which, after all, had yielded the state of Israel. Where to say, "Gentlemen, the Queen," was to offer the obligatory toast to Elizabeth II at an affair, not to begin a discussion on Andy Warhol. Where smack was not habit-forming, but what a disrespectful child deserved; pot was what you simmered the chicken soup in; and camp was where you sent the boys for the summer. It was astounding, Jake was incredulous, that after so many years and fevers, after Dachau, after Hiroshima, revolution, rockets in space, DNA, bestiality in the streets, assassinations in and out of season, there were still brides with shining faces who were married in white gowns, posing for the *Star* social pages with their prizes, pear-shaped boys in evening clothes. There were aunts who sold raffles and uncles who swore by the *Reader's Digest*. French Canadians, like overflying airplanes distorting the TV picture, were only tolerated. DO NOT ADJUST YOUR SET, THE TROUBLE IS TEMPORARY. Aunts still phoned each other every morning to say what sort of cake they were baking. Who had passed this exam, who had survived that operation. A scandal was when a first cousin was invited to the bar mitzvah *kiddush*, but not the dinner. Eloquence was the rabbi's sermon. They were ignorant of the arts, they were overdressed, they were overstuffed, and their taste was appallingly bad. But within their self-contained world, there was order. It worked.

As nobody bothered to honor them, they very sensibly celebrated each other at fund-raising synagogue dinners, taking turns at being Man-of-the-Year, awarding each other ornate plaques to hang over the bar in the rumpus room. Furthermore, God

was interested in the fate of the Hershes, with time and consideration for each one. To pray was to be heard. There was not
even death, only an interlude below ground. For one day, as
Rabbi Polsky assured them, the Messiah would blow his horn,
they would rise as one and return to Zion. Buried with twigs
in their coffins, as Baruch had once said, to dig their way to him
before the neighbors.

Phoning Hanna, in Toronto, Jake had to cope with Jenny first.

"Sitting *shiva* with the hypocrites, are you?"

Oh, God.

"I suppose whenever my name's mentioned they cross themselves, so to speak," she said, giggling at her own joke.

He hadn't the heart to say her name had not been mentioned
once, and next thing he knew Doug was on the line.

"I want you to know why I didn't send flowers."

"You're not supposed to," Jake said wearily.

"It's not that. You know I'm beyond such ethnic taboos. Instead of flowers, I've sent a check in memory of your dad to
SUPPORT in Hanoi."

"You did?"

"It goes toward buying artificial limbs for children maimed
in the air raids."

"I knew you'd always come through in a crunch, Doug. Now
may I please speak to Hanna?"

"So, Yankel?"

"Hanna, how are you?"

"I'm sorry. You know we were never friendly in the old days,
but, after all, he's your paw, and I'm sorry." She inquired about
Nancy and the baby and demanded photographs of Sammy and
Molly. "I wanted to come to Montreal, but you know how
Jenny feels about the Hershes. She wouldn't give me the fare.
Big deal. I'll hitchhike, I said, like the hippies . . ."

"I'd send you the fare, Hanna, you know that, but . . ." He
feared the family would treat her shabbily.

"I know. Don't explain. Couldn't you come here for a day?"

"There's the new baby, Hanna. Really, I . . ."

"It's O.K. Next time, yes?"

"We'll go to a hockey game together."

"Hey, Red Kelly's in parliament. He's an M.P."

"Who?"

"What do you mean, who? The Maple Leafs' defenseman. You remember, Imlach traded with Detroit for him."

"And he's in parliament now?"

"*Aquí está nada.*"

"*Aquí está* Hanna."

"Yes, sir. Alive and kicking. A living testimonial to Carling's beer. How's Luke?"

"The same."

"You two; you give me a royal pain in the ass. When will you make it up?"

His mother made Jake lunch in her apartment. She said how sad she was his father had died. He was not to blame if he had not been intelligent enough for her and she was certain he would have been a good husband for a simple woman. And that done, she asked, "How's my new baby?"

"Nancy's baby is fine," Jake replied.

Again and again he was driven back to St. Urbain to linger before the dilapidated flat that had once held Hanna, Arty, Jenny, and, briefly, the Horseman. More than once he strolled around the corner and into the lane. To look up at the rear bedroom window, Jenny's window, that had used to be lit into the small hours as she applied herself with such ardor to her studies, the books that were to liberate her from St. Urbain, the offices of Laurel Knitwear, and all the oppressive Hershes.

"You know what she's plugging away at in there?" Issy Hersh had said. "Latin. A dead language."

Through a hole in the fence, Jake contemplated the backyard where the Horseman had once set up a makeshift gym, doing his stuff for admiring girls, high-quality girls. He and Arty, Jake recalled, had used to watch from the bedroom window and once they had seen Joey, his eyes shooting hatred, strike a stranger ferociously in the stomach.

Suddenly, a dark-eyed, olive-skinned boy appeared in the yard, ran to the fence, and confronted Jake. "Fuck off, mister."

Duddy, he remembered, Arty, Gas, and me.

Everything happened so quickly. One day Arty, Duddy, Stan, Gas, and Jake were collecting salvage, practicing aircraft recognition, and the next, it seemed, the war was over. Neighbors' sons came home.

"What was it like over there?"

"An education."

IS HITLER REALLY DEAD? was what concerned everybody. That, and an end to wartime shortages and ration books. One stingingly cold Saturday afternoon a man came to the door. Leather cap, rheumy eyes, an intricately veined nose. Battle ribbons riding his lapel. One arm was no more than a butt, the sleeve clasped by a giant safety pin, and with the other arm, the good arm, the man offered a Veteran's calendar, the Karsh portrait of Churchill encased in a gold foil V. "They're only fifty cents each."

"No, thanks," Mr. Hersh said.

Reproachfully, the man's bloodshot gaze fastened on his battle ribbons. "Ever hear of Dieppe?" he growled, flapping his butt.

Jake looked up at his father imploringly.

"And did you ever hear of the Better Business Bureau," Mr. Hersh demanded, "because it so happens they have broadcast a warning for law-abiding citizens not to buy combs from cripples *who just claim to be war veterans.*"

"Jew bastard."

Mr. Hersh slammed the door. "You see what they're like, all of them, underneath. You see, Jake."

"But did you see his arm? He lost it at Dieppe maybe."

"And did *you* see his schnozz? He's a boozer. The only battle he ever fought was with Johnny Walker. You've got to get up early in the morning to put one over on Issy Hersh."

Or, Jake thought—remembering Tom the gardener with a chill of shame, Sammy watching, all eyes—or his first-born son Jacob.

The old friends Jake sought out, were, to his dismay, churlish or resentful.

"What's the famous director doing here, back on the farm?" Ginsburg demanded. Arty's enthusiasm for Jake's film iced over with three drinks. "If you had asked me when we were kids, I never would have picked you to make it. Stan maybe." Witty, corrosive Stan Tannenbaum, with whom Jake had sat in Room Forty-one, at Fletcher's Field High. Stan was a professor now, his long greasy hair bound by a Cree headband, a pendant riding his barrel belly. "I'm the leading authority on Shakespeare in this country and I adore teaching it, but it humbles a man, you know. I don't flatter myself into thinking I have anything to add. There's so much crap being written today. Take your buddy, Luke Scott, for instance."

Gordie Rothman, another old schoolmate, who had forsaken teaching for corporation law, insisted they meet for a drink at Bourgatel's. "The truth is the money's rolling in . . ." He was happily married with two children, a house in Westmount, and what he called a shack in Vermont, just in case the French Canadian business got out of hand. "There's only one thing." Gordie slid a plastic-covered, leather-bound folio out of his attaché case. "I'd like to get my screenplay produced."

"You mean to say you've written a . . ."

"What the fuck, don't come on with me. Before you were well known who ever heard of you?"

"Nobody."

"I've sent the script to agents in New York and even London, but naturally they couldn't care less about anything set in Canada. You've got to have connections in this game, I realize that, and somebody like you . . ."

"I'll read it, Gordie. But I've got high standards, you know."

"Listen here, me too. But not everybody is James Joyce. I mean I'm sure you'd like to be able to direct as well as Hitchcock or . . . or Fellini . . ." Suddenly agitated, he glared at Jake. "I knew you when you were nothing. Nobody ever thought that much of you here. How in the hell did you ever get into films?"

"Sleeping with the right people," Jake said, winking.

After prayers each evening, the comforters streamed into the apartment. Dimly remembered second cousins, old neighbors, business associates. They compared Miami hotels for price and rabbis for oomph, but, above all, they marveled at the miracle of the Six-Day War and followed, with apprehension, the debate over the ceasefire continuing at the U.N. One rabbi, a suburban mod, wanted the Israeli victory enshrined by a new holiday, a latter-day Passover.

Uncle Lou accosted each visitor with the same question. "What kind of tanks were the Egyptians using in Sinai?"

"Russian."

"Wrong. Not rushin'. Standin' still."

Whenever guests celebrated the feats of the Israeli air force, Lou taunted them with the impending Bond drive. "Never before in the history of man," he was fond of saying, "will so few owe so much to so many."

Jack assured all comers that the Egyptians had used gas in Yemen only to test it for the Jews.

"But the Israelis were using napalm," Jake protested.

"By Jake here, whatever we do is rotten. Whatever they do is A-1. Do you know they had ovens ready in Cairo for our people?"

Only Uncle Sam was not surprised by the Israeli victory. He reminded everybody that it was the Jews who had turned the tide against the Nazis in World War II. At Tobruk.

"They stood against five Arab nations," Uncle Abe said again and again, "all alone. It has to be the fulfillment of divine intervention, even the most skeptical man must accept it was God's fulfillment to Abraham . . ."

One evening Max Kravitz drifted in, holding his taxi cap in his gnarled hands. Max's hair was white, his face grizzly. "Do you remember me," he demanded, driving Jake against a wall.

"Yes."

"What? You mean to say you remember me after all these years?"

"Yes. Of course I do."

"Well, I don't remember you," Max replied triumphantly.

Arty, long established as a dentist, came to pay his respects.

Arty had become a joker. Such a joker, they said. He told wonderful stories; then, as you laughed, Arty's head would shoot forward to within inches of your gaping mouth, his eyes scrutinizing, his nose sniffing tentatively, appalled by what they perceived and smelled, his smile abruptly transformed into a pitying headshake. The next morning you found yourself sprawled, gagging and struggling, in his chair. Joking, cunning Arty had drilled his way through Hersh family molars, shoving in an upper plate here and striking a buck-tooth bonanza there, working his passage into a split-level in Ville St. Laurent.

They mourned the passing of Issy Hersh for a week, the truculent rabbis surging in nightly to be followed by prayers and more guests. The sweetest time for Jake was the early afternoon, when, riding a leaden lunch, the drooping Hershes wrestled sleep by reminiscing about their shared childhood and schools, their first jobs, all on a French Canadian street.

"They're so dumb," Aunt Malka said, shaking her head with wonder. "There's one I used to tell a joke to on Friday and on Sunday in the middle of church service she would finally get it and begin to laugh."

What about the Separatists?

For them, birth control would be a better policy. They breed like rabbits.

Suddenly, the apartment darkened. Irwin's body filled the screen door to the balcony to overflowing, the transistor held to his ear. "Arnie's just shot a birdie on the fifteenth. That puts him only two down on Casper."

"That Arnie. Wow!"

"Where's Nicklaus?"

"Hold it."

Artfully, Jake brought the conversation around to Cousin Joey and Baruch.

"When they brought Baruch over, you know, the nut, he had never seen a banana before. Paw gave him a banana and he ate it with the peel."

Uncle Abe, chuckling with fond remembrance, said, "On the ship that gangster came over on, another Jew was robbed of his wallet. They searched high and low and couldn't find it. Two special cops were waiting at the foot of the gangway, looking into all the hand luggage. Baruch comes sailing down the gangway with his satchel already open for inspection. He is eating an apple and whistling. Inside the apple is the money from the wallet."

"That Baruch. Boy!"

And all at once, Jake, come to sit with the Hershes in mourning for his father, feeling closer to them than he had in years, felt obliged to honor the Horseman in his absence. Without preamble, he turned on Uncle Abe, reminding him of Joey's last visit to Montreal, the men waiting in the car outside the house on St. Urbain, the gutted MG in the woods, and Jenny's abiding hatred. "You turned him in, didn't you, Uncle Abe?"

Uncle Abe's face flamed red. "What are you talking about, you drunken fool?"

"All I want is a straight answer."

"Here it is, then," and he slapped Jake hard across the cheek, stomping out of the living room.

"Well," Jake said, startled, trying to smile into hostile faces, faces all saying you deserved it.

The room was choked in silence.

"Hey," Uncle Lou said, "have you heard the one about the girl who wouldn't wear a diaphragm because she didn't want a picture window in her play room?"

"I've had enough of your puerile jokes, Uncle Lou."

"Well, pip pip, old bloke. And up yours with a pineapple."

Rifka shook a fist at him. "You come here once a year maybe and you booze from morning until night and stir up trouble. Then you fly off again. Who needs you anyway?"

Herky, roused, demanded, "What ever happened to that James Bond film you were supposed to direct? Big shot."

"Flush, flush, flush," was the most dazzling retort Jake could come up with before he fled indignantly to the balcony, lugging his brandy bottle with him.

Unfortunately Cousin Irwin was already there. Mountainous Irwin, huffing, as he clipped his fingernails. Irwin, having once peered into Jake's hot indignant face, retreated, wiggling his eyebrows ingratiatingly.

"Say something, you prick. Say something to me."

"Can do."

"Well. Go ahead."

Irwin pondered, he screwed his eyes. Briefly, he contemplated a gasoline pool in the Esso service station opposite. He scratched his head and studied his fingernails. Finally, as if pouncing on the words, he demanded, "Got many irons in the fire?"

Oh, my God, Jake thought, and he bounded back into the living room, where heads bent together to whisper leaped apart.

"Look here," Jake pleaded, "we're all going to die—"

"What have you got?" Sam asked.

"—sit down, you fool, it's not contagious. Oh, hell, what am I sitting *shiva* for anyway. I don't believe in it. Why should I try to please any of you?"

"Out of respect for your father."

"I never respected my father."

"Whoa, boy."

I loved him, Jake added to himself, unwilling to say as much to them.

"He's not dead a week," Rifka howled, "and he doesn't respect him. You hear, do you all hear?"

"He didn't leave any money, dear. There's no need to come on."

"Rotten thing. Animal. The day you married that *shiksa* you broke his heart."

Uncle Abe was back, his slippers flapping.

"I shouldn't have slapped you. I'm sorry, Jake."

"No. You bloody well shouldn't have slapped me. You should have given me a straight answer to my question."

"Can you not," Abe asked wearily, "take an apology like a gentleman?"

"Did you tell them where they could find Joey?"

Sighing, Uncle Abe led him into the kitchen, shutting the door after them.

"Do you see Joey in London?"

"I think he's in South America now. I haven't seen him since I was a boy."

Uncle Abe's eyes flickered with relief. Or so it seemed to Jake.

"You're lucky, then. Because he's rotten."

"Tell me why."

"You think the world of your cousin. Is that right?"

"Maybe."

"Joey did fight in the International Brigade in the Spanish Civil War, I'll grant him that—"

"And in Israel in forty-eight. He rode in the last convoy into Jerusalem."

"Good. Fine," Uncle Abe said, his smile dubious. "And if that's enough to make him a hero for you, let's leave it at that, shall we?"

"No. Let's not."

"Tough guy. O.K. He came crawling back to us, in 1943, with his tail between his legs, because he was in trouble with gangsters. He drove all the way from Las Vegas, without daring to look back."

"What sort of trouble was he in?"

"Nothing grand, Jake, nothing stylish. Squalid trouble. With bookmakers, mostly. He gambled, O.K., so do a lot of people. He didn't pay his debts. O.K., he's not the first. But he was also a gigolo. He was a blackmailer. He squeezed women for money, sometimes even marrying them. Do you remember the women who used to come to the house on St. Urbain?"

Jack nodded.

"Well, to begin with they were fast types, bar flies, with husbands overseas in the army. Then there was a young Westmount girl, he met her at a horse show, I think, and that led to more society types, looking for kicks. After all, Joey was a colorful fellow. He'd been a stuntman in the movies. He'd played professional baseball. And when it came to horses, he could ride with the best of them. But he was also a roughneck, you know. No education. He got too ambitious for his own good, he got beyond himself. He began to hang out at the Maritime Bar, in the

Ritz, you know, making time with married women. They bought him clothes, they gave him money, and when he didn't have enough he signed for credit, using me as a reference. I must have settled more than two thousand dollars in debts after he skipped town."

"You put the men on to him after the trouble at the Palais d'Or. You betrayed him."

"Cock-and-bull, that's what you're talking. It wasn't like that, Jake. Your cousin suffered from a swelled head. He got involved with the wife of somebody important here, a man of real quality and position, with an influential family. The wife had a drinking problem and hot pants for Joey. She was most indiscreet, to say the least. When the husband was out of town, Joey stayed in the house. Right on top of the hill. He didn't leave with empty pockets. Jewels disappeared, so did some of the family plate. The husband came to see Joey. He offered him money, but it wasn't enough. They quarreled. Joey hit him. Then your hero got cold feet, but it was too late to run. The woman's husband wanted him taught a lesson. What could he do, he had become a laughingstock. So he hired some ruffians to give Joey what for."

"I've been to see Joey's wife in Israel," Jake said, hoping to startle him.

"Joey's wife. One of them, you mean. There are others."

"He told her the family was responsible for his father's death and his, almost."

"His words. Golden words. The man is a congenital liar."

Jake told Uncle Abe about the Mengele papers he had discovered on the kibbutz. He told him about Deir Yassin, the Kastner trial, and how, after seeking the Horseman in Munich and Frankfurt, he had become convinced that Joey was trying to track down Josef Mengele in South America. To his immediate regret, he also told him about Ruthy.

Uncle Abe shook his head, amazed. He guffawed. "De la Hirsch," he said, "that's a hot one."

"I am not amused. Neither am I convinced by your tales of Joey's philandering. You turned him in, Uncle Abe."

"I wish I had. I could have done it without batting an eyelash."

"In God's name, why?"

"You have no idea how close we were to a race riot here. Those days weren't these days. Those days they were painting *À bas les juifs* on the highways, the young men were hiding in the woods, they weren't going to fight in the Jews' war. We could all be shoveled into a furnace, as far as they were concerned. And now, they have the *chutzpah* to say how much they admire the Zionists. The Separatists say they are no more than Zionists in their own country and the Jews should support them. Over my dead body, Yankel. They get their independence today and tomorrow there's a run on the banks. Why? Because of the Jews; and it will be hot for us here again. Listen, you don't live here. In your rarefied world, film people, writers, directors, actors, it hardly matters this one's a Jew, that one's black. God help me, I almost said Negro. You lead a sheltered life, my young friend. We live here in the real world, and let me tell you it's a lot better today than it was when I was a youngster. I rejoice, I celebrate it, but I remember. And how, I remember. And I'm on guard. Your *zeyda*, my father, came here steerage to be a peddler. He couldn't speak English and trod in fear of the *goyim*. I was an exception, one of the first of my generation to go to McGill, and it was no pleasure to be a Jew-boy on campus in my time. Those days weren't these days. In my time we were afraid too, you know. We couldn't buy property in the town of Mount Royal, we smelled bad. Hotels were restricted, country clubs, and there were quotas on Jews at the universities. I can remember to this day driving to the mountains with Sophie, she was four months pregnant, a young bride, I got a flat tire on the road and walked two miles to a hotel to phone a garage. No Jews, No Dogs, it said on the fence. I close my eyes, Yankel, and I can see the sign before me now. But today, I'm a Q.C. I serve on the school board. The mayor has come to an anniversary dinner at our synagogue, he wore a skullcap. Ministers from Ottawa, the same. There are Jews sitting on the bench. Why, today we even have Jews who are actually members of the University Club. Three members already."

"And you're flattered, are you?"

"Flattered, no, pleased, yes. My Irwin hardly knows anything of anti-semitism. He's a fine boy, you know, you should have a chat with him. He's serious, and he's got respect for his elders, not like some of them, his age, they're on drugs now. I lectured at McGill, you know. The peddler's boy, how about that? I spoke on Talmudic law, and those kids, my God, my God, Jewish children, I see them, they're taller than we were, big, healthy, the girls a pleasure to look at, dressed like American princesses, the boys with cars, and I think to myself, we've got reason to be proud, we've done a fine job here. The struggle was worth it. And what do they want, our Jewish children? They want to be black. LeRoi Jones, or whatever his name is, and this Cleaver nut tell them the Jews are rotten to the core, and they clap hands. It's a *mechaieh*. Not that they know a Yiddish word; French, that's what's groovy. Their hearts are breaking for the downtrodden French Canadians. Well, only two generations earlier, these same French Canadians wanted only to break their heads. And if it's not the blacks, or the French Canadians, it's the Eskimos. They can't sleep, they feel guilty about the Indians. So there they are, our Jewish children, wearing Indian head-bands. Smoking pot. It's the burden of being white, it bugs them. How long have we even been white? Only two genera-tions ago, who was white? We were kikes, that's all.

"Some bunch. What's Israel to them? An imperialist outpost. And World War II; that's when we wiped out Hiroshima, and the beautiful city of Dresden, we poor old sinners. We Philis-tines. You know I saw a Jewish kid on a motorcycle, Bernstein's boy, wearing his hair Ritz Brothers style and on his head there's a German soldier's helmet. Shame, I said, shame. 'It's campy,' the girls squeal. 'Why are you so uptight, Mr. Hersh?' And they lay into me about Harlem, the *tzoris* of the Eskimos, Indian braves without hope. Vietnam. Cuba. Look here, I said, this is Abraham Hersh you're looking at. I am a reasonably good fellow. I am responsible for none of the world's ills. Whatever I got, I earned. Napalm's not my invention. I never lynched anybody. I'm sorry you're not black and beautiful, but only a Jewish child. For me, it's the thoughts of Rabbi Akiba, not Chairman Mao. And this *pisherke* pipes up, he says, they're the love generation, they're for peace, they give each other flowers. Big news, eh, Yankel? What am I, I say, the hate generation? A war-monger? When I was chasing after girls, did I hand out poison ivy, I said it with flowers too. No, no, I don't dig it. This kid says when they have a rock concert, thousands of them from miles. around, there's no rough stuff. I answered him, listen here, shmock, if I go to an affair at the synagogue, or a Mozart concert, we don't pour out of the halls with clubs, splitting heads. Why should you be amazed that your concerts don't end in a riot? What's so special? But he's not finished yet, this latter-day savant. After all, I don't strut down Sherbrooke Street with FUCK painted on my forehead. If I jerked off, I'd feel guilty. I wouldn't kiss another man. Feh, I said. Their bodies are beautiful, he tells me. When they swim nude, the sun shines out of their asses. Listen here, you little prick, you think I was born fat and bald, with a heart condition. Wasn't I young once, and aren't you going to grow old too? Aren't we all made of flesh?

"Oh, it was exasperating. Beyond belief. But my Irwin's got a head on his shoulders," Uncle Abe said, knocking wood, "and both feet planted on *terra firma*. I must remind you once more, Yankel, this is our home. We live here, you don't. I am a respected citizen. My daughter has married well, she doesn't lack for comforts. She phones her mother every day, she calls me at the office. We adore our grandchildren. One day Irwin will marry a good girl, God willing, and there will be more grandchildren. I brought them up, Irwin and Doris, and when the day comes they will bury me. I wear my father's *talith* in *shul*, next Irwin will wear it, and then his son and his son's son. It's a good life. I enjoy it. I am not one of your bitten Hershes, a wanderer, coming home only to poke snide fun and stir up trouble. A shit-disturber."

"Like Joey," Jake asked, "or me?"

"I do not compare you with him. You're a good Jewish boy. Look inside your heart, Yankel, and there's *yiddishkeit*."

"Don't claim me, please. At least not in that fashion. Because as amusing as you are, and plausible, the Hersh family honor rides on Joey's back, not your complacent shoulders, and my heart belongs to him."

"In Paraguay?"

"Yes."

"*Putz.* Let me ask you this, as I'm the villain in your books. What has Joey ever done for his wife? Or Hanna? Or Jenny? Or Arty? Me, the complacent one, I took them all in when they were in rags, Arty's head crawling with lice. I paid the rent and the doctor's bills. I put Arty through dentistry school, and I'm not sorry, let me tell you, because he's turned out a respectable man, highly thought of in the community."

"Don't you community me any communities. Because you, my dear, the peddler's number one son, were one of the community leaders who signed an obsequious letter to the *Star* saying no stone would be left unturned to find whoever had beaten up the French Canadian student."

"Yes, I'm the guilty one. All he did was beat up an innocent boy and leave him lying unconscious in an alley."

"When Jenny left town she said no more money from Uncle Abe, sweet fucking Uncle Abe. Why?"

"Because she's a foul-mouthed whore and she hates us. Don't you even know that much?"

"You had Joey beaten up and ridden out of town, Uncle Abe. You know it and I know it."

"I sleep with a good conscience. The only thing that ever keeps me awake is heartburn."

"Oh, what's the use?"

"Yankel, let's get something straight here. We are talking about a blackmailer. About a gambler and a bigamist and a liar. You and I are discussing a gigolo. A man who moves from country to country under assumed names, certainly with good reason. De la Hirsch," he said, snickering. "Josef Mengele yet. Paraguay. O.K., no more burning looks from you, please. Joey is the Golem. He's Bar-Kochba. A one-man Maccabee band. He is searching the jungles for Mengele. After all, somebody caught Eichmann. But if he finds him, what then? How old would this obscenity be? Sixty? Seventy? Joey finds him, he slits his throat.

Does that balance any books? No, sir. It makes trouble for the Jews in Asunción, that's all."

"Like Joey made trouble for you here?"

"All right, then. Chew on this, my young friend. From what I know of your cousin, if he is actually searching for Mengele, which I don't believe for a minute, if he is hunting this Nazi down and finds him," Uncle Abe shouted, pounding the table, "he won't kill him, he'll blackmail him."

Outside, it was still stifling. But it looked like rain. Cousin Irwin was leaning against the family Cadillac, umbrella in hand, waiting to drive his parents home. Irwin was licking a triple-scoop, double-coned ice cream. Strawberry, chocolate, and pistachio. A baseball cap (*Go*, METS, *Go!*) hooded his eyes. His arms had been boiled lobster-red by the sun. Instead of elbows, dimples. He wore a yellow jersey, his nipples showing through. His enormous belly spilled over his tartan Bermuda shorts.

Jake bore down on him, glowering.

"Want a lick?" Irwin asked, heaving with laughter.

Jake knocked the ice cream out of his hand. It spattered against the Cadillac, sliding to the pavement. "How many states in the Union?" he demanded.

"Forty-eight."

"Fifty," Jake shot back.

"Fifty, then."

"Name them."

"*What?*"

Jake raised his foot and brought his heel down as hard as he could on Irwin's toes.

"Oregon, Idaho, North Dakota, Nebraska, Wyoming, Illinois, Michigan, New York, North Dakota—"

Jake let him have an elbow in the stomach. "You said North Dakota."

"—South Dakota, Vermont, New Hampshire, Texas, Nevada. How many does that make?"

Jake whacked him across the face with the flat of his hand.

"Arizona, California, Utah, New Mexico, Missouri, Miami,

Georgia, Florida, Alabama." Driven back against the hood of the car, his balance precarious, his eyes bulging, Irwin began to quiver. "Kansas, Virginia, North Carolina, South Carolina, Alaska—"

Aunt Sophie, emerging from the apartment building, shrieked. "What's going on here?" Uncle Abe asked, aghast.

"My grandfather didn't come here steerage, Baruch didn't die in penury, Joey wasn't driven out of town, so that this jelly, this nose-picker, this sports nut, this lump of shit, your son, should inherit the earth," and Jake turned to stride down the street, fighting his rising stomach, praying that he would not be sick until he had turned the corner.

16

It was a giggle, coming across Nancy's love letters in Jake's bottom desk drawer. (". . . I never did that before, darling, not with any other man . . .") Oh, wasn't she the grand duchess! (". . . previously took precautions, because there was no man's child I wanted . . .") Such transcendental thoughts! Such high-flown sentiments! As if she wasn't made like all the others, with the answer between her legs.

Digging deeper into the drawer, Harry came up with some pages of script.

> CU GENERAL ROMMEL
> As he raises his field glasses to his eyes.
> POV ROMMEL (THROUGH FIELD GLASSES)
> The 8th Army retreating in disarray across the dunes.

Harry began to skip.

> INT. DAY. A DUNGEON
> reconstructed to resemble a child's nursery. MONTY, on his knees, stripped to the waist. Terrified yet enthralled as MAJOR POPPINS enters, wearing only a nurse's cap, a bra and corset, and high-button shoes.

. . .

Interesting. How very interesting. If Jake secretly fancied that sort of stuff, what right had he to have feigned such superiority, mingled with disgust, when Harry had trusted him sufficiently to show him some of the photographs he had taken. Mocking him. Bloody superior. Even when Harry had spoken more freely than he had with anybody else. Patronizing bastard. His smile so smug, Harry remembered, that he had had half a mind to clobber him with his tripod. After all, he had everything. Beautiful wife. Three kids. House in Hampstead. Numbered Swiss account. Fuck him, Harry thought, suddenly unable to endure even another minute in the house.

Outside, it was raining. Once more into the breach, Harry, for England and cunt. He tried his charms to no avail in the coffee bars along the King's Road and Kensington Church Street, feeling despondent by the time he returned to Finchley Road and managed to elbow his way into The Scene just before closing time.

The girl who caught his eye was sullen but certainly pretty, with lazy blue eyes and long blond hair. Sitting alone, puffing on the butt of a handrolled cigarette. Tit-hugging sweater, miniskirt. Whoever had been sitting with her had gone, leaving his coffee unfinished and cheesecake uneaten.

"I don't know how to put this, actually," Harry said shyly, "because you won't believe me."

"That is right," she agreed, the accent German.

"I am a film director."

She tittered, seemingly drifting.

"You see," Harry began, sliding into the empty chair beside her.

"You are not invited. Hey, I do not recall . . ."

"Give me two minutes and then just say it and I'll be off," he said, flicking his fingers, "like that," and he held his light meter close to her, studying it. "You are absolutely beautiful."

"Tick-tock, tick-tock."

"I've been searching all night and without a doubt you're it."

"Tick-tock, tick-tock."

"Now then, I *am* a film director, as it happens. Look here," and he shoved a credit card at her.

"Jacob Hersh," she read aloud, indifferent.

"And look at this."

Not without effort, blinking, she read a review of Jake's last film and scrutinized his union card. Then she picked up the clipping once more, reading it more slowly this time, moving her lips, and absently passing him her cigarette butt. Pretending to inhale deeply, Harry said, "Lovely."

"And so. What is it you want?"

"Let's split and go to my pad for a drink. It's not far," he said, half rising.

But she didn't budge.

"Are you an actress?"

She nodded, no.

"Beautiful. Fab."

"I am a student. An *au pair* girl."

"Would you believe it?" Harry shook his head; he smacked a fist into his open hand. "Would you believe it?"

"Believe what . . .?"

"Lightning strikes twice."

"I do not understand."

"Elke Sommer. She was an *au pair* girl, you know, right here in Hampstead. When she was discovered."

This time, when he took her arm, raising her from the table, she did not resist.

"Mind you, I can't promise anything," Harry continued. "Your English isn't bad, it's charming in fact, but there are some lines I'd like you to read for me. Are you up to it?"

Shrugging, she said, "Why not?"

Outside, giddy with achievement, his heart pounding, Harry said, "Walk ahead of me."

"Why?"

"Do as I say. Please."

She floated on ahead of him.

"Smashing. Absolutely smashing," Harry said, catching up to take her arm. "Let's go."

17

Jake didn't last the prescribed week of mourning, but left a day early, undone by his excruciating and heated quarrel over the Horseman. It rankled. Oh how it rankled. On the flight back to London, bouncing in blue skies over Labrador, dozing fitfully as he cruised over the rippled, steely Atlantic, Jake thrashed through his altercation with Uncle Abe again and again, coming out best in retrospect.

England was signaled by earache, the lowering jet, and the usual bank of snotty cloud. Jake disembarked at Heathrow in a black mood, with tomorrow's drive to Cornwall, Nancy and the kids, still ahead of him.

There were lights on in the house. Could he have forgotten to . . .? No, Harry would be there, damn it, he thought, damn it, as he turned the key.

The hall smelled sweetly of incense.

Once in the living room, he saw the girl. Lazy blue eyes. Lank blond hair. Coltish. He had surprised her, drifting out of the study, and now it was with a measured insolence that she stooped to retrieve a shawl from the floor, gathering it to her breasts. As in a frozen frame, he was to remember, they scrutinized each other, Jake seething with impatience, the girl leaning against the door, the opening picture in a *Playboy* spread sprung to life.

"Yes," she said.

"This is my house," Jake snarled, "my name is Hersh," and, as if to establish his proprietorial rights, he flung his flight bag on the sofa, self-consciously aware that his manner was as bellicose as an A. J. Cronin father returned to the manse.

The girl withdrew into the study, there was a giggle, some whispering, and then an agitated Harry appeared.

"Oh, for Chrissake! Put something on, will you!"

Harry slid into his trousers, grinning idiotically. "But you weren't coming back until tomorrow."

"I changed my mind."

Beseechingly, he squeezed Jake's arm. "I told her I was in films. A director. Don't ruin it for me, Jake."

She was there again, standing in the doorway, the shawl wrapped around this time.

"Do you want her?" Harry whispered. "She's crazy for it. All ways."

"At the moment, Fellini, I'm crazy for only one thing. A drink," and he turned smartly, taking the stairs to his bedroom two at a time, stumbling but once.

Cunning Harry sent Ingrid with a tray. Remy Martin and a glass. "You are angry with us," she said.

"And you are very observant."

"You're the intellectual type."

"That's the ticket."

"But you keep a gun."

So Harry had treated her to a tour of his aerie. The little German bitch would have seen the photographs on the wall. Frau Goering, the Von Papens, "Sepp" Dietrich.

"For a good reason," he said. "Now would you just set the drink down over there and go."

She reeked of sex, and he, equally palatably, of death. Gratuitously, he added, "I'm going to have a bath."

"What reason?"

"The gun or the bath?"

"The gun."

"I might be planning to shoot some Germans. Maybe even you. Who knows?"

Ingrid giggled, pointing, but it wasn't his prowess she was mocking. It was the Y-front underwear he was standing in. Powder blue. Pilar had stupidly put them in the machine with Sammy's jeans and the colors had run.

Spitefully, Jake pulled at the shawl, which came away easily. Then just to show he wasn't utterly unappreciative or a prude, he ran his hand over her breasts and passed it angrily between her legs. Glaring at him, she locked him there. Jake, to his astonishment, responded by pinching her as viciously as he could. Which set her to trembling all over. The next thing he knew she was on her knees, her head bobbing between his legs. Uprooting her, Jake feigned lofty disinterest, betrayed by a throbbing erection. Even so, he said, "Go back to Harry, will you. He must be getting impatient."

At five thirty in the morning, Ingrid started up Haverstock Hill, heading for home, her gait uneven, almost a totter. Sobbing, she steeled herself against the car creeping toward her, unaware as yet that it wasn't an attempted pick-up but a police car, coming from scouring the Heath for Hampton flashers: Echo-1 from E Division.

"Everything all right, miss?"

Her inchoate tale, choked with sobs, sounded like the usual guff. Although Sergeant Hoare was skeptical, for at that hour most girls surprised in her state fell back on the same sort of wild sexual charges, especially if they were frightened, he parked, his engine idling. Policewoman Everett invited Ingrid to sit down beside her in the back of the white Jaguar. Wearily, she asked the girl to begin again. It was no use. Once more she rambled hysterically, weeping, and lapsing into German.

"What was the other man's name again?" Sergeant Hoare asked, glancing sharply at policewoman Everett, who took out her notebook for the first time.

"Hersh."

"Have you been taking drugs?"

"*Niemals*. Not me."

"Not you. But the others?"

Ingrid fell silent, more shrewd than hysterical now, and protested that she felt better and was capable of walking home.

"It's no trouble. We'll drive you. But what would you say to a nice cup of tea first?"

18

Jake appeared with Harry in Magistrates' Court, Great Marlborough Street, at ten thirty in the morning. Harry was charged with sodomy, rape, and the possession of cannabis. Jake was charged with rape, aiding and abetting sodomy, and the possession of cannabis. They both pleaded not guilty. Detective Inspector Mallory, the officer in charge of the case, did not object to their being released on bail, which was set at £1,000 for Jake and £2,500 for Harry. Mallory pleaded for a remand of eight days to allow the police sufficient time to collect all the necessary evidence. This, too, was granted by His Worship. And Jake, bewildered by events that were succeeding each other with benumbing swiftness, retired with Harry to the pub across the street.

"Now we'll see what sort of friend you are," Harry said.

Jake stared at him, puzzled. He had quite forgotten Harry was there.

"Now we'll see if you're my friend or if you run."

"Don't panic. I'm not going to run, Harry."

"You can't. You'd be ill-advised, mate. Because you're in this up to your neck. Just like me."

"The hell I am. I just walked in on the two of you," he pleaded. "I'm a bystander."

"Hullo, hullo, hullo."

Jake was elsewhere. "I am insulted," he said. "I am insulted to my very bones."

"There, there, luv. It hasn't even started yet. You haven't seen anything yet."

"Bastard."

Harry clucked his tongue. He waved a finger in front of Jake's ash-gray face. "No, you don't. Because I'm not the bastard. You are. If not for you, mate, none of this would have happened."

Jake began to tremble. He hid his hands.

"If you hadn't heaved her out of the house, she never would have gone to the cops. She wouldn't have had a case. If she had been allowed to stay the night, as she expected—if she had eaten breakfast with us—there isn't a magistrate in the land who wouldn't have laughed her out of court. But then we didn't want her soiling your precious fucking sheets, did we?"

"No."

"Better this, wouldn't you say?"

But Jake wasn't with him; he was still struggling awake to the clamor of heightened voices and a dog's persistent barking, starting downstairs in his dressing gown, baffled, his mood irascible, to discover Harry locked in a heated exchange with Sergeant Hoare.

"Why did they take my jar of vaseline with them?" he asked.

"Because the police doctor's been up her ass hole with a swab, and what do you think he found, duckie, the Northwest Passage?"

"Did you force her, Harry?"

"Not bloody likely. She couldn't get enough. But it doesn't matter. Because sodomy is a felony even among consenting adults. Your wife can charge you with it. Or doesn't she fancy the back door?"

"Go to hell."

"Driving out to see her now, are you? Well, here's to you. The best of British luck."

Jake said he would be in touch with Harry again in the morning. They should go to see solicitors together.

"If you let them talk you into making me the sacrificial lamb," Harry said, "I'll have you in court, mate. I'll do anything I can to see that you get sentenced."

"I'm sure you would."

"I've got nothing to lose, don't you see?"

On the road to Newquay, Jake's mood oscillated between seizures of fear, obliging him to pull to on the soft shoulder, resting with his head against the steering wheel until his nausea passed, and long stretches of lightheartedness, even incredulity, wherein he all but convinced himself none of this had happened to him. It was altogether too absurd.

Nancy, who had been trying to reach him at the house all through the night, was in a state. "Where have you been, Jake?"

"In jail."

He had prepared a speech.

"When I was at university, we used to play something we called the Values Game. We set ourselves moral dilemmas. In one of them, which I remember rather well, you are crossing a bridge, you pause to stand by the railing, and you see a man drowning. He's a total stranger. Maybe you can save him. But if you jump in after him it is equally possible that you may go down with him in the ensuing struggle. There is nobody else on the bridge. So if you choose to walk away and pretend you haven't seen him, nobody will know but you. What do you do?"

Then he told Nancy that he had lied to her; Harry had indeed been staying in the house and he was there the night of Jake's return from Montreal. He had a girl with him, somebody he had picked up in a coffee bar. Harry and the girl had played all manner of sexual games in which he had not taken part, he said, but he had joined them downstairs for a drink, and something the girl had said outraged him. He had thrown her bodily out of the house in a paroxysm of anger. Vengefully, the girl had gone to the police and sworn out a complaint. Jake told her what he was charged with and what Harry was charged with. He assured her he was innocent and that the case against him, if not Harry, was bound to collapse in Magistrates' Court in eight days' time, but reporters would be there, there would be publicity, obscene publicity, and they would have to stand up to it.

Nancy didn't cry. Neither did she admonish him. With the utmost calm all she said was, "I think we should return to London immediately."

"You could stay here with the kids. It might be better."

"No."

He told her that Harry blamed him and confessed that there was some justice, however convoluted, to his complaint. He would pay for Harry's defense, he said, but once the hearing was over he would never see him again. That was a promise.

"It could go further than Magistrates' Court, Jake. I think you should be prepared for that."

"It won't," he cried. "It can't."

"If it's going to be in the newspapers, you'd better write to your mother before she reads it herself."

Canada. He told her about his father's funeral, light years ago it seemed, on the other side of the moon, and about his quarrel with Uncle Abe over the Horseman. Which was the only time she revealed how fragile was her composure.

"You've got him to thank for this, you know. If not for Joey," she said, "you would never have met Ruthy or . . ."

"Don't," he protested, appalled.

"I'm sorry."

It was dawn; and the packing was done.

"We can start back as soon as the kids are up," he said. "I don't need any sleep."

In London, the following evening, Jake had his first meeting with Ormsby-Fletcher. In the morning, Detective Inspector Mallory came to call with two policemen, one of them a photographer, and Jake hastily sent Nancy out with the children. Mallory's affable men measured the house from end to end. They took pictures, discussing lenses with Jake, and exposures, for after all he was a professional. Jake served drinks.

"I've got some good news for you," Mallory said amiably.

"What's that?"

"I shouldn't be telling you this, but it will all come out in the wash. We found a small quantity of cannabis in her room. She claims Stein gave it to her, but . . ." He shrugged. ". . . It might not hold up."

"I should hope not," Jake replied fiercely.

"You're too worried, Mr. Hersh. In my opinion, you haven't much to fear."

"Oh," Jake said cautiously.

"It's bad luck your being involved with Stein. He's a villain. He's got a nasty record. Did you know that?"

"I don't think we should discuss the case any more."

"Not to worry. This is all unofficial. We didn't find any cannabis in Stein's flat, you know."

"Harry doesn't smoke pot."

"Maybe not. He could keep it for his girls. He's a very fancy fellow, you know. Something of a photography buff."

"Mmmn," Jake said.

"I should think pot will be legalized soon enough, wouldn't you?"

"The sooner the better."

"You ever tried it yourself?"

"I shouldn't discuss these things with you."

Mallory looked wounded.

"I will say one thing and no more," Jake said. "Harry did not rape that girl."

"Maybe not this one," Mallory allowed, rising. "Well, we shan't be bothering you again."

"Sorry we didn't meet under more pleasant circumstances," Jake said.

"Good luck in court."

It was all so agreeable, so bracingly civilized, that Jake was lulled into a sense of well-being until he saw that instead of getting into his car and driving off, Mallory strolled next door to see Lady Dry Cunt. He emerged an hour later to ring the Clarkes' bell.

Jake and Harry met with Ormsby-Fletcher every afternoon and most evenings, mulling over the police depositions, as well as the brief Ormsby-Fletcher was preparing, in the days leading up to their hearing in Magistrates' Court, Great Marlborough Street.

The hearing got off to a rocky start. Once the barrister who was appearing for the Director of Public Prosecutions had opened the case, outlining the charges against Stein and Hersh, Ormsby-Fletcher rose for the defense.

"Your Worship," he began, "as you may know, my client is a well-known film director, particularly vulnerable to bad publicity. As I strongly feel the case against him will go no further than this court, I ask that this examination should be conducted in private as you are allowed to do by section 4 (2) of the Magistrates' Courts Act, 1952."

His Worship didn't ponder. He hardly blinked.

"I am afraid I cannot accede to your request. It is the general practice of the courts to hold these preliminary examinations in public, and I see no reason at this moment for departing from that practice."

The barrister for the Crown concluded his opening speech without any further interruptions. Then the depositions of the witnesses were taken and read aloud to them by the Clerk of the court. Ingrid signed hers, then Detective Inspector Mallory signed, followed by Sergeant Hoare and the police doctor. They all entered into a recognizance to give evidence at the Old Bailey, if the case were committed for trial.

Gilbray, a colleague of Ormsby-Fletcher's appearing for Stein, pleaded not guilty and reserved his client's defense. Then Ormsby-Fletcher, simulating impatience, bravely raised the flag for the defense once more.

"Your Worship," he said, "I submit there is no case here for my client to answer and none to justify a committal for trial. The evidence against my client is thin and inconclusive. Even supposing the girl was raped, there is nothing to show my client was anything more than a bewildered bystander to the act. Surely such evidence does not justify you putting my client to the expense and anxiety of a trial."

His Worship did not agree.

"As you well know," he said, "I have not to be satisfied beyond reasonable doubt that the defendant raped Ingrid Loebner. That is a much higher standard of proof which must be attained before a jury can convict. I must be satisfied only 'that there is sufficient evidence to put the accused upon trial.' As the case now stands, I am so satisfied unless the prisoner in giving evidence himself or by calling witnesses is able to convince me that the evidence is insufficient."

But the prisoner, Hersh, remained silent. He made no statement. He gave no evidence.

"My client," Ormsby-Fletcher said, "pleads not guilty and reserves his defense."

"Very well." His Worship turned to Jake. "You will be committed for trial at the next sessions of the Central Criminal Court."

19

More than three months passed before Jake actually stood with Harry in the dock of Number One Court of the Old Bailey, or more properly the Central Criminal Court, at 2:30 on a Thursday afternoon in October. The dock, an octagonal-shaped structure with glass panels in black wooden frames, measured sixteen feet by fourteen feet, sufficient to hold up to twenty prisoners. It faced the bench.

The presiding judge, Mr. Justice Beal, sat on the bench. Not on the center chair, under the elegant Palladian arch, flanked by pillars, with the coat of arms of Edward VII at the top and the Sword of Justice, pointing upwards, in the center, for this seat was traditionally reserved for the Lord Mayor of London as senior Commissioner. Mr. Justice Beal filled the chair next to it, resting his enormous bottom on a green velvet pillow.

The necessarily somber, oak-lined Number One Court was really astonishingly small, measuring forty-four by fifty-six feet, but this did ensure that the tone of the proceedings was subdued, conversational, as it were, rather than overblown. Below the bewigged judge there was a table for the Clerk of the Court and below that the well of the court. To the left of the well, there were benches for counsel, those for the prosecution being nearest the judge and those for the defense being closest to the prisoners. Counsel for Regina, instructed by the Director of Public Prosecutions, was Mr. Peregrine Pound, Q.C., assisted by Mr. Henry Fraser. Counsel for the defense, instructed by Messrs. Ormsby-Fletcher & Co., Solicitors, was Sir Lionel Watkins, Q.C., and Mr. Guy Harrington, on behalf of the prisoner Jacob Hersh; Mr. William Coxe and Mr. Julian Fowler on behalf of the prisoner Stein. On the right of the well of the court, there were benches for officials and the press, and to the right of the press benches, there was the jury box. The witness box, supplied with a microphone, was set between the bench and the jury box. There were also a number of benches, as well as a gallery, available to the public, who were free to drift in and out as they liked.

The Clerk of the Court charged Harry Stein with sodomy, rape, indecent assault, and the possession of cannabis. "Harry Stein," he said, "are you guilty or not guilty?"

"Not guilty."

Jacob Hersh was charged with aiding and abetting sodomy, a reduced charge of indecent assault, and the possession of cannabis. He, too, pleaded not guilty.

"May it please your lordship, members of the jury," the avuncular Mr. Pound began, opening for the prosecution, "there is a letter and some pages of film script which I think I shall have to refer to in my opening address."

Mr. Justice Beal allowed him to pass out some pages of film script to the jury, pages from *The Good Britons*, and then he read the pages aloud.

Peregrine Pound described how Ingrid Loebner, an *au pair* girl, had been picked up by Stein in a coffee bar, The Scene, on Finchley Road, and had been tricked into accompanying him to Hersh's house. A detached nine-room dwelling, with a walled garden, in the most enviable part of Hampstead. "Stein promised her there would be no 'funny stuff' and even assured her that his wife was at home. He further alleviated the girl's suspicions by purporting to be Hersh, a reputable film director, and showing her such *bona fides* and press clippings as would support this claim."

Here Mr. Pound graciously apologized for a digression. "But I should make it clear, members of the jury, that the *au pair* girl is no common domestic. She is normally the well-brought-up daughter of a respectable middle-class family, come to this country to learn the language, paying her way by being a mother's help, living as one of the family. Dame Joan Vickers, Conservative M.P. for Devonport, and for years," Mr. Pound ventured, "a veritable Joan of Arc of the *au pair* girls, has only recently spoken of the hazards into which a green girl, inexperienced and far from home—under an alien sky, as it were—might fall."

Mr. Pound paused to peer at the jury over his bifocals.

"Stein's 'wife' was not at home when Miss Loebner arrived, but he assured her she would soon be with them. Meanwhile, he offered her a drink and what she took to be a cigarette, but what was actually cannabis. He showed her the pages of script I have read to you. She protested she could not read for a part which obliged her to appear in no more than a bra, a corset, and high-button shoes. He was reassuring. It would not be necessary, he said."

But Miss Loebner, he went on to explain, her resistance weakened by drink and drug, soon found herself reading for Stein clad only in her bra and panties.

"Even so," Mr. Pound said, "she would not acquiesce to anything more, and when he made physical advances to her, she resisted. She threatened to scream for help. Which is when he put a record on the player, *Lumpy Gravy* by Frank Zappa, playing it very loud indeed. Stein became menacing. He brandished a riding crop. He warned Miss Loebner that if he beat her with wet towels they would leave no marks on her body. She discovered that her clothes were hidden. Even then, frightened as she was, under the influence of drugs, she resisted Stein when he attempted to have intercourse with her. She resisted as well as she could under the circumstances, which the medical evidence will abundantly support. Once he had taken his pleasure, Stein seemed to calm down. She hoped that he would pass out, she could retrieve her clothes, and flee. So imagine her consternation when Hersh arrived and instead of the games breaking off, they were to take an even more unpleasant turn."

Mr. Pound described the games, such as they were, calling the jury's attention once more to the saddle and riding crop kept by a man who was no equestrian himself. He told them how Hersh, seizing Miss Loebner by the hair, had forced his erect penis into her mouth and ejaculated therein. And how Stein, inflamed by Hersh's presence to even greater acts of perversion, penetrated Miss Loebner *per anum.*

"It is the case of the Crown," he concluded, revealing a sudden flash of temper, "that Miss Loebner accompanied Stein to the house, expecting to read for a part in a cinema production. Naïve, perhaps, but not an uncommon dream for a comely young girl. She most certainly did not go to the house with Stein anticipating that she would be beaten—raped—buggered—and be held prisoner until five in the morning by two men, each of them almost twice her age."

The amiable Detective Inspector Mallory was the first witness to be sworn in by the prosecution.

"What," Mr. Henry Fraser asked him, "did Hersh say to you when you told him he was charged with aiding and abetting sodomy?"

"He said, 'What can I get for that?' I told him seven years to life."

"What did he say to that?"

"He said as British law seemed to value property above everything else, and he quoted the thirty-year sentences of the Great Train Robbery as an example, then it would seem to follow that there was no property on this island quite so precious as Miss Loebner's bottom."

Eventually, they got to Mallory's second visit to the house.

"Did you then discuss cannabis with him?" Mr. Fraser asked. "Yes."

"What did he say?"

"I asked him if he thought it should be legalized. He said the sooner the better."

Cross-examining, Mr. Guy Harrington asked, "Did you find any cannabis in Hersh's house?"

"We found the butts of three cigarettes."

"In your search, did you find cannabis or even traces of it in drawers or on shelves or anywhere else?"

"No."

"Could the butts you found have been the remains of cigarettes brought into the house by Miss Loebner?"

"Yes. That's possible."

Then Sir Lionel Watkins, manifestly bored, skewered Inspector Mallory.

"You say Hersh said cannabis should be legalized. The sooner the better. Is it possible you led Hersh on, suggesting to him that pot would be legalized soon enough, and then inviting his opinion?"

"No. I did not."

"Did you, on your visit to Hersh's house with a photographer, properly caution him or did you say," and here he mocked the inspector's bluff manner, "this is all unofficial, old chap?"

"I cautioned him."

Sir Lionel smiled. He nodded. "That will be all, Inspector."

Sergeant Hoare, called to the stand, substantiated Mallory's testimony and told of his initial difficulties with Stein at the door. The police doctor testified that Miss Loebner, when brought to him, had been in a state of shock, and that on examination he had discovered evidence of both vaginal and anal penetration. Entry of the penis into the anal passage had been eased with vaseline.

"Would you say entry was forced?"

"It could have been forced. But it is not necessarily so."

"Would you care to explain?"

"The passage is narrow. If the member were large, and erect, this could account for the bruises."

Cross-examining, Mr. Harrington asked, "Were there any scratches on Miss Loebner, indicating a struggle?"

"There were no anal bruises that would establish beyond doubt that entry was forced. On the other hand, she has a nasty bruise on her forearm. One inner thigh was slightly discolored immediately below the vagina. Her left buttock was also discolored."

"Could the last discoloration have been the aftermath of a love tap?"

"Yes, but rather a strong one."

"You say she was in a state of shock?"

"Yes."

"Is that not natural, considering she had been picked up by the police at five-thirty in the morning, high on cannabis, and was then asked to submit to a rigorous examination of her private parts?"

"Yes."

Old Lady Dry Cunt was the next to be sworn in.

"Did you hear or see anything unusual emanating from the Hershes' house on the night of June twelfth?"

"I heard music playing loudly."

"*Lumpy Gravy* by Frank Zappa?"

"I wouldn't know," she said sniffily.

Ingrid Loebner's employer, a Mr. Ungerman, was sworn in, and testified to her good character. But, cross-examining, Sir Lionel instantly established that though Miss Loebner had only been with the Ungermans for three months, she had stayed out all night at least four other times.

"Does she, to your knowledge, smoke cannabis?"

"No. Not to my knowledge."

"What is it you said she burns in her room some evenings?"

"Incense, I think."

"Are you not aware this is burned to conceal the smell of cannabis?"

Mr. Pound objected strenuously. Sir Lionel withdrew the question.

Then Ingrid was sworn in.

"Did your father serve in the war, Miss Loebner?"

"He was with the medical corps. On the Russian front. It was terrible for them. They had no winter clothes."

"Was he a member of the Nazi party?"

"Never," she protested vehemently. "I told Hersh. My father disapproved."

"Did you also tell Hersh your father was a dentist?"

"Yes."

"What did he reply?"

"If that's the case, he said, he must have been very busy during the war, extracting gold fillings from Jews."

Ingrid described how she had been enticed to Hersh's house, where she had been plied with liquor and cannabis. Hersh's actual arrival had been a surprise, she allowed, and she had immediately looked to him for help.

"What did Stein say when he arrived?"

"He said, Do you want her now? She's crazy for it. All ways."

"And what did you say to that?"

"Nothing. I was very frightened."

"And then what happened?"

"Stein sent me to Hersh's bedroom, carrying a tray with brandy."

"What were you wearing?"

"I was naked."

"Isn't that unusual, rather?"

"He had hidden my clothes," she protested.

"Who had?"

"Stein. He forced me. He warned me, yeah, Hersh was very important. He said he could make me a star, yeah, but he would have to see what I looked like naked. He said I was to please Hersh or they would both be very angry with me."

"And you were willing?"

"But he had hidden my clothes," she cried. "He had a wet towel in his hand. He had already hit me with it. He warned me the marks didn't show. I thought I would play for time. I didn't want him to hurt me again."

"What happened when you entered Hersh's bedroom?"

"He was in his underwear, yeah? They were blue ones. I asked him why he kept a rifle."

"How did you know he had one?"

"Stein had taken me to see it. He said it didn't pay to be a disobedient girl in this house."

"I see. And what did Hersh say when you asked him why he kept a rifle?"

"He said he might be planning to shoot some Germans. Maybe you. Who knows."

"Then what happened?"

"He grabbed me by the hair and forced me on the bed and made me take it in my mouth."

"He obliged you to commit *fellatio?*"

"That's to suck the cock, yeah?"

Mr. Pound nodded reprovingly. "Yes," he said.

"Yes. It was so."

"Did you struggle?"

"I was too frightened."

"Did you scream for help?"

"But my mouth was full, yeah? How could I?"

"What happened next?"

"I said to him, yeah, why do you treat me like an animal? He said, because I am kind. It's more than your father would have done for mine, he said, if he had the chance."

"And then what happened?"

"He was drunken. He wished to sleep. Go away, he said. Go downstairs. You do everything Harry asks or there will be trouble."

It was time to adjourn the court.

"Members of the jury," Mr. Justice Beal said, "I need hardly say you will take care not to speak to anybody about this case, and tell me if anybody approaches you about it."

Ingrid resumed her testimony at 10:30 on Friday morning. She told the court about the saddle and the use Harry had put it to. She said he wanted to take photographs and threatened her with violence.

"What did Stein do then?"

"He forced me on to the rug, facing downwards."

"And then what happened?"

"He forced his cock up my ass hole."

"Did you resist?"

"But, naturally. It hurt me. But he held the riding crop in his hand."

"How long did this go on?"

"I can't remember. I think I passed out."

"When did Hersh appear again?"

"It was four o'clock. I remember that."

"Was he dressed?"

"He was wearing a dressing gown, but you could see it."

"See what?"

"His gown was not belted. It hung open."

"What did he do?"

"He was very angry with Stein."

"Why?"

"Not because he had done it to me. He didn't care, the fucking." She stopped, flushing. "Excuse me, your lordship."

Mr. Justice Beal waved her on.

"The witness's grasp of English is imperfect," Mr. Pound said. "She doesn't realize which words are offensive."

"Carry on, please, Mr. Pound."

"Yes, your lordship. Why was he angry then?"

"Over the rifle. And the saddle. Especially the saddle. He took Stein into another room and shouted at him, and when Stein came out, yeah, he put the saddle aside."

"Could you not have taken advantage of their absence to escape?"

"I had no clothes. They had a gun. They had the riding crop. And they were back presently, yeah?"

"And then what happened?"

"At first Hersh was very kind. He poured drinks. He sat down beside me and all he made me do was, well, he took my hand and put it on his thing."

"His penis."

"Yes. It was so. Then his mood changed. He asked me had I

ever been in the Hitler Youth. I said I was born too late. This
made him laugh. I said my older brother had been in the *Hitler
Jugend*, it was all a nonsense. My father saved Jews in the war.
This made him laugh even more. He thought it was funny."

"Did you know Hersh was Jewish?"

"It's a drag. Who cares?"

"Answer yes or no, please."

"I did not know. Then he told me. I said you are so nice,
I would not have guessed. He didn't look, you know. Well,
maybe my English was not right. But he turned very, very angry
in the face."

"And then what happened?"

"He pushed me. He shoved me. He grabbed me very, very
hard here," she said, indicating her arm, "and he told Stein get
her dressed and out of here immediately."

"Then what happened?"

"Stein thought this was a bad idea. He said to keep me prisoner
until the morning. I have marks on me, he said. Hersh shoved
him too. He shouted I want her out of here right now."

So Stein, in spite of his misgivings, at last allowed Ingrid her
clothes and she escaped.

"It was a nightmare," she said, breaking down.

Cross-examining, Sir Lionel Watkins was swift but lethal.
He established, in short order, that it was not unusual for Miss
Loebner to sit in The Scene until midnight. He confronted her
with the fact that the police had found a small quantity of
cannabis in her room; and so, possibly, she would recognize a
joint when and if she was offered one.

"It was not mine," she cried. "A student friend left it there
with his sleeping bag, yeah. I did not even know it was there."

He also got her to admit that she had not gone to the police
station herself, but had been stopped by a cruising patrol car.
Then, without warning, he demanded, "Are you on the pill,
Miss Loebner?"

She looked to the bench where Mr. Pound sat.

"Miss Loebner, do you understand my question?"

"Yes."

"Yes you understand my question or yes you take the pill?"

"Yes. The pill. I take it."

"Were you on the pill the night of June twelfth?"

"I don't remember."

"Odd. I should have thought that would be most important to you."

Why, Sir Lionel demanded, had Ingrid not thrown a vase through a window and screamed for help? Or a chair? Why, once left alone in the living room, had she not fled into the streets nude rather than suffer gross indecencies?

She quit the stand, visibly shaken, holding a handkerchief to her face. Then Mr. William Coxe opened for the defense, on behalf of Stein. Mr. Coxe expressed sympathy for the jury, decent people, who had already been subjected to some plainspoken testimony, especially from the aggrieved Miss Loebner, whose uncertain grasp of the Queen's English encompassed an exact knowledge of those words that were usually associated with the gutter. "The charge brought against Stein," he said, "has always been easy to bring, but terrifyingly difficult to prove and, contrary to what you have heard from my learned friend, the medical evidence does not support the charge of violence. You are asked to believe, members of the jury, that Miss Loebner was raped, violated, and held a prisoner, but it is the case for the defense that she went happily with Stein to Hersh's house and . . ."

Jake began to drift, his mind elsewhere, until Sir Lionel Watkins, a spare man with a severe manner, stood at the bar, and opened the defense on his behalf. Sir Lionel's main point was that Miss Loebner had lied for two reasons. "When the police discovered her, she was high on cannabis, an offense for which she could be deported forthwith. She was also fearful of her employer's ire, for this, as we have heard, was not the first, or indeed the second, time she had been out all night, but her employer had warned her it would be her last. Unless she had a cracking good story to explain her absence."

On and on Sir Lionel rolled, inevitable as the tide, his wrath rising to crash against the jury in a splendiferous crescendo. "Her last words, on being flung out of Hersh's house, were, I'll fix you for this, you mother-fucker bastard. I will fix you for this, you mother-fucker bastard."

As Sir Lionel sat down, Jake surged with hope, he basked in the jury's rueful glances. Jacob Hersh, the ill-used bourgeois, a good white colonial type, albeit a Jew, victimized by a scheming foreign tart. All Jake's antennae screamed reprieve, reprieve, and then Harry was called to the stand, and even as he padded across the well of the court, his complexion sallow, his fixed smile scornful, Jake felt the wind change. He shuddered with apprehension himself.

Mr. Coxe smiled reassuringly, trying to put Harry at ease.

"Could you tell us exactly what happened when you entered The Scene coffee bar on Finchley Road?"

"I sat at a table, ordered a coffee, and then this bird sat down beside me, high on pot. We got to talking."

"Did you tell the *girl*," he said, flashing Harry a warning look, "who you were?"

"I did not say I was Jacob Hersh. I'm attractive to women, you see. I don't need to chat them up. Or write to them on House of Commons notepaper, like John Profumo."

Mr. Justice Beal's hands fluttered. Mr. Pound sat back, beaming; he whispered something to his junior, who smiled, holding a hand to his mouth.

"*My question was—*"

"I told her my name was Stein."

"And then what happened?"

"I did not offer her a part in a film. I invited her back to the house for a drink and some fun."

"And then what happened?"

"She couldn't wait, that's what happened."

"But she did read from the script we had all seen?"

"We played a game or two."

Harry denied using force. Miss Loebner was more than eager

for it, he said. He did not strike her with a riding crop. "But she asked me to. A lot of them like it, you know. Especially your Kensington Gore types. It excites them."

"I would appreciate it immensely if you would confine your remarks to the events that took place in the house."

He had not committed sodomy with Miss Loebner. "She begged me to, but it's not my line. I'm not an establishment type. I was nobody's fag at Eton."

Mr. Pound rose to cross-examine Harry, his appetite mingled with pity, and he quickly pointed out that the medical evidence had shown traces of sperm in Miss Loebner's anus.

"On her impassioned urging, I attempted entry. I teased her backside, but I couldn't bring myself to actually do it."

"Then you did not commit sodomy with Miss Loebner, in spite of her invitation?"

"No. The proof is when Jake—Hersh—came downstairs again she said to him, Hey, man, your friend won't bugger me, he's not the back-door type, what about you?"

Jake, who was to testify next, cringed in the dock.

"Could you tell us," Mr. Pound asked, "how Miss Loebner left the house?"

"Like I said, we wanted her to stay to breakfast, but, suddenly, she panicked. She said she had to get back to her place before her employer wakened, but would we like to see her tomorrow night."

"She offered to return?"

"She said she hadn't had such a ball since she'd had it off with a couple of West Indians."

Then Mr. Pound shifted to the question of Sergeant Hoare. "Did you say to Sergeant Hoare, when he came to arrest you, that No Cossack is going to plant a bloody brick on me?"

"It has happened, hasn't it? It's a matter of record."

"You did say it to him, then?"

"Yes. I'm experienced in these matters, don't you see?"

Mr. Pound faltered. He turned to Mr. Justice Beal for instruction. Leaping up, Mr. Coxe asked, "Would your lordship permit me to have a word with my client? I did already caution him, but . . ."

"Will it be necessary for the jury to leave the court?"

"No, your lordship."

"Do you wish to have a word with him here or below?"

"Here, your lordship."

Mr. Coxe warned Harry that nobody knew of his previous record; it could not be introduced until after the jury had reached their verdict. Even then, only if he were found guilty.

Resuming for the prosecution, Mr. Pound asked, "You say you played a game or two with Miss Loebner. *Did that include concealing her clothes?*"

"No. It did not. She was free to leave at any time."

As Harry quit the witness box, bristling with defiance, Jake sensed the jury's revulsion.

Jake was overcome with despair, he felt undone, as he himself was sworn in.

Sir Lionel asked, "Were you expected at your home on the night of June twelfth?"

"No. I was to arrive the following day."

"Where were you coming from?"

"Montreal."

"What were you doing there?"

"I was on family business."

Questioned more closely, Jake allowed he had gone to attend his father's funeral and, as is the religious custom, was observing a week of mourning.

"What happened when you arrived at your house?"

"I'm afraid I took Stein and Miss Loebner by surprise."

"Did Miss Loebner seem distressed?"

"She most certainly did not."

"What was she wearing?"

"She was nude."

"Didn't this embarrass her?"

"Far from it."

"Did Stein then offer you the girl? Did he say, Do you want her now? She's crazy for it all ways."

"No. He did not."

"And then what happened?"

"She came to my bedroom, with brandy on a tray."

"At your request?"

"No. Of her own volition."

"Did you discuss your rifle with her?"

"No. I did not."

"What happened in your bedroom?"

"She attempted to fondle my penis, but I told her I was tired. I wished to have a bath. I sent her downstairs."

Jake said it was four o'clock when he wakened and went downstairs himself.

"Did you waken because you heard disturbing sounds from downstairs?"

"I wakened with a headache. I heard laughter from downstairs. Moans of pleasure. That's all."

They skipped Jake's quarrel with Harry over the saddle and the rifle. Jake admitted he couldn't remember whether his dressing gown was belted or not.

"You were still in a distressed state."

"That is correct."

"How did Miss Loebner greet you?"

Jake hesitated. He bit his lip. "She called out, Hey, man, your friend won't bugger me, he's not the back-door type, what about you?"

"What was your reply?"

"Some lame joke. I don't remember."

"What happened then?"

"I sat down on the sofa. She sat down beside me."

"And then what happened?"

"She began to stroke my penis."

"And what did you do?"

"Nothing."

There was a pause.

"I was tired," Jake said. "It was soothing."

"Then what happened?"

"She got overexcited. I made her stop."

"And what happened next?"

"She was insulted. We quarreled. Suddenly, I had had quite enough. I insisted she leave the house."

"Did you handle her roughly?"

"No. Not roughly. Well, I did shove her, perhaps."

"And then what happened?"

"She said, I will fix you for this, you mother-fucker bastard."

It was time to adjourn, and Mr. Pound deferred his cross-examination of Hersh until Monday morning.

Harry, who had begun to flake and peel ever since they had first appeared together in Magistrates' Court, had no skin left now. Only flesh. Over the long and agonizing weekend, a largely sleepless weekend, Jake was in and out of Ruthy's flat, where Harry was staying.

"You looked at me like I was a lump of shit," Harry charged. "When I finished my testimony, I looked at you in the dock, my friend, and I saw it in your eyes, no different from the others. Harry Stein is a lump of shit."

Ruthy, whatever resources she had being exhausted, was perpetually in tears.

"If they put this man behind bars, I'm going to wear black until the day he comes out. I will stand in front of your door every morning dressed in black."

"I mightn't be home, Ruthy. We may be tossed into prison together."

"I've been a widow once. I don't deserve this. God shouldn't let me be a widow a second time."

Harry broke out in shingles. He had a cold sore on his lip. He vacillated between castigating Jake, threatening him, and then suddenly revealing the gentle side of his nature, the crushed soul within. He was exhausting, his mood changing from moment to moment.

"If they find me guilty, and not you, I'm going to alter my testimony. I'm going to say you challenged me to bugger her."

"That would be a lie," Jake replied wearily.

"Oh, listen to that! I say! Aren't you lying in there?"

"Yes. Like a trooper."

"Didn't you have any fun with her?"

"Yes, Harry. I did."

Harry assumed a falsetto voice. "Did she place her hand on your cock? Yes, Sir Fuck Face, it was ever so soothing. Soothing, was it? Is that what it was?"

"Shettup, Harry."

Then, as Jake seemed despondent, Harry said without rancor, "Not to worry, mate. It will all be over for you tomorrow."

"Will it?"

"In the end, it's class that counts in this country. There are only two rotters in there. Me, and Ingrid." He ruffled Jake's hair. "Hey, remember that day we had champagne together at the White Elephant?"

"Yeah. That was fun."

"Out of all the people you knew, you chose me to celebrate your son's birth with."

"Yes," Jake lied.

"You said not everybody's rotten. Well, I don't think you're rotten. You've been a friend to me, just like you said."

And, all at once, he was seized with indignation again.

"It's the marks on her arm that's going to do us in. You made them, throwing her out. Not me. If you hadn't lost your temper, neither of us would be in court."

Sunday night Jake did not even attempt to sleep. He lay in bed with Nancy, chain-smoking and drinking cognac.

"My life seems to function in compartments," he said. "When I'm in Montreal, I don't believe in my life here with you and the children. In court, it seems I was born in the dock, there was no life before and there will be nothing after. But lying here with you, I can't even believe that I'm expected to turn up in court again in the morning."

Maybe to be sentenced, she thought.

"They're skinning me alive in there, Nancy. I am insulted. I have never been so profoundly insulted."

"It will all be over tomorrow evening."

"The lies. My God, we're all lying. The barristers. Harry, me, Ingrid. Everybody's lying. It's incredible."

In the morning, he walked Sammy to school, holding his hand all the way. He returned to the house and took Molly to school, telling her a story about Rabbi Akiba. Once more, he refused to allow Nancy to come to the Old Bailey. He absolutely forbade it. Ormsby-Fletcher arrived in his black Humber.

"I am expecting you for dinner," Nancy said.

"Yes. Certainly. See you later, darling."

Mrs. Hersh's head darted out of the door.

"Good luck, *ketzelle*."

"Thanks, Maw."

At 10:30, Jake was sworn in again, and Mr. Pound began his cross-examination.

It went well to begin with, but then Jake had had enough. He was undone by nerves and indignation.

"You have told us," Mr. Pound said, "how you found it . . ." here he paused, determined to find the exact word . . . "how you found it . . . *soothing* . . . to have Miss Loebner stroke your penis."

"Yes."

"Would you not then have found *fellatio* even more . . . soothing?"

"I did not allow her to take me in her mouth."

"That was not the question."

"If," Jake replied, seething, "we are now discussing sexual pleasures, in the abstract, as it were, well, yes, I do not hold *fellatio* to be a disagreeable act."

"But not with Miss Loebner?"

"No."

"Because she's German?"

"Because she did not appeal to me."

"Have you ever smoked cannabis?"

"I'm a gin man. It's a question of generations, I suppose . . . different tastes . . ."

"But have you ever smoked it?"

"Yes, I have," he replied sharply. "Once or twice."

In his closing speech for the Crown, Mr. Pound, his style florid, excoriated the permissive society, warning the jury that the very foundations of society as they knew it were threatened, unless somebody had the common sense to call a halt. He raked over Harry's testimony and demeanor with scorn. "Stein's case," he said, "is pathetically clear-cut. He is a disappointed little fellow, clearly not attractive to women, who forced his gross attentions on an innocent girl. Lying to her, drugging her, and finally beating her. Stein has not had the benefit of a first-class education or upbringing. I daresay my learned friend will play on this stale tune soon enough, telling you about this man's deprived background, as if it were a license for rape and sodomy. The defense will try to bring tears to your eyes, members of the jury, telling you that though this poor little chap could get glasses on National Health, the welfare state failed to provide him with girls." Mr. Pound clucked his tongue. He shook his head. "And, after all, these are permissive days, and everything the prisoner has seen in the so-called adult cinema, or in Soho strip clubs, tells him that he has a right to everything. Even to satisfying his very special tastes. For Stein, you know, is something of a photographer. As you have heard, he regularly photographs nude girls in chains. The sort of girls available for such work in squalid Soho basements. Oh, yes, Stein's case is all too familiar. He is flotsam. The driftwood that floats in the brackish waters of the I'm-all-right-Jack society. Stroll through the streets of Soho, the back alleys of this once proud city, and within the shadow of Nelson's column you will uncover a plethora of Steins, lingering outside pornography shops and strip-club displays . . ."

Mr. Pound reminded the jury of Jake's affluence and called their attention once more to the saddle and riding crop kept by a man who was no equestrian himself. "You must ask yourselves why, members of the jury, and to what purpose." Hersh, he suggested, was possibly the true villain of this sordid affair. "At once more privileged, I put it to you, and more blameworthy. He is not an embittered little man, like Stein, denied his share of materialism's cornucopia. He is well educated, successful, talented, married, with three children. He lives in style, mingling with cinema stars in Mayfair's most fashionable restaurants. *Look at it this way. He is so successful in his chosen field that he earns rather more annually than the prime minister of this country.* Why, oh why, you must be asking yourselves, would such a man, seemingly blessed with all that this world can provide, stoop to such perversions? Let me suggest this to you, members of the jury, he is so arrogant a man, accustomed to directing fantasies under set conditions, that this time he attempted to carry over into actuality the prerequisites of his trade, *he wished to direct real people in x-certificate scenes, as it were.*"

Overflowing with self-content, Mr. Pound smiled at Sir Lionel Watkins. Sir Lionel nodded, acknowledging a goodie.

In conclusion, Mr. Pound suggested that Hersh, like those overpaid pop stars who sprang up overnight, felt there was one law for him and another for squares, their contemptuous word for God-fearing people. He reminded them of the medical evidence. An act of sodomy had been committed. Miss Loebner, however *charming* she had found Stein, however *soothing* she had proven to Hersh, had been drugged. She had been raped. It was the jury's duty to find Stein and Hersh guilty as charged.

Rising on Stein's behalf, the mellifluous Mr. William Coxe complimented the jury for their attentiveness and self-evident intelligence. He advised them, "You are not here to judge Stein for his erotic tastes. It is no crime, members of the jury, to take artistic photographs of nude ladies. Indeed, I have seen them in the color supplement of the *Sunday Times.* Whether we like it or not, the blushes that one once saw at the very whisper of the word 'sex' have disappeared from the cheeks of young people." He told them that it was not necessary to be enamored of Stein to find him innocent. He was not an entrant in a popularity contest. He was not on trial for his character. Promiscuity, however distasteful it was to the jury, as it was to him, was no crime. Stein was charged with sodomy, rape, indecent assault, and the possession of cannabis, and it might go very hard for him if he were found guilty. He should not be so found if there was any reasonable doubt. "You are asked to believe, members of the jury, that Miss Loebner was raped, violated, and held a prisoner. Oh dear, oh dear. How did this dreadful thing come about? She was picked up at midnight in a coffee bar and went to Hersh's house, expecting . . . not to be seduced, heavens no . . . but a screen test . . ."

Sir Lionel Watkins stood at the bar next.

"Members of the jury," he pointed out at once, "this much abused man does not stand in the dock because he owns a house in Hampstead with a walled garden. He did not acquire this house illegally, but by dint of hard work and talent. Neither does he stand before you because he dines in fashionable restaurants or moves in glittering company. It is only ill luck, a combination of fortuitous circumstances, that have brought this man where he stands now. Had he not returned a day early from Canada, he would not have intruded on his friend, enjoying a liaison with a compliant girl. Had he not found this girl disgusting, and tossed her out of his home in anger, she would not have complained to the police, bringing him here before you, the innocent victim of an amoral girl's vindictive fantasies . . ."

Sir Lionel concentrated on Miss Loebner's story, denigrating it with zeal.

"How was this shrinking prisoner of love taken?" he demanded. "Was she abducted in a motorcar? Frog-marched to the house in Hampstead? Was she seized and overcome by force in a dark alley? No. She sailed out of a coffee bar, arm in arm with Stein." He reminded the jury of Ungerman's testimony and the cannabis that had been found in her room. He insisted that nothing was proven against Hersh, except foolishness, perhaps, and the jury should discharge him forthwith.

Mr. Justice Beal, fiddling with his notes, sympathized with the jury, who had, he said, to search for the needle of truth within a haystack of contradictory testimony. Somebody, obviously, was dissembling. But who? "In deciding that question, I daresay you will not be swayed by emotion or prejudice one way or another. You will cogitate and come to a conclusion based on reason." He sifted through the evidence for them again. "If your state of mind after you have reflected on these matters is this: 'We are suspicious. We are inclined to think they did it, but we are not quite sure,' then the prisoners are entitled to what is called in English law the benefit of the doubt, and you are bound to return a verdict of not guilty. It is for the prosecution to prove a man guilty. They must satisfy you. It is probably unnecessary for me to say to you that you must not approach the matter in the attitude of the juryman who said when he saw the prisoner in the dock, 'If he had not been doing something dodgy he would not have been there.' The prisoners in the dock are presumed innocent until the prosecution has proved them guilty."

The court adjourned for lunch and when it assembled again, at 2:30, the jury was ready with its verdict.

The Clerk of the Court rose and asked, "Members of the jury, are you agreed on your verdict?"

"We are," the foreman replied.

"How say you then—do you find the prisoner, Jacob Hersh, guilty or not guilty of aiding and abetting sodomy?"

"Not guilty, my lord."

"Do you find the prisoner at the Bar guilty or not guilty of indecent assault?"

"Guilty."

"You say that the prisoner at the Bar, Jacob Hersh, is guilty and that is the verdict of you all?"

"Yes."

"Do you find him guilty or not guilty of possession of cannabis?"

"Not guilty."

"And so say you all?"

"Yes."

"Prisoner at the Bar, you stand convicted of indecent assault of Miss Ingrid Loebner."

Then the charges against Harry were dealt with.

"How say you then—do you find the prisoner, Harry Stein, guilty or not guilty of sodomy?"

"Guilty."

"Do you find him guilty or not guilty of rape?"

"Guilty."

"Do you find him guilty or not guilty of the possession of cannabis?"

"Not guilty."

"And that is the verdict of you all?"

"Yes. It is the verdict of us all."

"Prisoner at the Bar, you stand convicted of the acts of sodomy and rape against Miss Ingrid Loebner."

Before Jake was sentenced, Lucas Robin Scott was summoned to the witness box to testify to his character.

It was quickly established that he was the son of Senator James Colin Scott, O.B.E., and that from Upper Canada College he had gone on to Victoria College, University of Toronto, graduating with an Honors Degree in English Literature. He was a playwright and script writer. He had won the Governor-General's Award for Literature, he was a former Guggenheim Fellow, and the author of two prize-winning scripts. His voice breaking, Luke testified that he had known the prisoner for twelve years. They had shared an apartment in Toronto and had come to England together. He was a man of singular good character, a model husband and father, and the most generous of friends. "I cannot imagine him," Luke said, his voice filled with anger, "being guilty of any of the things he has been charged with in this court."

Jake watched, stunned, with a tendency to giggle, for it was all happening to somebody else. It wasn't him they were going to sentence.

"Prisoner at the Bar, have you anything to say before sentence is passed."

"No, my lord."

Mr. Justice Beal sighed heavily. He consulted his notes. He motioned for the Clerk of the Court to step up to him and they whispered together. Mr. Justice Beal nodded, he cleared his throat.

"You have been a confounded fool, Hersh. You are a man

with every advantage, obviously intelligent and talented, yet today you stand here disgraced." He shook his head, appalled. "Through folly, and sheer egoism, perhaps, you have formed an association with a man of obvious disreputable character, placing your family and your property in jeopardy. How in God's name could you form an association with Stein in the first place?"

Jake made no reply.

"If I'm not sending you to prison today, which could be a mistake, it's out of pity for your family. Not you. I do believe your wife and children have suffered enough for your folly. I do not see how your imprisonment would serve any useful social purpose. On the contrary. It would only exacerbate your family's suffering. You have been a party to some disgusting acts, Hersh, but I'm going to give you a chance. I hope you have learned a lesson. I am fining you £500 and costs of the prosecution." With a pained expression, Mr. Justice Beal added, "It remains to be seen if I have made a silly mistake. Do you understand me, Hersh?"

"Yes, my lord."

"The prisoner is discharged."

Harry had brought nobody to the Old Bailey to testify to his good character. He said he had no friends. So, without preamble, the Clerk of the Court called on Detective Inspector Mallory to testify as to his previous convictions. Three years for attempted blackmail in 1952. Another two years for attempting malicious and grievous bodily harm to a young lady in 1957.

"You are a humbug, Stein, and a troublemaker of the most reprehensible sort. In my opinion, what we need is an island, somewhere where people like you could be sent. Not so much out of sight, out of mind, but to protect the public. For you are a menace, a persistent public menace. I know very well that I will be criticized for this in the liberal press tomorrow morning, but it seems to me that men like you are let out of prison only to prey on other members of society. Your record is a prime example of the unfortunate fallacy of passing light sentences by the Court of Criminal Appeal. I think the wrong policy has been adopted in the past with respect to men who obviously intend to lead a life of sexual perversion and crime. Unduly light sentences in the past, in my opinion, are responsible in no small part for the present serious increase in sexual perversion and crime."

Handed some papers by the Clerk of Court, Mr. Justice Beal combed through Harry's record in excruciating detail; and then he sentenced him to seven years' imprisonment.

Harry opened his mouth, he closed his mouth. He opened his mouth again, the obscenity dying on his lips, inadequate. Jake grasped him. On his other side, a warder grabbed his arm.

20

Following the trial, Jake didn't read his mail. There was nobody he wanted to hear from. So Jenny's letter lay unopened like the rest.

The day after Mr. Justice Beal pronounced, Nancy suggested they go to the country for a week, taking the baby, but leaving Sammy and Molly with Mrs. Hersh. Jake wouldn't have it. "This will just about clean us out. I should look for work."

But whenever his agent called, he asked Nancy to say he was out. He didn't look at any of the scripts that were delivered by hand. Instead, he sat on the garden bench, under the horse chestnut tree, watching Sammy and Molly at play, doing the *Times* crossword in the morning and burning leaves in the afternoon. Prey for Mrs. Hersh.

". . . then I feel this pain in the right armpit, so I rush to make an appointment with Dr. Bercovitch, you know, the one who did the biopsy on my breasts. He said not to rely on my feeling for lumps. There was a swelling in the glands of my right arm, but Dr. Bercovitch said it was there three years ago. You're not listening, Jake."

When Luke came, as he did almost every afternoon, Nancy sent Pilar out with a tray of drinks and drove Mrs. Hersh and the children out of the garden, so that the two old friends could be alone. But each afternoon, it seemed to Nancy, Luke did all the talking and Jake sat comatose. One afternoon, as soon as Luke had gone, Jake came into the kitchen and said: "Luke's given me his new script. He wants me to do it."

That night in bed Nancy was encouraged when he switched on his bedside lamp and actually read the script right through. "It's not bad," he allowed grudgingly.

"Your enthusiasm overwhelms me."

"But I've been waiting for this moment for years, you know. I dream about it. Ever since he got another director to do his play, I said to myself one day he's going to come to me, the bastard, he's going to come script in hand, because he needs me, and I'm going to tell him to stuff it."

"That settles it, then, does it?"

"No. It doesn't. Because Luke can have his pick of directors. He doesn't need me at all. He's being kind."

"You're as talented as any of them," she said by rote.

"Am I?"

"All right, then. Are you, Jake? Are you really? You're arrogant, I'll grant you that. But I don't know if you're a really fine director, because you've never had a proper chance."

Startled, he protested, "I thought you liked my first film."

"Yes. As a first film. A young man's film. But you haven't done anything better since."

"I see."

"You have a choice, Jake. I can be your wife or your nurse. You tell me which you want."

"Wow."

"I've put up with a lot, you know. It hasn't been fun. I'm not going to spend the rest of my life in mourning for Harry. Or reading alone in bed while you commune with the Horseman in your aerie. Even the children are upset now. 'Don't bother Daddy, he's depressed.' 'Don't ask Daddy for anything now, he's troubled.' I'm not bringing them up like that."

"What would you like me to do?"

"If the script's good, do it. You owe it to all of us."

"I haven't noticed that any of you have gone without because of my self-indulgence. I haven't been such a bad provider over the years."

"I didn't marry you because of what you could provide. There were infinitely better providers who wanted me. I married you because I loved you."

Jake started to read the script again. He had only reached page ten when she began to sob brokenly. He tried to take her in his arms, but she drew away from him.

"Was it in this bed?"

"I did not make love to her."

"You were naked together on a bed. I read the papers, you know. And if I didn't there were enough friends to phone me. Did you know that Natalie was at the Old Bailey every day? And Ethel?"

"I didn't notice. I had other things to worry about."

"Were you with her on this bed?"

"I am not answering any more questions. I'm sick of answering questions."

"Did she take you in her mouth?"

"Yes, your lordship. No, your lordship."

"Don't you dare."

"Yes, she took me in her mouth, but I shoved her off."

"She's pretty."

He laughed dryly.

"Did you feel her breasts?"

"Yes."

"She hasn't had any babies."

"Oh, Nancy, my darling, please."

"Did you touch her between the legs?"

"No."

"Liar."

"Ben's crying. You'd better get him."

"We never go to a restaurant that you don't devour the other women with your eyes."

"I'm human. Big news."

"Do you find me ogling other men's crotches?"

"Ben's crying."

"Would it excite you if I wore a blond wig?"

"You'd better get Ben."

"What gave Harry the idea you'd want her in the first place?"

"I sent him out every night to fetch me girls. I can't find any myself. Now you'd better get Ben or next thing you know, *ketzelle*, we'll have my mother in here."

"You are dreadful to your mother. You don't need her any more. What happens when you decide you don't need me any more?"

"*Would—you—get—Ben—please?*"

"Here," she shouted, pulling out her dressing table drawer so savagely that it was knocked to the floor. "Here. And here. And here."

They were letters from Harry, describing in lascivious detail all the acts Jake was supposed to have performed with Ingrid. Saying how they had gone to C. Bernard Farber's together, looking for cunt. When he was released from prison, Harry wrote, the three of them must go to bed together; he would lick her until she passed out, satiated, and then he would ram it up her ass. She would discover a real man in Harry and could taste him as far as the back of her throat. He would come with a riding crop. He would bring handcuffs. Anything she desired. If you beat a woman with wet towels, it left no marks. Ask Jake.

"Oh, my God, I'll kill him. Somebody must have smuggled these out for him. He's only allowed one letter a week."

Nancy was rocking on the edge of the bed, whimpering softly as she nursed Ben. Even though it was dark, she sat with her back to him, so he could not look on her breasts. Her back was beautiful.

"It's all lies, Nancy. He's psychotic, you know that."

"Yes. But you'd say it was lies anyway. Wouldn't you?"

"Yes."

"You'd have to."

The next afternoon, Luke didn't come, and, for the first time since the trial, Jake ventured out of the house, absently wandering as far as Swiss Cottage. When Ruthy rapped on the dress shop window, claiming him.

At the King's Arms (*their* pub, he mused), Ruthy peeled the label off an Orange-Kool bottle and announced that she had met a wonderful, wonderful man, highly sensitive, keen on classical music and well versed in Jewish lore. There was only one problem, she added lugubriously. "He's an inveterate masturbator. He can drive a woman bonkers until he satisfies himself and then she ends up in a frightful state. It's diabolical."

"Ruthy, I am no longer interested in your love life."

"Oh, that's nice. That's ever so nice. After all we've been through together."

"I don't want to hear any more."

"He says intercourse is not necessary, it's only the preliminaries that count. It's like climbing a mountain, he says, it's not necessary to reach the top, it's enough to look up and know that it's there. What's your frank opinion?"

"My frank opinion is you will survive, Ruthy. And now," he said, rising abruptly, "goodbye."

When he got home, Nancy said Luke had called to invite them both out to dinner.

"I'm too tired. You go."

So she called back to say no. "Poor Luke. He's not saying anything, but I'm sure he's dying to know what you think of his script."

Let him suffer, then.

"Couldn't you phone him?"

"Tomorrow."

But tomorrow Jake didn't phone and Luke did not come in the afternoon.

"Couldn't you at least call to say you've read it?"

Sammy and Molly began to fight upstairs. "Mommy, mommy," she hollered.

"Coming, precious one," Mrs. Hersh replied.

"Haven't you ever behaved badly toward someone who trusted you?" Nancy asked just before she quit the living room.

Pouring himself a drink, Jake suddenly wondered if the Horseman, wherever he was, had read of his trial in a newspaper.

Stiff-collared, cherub-mouthed Ormsby-Fletcher came, lugging his black briefcase and looking severe. He and Jake conferred behind closed doors for more than an hour and then he strode out of the house, belted himself into his black Humber, and was off again.

"Guess what," Jake said. "Hershel's appealing."

"On what grounds?"

"Well now, for openers, I got my doctor to drug him before he went into court each morning. Then Ruthy was my mistress, which explains why I deposited seven hundred pounds to his account. I also bribed Ormsby-Fletcher to misrepresent him in his brief. He wants Ormsby-Fletcher disbarred." Jake laughed, he shook his head. "I phoned Luke. He's coming tomorrow."

Luke and Jake sat in the garden all afternoon. Nancy served them sandwiches and then slipped upstairs to nurse Ben. When she looked out of the kitchen window again, Luke was gone. He hadn't even said goodbye.

"Did you quarrel?"

"No. I even told him I liked the script."

"With reservations, though?"

"Yes," he snapped back.

"Are you going to do it, then?"

"I don't even know what I'm going to do tomorrow. I plan on waking up, that's all."

"Did you say no, then?"

"I said I wanted time to think about it. Don't bug me, Nancy."

In the morning they all piled into the car and drove Mrs. Hersh to the airport. She did not break down until she was alone with Jake at the passport barrier.

"When you were a child you needed my love and protection and now that I'm approaching old age, I'm going to need yours."

"I'll do everything I can for you, Maw."

"Oh, I realize you would protect me against illness and old

age, with all that money can buy, but it goes deeper than that with me. I am not stupid. I am a woman with pride and dignity and intelligence. Isn't that right?"

"Yes, Maw."

"So it goes deeper than money with me."

"I understand."

Her face erupting in tears, she grabbed him, pelting his face with kisses. He responded as lovingly as he could, but it was insufficient to the moment. Suddenly, Mrs. Hersh thrust her son from her, heaving, her eyes brimming with rage. "You have children too," she declared fiercely. "You have children, Yankel," and then she turned to pass through the barrier. He lingered, but she did not turn back. She didn't wave.

Then Duddy, prospering Duddy Kravitz, rode into London. Before lunch, he and Jake strolled down the King's Road together, the girls streaming past in their miniskirts and leather boots.

"*Oy.* Who could blame you? How can you stand it here?" Duddy asked. "All that quim out taking the air in those short skirts. Short? I tell you, Yankel, if one of those chicks had a Tampax inside, you'd see the string dangling. It's enough to drive you crazy. Walking down the street here, if you swung your arm like a hook, the fingers extended, you could lick hot pussy off your hand for hours."

They ate at Alvaro's. Duddy, as was his habit now, ordered Beluga caviar for both of them, double portions, with a side order of chopped eggs and onions for himself. For the truth was Duddy didn't care for caviar and only by mashing egg and onion into it could he make it taste almost like chopped liver.

"These skirts—Christ—when I think of the agonies we suffered in our day before you could get a girl to hike her skirt that high. When I remember the double features at the Rialto you had to sit through, the coaxing, the toasted tomato sandwiches you had to pay for, the sundaes, gaining an inch here, losing two there. Why, you could put in a month of blue-balls and lies before you even got a peek at a stocking top, never mind some real stink-finger. But the kids today, shit, do they know what struggle is? They take out a chick and, for openers, her skirt is riding her crotch. All you have to do is flip it over and shove it in."

Ordering another bottle of Veuve Clicquot, Duddy excoriated the new-style books and movies. "When you come down to it, I'm a traditional Jewish boy. For me to enjoy sex, I've got to feel, well, you know . . . a little bit guilty. The first time Marlene blew me I was actually ashamed for her. Never mind she wanted to kiss me on the mouth afterwards with all my come still dribbling down her chin. Feh," he said, making a face. "What's the matter. Am I embarrassing you?"

"Certainly not."

"Well, the first time she sucked me off I thought, oh boy, lucky Duddy, you're really marrying a hot one. This is something really special. Now you open a novel or go to a movie and they're all going down on each other from the opening chapter or scene. The whole world going gobble, gobble, eat, eat. So what's so special about my marriage any more? What makes my life such a rare item? It's ruining sex for me, I tell you. All this new outspokenness in the arts is taking the kicks out of it for me. Gone are the guilty pleasures, the dirty secret joys."

"Duddy, I realize you're trying to make me feel better, but the truth is there's nothing in it. There was no orgy at my place."

"In that case, you're a bigger prick than even I gave you credit for. You mean to say, after the trial, all you've been through, the whole *tzimmis*, you didn't even get laid out of it?"

Jake nodded.

"I hope I'm the only one you've bothered to tell. Because I remember from way back. I know you're a shmock. But nobody else would believe you."

"Do you believe me?"

"Unfortunately, yes. But, you know, you give off a guilty smell. You look like shit warmed over, Jake."

As Duddy leaned forward to light his cigar, Jake noticed the hair slicked back over the spreading widow's peak. His sideburns were gray. There were deep, dark pouches under his eyes.

"Is Nancy raising hell?" Duddy asked.

"She is somewhat displeased."

"Buy her a coat."

"Oh, for Chrissake, Duddy, she's not that kind of woman."

"What's to be done with you? Crap artist. You broke?"

"I'll make out."

"When I was up the creek in Toronto, you helped me out, remember? How much do you need?"

"What if I were to say ten thousand dollars?"

"In that case, I'll only have to dip into the petty cash."

Jake laughed, incredulous, as Duddy wrote out the check. "It's good to see you again," he said.

"Hoo haw. It's good to see anyone who would lend you ten bills. Here," he said, thrusting the check at him, "and now tell me what your so-called best friend Lucas Scott, Esq., has given you recently?"

Jake told him about Luke's script and the conundrums it made for him.

"Do it, do it. If it's good, do it. Then tell him to get fucked."

Jake laughed and called for a round of brandies, but Duddy said no, not for him, he couldn't take it any more. It kept him awake. He swallowed a pill with his coffee.

"Hey, Yankel, what if I held a class reunion? Could I count on you?"

"Sure. But why would you want to do that?"

"I had my secretary check out everybody who was in room forty-one with us. Of all the guys, I'm the only millionaire. Let them come to my place and choke on it, don't you think?"

Duddy's check stuffed into his jacket lapel pocket, Jake felt resuscitated, even lighthearted, for the first time since the trial had ended. Driving home, he realized he did not have his mother to contend with any more.

Or lawyers.

Or Harry.

Or Mr. Justice Beal, in the morning.

Now he was no longer obliged to do Luke's script. If he

wanted to say yes, O.K., but if he decided against it, he could cash Duddy's check. The trial's over, Yankel. You did not behave badly. Nancy won't leave you. She can't. He resolved to be good to Sammy when he came home from school. Molly wouldn't irritate him today.

Jake found Nancy in the kitchen. "These are called flowers," he said, "and they're for you."

"Oh," she said, not displeased.

"If Duddy Kravitz believes me, why can't you?"

"But I do, most of the time."

Jake scooped up the carton with his backlog of mail and sat down at the kitchen table. Bills, magazines, his bank statement. Letters from actors, scripts, some invitations.. He read aloud to her whenever he struck anything outlandish. Once, she laughed aloud.

"You said you married me because you loved me. Do you still?"

"Yes."

"I love you too."

Then he ripped open Jenny's letter, reading it impatiently, nodding, and, as she watched, he turned a page and all at once the color was sucked from his face. His hands began to tremble like an old man's. He moaned. He looked up at her, shaking his head, his eyes imploring, but unable to speak.

"What is it, Jake, for heaven's sake?"

"Joey's dead."

"Oh, I'm sorry. I'm so sorry."

"He's been dead for more than two months. Oh, hell. Bloody hell."

Nancy, coming up behind him to stroke his head, found him drenched in sweat.

"Better shut the kitchen door."

"The children are in the garden," she said. "It's all right." She poured him a brandy.

"He's been dead for more than two months. Oh, Joey. Joey, Joey. There's so much I wanted to ask him."

"I know, darling."

"It took all this time for the Canadian consul in Asunción to contact Hanna."

Jake drifted over to the window to watch Molly in the sandbox. Sammy was crouching in the long grass with his action man, the one he called the Horseman, after Jake's stories.

"How did it happen?" Nancy asked.

"What?"

She repeated her question.

"An air crash. He was in cigarette smuggling, they say. That's very big stuff in Paraguay, you know. There's no duty on American cigarettes. They import millions and millions and fly them by night into Argentina, Brazil, and Bolivia. They land on makeshift fields. He was burned to a crisp."

"Poor Hanna."

"His body was beyond . . . Why did it have to be Joey? There are so many bastards in this world I could do without."

She passed him a cup of coffee.

"There's a small policy. Five thousand dollars for Hanna. They found his papers in an hotel room in Asunción."

Briefly, Jake slumped forward, resting his head on the table. Nancy massaged his neck.

"He crashed in a clearing between the Mato Grosso and the Brazilian Highlands, not far from the Paraná River."

Neighing, the stallion rears, obliging the Horseman to dig his stirrups in. Eventually, he slows to a jog. Still in the highlands, emerging from the dense forest to scan the scrub below, he strains to find the unmarked road that winds into the jungle, between Puerto San Vincente and the border fortress of Carlos Antonio López.

"You know," Jake said, standing up, "according to Simon Weisenthal, who runs the Documentation Center on Nazis in Vienna, when Dr. Mengele fled Buenos Aires, going to Barloche, in the Andes, where so many of them live in opulent villas, it happened that an Israeli lady was visiting her mother there. Both of them had been in Auschwitz, Mengele having sterilized the Israeli lady. One evening, in the ballroom of the local hotel, she suddenly found herself face to face with Mengele. Naturally, he didn't recognize her, after all he had sterilized thousands. But he did take in the number on her lower left arm. Not a word passed between them, according to eyewitnesses. A few days later however, the Israeli lady did not return from an excursion in the mountains. It was several weeks before her body was discovered near a crevasse. A mountain climbing accident, the police said."

"Hold on, Jake. What if he was no more than they say? A cigarette smuggler."

"I don't know. I'll never know now," he cried, "don't you see?"

"Yes," she replied, alarmed.

"Weisenthal writes, I've got his book upstairs somewhere, he writes that the Jewish community in Asunción has been apprehensive for years. They've had many anonymous letters. If Mengele should be kidnapped, the letters threaten, not one Jew in Paraguay will survive . . . Oh, hell, who knows what the truth of the matter is. Some guys, you know, they don't understand $E = mc^2$, it drives them crazy. I don't understand anything. I'm going upstairs," he said, picking up his carton of mail.

"Will you be all right?"

"Certainly."

Opening the cupboard, he plucked the Horseman's journal from the shelf and flipped it open.

LEVKA: You're an idiot, Arye-Leib. Another week, he says. Do you think I'm in the infantry? I'm in the cavalry, Arye-Leib, the cavalry . . . Why, if I'm even an hour late the sergeant will cut me up for breakfast. He'll squeeze the juice out of my heart and put me up for court-martial. They get three generals to try one cavalry man; three generals with medals from the Turkish campaign.

ARYE-LEIB: Do they do this to everyone or only the Jews?

LEVKA: When a Jew gets on a horse he stops being a Jew . . .

• • •

On the first page, Jake found the entry that read, "The Horseman: Born Joseph Hersh in a miner's shanty in Yellowknife, Yukon Territories. Exact date unknown.", and added, "died, July 20, 1967, in an air crash, between the Mato Grosso and the Brazilian Highlands, not far from the Paraná River."

What are you going to do about it, a voice demanded.

He wept, that's what. The tears he couldn't coax out of himself at his father's graveside or summon up for Mr. Justice Beal's verdict on Harry or his mother's departure flowed freely now. Torn from his soul, the tears welled in his throat and ran down his cheeks. He whimpered, he moaned. He sank, trembling, to the sofa. He wept for his father, his penis curling out of his underwear like a spent worm. His penis, my maker. Rotting in an oversize pinewood casket. He wept for his mother, who deserved a more loving son. He wept for Harry, fulminating in his cell and assuredly planning vengeance. He wept for Nancy, whose stomach was seamed from childbearing. Who would no longer make love with the lights on. He wept because the Horseman, his conscience, his mentor, was no more.

Unless, he thought, pouring himself a brandy at his desk, I become the Horseman now. I seek out the villa with the barred windows off the unmarked road in the jungle, between Puerto San Vincente and the border fortress of Carlos Antonio López, on the Paraná River. I will be St. Urbain's avenging Horseman. *If,* a more skeptical voice intruded, *there ever was one.*

Why did he return to Montreal? He came to fuck me, Jenny said. "If he is hunting this Nazi down and finds him," Uncle Abe shouted, "he won't kill him, he'll blackmail him." What if the Horseman was a distorting mirror and we each took the self-justifying image we required of him?

> I am the LORD thy God, which brought thee
> out of the land of Egypt, from the house of
> bondage.
> Thou shalt have none other gods before me.
> Thou shall not make thee any graven image,

or any likeness of any thing that is in
heaven above, or that is in the earth beneath,
or that is in the waters beneath the
earth:
Thou shalt not bow down thyself unto them,
nor serve them: for I the LORD thy God am
a jealous God, visiting the iniquity of the
fathers upon the children unto the third and
fourth generation of them that hate me.

No, no, Jake argued, and he pulled the Horseman's saddle out of the cupboard, heaving it onto the floor before him. It wobbled briefly and then fell on its side. With a distinct metallic clunk.

Jake lunged at the saddle, upending it, and probing its innards he found the pouch. "That's where he keeps his gat." There was indeed a revolver, and alarmed, his heart hammering, Jake took it in his hand. Feh, he thought, shrinking from it, setting it down gently on his desk, pointing it away from him. Jake poured himself another brandy and contemplated the weapon. He knew almost nothing of such things, but even to his untrained eye it seemed an archaic gun. *Pick it up, chicken.* So he took it in his wet palm again, raised it, and pointed it at the window.

Look sharp, Mengele. *Die Juden kommen.*

Then, demonstrating his courage to himself, Jake gritted his teeth and turned the revolver, pressing the barrel to his forehead.

Putz, you can hurt yourself.

I want to find out who I am, he had told Issy Hersh. It's taken years, but now I know. Who am I? Well, I'm not Hedda Gabler. I'm Aaron maybe.

Now Jake pointed the revolver at that discolored square on the wall where "Sepp" Dietrich's photograph used to hang. He pointed it, squeezed his eyes shut, and fired. There was a tremendous report, a kick, but, to his astonishment, no hole in the wall.

Nancy bounded up the stairs and charged into his office, "Jake! Jake!" the tears actually flying.

He seized her, holding her tight, and explained.

"Watch this," he said, taking up the revolver again. With more confidence now.

He fired at the wall once more. Eyes open this time. A tremendous bang, but no hole.

"It only fires blanks. It's an actor's gun. A souvenir of his film days, probably."

Jake poured himself another brandy and slumped on the sofa. "I'll just finish this and try to get some sleep. I'm all right, Nancy, honestly."

She woke him at six to say, "Luke phoned. He wants to take us to dinner."

"Say yes."

"Really?" she asked, startled.

"Yes, really."

For sentimental reasons, they met at Chez Luba. Jake told Luke he would like to direct his script. Ostensibly, Luke was overjoyed. So was Nancy. So was Jake. But their shared gaiety was forced, a fragile cork bobbing on currents of doubt.

Even as Jake basked in their concern for his well-being, his belated return to the land of the living, his mind rode with the Horseman. He told them about the other letter he had found, Hanna's letter. "She doesn't believe Joey's dead. She thinks he may be in trouble with the police again and staged the crash to evade arrest and because he needs the insurance money. She's not touching the money. It's being kept in a special account, until Joey sends for it."

Luke set down his glass wearily. Nancy toyed gloomily with a fork.

"Of course, it's absurd," Jake said.

They parted, agreeing to meet for lunch tomorrow. To discuss the script. And then, for the first time since the trial's end, Jake and Nancy made love, shy with each other.

In his nightmare, he was the Horseman now. It was Jake who was St. Urbain's rider on the white stallion. Come to extract the gold fillings from the triangular cleft between Mengele's upper front teeth with pliers. Slowly, he thought, coming abruptly awake in a sweat. "I've come," Jake proclaimed aloud.

Beside him, Nancy stirred.

"It's nothing," he said softly. "Just a nightmare. Go back to sleep."

Careful not to disturb her, Jake slid out of bed and into his dressing gown, sucking in his stomach to squeeze between the bed and the baby in the bassinet.

Once in his attic aerie, he retrieved the Horseman's journal from the cupboard, found the page where he had written "died July 20, 1967, in an air crash," crossed it out, and wrote in over it, "presumed dead." Then he returned to bed, and fell into a deep sleep, holding Nancy to him.